# Vindaguar's Prophecy

Patrick Madden

"Vindaguar's Prophecy" second edition by Patrick Madden. ISBN 978-1-63868-118-2 (softcover).

Published 2016, 2023 by Virtualbookworm.com Publishing Inc., P.O.Box 9949, College Station, TX, 77842, US.

# Dedication

I would like to dedicate this book to the very lovely Lucia. Lucia is Spanish and works at the Cork Railway Station coffee bar. This pretty senorita was my absolute inspiration for writing this story.

Gracias por tu encantadora sonrisa, Lucia.

# Vindaquar's Prophecy

O ne August evening, in the year 1899, Gwydion Llewellyn, a six-foot eighteen-year-old teenager, was riding his old and retired pit pony across Blaenafon's Elgam Mountain, checking on his grandfather's sheep.

High on the slopes of Elgam Mountain, once stood a small Roman Garrison. It was abandoned by General Titus Andronicus and his legion of centurions in 62 A.D. The fortress stayed uninhabited until the year 1220 when, according to the legend, it was taken over and rebuilt by a Welsh wizard named Bleddwyn. After repairing the surrounding battlement and barracks, he replaced the crumbling keep with a small castle. He was a generous peace-loving wizard, living alone until he met Eluciana, an exceptional Spanish Soothsayer. They met at a festival while Bleddwyn was visiting his cousin Brynmoroc, in Spain. Three years later, on the twenty-fourth of February 1262, they were married in Llanwenarth Baptist Chapel, Govilon, South Wales.

The happy couple enjoyed life and spent most of their time helping the poor set up self-sufficient farms throughout the valleys of South Wales. They became well known and loved and were often visited until on their fortieth wedding anniversary, they disappeared never to be seen again. Consequently, over the centuries, this sadly led to the ransacking of their beloved Roman fortress. All that remains now are the slab stones that formed the base of Bleddwyn's castle and the old Roman road running across the mountain.

In the year 1787, because of the vast amount of iron ore in the valley below the old ruins, Thomas Hill, a wealthy man from Staffordshire, constructed a foundry with a series of furnaces to extract the iron. It's the only Ironworks in the country. There were already working coal mines in this valley, so along with the construction of the Ironworks, men, women and children came from all over Wales and England for employment. Hence, a new town emerged, with schools, churches, shops and homes for all the workers. They call this town Blaenafon, being Welsh for "Beginning of the river." A river that flows, winding its way through the valley to the sea. So, like the beginning of the river, I'll begin my story.

My name is Gwydion Llewellyn, and I was that teenager. It was on that summer's day that my pony, Mad Luke, suddenly bolted as we crossed over the ruins of the fort. In doing so, his hind legs moved a slab stone, revealing a gaping hole in the ground. Taken by surprise, I was catapulted back onto the slabs. I remember feeling very dizzy, and as I rose to my feet, I staggered backwards, toppling down into the hole. I must have hit my head as I fell, rendering me unconscious. When I came to my senses, I found myself looking up at stone steps. I was still groggy, but as soon as my head cleared a sudden fear came over me. I realised that I was in some creepy dark room, making me quickly scamper up the steps, back out into the light again.

"Blimey! What the heck's down there?" I said while peering down into a dark hole. "It must be some kind of cellar or a secret passageway under the old fort. Brilliant! I wonder if there's any treasure down there."

It was a struggle, but I managed to cover the hole by sliding the slab safely back over it.

"I'll keep this a secret and come back tomorrow with some candles," I thought.

I looked across the mountain for my runaway pony, but Mad Luke was nowhere to be seen. I thought I'd never catch the fool now, but he'd be okay. I'd fetch him after work tomorrow. I was so excited walking back down the mountain that I couldn't help quietly shouting, "Yahoo! Ya beauty you."

I arrived home at my Granddad's cottage where I had lived ever since my parents were tragically killed in a mining accident. I was three years old at the time and have no memory of them. Granddad told me that their bodies were never recovered. Some say they were never there that day of the accident. Others say they were, but it was impossible to reach them. Either way, that part of the mine has been sealed off ever since.

"Don't tell me you've lost that mad pony of yours again Gwydion. Are the ewes and lambs okay?" asked Granddad, as I walked in.

"Yes," I replied taking off my boots, "They are all okay, and yes Mad Luke bolted again. There's something about that old fortress ruins. He hates going past them. He'll probably turn up in the morning for his oats. If he doesn't, I'll find him tomorrow after work."

"Ah Gwydion, I don't know why you bother riding that crazy pony. I told you I'd buy you another one, a quieter one."

"Yeah, I know Granddad, but I like him. Is dinner ready?" I asked tapping him on the shoulder.

"Yes, I've had mine, you're cabbage is still in the pot," he joked.

"Haha Granddad, very funny. Watch I don't hide that old pipe of yours, ya old joker you."

That night, while we were sitting by the fire, I asked him if it was true about the wizard Bleddwyn living in a castle up at the old Roman fortress, and that he and his wife suddenly disappeared without a trace.

"Well, according to my father and for what I heard one day up there by the old ruins, it must be."

"What did you hear Granddad?" I quickly asked while he was filling his pipe.

"Well if I told you, you'd probably never go up there again Gwydion."

"Ah, don't be silly Granddad, I'm not afraid. You are up there all the time, so it couldn't be that scary now, could it?"

"Well if you really want to know, then I'll tell you," he replied, lighting his pipe.

"It was on a sunny day in May 1824, the day of a total solar eclipse. My father was worried about his sheep up on the mountain and how they would behave during the darkness. So I decided to take Shep and fetch the flock over to the old ruins and stay with them until the eclipse passed. It was about four o'clock before we rounded them up. I was tired by then and sat down close to the ruins, holding my hand to my eyes. I peered through my fingers at the sun, but it was far too bright for me. So I sat until a shadow began creeping across the mountain. I knew then that the eclipse was about to happen. The sheep were all stood quietly because they could see old Shep watching them from on the top of a bank. However, within minutes of the shadow catching up with us, there was total darkness. It stayed that way until after about a minute the sun slowly began to appear, and that's when I heard it."

Granddad stopped, sat up and shook his head as if afraid to tell me. I was anxious now, and as he looked at me with creepy eyes, I asked, "What Granddad? What did you hear?"

"I heard my father shouting boo. He was right behind me," he replied before doubling up with laughter.

"Ah, you old codger you," I shouted, jumping up. "I'll get you for that. You, you're nothing but an old joker."

We laughed and laughed for a long time until we went to bed. Yes, I went to bed, but all I did was toss and turn thinking about the cellar and how I was going to investigate it. Eventually, through sheer exhaustion, I fell asleep.

I was up early to start work at five o'clock. My job was to shovel iron ore into the blast furnace of Blaenafon ironworks. All through the day I was dying to tell my pals Barry Protheroe and Lawson Allcock about the cellar, but being jokers like my Granddad, they would have probably made some silly wisecrack. Besides, both of them were not very brave. I remember one night, while we walked through the cemetery for a dare; they ran away leaving me in the middle of all the graves.

Prothy, being Barry's nickname, works as a foreman at the Ironworks but spends most of the shift asleep around the back of the furnace. Lawson is a school teacher, and according to his pupils, even he does his fair share of sleeping.

I couldn't wait for the shift to end and after the whistle finally blew, I hurried home as fast as I could.

"You're home early son," said Granddad. "What are you up to? Oh, I know, you're off to find Mad Luke. I forgot about him."

"I take it he hasn't come home yet then, Granddad. I'll go on up and find him."

"Yes, and I'll have your tea ready by the time you come back son. Don't be too long up there. If you can't find him, leave him, he'll be alright. I'll fetch him tomorrow."

I went outside to the shed, quickly grabbed and put a couple of candles and matches into my pocket.

"I shouldn't be too long Granddad," I shouted and walked off up the mountain.

I caught sight of Mad Luke above the Balls Pond. He was okay, so I thought I'd catch him later. I walked on up to the old ruins and sat down for a while, trying to stop my heart from racing. It was a waste of time taking deep breaths, for no matter how many I took, it just wouldn't slow down. Finally, I plucked up some courage and walked over to the large slab. With a bit of a struggle, catching my fingers in the process, I managed to lift the slab and slide it over.

"Good grief!" I said to myself. "That's one creepy-looking hole. I must be crazy to go down there, but that's what I came here for, so come on, let's do it."

It was a beautiful sunny day, and as I slowly descended, I could see the steps. They were running down along the wall, but there was no rail to hold onto. I stopped halfway down, sat on the steps and lit a candle. I waited for it to brighten up before I carried on down. It may seem strange to you, but for some silly reason, I counted all the steps. There were eighteen in all, each one about a yard wide.

"Wow!" I said as I reached the bottom. "This is some kind of cave or cellar."

I walked on a little and to my surprise; in front of me was a wooden stand holding six candles. I nervously lit them with my candle and once again waited until they brightened up. I found now that I was standing in an exciting-looking room. The ceiling was sparkling as if lined with diamonds and on the wall were paintings of people and scenes. After looking closer, I thought one of the scenes seemed very familiar. I walked further into the room, holding the candle stand in front of me. Then to add to my amazement, I saw beautiful wooden furniture, carved with designs I had never seen before. One of these was a partially opened wardrobe. I put down the stand and was about to look inside when I noticed a dusty-looking chest alongside a chair. I walked over and after wiping off some of the dust, I whispered, "Yes, oh yes, it's gold. It's made of gold."

I didn't open it because I wanted to look further around. I was excited but at the same time a little uneasy about it all. By now the candles had brightened up the room revealing a table with a chair at each end facing one another. I walked over to the table, and as I did, an eerie feeling came over me. I noticed that the lovely-looking oak chair at one end of the table was carved in the shape of a woman. The table was oval, made of solid oak about six inches thick. Engraved around the edge of the table were letters forming words I thought maybe Welsh, but they weren't. It was some other language, one that I had never seen before. Standing in the centre of this unique table, was a wooden figure of a snarling dragon. My first thought was of the mythical dragon, Ohibronoeler, who is said to inhabit the nearby Dragons Pond. Ohibronoeler or not, it was a fabulous-looking carving. Then, as I slowly walked towards the other chair at the head of the table, a cold shiver ran down my spine. The chair was carved in the image of a wizard, holding a staff in his hand. He looked so real, and as I studied his eyes, I felt that he was looking back at me.

"Strewth!" I said, backing away against the wall. "I don't like this at all."

I stood there for a while slowly looking around but keeping one eye on that creepy-looking chair. My heart was beating fast now, and with it being so quiet down there, I could even hear it. I tried to calm myself by taking slow deep breaths, but it was of no use. You will never believe how anxious I was, for as I looked, the wizard's head slowly turned towards me and the whole chair began to move. I felt the blood drain from my face, and my head felt as if someone was sticking a million needles in it.

"This really can't be happening," I said to myself. "It couldn't be?"

I was frozen to the spot, not knowing what to do. I thought if I made a run for it, he'd probably grab my legs as I climb the steps. Even so, I wasn't going to stay there. I decided to make my way out, and if he was going to get me, he was going to get me. So, with my eyes blurry from looking at the staring wizard and my throat dry as dust, I slowly slid across the wall towards the steps, but as I crept, I got the fright of my life. The wooden wizard stood up, held out his staff towards me and shouted, "NO!"

To add to my horror, the candles went out, and there was a rumbling noise above me. My legs felt weak, and as I staggered towards the steps, I saw what was causing the rumbling. It was the stone slab sliding back across the opening, turning the whole cave into darkness. I stumbled backwards falling to the floor and crouched alongside a chair.

"Why, oh why did I ever come down here?" I whispered, covering my face.

"Piediwch a bodofn," said the wizard in a deep, but kind-sounding voice.

He was speaking in Welsh, meaning, 'Do not be afraid.' I then, but slowly, looked up into the blackness and gave a small sigh of relief. I didn't move; just stayed there crouched down, trying to keep still and quiet waiting for him to speak again. Thoughts were beginning to run through my mind now.

"A wooden wizard! Surely this can't be true? Surely not?"

Yet, incredibly as it may seem, the creepy-looking wizard was there, and I could hear him breathing.

"I can't believe this is happening to me," I muttered. "He told me not to be afraid, so what's he going to do now? Oh, Granddad! How will I ever get out of here?"

It seemed hours but was probably only a few minutes when I heard the same rumbling noise again. It was the slab stone opening back up. Then as I looked up, beams of sunlight flashed in, turning the whole room into a mass of colour. The shock of the flash and the beautiful bright colours dazzled me, making me close my eyes. I kept them closed until I heard a roar of thunder followed by cracks that sounded like firewood, sparking. I crouched beside the chair and with my head down, put my hands over my ears. Although my ears were covered, I could hear men shouting at one another. So I opened my eyes, and as I looked over the side of the chair, I was looking at an incredible vision. There was a castle inside a fort; I assumed being the old Roman fortress. It had to be because I recognised the surrounding area. The crackling and thunder were coming from two battling wizards, one of them a giant about six feet taller than the other. To me, the giant seemed to be shimmering like heat waves rising from a furnace. The wizards were on top of the castle and in a ferocious battle against one another. I quickly stood up and turned to look for the steps, but to my dismay, they were gone. Then as I turned back around, an amazing thing happened. I was there on top of the castle, watching the battling wizards. There was nothing I could do only stand back and witness this incredible conflict. Both wizards were shouting in Welsh with the smaller of the two, pleading with the giant.

"Stop! Stop Brynmoroc! I beg you. Don't be a fool, cast him out. Please cousin, before it's too late. The prophecy says that he who violates, by stealing the power of the stones will be obliterated by the eyes of a lady and the hand of a young man."

YES!!" replied the angry giant. "But I'm no fool Bleddwyn. I know the prophecy, and I'll see that no one will ever find the stones. I'll take that wife of yours and close her eyes forever. She'll never see the light of day again, and neither will you."

It was no use Bleddwyn pleading with the giant for his pleas were only making the giant worse. With a screwed-up face, Brynmoroc pointed his staff towards Bleddwyn, and another shearing crackle of thunder and lightning sent the wizard tumbling over the castle turrets down into the courtyard.

All through this thunderous flashing battle, the wizards continuously cursed each other. Incredibly, as they clashed throughout the fortress, I was with them where ever they went. The final battle was again at the top of the castle, where the weakened Bleddwyn, after a savage blast from the giant, fell tumbling down the stone spiral staircase to the bottom where he lay exhausted. I then watched as Brynmoroc lifted a slab stone, opening an entrance to a cellar much the same as the one I had been in earlier. The gleaming giant, after dragging the stricken wizard over to the entrance, threw him down the steps into the dark cellar below.

"Now, dear cousin, we'll soon see who's the fool. Eluciana will belong to me now and so will her eyes. As for you my wretched kin, this shall be your home and only in our world of darkness shall you roam."

With ease, Brynmoroc slid the slab stone back over the hatch and stamped on it. He stood there for a moment, and as I watched him shimmer and shake, he shrunk to about six feet tall.

"NOW." he roared and took off through the castle until he found what he was looking for. It was a stern-looking woman with long black hair. She was wearing an orange dress, a long yellow cloak and holding a dazzling silver shield in front of her. She stood facing him as he entered what looked to be her living room. The wizard glared, and as he carefully approached the woman, he was sent hurtling backwards, thumping against the wall. Each time he advanced, the same thing happened. It seemed that every time he caught sight of his reflection he was hurled back across the room with tremendous force. The angry wizard then backed away to the door and stood there scowling, sneering at the woman.

"Ah, ingenious my dear. Yes, very clever my sweet Eluciana, but I've had just about enough of this nonsense."

With eyes half-closed and a look of contempt on his screwed-up face, he gave a terrible roar, ripped up a large stone statue and flung it across the room, smashing it into the wall. This shook the whole room, causing the disoriented Eluciana to fall, dropping her shield as she fell. Like a flash, the wizard swept her up into his arms.

"You are mine now Eluciana. Mine now, forever," roared Brynmoroc, wickedly.

I watched as he ran with her, slumped in his arms, down towards the Black Ranks Lake. By then he had since reverted to his giant size, and with one enormous leap across the lake, he leapt towards the setting sun and was gone. I quickly turned to run, but to my disappointment, instead of me running home from the Black Ranks, I found myself back in the dark cave again.

"Oh, no! What's happening now?" I said, slumping down behind the chair again.

I stayed there for what seemed like an eternity until I heard movement.

"Gwydion, you are my body and soul, my equity of blood," said a voice in the dark.

"It's the wizard. What's he talking about? What does he want?" I muttered.

Suddenly, I began to shiver as a cold breeze swept through the cave, followed by a creepy silence. Once again, it seemed forever crouching there, wondering what next. Eventually, the place lit up with candles and there, sitting in the wizard's chair, was the wizard himself. It was Bleddwyn, the same stricken wizard I saw in the battling vision.

"Sit, Gwydion," he said, pointing to the chair I was crouched by.

I sat and was thankful he didn't ask me to sit on the wooden woman's chair. The wizard had a kind face, and his long wavy auburn hair fell over his shoulders to the same length as his long wavy beard. What I could see of his cloak was dark red with small streaks of yellow lightning running through it. In his left hand, he held a staff about six feet tall which was black and knobbly, probably cut from a blackthorn tree or similar. He had a gentle smile on his face as if pleased to see me. This made me feel a whole lot better.

"Gwydion, my name is Bleddwyn. I have been waiting almost six hundred years for you, and now, finally, you are here."

I squinted in bewilderment thinking once again, "What's he talking about?"

"Why? What do you want from me?" I asked, but with a quiver in my voice.

"You are the instigator of a prophecy," he replied. "A prophecy set by the great and all-powerful wizard, Vindaguar."

"How can this be?" I asked. "I'm Gwydion Llewellyn from Blaenafon, and I don't even know you or Vindaguar."

"Vindaguar is the sole instigator of wizardry," replied the wizard, leaning forward. "Now, listen carefully, Gwydion. As you may or may not know, this planet Earth is three-dimensional, but what I am about to tell you no human knows. Earth has a fourth dimension, a single dimension, one that is impossible for humans to see unless we so wish. This dimension is the world of energy where we enchanted wizards, giants and creatures abide. Incredible as this may sound, wizards, can live along with humans in their three-dimensional world and at the same time, in our own. We enjoy the same benefits as you, except that in our dimension, it never snows."

He then paused to slowly sit back in his chair. I was wholly baffled now but fascinated as he continued.

"All wizards have their energy replenished by an enchanted spiralling rainbow. Unlike others, the source of this rainbow comes from seven different coloured gemstones. These stones are enchanted and sit somewhere in seven different locations around the world. They were placed there by Vindaguar at the beginning of wizardry. No one knows where they are, soothsayers could possibly find them, but no one would ever dare for fear of the prophecy. The gemstones are ruby, fire opal, citrine, emerald, sapphire, tanzanite, and amethyst. During the first year of every new century, a total solar eclipse occurs with the new moon completely blackening out the sun. This only happens over certain parts of the world, but before it does, it begins to rain all over the Universe. Every wizard knows when this is happening, and when it does, we all stand to point our staff, topped with a crystal, towards the night or day sky. The very moment the sun reappears, its bright beams shoot through the rain, seeking out the seven enchanted gemstones. Their sparkling colours are then reflected into the sun where they are deflected, spiralling down to charge a black diamond called a collector. This diamond is held in the outstretched hand of the Sun Giant standing high up on a mountaintop. He quickly absorbs this enchanted energy and distributes it to every wizard throughout the world. All this happens in a blink of an eye."

The wizard sighed a little then gently shook his head before carrying on.

"The vision you have just witnessed happened in February 1302 AD twenty-one months after our total solar eclipse. The giant wizard is my cousin, Brynmoroc. Since the great Vindaguar passed away in the year 1150 AD, the Sun Giant was the only one who knew the location of the black diamond."

"Sun Giant! I don't understand," I said interrupting. "Who or what is the Sun Giant?"

"The Sun Giant is a visible mass of rippling energy, created by Vindaguar. He receives this energy all year round from the sun. However, although his appearance is that of a human, the giant longed for a human body. Before Vindaguar died he enrolled Brynmoroc as the highest-ranking wizard. Brynmoroc was happy with this, but he was already a very powerful wizard in his own right. Also, before Vindaguar died, he voiced a prophecy, warning all wizards of the consequences of stealing the power of the precious stones. Unfortunately, Brynmoroc became restless and dictative. This newly ordained authority created in him a desire for more, to rule the entire enchanted kingdom. Yes, my rapacious cousin knew that if he were in possession of the black diamond, he could receive all the power of the jewels. Henceforth, in defiance of the prophecy and because he lusted for total power, he conjured up what he thought to be a foolproof plan of counteracting the prophecy's fulfilment and set out to trick the Sun Giant. My crafty cousin promised the giant, that if he was to let him hold the black diamond to absorb its energy, he would then have the power to give him a wizard's body. The Sun Giant was delighted and happily agreed, but what the giant didn't know was; he would also be absorbed along with the energy of the jewels. The body my crafty cousin promised him, was none other than his own. So, in May of the year 1300 during the centenary total solar eclipse, that's precisely what happened. Immediately Brynmoroc grew to twice his size and was a powerful force of enchanted energy. However, unfortunately for my devious cousin, not only did he absorb the trusting Sun Giant, he also absorbed the sacred black diamond. The violating wizard suddenly found himself in an unexpected situation. Realising this, Brynmoroc knew that he'd be okay and would still be able to receive the power of the jewels as long as no one ever found them. Not one person or any living creature knows where these precious jewels are hidden, and no one would ever dare go looking, either. In Vindaguar's prophecy, he stated that the lady with all-seeing eyes would be Spanish. Brynmoroc knew this and it was part of his plan but he made a big mistake in thinking that my wife, being Spanish and a high-ranking Soothsayer, was the lady in the prophecy. Without her, the prophecy would be null and void. So, out of ignorance, he came here to capture her, the rest you have already seen. Then, in thirteen hundred and ten, with his power and wealth, he compiled a human army, conquered the Spanish city of Murcia and took over Lorca Castle. Over the centuries, the Spanish people have called this castle the Fortress of the Sun. Brynmoroc lives there, ruling our world as the powerful gleaming giant and at the same time in your world under the pretence of being the people's kind and generous Lord."

I was more than curious now and politely interrupted him.

"Surely the people of Murcia must think it strange him being a gleaming giant, twelve feet tall and over five hundred years old?"

Bleddwyn replied, "In the three-dimensional world, Brynmoroc can take on many forms. The real Brynmoroc, the gleaming wizard, people have never known or seen. To achieve this, down over the centuries he has manipulated people's minds with illusions of his death and funeral, leaving behind false images of a wife and an identical son bearing the same name. Down over the years, the evil wizard has faked his death eight times."

To me, that was crazy and unbelievable, but I said nothing, but thought, did it all mean that Bleddwyn had no power now and never would? So I asked him.

"That's not quite true, Gwydion. No more enchanted energy, yes, but we still have the natural source of energy we were born with. To explain enchanted energy in-depth would be more than complicated for you to understand, but I'll give you an idea. In your world, you call it magic, something fabricated, something written in children's stories or a magician's trick. To us, it is the ability to create by using the very source of life called atoms. That is all I can say other than without our supply of enchanted energy, we have no dynamic force, nor can we create to our usual strengths. So, with Brynmoroc being all-powerful, especially during the day, and with me now confined solely to our one dimensional, I can only venture out at night, though sadly, only local…."

Once again, I interrupted him, "Excuse me Sir, but I was wondering. If you were confined to this area, and only venture out at night, how could you possibly know what was said and happening elsewhere?"

"Night birds Gwydion. The birds have informed me of every step Brynmoroc has ever taken, and every word my wife had ever spoken."

"Excuse me again Sir. But why have you been waiting nearly six hundred years just for me? You tell me that I am your instigator of some prophecy. How can this be? I am no one special. All I do is shovel iron ore and coal every day. You are a wizard; how can I possibly help you?"

Without answering, he leaned forward in his chair, tapped the base of his staff on the floor, pointed it towards the wall, and another vision appeared. It was a beautiful young lady with long black hair, serving hot drinks in what looked to be a train station.

"This young lady Gwydion is the last of my bloodren. Her name is Lucia. When Brynmoroc kidnapped Eluciana, she was pregnant with my daughter Natalia, who in August thirteen hundred and two, was born in the dungeons of his Spanish castle. When my child reached the age of six months, Brynmoroc gave her to some passing peasants who then sold her to a childless couple, Alberto and Diana Lavanatti. Alberto and Diana, before Brynmoroc invaded the city and evicted them from Lorca castle, were the Emperor and Empress of Murcia. Unknown to Brynmoroc, after Natalia was born, Eluciana placed in the young eyes of my daughter the knowledge of how to seek out the enchanted jewels. This knowledge has been secretly passed down through the ages and is now in the beautiful eyes of Lucia."

He then paused and frowned a little before answering my earlier question.

"You are who I say you are, Gwydion. During my wife's captivity, she had foreseen that on this day I would meet the instigator, a young son of a coal miner. Together with Lucia, you must fulfil the prophecy's revelation by seeking out, not Brynmoroc, but the seven enchanted jewels. However, because of the ongoing secrecy, Lucia does not know about myself and Eluciana being her ancestors. This and whatever else you may discover about Lucia, you must promise to keep it secret. She will know everything when the time comes. Also, as you carry out your mission, you may develop feelings for her. If so, you must never show or reveal them to her. It may also happen that she develops feelings for you. In that case, you must do all you can to discourage her."

I promised him, though I don't know why for it all seemed crazy to me. I then asked how he had managed to live for hundreds of years, but his wife Eluciana and his many grandchildren hadn't.

"Wizards live for thousands of years and so too can a wizardess, soothsayers' and the likes. Unfortunately, our daughter Natalia, although born of pure wizard blood, was also born in an era without enchanted energy. Without this energy we wizards provide to our newborns, Natalia's lifespan was that of a human."

That also seemed a little crazy, but feasible. Before carrying on, the wizard let down his staff, and the vision disappeared.

"The finding of the jewels must be achieved before the next total solar eclipse, the twenty-eighth of May nineteen hundred. After you have located them all, what happens then I know not. Lucia is the only one with the knowledge of completing the prophecy on the day of the eclipse. Only then, will the enchanted energy be restored to all wizards and our world of enchantment?"

He now pointed to the gold chest that I had noticed earlier and asked me to open it. I walked over and very carefully lifted the lid.

"Wow!" I said as two gleaming silver shields dazzled me for a moment.

"Take out the shields, Gwydion. Give them to me then take out the rest."

I lifted out the shields and nervously placed them on the table in front of him. As for the rest, I was a little disappointed. All that was in there was a single black cape, neatly folded. I took it out and placed it alongside the shields which were no longer bright.

"Sit Gwydion. Please sit and listen?" He asked, holding his hand out in front of him.

I turned to sit but staggered back in shock. Alongside the table was a wooden chair carved in my image. So I gently sat down on myself and listened.

"This shield, as you have probably guessed, belonged to Eluciana. It is now Lucia's. The cape is mine; now it's yours. So too is the other shield."

He then sternly looked at me as if making sure that I was listening.

"Lucia has recently moved from Spain to the City of Cork and works there as a waitress in the tea room of Cork train station. Lucia knows of the prophecy and will be expecting you. Once you make yourself known to her and her to you, the rest will fall into place."

He lay down his staff on the table and went over to a little box on the dresser. While he did so, I happened to notice that on the wall was a painting of a young man riding a dappled grey horse. I recognised it being the fabulous wild horse roaming our mountains. Alongside them was a beautiful queen riding a sizeable white elk. She was wearing green riding clothes and on her head was a white crown with a green emerald in the middle that was actually twinkling. The wizard noticed me looking at it, and as he sat back down in his chair, placed a small pouch on the table. He stayed seated for a while, saying nothing, until I heard the slab stone rumbling.

"Now go!" He said in a stern voice. "Go, prepare yourself and return here at noon on the first day of the new week."

I was puzzled now, so as I made my way to the steps I turned and asked him to explain.

"What do you mean, prepare yourself? How can I prepare myself for such a journey?"

"The best way you can, son. The best way you can," was his reply.

With that and after stepping out into the sunlight, I sighed in relief hearing that slab stone rumbling shut behind me.

"Dew!" I said to myself. "If he thinks I'm going all around the world looking for some gemstones that no one has ever found, he's got another think coming. That's just crazy; it takes me a week to walk to Swansea, never mind ten months to go around the world. I'm off home and never coming back up here again, ever."

I sighed again and walked off down the mountain, happy to be free. I looked over to the Balls Pond to see if Mad Luke was still there, but he had gone. My old school pal Tony Brown was sitting beside the pond. So I called out to him.

"Hey, Tony, I don't suppose you've seen Mad Luke about, have you?"

"Yeah, your Granddad caught him not so long ago. Are you coming fishing down over tomorrow night? Those eels we caught last week, were some size, eh?

"Yeah, I might. I'll let you know after work, but those eels, you can have them old things, I'll have the fish," I replied and laughed.

I walked home and found Mad Luke munching away in his stable, so I shouted in on him.

"You caused me some trouble. I've got a good mind not to give you any carrots tonight; I'll eat them all myself."

He took no notice and carried on eating while I walked away, laughing.

"What happened to you, Gwydion? Mad old Luke was roaming around the Balls Pond. Didn't you see him?" asked Granddad as I walked in.

"Yeah, I saw him, but I met someone and started talking. I was going to fetch him later. Is there anything to eat?" I asked, to change the subject.

I looked at him and the way he looked back I just knew he was going to say something corny.

"No," he replied. "You'll probably be full up after Mad Luke's carrots. They are over there in the bucket."

"Ah! Ya menace Granddad," I said, pulling his cap down over his eyes. "I knew you were going to say something daft."

After dinner and checking on Mad Luke, my Granddad and I had an early night.

I lay in bed for a while thinking about the wizard and my incredible day.

"Six hundred years he said. So why is it that no one has ever seen him? But there again, according to Brynmoroc, Bleddwyn was confined to their world, unable to enter ours. It's crazy but I suppose it makes sense."

Then as I was about to blow out the candle, the framed painting of a castle hanging on my wall made me jump out of bed. I had never taken much notice of it before. So I studied it more closely and found that it was very similar to a castle painted on the wall of the wizard's cave. My Granddad's room was next to mine, so I tapped on the wall and called out to him.

"Hey Granddad, are you asleep?"

"Why, what's the matter?" he replied.

"This old painting of a castle in my room, what do you know about it?" I asked.

"Oh yeah, the castle. It was the only painting in your old house. I put it in your bedroom. Why? Why do you want to know about it anyway?"

"Oh, I just wondered, that's all," I replied, getting back into bed. "Goodnight".

While I lay there thinking about the cave and that castle, I suddenly remembered the painting of the beautiful queen and the young man riding that dappled grey horse. I thought for a while, then suddenly sat up remembering a book I had read in school. The young man was Welusa, the storyteller, who after publishing his book, disappeared along with his parents. The lady on the elk had to be the beautiful Emerald Queen of Children, the Fairy Queen, who according to a girl down in the village of Afon Llwyd, Welusa had been supposed to have married. I knew where Welusa lived and walked past his empty house many times. No one would ever go in there. They were afraid to.

Trying to sleep that night was as frustrating as doing a puzzle. It was hopeless. I felt as if I was battling with the wizard who was playing with my mind. Funny thing though, I wasn't tired getting out of bed in the morning for work.

# Chapter 2

It was Saturday and my shift finished at one o'clock, but all that morning I was so far away in thought that I must have shovelled a record amount of iron ore and coal. I remembered the wizard telling me to come back on the first day of the week, which happened to be the next day. I was so tormented by not knowing what to do that I decided to have a chat with Cindy, a trusted friend of mine.

Afon Llwyd was no more than ten minutes away so after work, I called around to her house in Staffordshire Row and lucky enough she was in. I told her that I wanted to ask about Welusa's book 'The Lock of Tianaju's Hair.' She made up a pot of tea, and before I could even say a word, she went right into telling me all about her best friend and his story.

"There now, Gwydion. Is there anything else you would like to know?"

I took a deep breath and replied, "No, but I would like to tell you about something that happened to me yesterday up at the old Roman ruins."

I told her everything, and when I had finished, she rose, went to the kitchen and brought in another pot of tea. She then sat down and looked into my eyes as if looking to see if I had been truthful or not.

"I believe you, Gwydion. Now you must believe me. Every bit of Welusa's book is true, right down to the very last word it is. Now, as for this giant wizard. He violated Vindaguar's law much the same as Ohibronoeler violated Fairyland's. He must be brought to justice."

After finishing our tea, and before I stood up to leave, she leaned over and held my hand.

"Gwydion, for some reason the wizard has either chosen you, or you are the true instigator of the prophecy. If you have any doubts at all, let the wizard know, and he will assure you. The only piece of advice I can give you is, to do as Welusa did, follow your heart. Then if you do decide to take on the wizard's quest, once again, follow Welusa and write a journal."

I thanked her for everything and asked her not to mention our conversation to anyone.

"Your secret is safe with me Gwydion, and I trust mine is with you?"

I assured her that it was and always would be. She then kissed me on the cheek and said, "Good luck Gwydion. I'll tell Welusa the next time I see him."

On the way home, I met Ross Price, an old-school prefect from my class.

"Hi Ross, you old dog. Are you playing rugby on Saturday?" I asked.

"Hopefully, well if I can borrow a pair of boots, that is," he replied and laughed.

"Yeah, and a pair of boxing gloves too!" I said. "Anyway, what did you do with the last pair you had? Worn out from kicking everyone, no doubt."

"No, that's not like me. I hate that kind of stuff," Ross shouted and laughed

In bed that night, all I did was think and the more I thought the more I convinced myself that the whole idea was more than ludicrous.

"How could I go around the world? I'll probably get beaten up and thrown overboard before I even reach Ireland. Besides, I have a good job and if I give it up, I may never get another. What about Granddad? What will I say to him? How can I possibly tell him that I'm leaving and if I did, where will I say I'm going? Ah! It's crazy. I'm going to tell that wizard tomorrow that I can't go."

I was up at seven and after breakfast, Granddad and I hitched up Mad Luke to the cart and went off to church. Making our way across Queen Street, we stopped to give Sheila and Theresa Morgan a lift. There was always someone wanting a lift to church. Going home was just the same. Even that very day, Roger Regan and Les Schofield wanted a ride as far as the Pottery. So it was eleven o'clock before arriving home. Granddad went away off up the mountain, checking on his sheep while I paced around the house and yard thinking of what I was going to say to the wizard.

Fifteen minutes to twelve, I made my way up to the old ruins, hoping I wouldn't meet Granddad on the way. Thankfully, he was nowhere in sight. It was almost noon and once again as I began to slide back the slab stone, my heart began to race. I was kind of hoping that the cellar wasn't going to be there, but it was, and just as dark. I took a deep breath and slowly descended the steps, reaching the bottom just as the hatch closed above me. I stood there in the darkness for a moment or two until about fifty candles lit up the whole place. I looked, expecting the wizard to be there but he wasn't.

"Oh no, here we go again," I muttered. "Where is he? What's he up to now?"

"Here I am," said the wizard, appearing in his chair. "Sit Gwydion and drink."

There was a small glass of wine on the table in front of me, so I walked over, sat and took a sip. I noticed that the cape, both shields and pouch were still on the table in precisely the same position when I left. I half smiled and waited for him to say something, but he didn't. He just sat there, smiling, looking at me as if expecting me to speak.

"Okay," I said to myself, "Here goes, let's give him the bad news."

Suddenly, a fear came over me. I was afraid now of what he might say and do after I told him. So I took another couple of deep breaths before squeaking out, "Excuse me……"

"Gwydion," said the wizard, interrupting me. "I know of your worries and fears, so I am going to assure you. Pick up the cape and put it on."

I slipped it on and as I did, a strange sensation came over me, and my fear left.

"As long as you wear the cape Gwydion, you will have exceptional strength, and no human can harm you. Now pick up the pouch and take out what's inside and give it to me."

I reached over, picked up the pouch and opened it. There was a guinea inside, so I took it out and gave it to him. He then told me to look inside again. I did and found another guinea.

"You will never want for money ever again," said the wizard and smiled. "No matter what happens, there will always be a guinea in your pouch. Now, firmly take hold of my staff."

He stood up, held out his staff and as I grasped it a sheering pain went through my hand up to my shoulder making me quickly push the staff away. Then before my very eyes, a blackthorn staff quickly began to grow in my hand to about six feet long. The pain in my hand was so unbearable that I grabbed the staff with my left hand and pulled it away. As I did, a large thorn about the thickness of a knitting needle came away from the staff and was left sticking out of my middle finger. I hollered in pain, pulled it out and threw it away.

"Gwydion, the prophecy says that you must use this staff to extract and absorb the colours from each of the seven enchanted jewels. To absorb these colours, simply place the base of the staff on each and every one of the jewels as you find them. The rest of the prophecy is in the eyes of Lucia. The staff is also your means of transportation, but remember this; you can only fly once. There is only enough energy in the staff to do so. Energy that I have been saving especially for this day. Use it wisely Gwydion."

I was astonished by it all and my hand was paining like mad. I mentioned it to him and asked him why the thorn had stuck in my finger. Before he replied, he leaned forward, held my hand and the pain went away. He then gazed into my eyes and with a puzzled look he shook his head.

"I know nothing about the meaning of the thorn. All I know is that it is part of the prophecy. Take care of the staff Gwydion; never give it to anyone, especially Brynmoroc, for without the staff the prophecy is null and void."

I half-looked him in the eye and said, "You say that I am the instigator of some ancient prophecy, why, I don't know. Wizards and magic, as you said, I thought were only in books and imaginative minds. How wrong we were and because of this, and the very fact you seem to have faith in me, I accept the mission and only hope that I can fulfil it. Also, I feel a lot better, knowing that I will have protection and enough money."

"Now go. Go tell who you must and only return here when you are ready," was all the wizard said, not even a thank you.

I was a little worried about protecting the staff because it would have to be in my possession at all times. What would people think and how would they react to me carrying a six-foot staff all around the world? I thought this to be undeniably awkward and mentioned it to the wizard.

"I was waiting for you to ask me that," he replied. "I fully understand the dilemma you face, so to help you on your travels and to avoid unwanted attention, the staff will automatically reduce to the size of a normal walking stick as the occasion arises. Also, I would like you to know that apart from Brynmoroc, no one can take the staff or cloak from you against your will."

Within an instant, I was outside looking down the mountain. My cape was gone but I still had the staff in my hand. It was just an ordinary staff, not like the wizards with a crystal tip. It was weird and I had to laugh because, with this six-foot staff of mine, I truly felt like a wizard.

Walking home, I put my hand in my pocket and felt something inside. It was the pouch and after opening it, the guinea was still in there. I took out the coin and thought I'd give it to Granddad. Then just as the wizard said, there was another one inside. So I took it out, put the two coins in my pocket and walked down the mountain.

That evening, while Granddad and I were sitting down, talking about the local gossip, I thought it was a good time to tell him that I was going away for a while. I waited for him to light his pipe before telling him.

"Granddad, I've recently been thinking about going to sea. There's someone in Cork who has work lined up for me, so there is no need to worry.

I've saved enough money to keep me going for a while. There's a boat sailing every day from Swansea and I intend to take it as soon as I can. I'm sorry to spring this on you Granddad but it's only until next summer. The Iron Works is coming to an end anyway. When I come back, I'll get a job down the mine."

He took his pipe out of his mouth and to my surprise, he liked the idea.

"Good for you Gwydion, I'm pleased for you. You are a bright young lad, and I know you'll do well. As for the coalmine, ah, you don't want to be going down there, son. Maybe after you return, we'll buy ourselves a little more land and breed a few horses, eh? Would you like that?"

"Yes, that'll be great Granddad, thank you for understanding. Funny you suggested buying more land. I have also saved another two guineas for special occasions. Here, you can put them towards it."

"Wow!" He said in astonishment. "I wondered what you were doing with your money. I'll put them away until you come back. Now we had better get to bed."

As usual, I was up early in the morning and arrived well in time for work. During our break, I told my mates that I was off working overseas until next summer. Prothy wanted to come until he remembered that his mother probably wouldn't let him. That was lucky, for I wouldn't have known how to tell him he couldn't come. Next, was my boss, Fenton Coles. He wasn't too happy at first but later wished me luck.

"You are probably doing the right thing Gwydion. This place, as you know, looks as if it will be closing down shortly. So good luck son, I hope you come back a rich man."

He then joked, "If you do, I may want to borrow a coin or two."

When I left my shovel beside the furnace that evening, I never felt so miserable in all my life. I didn't realise until that moment that I would never work there ever again.

After supper, Granddad asked if I had told my boss that I was leaving. I said that I had, but it was terrible saying goodbye to everyone.

"Ah, don't be sad son. You just go and enjoy yourself. They'll still be here when you come home, and you'll have plenty to tell them too, won't you?"

I told him that he was the best and that I'd bring him back a new pipe and some foreign bacci. He just laughed and after that, I went upstairs and packed, but very little for I knew I would have plenty of money to buy whatever I needed.

Once again, I found it hard to get to sleep from thinking, worrying about Granddad and the mission. Finally, when I did drop off, it only seemed five minutes before Mad Luke woke me up, whinnying.

I dressed and went downstairs. Granddad was just coming in from feeding Mad Luke.

"Haha, did he wake you, son?" He said and laughed. "Come on, let's have some breakfast before the mice eat it all."

"I'm going to miss you Granddad," I said, feeling sad. "You know I will, don't you?"

"I'll miss you too son, but it'll soon fly by," he said, tapping my shoulder.

After we had eaten, Granddad told me that he was off to check on the flock and would see me later. I watched him go, collected my staff from my room and headed up to the wizard. When I approached the ruins, the slab stone slid open without me even touching it. Happily, the cellar was already lit up.

"Good morning Gwydion. Come, please sit down?" beckoned the wizard as I entered.

"Good morning Sir," I replied as I sat on myself.

"Tell me Gwydion, are you ready and willing to fulfil the prophecy?"

"Yes Sir, I am," I replied.

Bleddwyn smiled, looked at the cloak and shields on the table and asked me to pick them up and surprisingly told me to order them into my pocket. I did as he asked and all three disappeared into my jacket pocket. I was amazed and looked at the broad smiling wizard.

"The shields will help defend you and Lucia against Brynmoroc and his wizardry."

That was when the seriousness of the mission dawned on me. The very word defend made me think that we were going to do battle with the giant. If so, all we had was a shield and a stick.

"A battle, yes," said Bleddwyn, who had obviously read my mind. "One in which no wizard, not even Brynmoroc, can apply energy directly towards a human, if so, it will recoil. So yes again Gwydion, once the prophecy has been initiated Brynmoroc will do his utmost to prevent its completion. During this time, he can and will, conjure up many forms of creatures to seriously hamper your progress, and sad to say, physical contact with them could be fatal. Fortunately, apart from his wizardry, because he is one with the Sun Giant, Brynmoroc can only maximise his enchanted energy during the midday sun, but heed me now Gwydion, after the sacred jewels have all been drained, there is nothing to stop Brynmoroc from engaging in physical contact for the possession of your staff, and this he will surely do."

Bleddwyn hesitated, and before saying another word, he looked carefully and seriously into my eyes, making me think that something terrible was going to happen.

"Knowing this and all that I have told you, do you still want to take on the assignment?"

I couldn't have been any more baffled than I was a few days ago. But this time, death was mentioned. Nevertheless, I was determined to carry on regardless, so I assured him that I was.

"That's good," he replied. "Now as I have already told you, wizards live in the three-dimensional world of Earth and at the same time in our singular-dimensional world of Enchantment, making it four-dimensional. On your mission, you and Lucia will also travel in this four-dimensional world, but you will not be aware of it. Now, as for your staff Gwydion, once you absorb the power of the first stone, the staff will become a powerful source of energy, more so after you have absorbed them all. Until then, it can only be used for whatever means of travel you so wish. To do this, hold out the staff in your left hand and either command it with your thoughts or cry out, 'gofynnaf i chi. The staff will then analyse your command accordingly. If it is of animal nature, the creature will understand and obey you. Use it wisely, Gwydion."

I knew gofynnaf i chi was Welsh for I ask you. So I took hold of my staff, looked into his eyes and told him that I wasn't afraid, but worried about letting him down."

"You are a good lad Gwydion. Now once you have found Lucia, you must take good care of her. Never let her out of your sight unless absolutely necessary. Also, remember the promise you made to me. Now go, don't worry, for in you I have every faith. Go, do what destiny has ordained for you.

As I turned to walk away, Bleddwyn called out, "One more thing Gwydion. During your journey, you will meet many devious people, all claiming to be someone they are not. You have a kind heart son, don't let it be your downfall. Be especially aware of sweet loving ladies."

The next thing I knew; I was once again back standing on the slab stone, holding my six-foot staff in my hand. I looked at my watch and found that it was way past noon. I went home and made up a few sandwiches for myself and Granddad for when he came home.

That evening, Granddad suggested that if I was still determined to go, it would be a good idea to go the next day. Dai, the cockle man, who came from Swansea to Blaenafon selling cockles, was due in town that day. Granddad knew him well and said that he would have a word with Dai. That was good of him and I told him so. The boat sailed every day at midnight so we'd arrive in plenty of time. The next thing to do was to go down to the tavern and tell my mates.

"Don't have too much to drink son," said my laughing Granddad. "I remember one night down at the old tavern when I had too much to drink, your grandmother had to come and take me home in a wheelbarrow."

"Yeah, and all the other nights too," I joked and laughed. "I'm off. See you in the morning Granddad."

# Chapter 3

I was up at eight to help Granddad around the yard. After dinner, I put an apple in my pocket and to pass the time away I retrieved my staff, which I had hidden, and went for a walk up to the Keeper's Pond. While up there, something made me think of the mythical dragon. So, just out of curiosity, I walked over to the Dragon's Pond and sat on the bank. While taking a bite from my apple, I saw a ripple in the water coming towards me and the head of a small red dragon popped up in front of me.

"Strewth! It's a dragon. A real dragon," I said, jumping up and backing away.

"Of course, I'm real Gwydion," said the dragon. "Didn't the wizard tell you?"

I stood there in astonishment, thinking to myself, "He can talk. Really talk."

"Well?" asked the dragon," swimming a little closer.

"No, the wizard didn't," I quietly replied.

"Haha," laughed the dragon. "He knew you would make your way up here and was probably keeping it a surprise for you. Anyway, how is your Granddad getting on? I see him from time to time, rounding up his lovely sheep."

It was amazing to think that Ohibronoeler, the dragon, really existed and that he was actually here in the pond. Talking to him made me once again realise what kind of world I had entered. I knew from reading Welusa's book that Ohibronoeler was once a Lord, a tyrant Lord, and because of it, he was doomed to live as a dragon in that pond until he changed his ways. I also knew that he was full of blarney and was trying to trick me.

"Yes, you are right," I replied. "He must have wanted to surprise me. Thank you for asking about my Granddad, he's keeping well. How are you?"

"Oh, I'm fine. Just a little bored, that's all. That's a nice staff you have there. Did the wizard give it to you?" he asked.

"Yes, he did," I replied. "Do you like it?"

"Yes, I do Gwydion. Is it an enchanted staff?"

Going by what the wizard had told me, I knew the staff had some kind of power, but I didn't know what. Even if I did, I still wouldn't have told the sneaky dragon.

"I don't know. What do you think?" I asked, wondering what he'd say.

When the dragon heard me ask his thoughts, I could tell by his face that he was excited.

"No, it's probably just an old stick," he replied, swimming back out into the middle.

"Hey! I've got an idea; I like sticks, so why don't you throw it in for me to fetch? We can have some fun every day then."

I knew what he was up to. If the staff were to be enchanted, he could probably use it to escape from the pond.

"No, you don't want this," I shouted. "Sticks are only for dogs. Here, have my apple stump instead."

I threw it in, but much to his disgust and anger, he bellowed out abuse.

"Ah, you're as bad as that fool Welusa and that joking Granddad of yours."

He carried on shouting, but because he was spitting water at the same time, it was difficult understanding him.

"I don't know what you are saying. But I'm off home now, maybe I'll see you again one day," I said and began walking on over the heather.

"Hey Gwydion, hold on, don't go away yet. Don't leave before I tell you about ya mother, how she sold you to that fool of an old sheep farmer. She was a drunk, a lousy ugly drunk who sold you for a pint of stout. She met your father at the garbage dump where he lived, and he was just as ugly. Why they were so ugly, you cried day and night, and that's not all, they grew even uglier, so horrible that they ran away, terrified of each other. Oh yeah, one other thing, before you run away like them and that coward Welusa. Tell that cheapskate old farmer, who you think is your Granddad, if his stinking sheep come piddling in my pond again, he'll find them floating in it and his dog. Oh, and by the way, those old trousers you are wearing, they are so full of holes I can see ya dirty bottom. They must have been your fathers."

I carried on walking, laughing with him shouting, "Yeah, you can laugh, I forgot to tell ya, you even look like him, ya old toad, you."

He was so funny; I could have stayed there all day listening to him ranting and raving. I arrived home, dying to tell Granddad about him, but I didn't.

At seven o'clock, there was a knock on the door and I knew the time had come to say goodbye to Granddad.

"Here Gwydion, take my lucky penny with you. I used to take it with me when I went travelling. If it weren't for that, I wouldn't have met your Grandmother."

"Ah, no Granddad. You need it more than me. Besides, I have my own lucky charm, this stick."

He laughed and said, "Well, look after yourself son. Don't worry about me. See you next summer."

It was a sad goodbye, but Dai the cockle man was outside waiting. So I picked up my knapsack, pulled Granddad's cap down over his eyes and said, "Yeah, see ya. See ya, you old codger you, Granddad."

Dai and I travelled all through the night, stopping now and then to rest the two horses and to have ourselves a nap. It was eleven in the morning when we finally arrived at the port. I thanked Dai and gave him a guinea. The booking office wasn't open until ten that night, so I had to hang around for almost ten hours until the office opened. I paid for my passage, went aboard and found a seat inside. While I sat there, I began thinking about the dragon and couldn't help laughing at his crazy rants and wondered if he was still talking to himself.

The boat set sail and I was on my way to Ireland. It was my first time aboard a ship, so I ventured out onto the deck. It was a clear moonlit night, but windy. I stayed there watching the flickering lights of Swansea until they slowly disappeared in the distance. I went back inside, sat down and had a sandwich. Then after about an hour, the boat began to sway and rock.

"I'm going to be sick," I muttered, wishing I hadn't eaten that sandwich.

I quickly headed back on deck and for dear life, I hung onto the railings. The sea was rough now with large waves rocking the boat something terrible. One minute I was looking at the enormous waves; the next I was looking at the starry moonlit sky. I had never felt so nauseous in my entire life. The only way I could stop myself from being sick was to keep my head up looking only at the moon and stars. I stayed that way all night until we docked twelve hours later in Cork. By the time I stepped off that rotten boat, I was soaking wet with a stiff neck, smelling of fish, freezing cold and covered in slimy seaweed.

"There's no way I'm ever going back on that boat again," I said, rubbing my neck.

After I had rid myself of seaweed and warmed up, I asked one of the offshore crew if he knew of a place to stay for a few days. He told me that a lovely elderly lady, living a mile away, would surely put me up. The first thing I had to do was get rid of my wet and smelly clothes. On my way to the lady's cottage, I called into a store, bought a change of clothes and dumped my others. When I arrived at her cottage, she welcomed me and showed me to my room. Soon as I flopped onto the bed, I was asleep in no time but was surprised when I woke. I had slept for more than twenty-four hours. The little old lady was so kind and lovely that I stayed there another two days. Before I left, I paid the lady generously, checked out the route to the train station and caught the mail coach to Cork City. We stopped once to water the horses and arrived at the station mid-afternoon. I was nervous looking around for the stall where they sold hot drinks, even more so when I found it. I didn't know whether or not I could recognise Lucia from the vision, and even if I did, what was I going to say. Eventually, I plucked up a little courage and went over to buy a drink, but the girl serving the lady in front of me had short blond hair. I was disappointed, but suddenly, as I waited behind this lady, another girl stood up from down behind the counter. She had spilt something and had been cleaning it up.

"Can I help you?" she softly asked after giving me a lovely smile.

My mind suddenly went blank for I was now looking at a beautiful girl with dark eyes, lightly tanned skin and long black hair. I was stunned and couldn't remember what I wanted to drink until she asked if I would like tea or coffee.

"Is the coffee nice," I asked

"It is when I make it," she said and once again, beamed that beautiful smile.

I smiled back and said, "Well, in that case, I'll have one, please."

While she was pouring out the coffee, the blonde assistant tried to squeeze past her.

"Excuse me, Lucia," said the blonde. "Can I pass by, please? I need some sugar."

I now knew that the dark-haired girl's name was Lucia. Whether it was the Lucia I was looking for was another thing. So I took a deep breath and asked, as Lucia handed me the coffee.

"With a name like that, you must be from Portugal?" Hoping, of course, she wasn't.

"No," she replied. "I'm from Spain. I'm Spanish. What about you? Where are you from?"

"Wales. Yeah uh, Wales. South Wales," I replied, still mesmerised by her lovely smile

"Is it nice there?" she then asked.

"Yes, it is, though probably not as nice as Spain and definitely not as hot."

She then handed me the coffee, saying that I hope I'd enjoy it. I said that it looked nice and was sure that I would. I sat down at a nearby table and while sipping my coffee, I began thinking.

"Why didn't the wizard tell me what to say to her? She'll be expecting you, he said. Well, it certainly didn't look that way. So obviously, she doesn't know me. What can I do? I just can't walk up to her and say, I'm the one you are expecting. Perhaps it's not the right girl and then she'd think I'm crazy."

I was so deep in thought; I didn't notice that the stall had closed and the girls had gone. I searched all around the station but couldn't find them anywhere. I asked a couple of porters if they knew where Lucia lived, but sadly they didn't. I asked a few more workers, but no one knew until a young lad came up to me.

"Hello Sir. I heard you were looking for Lucia, the Spanish girl?"

"Yes!" I replied anxiously. "Do you know her and where she lives?"

"Yes, I know her and where she lives, but for a penny," he replied, holding out his hand.

After giving him a penny, he told me that Lucia lived on a Tinker's campsite. The boy then asked for another penny before he'd say where it was. I gave him a guinea and he told me where she lived. The kid was so happy with the money that he skipped off, shouting over and over that he was rich. Knowing where she lived, I sat down talking to myself until a dark-haired young lady came up to me.

"Excuse me. I hope you don't mind me asking, but are you a wizard?"

She was pretty with dark hair and about the same age as me, but her lovely eyes were green, so she wasn't Lucia.

"Oh, I'm sorry," she quickly said. "Let me introduce myself; I'm Emma Hill. I hope you don't think me strange asking you a question like that."

"Well, Emma. What makes you think I'm a wizard?" I asked the inquisitive young lady.

"It's your staff," she replied. "It's a wizard's staff. I know this because every blackthorn staff has staggered thorns, but on a wizard's, they are even. I love wizards and have a book on them."

"You are right," I said, looking at it. "I hadn't noticed that before, but unfortunately, I'm not a wizard. I didn't know there were any, but if I was, what would you like?"

"A job would be nice," she replied without even thinking

"Only a job!" I said and laughed.

"Well, somewhere to live would be nice too, but a job would do."

"You mean to tell me that you truly have nowhere to live Emma?"

"No, that's not what I meant," she replied. "I'm living with my auntie and have been ever since my parents died, but we don't get on. She doesn't like me and I don't like her either. So yes, I would like to have a place of my own."

"I am sad to hear that," I said, feeling sorry for her. "If ever I do find that this old stick has magical powers, I promise I'll remember you and come looking. But I have to go now, I'm meeting someone."

I said goodbye and went away before she asked any more questions.

That afternoon, I caught the jaunting car and we travelled out of the city, and up towards the campsite. I asked the driver to let me off about a mile from the camp. I wanted to think about how to approach Lucia and what to say. I walked on along the road until I arrived at the site where a field full of brightly coloured, round wooden caravans were strategically spaced. In the middle of the camp, I saw smoke and flames rising from a large fire. I had no time to study because four children came over and surrounded me.

"Who are you? What do you want? Give me that stick?" they demanded.

Then a bearded man, who was attending to a large white mare, shouted at them. "Leave him alone! Who are you stranger? What do you want?"

I told him that I was looking for Lucia and could he tell me which one of the caravans was hers.

"Why? What's your business with her?" he asked walking towards me.

"I don't want to sound rude but it's personal," I nervously replied.

He came so close, there was a distinct smell of drink on his breath.

"Well, in that case, she's over there around the campfire doing her usual tricks," he said, to my relief.

The campfire was in the centre of the site where a crowd of men, women and children were gathered. As I walked towards them, I could see Lucia pointing at one of the men. She was wearing a red dress with a red and white shawl around her shoulders and while shaking her long black hair, she asked a man, "Is this the one?"

They all laughed as the man shouted, "You know it is. That's another bucket of water I've to fetch you."

There was laughter again until they caught sight of me standing there, watching them.

"Who are you? Get away from here stranger, before I set the dog on you," shouted one of them.

Lucky for me, the bearded man I was talking to earlier, shouted out, "He's okay! Leave him be. He wants to speak to our Lucia."

Lucia looked across at the same time a young girl was pleading with her to do one more trick.

"Okay, I'll talk to him shortly," she said, dropping a rock to the ground.

I then watched as she walked over to a few pans and after turning them upside down, she asked the girl to pick up the rock and hide it under one of them. Lucia turned her back to the girl, but instead of hiding the rock under the pots the girl placed it in her pocket and shouted, "Ready!"

Lucia began scanning over all the pots, then laughed and said as she walked over to the little girl.

"Come on, Mary, take it out of your pocket, before you sit on it?"

"Oh, you were cheating Lucia," retorted Mary to the roar of laughter.

With that, Lucia walked over to me and said after beaming a lovely smile, "Hello, what's the matter? Didn't you like your coffee?"

"Oh yeah, the coffee," I replied. "Well, I must have. But to be honest, I can't remember drinking it. Perhaps I didn't?"

"Well, you are a funny one. Why ever not," she asked and laughed.

"I was trying to find you," I replied, looking into her lovely dark eyes.

Her facial expression changed now as she lovingly asked, "Whatever for?"

I stuttered, "Um, eh, well. There's something I would like to ask you, but it's complicated."

"Well, you had better tell me, before you lose your mind again," she said and chuckled. "Come on, let's go over to my little home where it's quiet."

She took me over to a beautiful pink and white wooden caravan with carved etchings around the roof. Three wooden steps were leading up to a lovely double door with the top half wide open.

"Well, what is it that's so complicated to ask me?" she said as she sat on the steps.

"Um, I bet you couldn't tell me where the enchanted jewels are?" I replied.

Hearing this, Lucia sprang to her feet, making me drop my staff just in time to catch her as she jumped, wrapping her arms around me. I staggered back and fell to the ground with her lying on top of me.

"It's you; it's you. You've come at last. I knew there was something strange about you," she said excitedly.

She clambered to her feet, grabbed my hands, pulled me upright and was back hugging me again.

"Wow!" I said in surprise. "What was I worried about? I wish I'd asked you at the station now."

"Come in; you must come in," she said, letting me go. "Are you hungry? I'll make you something to eat. Where are you staying? You must stay with me now. Oh, I have been so looking forward to meeting you. Put your pack and stick up on the shelf and sit down. What about a nice sandwich? Would you like that?"

"Yes, please. That would be lovely. I haven't eaten much since that old boat ride," I replied.

I was feeling a lot more relaxed now than earlier. So I sat down and looked around while she made up a sandwich. It was a cosy little caravan with a window at the front and another in the top half of the door. Opposite me were cupboards high above a soft bench seat, with pink curtains tied back on the sides. It was the same on my side. The table I thought was very clever, looking as if it would fold back up under the front window.

"There now," she said, putting the sandwiches on the table. "By the way, what's your name?" she asked, in her lovely Spanish accent.

"Gwydion. Gwydion Llewellyn," I replied.

Her eyes widened, "Gwydion! That's an unusual name, but it sounds nice. Would you like a glass of milk or a jug of cider with your sandwich?"

"Yes, please," I replied. "A glass of milk would be lovely. Cider would only start my stomach off again."

She laughed, poured the milk and sat down opposite while we enjoyed the sandwiches. After getting to know one another and after me telling her all about my encounter with the wizard, we agreed that we should get some sleep before making any plans. The benches were also two beds, so we made up our beds, blew out the candles and wished each other goodnight. Lying there, I remember thinking how lucky I was to be going all around the world with such a beautiful girl. She was so lovely that it made me feel warm and happy inside. The camp was quiet now and as I listened, I could tell by Lucia's breathing that she was asleep, so I turned over and I too drifted off.

# Chapter 4

"Wake up, Gwydion," I heard her say the next morning. "I have to tell my boss I'm finishing my job. I've made you a pot of tea and some bread and butter. I'm going now. We have a lot to discuss when I get back."

With no pony of her own, she travelled to work with one of the Tinkers' who would park up and sell on the roadside close to the station. With Lucia away, I tidied up her caravan before going for a walk in the afternoon. I hadn't gone far before I saw her coming up the road, swinging a stick. "Yoo-hoo Gwydion," she shouted.

I put my hand up to acknowledge her and then asked after we met, "Have you walked back on your own?"

"I had a lift to the turn-off. Come on; let's have something to eat. I'm hungry. How about you?"

She threw her stick away and gently slipped her arm into mine. I felt strange her holding my arm as if she had known me all her life. While we were walking, I remembered the wizard telling me not to leave her alone unless absolutely necessary. I mentioned this to Lucia.

She laughed and said, "Well, you had better not then, had you."

In the evening, we sat discussing our task of fulfilling the Vindaguar's prophecy. Although I thought it crazy, I once again went over everything the wizard had told me and that we only had until May to complete the seemingly impossible task. Lucia didn't think the same way and assured me that as long as we stayed together, it was possible. With this decision, I gave her the shield. She was astonished at how it shrunk every time she asked it to go into her pocket.

"Oh, this is just wonderful. My grandmother told me about this shield. I'll put it away in the cupboard."

With that done, we sat outside on the steps under a starry night sky.

"Now, Gwydion. Let's try and work out our complicated route. I can only see two jewels at any one time and each one has to be found in sequence with the rainbow's colours. The first one is ruby and I have a very good idea where it is."

"Okay, where is it?" I asked.

She shook her head a little, sighed and replied, "After we have crossed the Atlantic Ocean, it's two thousand miles across America. All I can see for now is that it's in the water on the edge of a falling rainbow."

"America! And then another two thousand miles!" I asked, hoping she was joking. "Are you sure?"

"Yes, I'm sure. So, you had better start thinking about using your staff."

"Oh yes, my staff," I said, remembering. "That should be interesting, but the wizard told me that it's only possible to fly once, so we'll have to sleep on it. Now, there is only one more thing that I have to tell you. I intend to write a journal as we go along. Is that okay with you?"

"That's fine with me," she replied. "Now, let's get some sleep because we'll have to move out early tomorrow."

We were up at dawn and after freshening up, we dressed and sat down. Lucia was anxious now.

"Well, Gwydion! Have you decided how we are going to travel?" she asked.

I said that my first thoughts were to find a ship that travelled to America, but I didn't know if I could stomach another sickening trip, especially with it being about two or three thousand miles. Plus, it would probably take us two weeks or more. The only other option was to fly, but we could only fly once. Then I thought, what if we land up with the last jewel being at the North or South Pole? So, much to my dismay, still thinking of my stomach, I had decided that we would have to travel by ship, but where from I didn't know.

"I think there's a ship that sails from Limerick to America, collecting lumber," said Lucia, tapping my hand. "I was told it's a very large ship, so perhaps they'll let us take the caravan? I can easily borrow a horse."

"Go by ship, yes. But take the caravan! I doubt it," I said and laughed. "Even if we were allowed, how could we take a caravan over mountains and goodness knows where else?"

Lucia suggested that we could take it so far, and then sell it. I was more than sceptical, but if we could, and as long as Lucia didn't mind leaving her caravan, I was happy.

"I don't mind," she replied. "At least we will have somewhere out of the weather and a place to sleep for a while."

That settled that, but before she borrowed a horse, I was going to see what my staff could do. So, I picked up my staff and we went outside. I then nervously held out the staff in my left hand and gave out the command. Then, to our amazement, a purple flash revealed a magnificent dark bay mare coupled with Lucia's caravan.

"Good grief!!" I said stepping back. It was so unreal that I couldn't stop shaking until Lucia caught hold of my arm.

"I can't believe it. She's fantastic, Gwydion. I knew you would be capable of many things, but I wasn't expecting this. Well, we are all set now so give me five minutes to tidy up, and we'll be away."

It didn't seem to have the same effect on her as it did on me, but I was still alive and thought, perhaps this could be fun.

It was a beautiful morning and with everything breakable packed away, we quietly set out on our assignment, leaving the sleeping camp behind us.

"Wee-hee!" shouted Lucia. "This is the first time I have taken my caravan out. Isn't it just wonderful Gwydion?"

"Yes, and it will be even better if our mare knows where she's going. What shall we call her?"

"Let me think, Gwydion How about Roslyn? It means beautiful in Spanish."

I thought it suited the mare so we proclaimed her Roslyn and laughed as she broke into a nice steady trot. It was lovely sitting up front with nothing to do only looking out at the beautiful scenery. We even went inside and had our breakfast while Roslyn trotted happily along, stopping now and then for a drink. The sun was behind and to the left of us, indicating that we were heading west across southern Ireland. On our way, we came across many busy people, all harvesting their precious crops. We stopped at one of the farms and bought a stock of hay, barley and oats for Roslyn. A couple of miles further on we stopped to eat. Roslyn enjoyed some hay while I collected wood for a fire. Our quaint little home had a fireplace with a chimney at the back, so with the fire burning nicely, Lucia warmed a pot of meat broth which we thoroughly enjoyed. Before heading on again, I wondered if perhaps Roslyn needed more extended rest.

"I would say Roslyn will be okay," said Lucia. "She's an enchanted animal and will probably never get tired."

So, away we went, with Roslyn breaking into a swift, smooth trotting action. She kept up the same speed for about an hour or so, only slowing down as we passed through Castleisland and Tralee. It was after leaving Tralee that Lucia and I began to panic. Suddenly, Roslyn began racing towards the coast.

"Whoa! Roslyn!" I shouted. "What are you doing? Slow down! Are you going the right way?"

Without warning, she veered off the road through a gap in the hedge, across open land heading for the coast. We didn't know whether to jump or not. Then as I looked over the side of our caravan, I was stunned to see that instead of four wheels, we now had legs, horses' legs. All we could do was hang on in desperation while Roslyn galloped across the cliffs, down onto the beach making her way to the sea. It was impossible to jump, so all we could do was hold our breath as she ploughed into the rippling waves. At that moment, we were expecting to be swallowed up and drowned only to find that we were now racing on top of the waves, out across the ocean. We were petrified, afraid to speak and as we held on to each other not knowing what to expect, we suddenly found ourselves falling onto a bed inside a cabin of a boat.

Lucia was as white as snow now, shaking from fright, "Oh Gwydion. That was terrible. What's happening now?"

"Your guess is as good as mine," I replied. "Stay here while I take a look outside."

"No! Don't leave me, Gwydion," she pleaded, grabbing hold of my arm.

I had forgotten about not leaving her, so I held her arm and opened the cabin door. After walking along a short passageway, up a ladder and through a door, we were out onto the deck of a medium-sized boat with a tall mast but no captain's bridge. The sails were folded up and tied, reminding me very much of a small Noah's Ark, but with a mast.

"Gwydion, look?" shouted Lucia excitedly. "Oh look at them Gwydion?"

I looked and laughed with joy, for to add to our incredible experience, we were being towed swiftly across the ocean by a school of tiger sharks.

"Oh, aren't they wonderful? And look Gwydion. The brown shark in front must be Roslyn."

"Yes, it has to be," I replied. "Yahoo, they must be travelling about thirty or forty miles an hour. If they keep that up, which I very much doubt, we should be in America next week."

"I hope the weather stays fine for us," said Lucia, holding my arm."

An hour on, my happy heart quickly thumped anxiously. Lucia was a little worried too. The thought of crossing the vast Atlantic Ocean in a small ark-like boat terrified me. We were committed now with no way of turning back. Although I felt this way, I had to be strong for Lucia. So, I told her that if the sea happened to get rough, as it undoubtedly would, I was sure Roslyn and her pals would see us through okay. If not, we could always fly; something I had forgotten about. Down below was another cabin with a comfy bed, drawers and a locker, also a small galley with a few cupboards, a fixed bench and table, and a nice size stove with a chimney. Next to the galley was a store full of sticks and logs. Lucia looked around and found that the food and drinks that were in our caravan were now in the cupboard, making us hungry. There was also an abundance of flints to light the fire which I did and later, after a nice cooked meal and while chatting, I asked Lucia what part of Spain she came from.

"Velez Rubio," she replied. "I have lived there with my grandmother since my parents were lost at sea. I was only three years old at the time and have no recollection of them. Long ago, my ancestors were the Emperor and Empress of Murcia and lived in Lorca Castle. In November, during the year thirteen hundred and ten, the horrid Brynmoroc, along with an army, took over the city and the surrounding area. He cast out the Royal Family and their daughter Natalia leaving them to live as peasants. At eighteen years of age, Natalia married a wealthy merchant who set her parents up in one of his mansions. Our family has lived there ever since. Unfortunately, over the centuries, people have grown to love Brynmoroc as their generous peace-loving Lord. I knew nothing about him being a wizard or my powers until I was seven years old. Unlike my ancestors, my powers are not of a Sooth Sayers' nature. I can only see where things are hidden or lost. I remember finding my friend's lucky charm that she had lost in the sand. It was then that my grandmother explained Vindaguar's prophecy to me and the reason why my powers had been handed down through the generations. My knowledge of the stones would lead me to meet a young man. Together we would avenge my ancestors and all the wizards of the world by bringing down Brynmoroc and his power. Eleven years and three months later, my grandmother told me that it was time for me to fulfil the prophecy. She paid my passage to Cork, where I was to wait for a young man. How about you? Where's your hometown? And tell me again how you met Bleddwyn?"

I was in a confused state of mind now because when I was three, a very similar thing happened to my parents and they were also never found. So I made up an excuse to have a cup of tea.

"Hmm, there's something strange about this," I thought and pondered while Lucia boiled the kettle.

"Well, come on then, tell me?" Asked Lucia after pouring out the tea.

It took me almost an hour to tell her about my life, for she would interrupt me, wanting to know every little detail. I told her once again about my encounter with the wizard, but I didn't want to say how my parents died and how old I was at the time, so I lied, saying that I was thirteen and that they died soon after one another, from what, I didn't know.

"Your town sounds very exciting and what a stroke of luck how you met the wizard. Surely that was no accident Gwydion. I think he must have spooked your pony purposely. Don't you?"

"Yes, come to think of it, I suppose he did," I replied. "But now it's late and I think sleep is calling."

Before we retired to our beds, we went outside to see our fantastic school of sharks. All I could see in the moonlight was the occasional movement of the ropes. Lucia couldn't see anything at all but shouted, "Goodnight, everyone, but please don't fall asleep?"

I gave her a look and we both laughed, then went below to our beds. I was about to undress when the pretty Senorita tapped on my door, so I opened it.

"You know you're not to leave me on my own, don't you?" She said to remind me.

"Yes, I know," I replied. "But you are not alone. You are here with me on a boat in the middle of the Atlantic Ocean. Surely nothing can happen to you here."

She then said as she looked at me with the most pleading eyes that I had ever seen, "Yes, but can we please keep our doors open and leave the oil lamps burning? I would like it better if we could see each other."

Our cabins were opposite one another, so I said okay but why leave the lamp burning?

"I don't like the dark," she replied.

I agreed and we opened our doors, but not until after she undressed and shouted ready.

It was hours before we fell asleep. The reason being; every now and then she would ask, "Are you alright Gwydion?"

"Yes, are you?" I would reply. To which she would answer. "Yes, I am now. Goodnight, go to sleep." Something I had been trying to do.

In the morning to our joy, the sharks were still there, speeding through the calm sea. They stayed that way until about midday when another school of tiger sharks came and took over. Lucia thought perhaps they had been doing it all through the night. I felt so too, especially when another school came in at three o'clock and a further three hours later. By this time, it was beginning to get cold. I could tell by the position of the sun that we were heading north.

"Look at those icebergs," I shouted. "We must be nearing Greenland."

"Oh, I hope it's not the North Pole," said Lucia as she shivered. Brrr, come on, let's go down and light the stove."

We lit it long enough to have some food and to boil the kettle. After that, we thought the only way to stay warm and make time go by, was to sleep. So we slept until nine the next morning only to be greeted with a gust of icy cold air. Looking out across the ocean, I saw land in the distance that could only be Greenland.

"I wonder if they ever get cold," said Lucia looking out at our towing pals. "I bet that water's freezing. How much farther do you think America is? I'm beginning to worry. It's so cold and the sea is getting really rough."

"Ah, don't worry. I'm sure that's Greenland over there," I said to assure her. "America's not far from Greenland and going by the speed of our pals; we should be there tomorrow. Come on, let's go down and have some breakfast."

All that day, we watched the incredible sharks as they pulled us effortlessly across the vast ocean. I knew from my geography at school that we would probably dock somewhere on the coast of North America.

"Look, Gwydion! There's a seagull. Surely that must be a good sign, don't you think? Yippee. I'm so happy, I could dance around the boat," said Lucia excitedly

"Well, watch you don't fall overboard then," I said as she began to dance and laugh.

She danced and laughed, even more when I joined in. Whatever kind of dance we were doing, I must have looked ridiculous. She was okay, but I was rubbish. We slept well that night, knowing that we were now not too far away from land.

Lucia was up first, giving me a poke. "Up you get, Captain. Let's go and check if there's land ahoy."

I dressed, met Lucia in the passageway, climbed up on deck and rushed to the bow of the boat.

"Oh, yes Gwydion! Land at last. Yahoo and look! The sharks have all gone except Roslyn."

Yes, all our faithful pals had gone except Roslyn who was now towing us past an island, heading for a bay where she disappeared from view as we entered. Then, with a gust of wind, our sails opened and we found that we were now sailing up the channel with a strong breeze behind us. With it being early morning there were no moving cargo or passenger ships only a few fishing boats. So we sailed through the channel okay and entered a large bay called Hudson Bay where passenger ships and many other boats were anchored. On a few of the ships crew members were walking on deck smoking their pipes, others watching us, curiously. We were nervous but sailed on quietly across the bay towards the docks until we began to pick up speed. Suddenly, two massive waves, shaped like hands, rose and wrapped their fingers around each side of the boat. In an instant, we were in a smaller boat being carried across the bay, up a narrow estuary and down a wide river. We were travelling at a tremendous pace that seemed as if we were floating on air. We travelled on, over and under its bridges, down its waterfalls, through multiple small lakes until we sailed into an enormous lake called Winnipeg. Then with a jolt, we were back sitting on the driving seat of our caravan racing across the water, up onto a bank and away down a forestry road.

"Dew! Thank goodness we are back safe on land again. That was some crazy ride Lucia," I said, looking out the window.

"I loved it. It was unbelievable Gwydion" she replied and we both laughed excitedly.

Roslyn trotted on through the forest and out into the country. When far enough away, I asked Roslyn to pull over onto the side of the road. With her being enchanted, one would have thought she could talk. She couldn't, but she understood every word I said. I sat back in my seat and asked Lucia where we were heading next.

"The ruby is somewhere on the edge of Rainbow Falls," she was happy to say. "Rainbow Falls are part of a river flowing into the large Chelan Lake, but there's a gold rush in that area, so we had better be cautious in our approach."

Hostile gold diggers were the last people we wanted to meet. The sun was beginning to go down, so I unhitched Roslyn and gave her some hay and oats. Roslyn is a super enchanted horse that never seems to get tired, but she liked her food. As for Lucia and me, we were that tired, we had our supper and went to bed.

The next day, I suggested that the best way to travel would be down rivers.

"Okay, let's go then," agreed Lucia and sighed. "But soon we are going to have to say goodbye to my little home, for later on there will be nothing but trees and mountains."

We climbed aboard and set off down a road that ran between two vast lakes until we came to a wide rough-looking river.

"Okay, this is it. Let's do it Roslyn," I shouted and in a few seconds we were running across the river until grabbed by two more waves. Then, as Roslyn disappeared, we found ourselves sitting on a soft bench in the cabin of a small boat not much bigger than a rowing boat. All we could do was hang on to one another as we made our way twisting and turning, following the windy river down and over all its waterfalls. It was so unreal that if natives or any settlers were watching, they must have run away terrified. We travelled on for hours clinging to each other until we found ourselves back in the caravan just outside a small town.

"Core-blimey that was crazy Lucia. I wonder where we are," I said after we stepped out and stretched.

While taking a walk to loosen up, we came across some children playing. Lucia asked them the name of the town; it was Saskatoon. I wanted a map of America and some rope, but by the time we had something to eat it was too dark to visit the town. We decided to wait until the morning, but we did manage a walk alongside the river. With a bright half-moon above us, it was light enough to see but as it went behind a cloud, Lucia quickly slipped her hand in mine.

"Gwydion, will you hold my hand, please? I am afraid of the dark."

So, hand in hand, we walked on, discussing the whereabouts of the ruby and how I could reach it. It sounded tricky and later while lying in bed, I heard Lucia sigh.

"Gwydion, this may be our last night in the caravan. So tomorrow we'll also have to buy a tent and a few other things."

"Good idea," I replied. "I'll buy one each and some sleeping bags too."

"Oh no, Gwydion," she said, quickly sitting up. "I mustn't be on my own. Besides, I can't see in the dark. That's why I asked you to hold my hand."

Once again I had forgotten and apologised, "I'm sorry Lucia, I forgot. What's wrong with your eyes, anyway? Why can't you see in the dark? They look alright to me."

"Ever since I can remember, I've never been able to see very well in the dark. My grandmother told me that after I find all the jewels, my sight will be fine."

"Well, we'll have to hurry up and find them then, won't we Senorita?" I said, lying back down.

"Okay, goodnight Gwydion," she said as I watched her turn over.

I must have slept well that night because morning seemed to come quickly. We were up at seven-thirty, had our breakfast and after giving Roslyn hers, we were off into town. When we arrived, the children were already making their way to school. We stopped outside a blacksmith's forge to ask the whereabouts of a general store.

"Firstly, are you a whiskey drinker by any chance?" Asked the Blacksmith.

"No, sir, I'm not," I replied.

"And what about the Lady?"

"No, she doesn't drink it either. Why? Why do you ask?"

"Well, in that case, Milligan's store is further on down the town," was all he said, pointing with his hammer.

He then walked over to Roslyn and remarked, "My word she's a lovely mare. Where did you get her? Did you buy her from them old Injuns camped up in the hills?"

I thought for a moment, "Eh; no, I acquired her from a gipsies' camp back in Ireland some time ago."

"Ireland!" he cried. "Well-well! My grandfather came from Galway. What part are you from?"

By the time I explained that we didn't live there and after being obliged to listen to his grandfather's Irish tales, it was about eleven o'clock before we finally arrived outside the store.

The attendant was an elderly, stern-looking lady who quickly asked the very same questions as the Blacksmith.

"Are you pair whiskey drinkers, by any chance?"

"No! We are not. Why?" I replied sharply.

"We don't have, or serve whiskey drinkers in this town," she declared. "Now, what do you want?"

I told her we were from Ireland, making our way west and if she sold tents.

"What size are you looking for?" she then asked, but in a much friendlier manner.

I smiled and replied, "Wow! I thought for a moment you were going to eat us."

"Ha-ha," she laughed, "This town is liquor-free and by the way, I'd have a difficult job eating you; all I've left are my gums."

That made us laugh, but we quickly stopped when her husband came in from the back room wondering what we were laughing at. With that, I asked the lady if she had a tent big enough for two and a knapsack. She had everything we needed, including rope, a map and more. I took out my pouch to pay but suddenly remembered that I only had guineas, but when I opened the pouch, to my surprise it was full of dollars and cents. So I handed her two dollars and five cents. She then wished us a safe journey and we left.

Making our way through the town and while passing a school, we could hear children reciting poetry. It reminded me of my old school days, though Shakespeare was definitely not my forte. We carried on trotting with me wondering what way, shape or form we were travelling next. I didn't have to worry, for as soon as we reached the river, we were back in a boat being carried by two waves over the river's ragging rapids, under its bridges, and down over multiple waterfalls until we found ourselves back in our caravan. We were now in the middle of a valley where we spent the evening studying the map, trying to find the easiest route.

"Well, this is it," declared Lucia. "From here on is four hundred miles of rough land and mountains. It's also bear country and other wild animals. So you had better think of another way of travel because bears are bound to attack us all."

It was going to take weeks, so I had to think of something quickly. I knew Roslyn could easily go a hundred miles or more, but that depended on how tired Lucia and I would get. So I suggested that if Roslyn were a bear, then perhaps bears wouldn't attack us, especially if she was larger than them.

"Brilliant idea," said Lucia. "That's what we'll do but let's wait until tomorrow."

# Chapter 5

The sun gave us a lovely morning to wake to. So after packing everything needed into my backpack, I tied the tent underneath it. The journey was going to take three weeks or more.

"Well, that's it," I said when finished. "Are you ready, Roslyn?" I asked.

She lowered her head and as I held out my staff towards her, I gave out my command, "Gofynnaf i chi."

"Where? Where is she? What's happened? Where's she gone?" Lucia asked, looking around for her.

Roslyn had completely disappeared until she gave us both a fright, playfully roaring behind us.

"Oh! Roslyn!" Lucia exclaimed. "That was a rotten trick. You frightened the life out of me, but look at you! Look at the size of you! You are magnificent!"

Yes, Roslyn was indeed a magnificent-looking brown bear, with a white nose. She standing there playfully growling, shaking her head. She was on all fours and well over six feet tall to her shoulders. Her lovely and shiny soft furry back was close to eight or nine feet long. She was absolutely awesome and we couldn't wait to sit on her, but she'd have to lie down for us to get on. I told Lucia to say goodbye to her lovely home, for this was where our mission was about to begin. I asked Lucia to sit up front so that I could carry the pack.

"No, I'd rather you sit up front," she replied. "I don't mind carrying the pack, and besides, it should rest nicely on Roslyn's bottom," she said and laughed

All that day, we trekked on through creepy-looking valleys and over their white rocky mountains. We met a few bears and other animals on the way. The sight of them quickly made our hearts race, but one look at Roslyn and they soon took off. The only time we stopped was to have a quick rest and some food. Finally, before sunset, we made camp in a sheltered valley. Lucia was a little sore and cramped. I said that it would soon pass and in a day or two she'd be used to it. It was a beautiful night, so after supper, instead of sleeping in the tent, we led down beside Roslyn. She was so soft and warm that we slept all night until the bright sun woke us in the morning. Roslyn rose, stretched, and then went off searching probably for food. By the time she returned, Lucia and I were ready to set out once more. No humans could ever live on the route we were taking, but after saying that, we did see two hunters who we had to hide away from.

It must have been more than a week of travelling over those massive rocky mountains before they changed to snow, making the going really tough. It was so cold that it was such a blessing each time we descended into the warm valleys below. Once reaching the valley floor, we had to cross many rivers, and with Roslyn partially submerged, we got soaking wet every time. Fortunately, with the weather in the valley being kind to us, there were plenty of dry sticks to make a fire. At one point when we reached a vast lake called Kootenay, we had to travel a few miles south before it was safe enough to cross its river. After that, it was another two weeks of climbing. Up and over rocky, wooded, snow-covered mountains we went. Weaving our way through pine tree forests, crossing fast-flowing rivers until we finally reached our goal, a beautiful waterfall.

It was now mid-morning and with the sun lying in the east, a lovely breeze was gently making trees swish and sway from side to side. The swaying branches created constant flickering beams of sunlight flashing through the flowing water as if a rainbow was slithering its way down over, crashing into a large white and blue pool below. We made camp in the woods nearby to get away from the thunderous noise of the falls.

"I'm so happy we made it," said Lucia. "We'll rest now and search for the ruby in the morning."

I too was happy until sitting around the fire, Lucia told me that the ruby was only half the size

Patrick Madden

of her little fingernail and is embedded in one of many jagged rocks on the side of the waterfall

"How am I supposed to find it, especially if it's that small?" I asked as my happy mood changed.

"Don't worry Gwydion. There is only one jagged rock with seven edges. I'll roughly point it out to you tomorrow."

I pitched our tent and as Roslyn kept watch, we settled down to sleep but not before Lucia nudged me.

"Will you hold my hand please Gwydion?" she asked.

"Why, what's the matter?" I asked.

"I'm afraid," she replied and swallowed. "As soon as you absorb the colour of the precious ruby, Brynmoroc will know about it. Once he finds out about me and the knowledge I have of the stones; our lives will be in danger. So will you hold my hand? It will make me feel a lot safer."

"Um, well yeah, alright," I stuttered. "But how am I supposed to hold your hand while we are lying down asleep?"

"Easy," she replied. "Just put your arm around me, and I'll do the rest."

So I gently put my arm around her and as I did, she held my hand, giving it a little squeeze. That's the way we stayed all night until I woke in the morning. She was still holding my hand, but now we were facing one another. I jumped up and crawled out of the tent with Lucia coming out behind me.

"Good morning Gwydion. Did you sleep well?" She asked as she stretched.

"Yes, I did," I replied. "Except for waking once. You were sound asleep so I assume you must have slept well too?"

"Yes, I did thank you. Now, let's have something to eat before we make our way to the falls."

We waited until mid-morning before we walked alongside Roslyn towards the river above the Rainbow Falls. I intended to hopefully tie my rope to an overhanging branch and use it to climb down and especially back up. Without it, it looked impossible. When we eventually reached the river, we found that because of the fine weather, it was calm. So we searched for a safe place to cross before swimming over on Roslyn. The opposite side of the river was completely covered in brambles. They were a nuisance, so we went through the woods to avoid them. I was lucky when we arrived at the top of the falls for there was a strong-looking overhanging branch that would do nicely. I slipped off my rope, but as I looked over the high falls, my legs went like jelly, and my head began to spin.

"Don't look over there Gwydion!" shouted Lucia as she grabbed me. "You'll fall if you do."

"Dew!" I said, dropping the rope. "Blimey, I felt really dizzy then. Thanks Lucia."

I sat there for a while with Lucia stroking my head until I felt myself again.

"Okay, let's do it," I said after giving Lucia my staff.

I picked up the rope, put one end between my teeth and asked Lucia to feed the rope as I climbed. To reach a decent place to tie the rope, I had to inch my way across the overhanging branch. It was so nerve-racking, especially with Lucia continually shouting.

"Watch you don't fall Gwydion. Oh, please don't fall. Whatever you do, don't look down you'll only get dizzy again and fall off."

I managed to secure the rope around the branch and was happy to be back on the bank again.

"Are you alright, Gwydion? You look so pale and shaky again. Quick, sit down before you fall down."

The things I could have said to her, but I didn't. She was only worried about me. I appreciated it really. Lucia now decided that she would cross back over the river to watch from the other side and would wave when I reached the rock where the ruby was embedded.

"Well, I had better get on with it then," I said, with a nervous sigh. "Wish me luck."

Lucia kissed my forehead, wished me luck and headed off with Roslyn. I waited until I could see her over on the opposite side of the falls before throwing the rope over the edge. As Bleddwyn informed me, my staff had shrunk for the occasion. So I slipped my small staff into my belt behind me and after taking a few deep breaths, I slowly began to climb down using the rope, but it was difficult trying to find a foothold. So, by using the rope, I monkey climbed it most of the way down while anxiously waiting for Lucia to wave. It seemed forever before she finally did. It was just as I reached a cluster of rocks. After managing to get a foothold in a crevice, I stood there and rested. Lucia was still waving excitely, meaning that I was in the right spot. When I recovered, I looked around and saw what I thought to be the jagged rock Lucia had described. It was in the middle of a cluster, a yard away from me.

"That must be it," I muttered, "And the ruby must be somewhere in it."

I was right, for as I looked, there it was, twinkling away in the middle of the jagged rock.

"Yes, there you are, you little beauty," I said, pulling my staff from behind me.

I was wondering, worrying about what would happen after I placed the staff on the ruby. There was only one way to find out. So after making sure I had a satisfactory foothold and wouldn't slip, I braved myself and shouted out.

"Come on! There's nothing to be afraid of. It's only a little ruby."

I took a firm hold of the staff and with great care, placed its base onto the twinkling jewel. The moment I did, the staff felt really warm and began to vibrate. Suddenly a red glow about six inches long rippled up almost to the top of my staff and stayed there glowing brightly until eventually going out like a candle. With that, I slipped the staff back into my belt. I then thought that I had better quickly head back up before Lucia returned, making me nervous.

I was soaking wet, but I didn't care. All I wanted to do now was get back to the top. This time, I could see where to put my feet. The climb was a lot easier now, but after about a quarter of an hour, my arms were aching, and my grip getting weaker. I had to rest and managed to find a foothold away from the falls. Then while I stood waiting for my arms to come back to life, I felt a tug on the rope.

"That's Lucia," I said as the rope tugged again. I yanked back and it slowly began to rise. I took a firm hold and found myself sailing up fairly quickly.

"Oh yes, this must be Roslyn now. Yahoo, go on girl!!" I shouted.

With all the noise of the falls, I knew she couldn't hear me, but I shouted anyway. It wasn't long before I was back on top, flat out on the bank being smothered with kisses from the very relieved and happy Lucia.

"Oh, I was so worried that you might fall Gwydion and with the pool full of huge rocks; you would have surely been killed. Did you hear me shouting?"

I muttered to myself, "No, and I'm glad I didn't because I probably would have fallen if I had."

"What did you say?" She asked.

"Yeah, um no," I replied. "I didn't. It was a shame, but I knew you were there wishing me well, but let's go back and make camp, shall we?"

"Yes, and I'll do you something nice to eat," she replied as Roslyn came trotting back through the woods with the rope in her mouth.

"Well done Roslyn," I said patting her. "Thank you, that was brilliant. Let's go now and have some food."

We crossed the river and set up camp away from the noisy falls. Then after a hearty meal, Lucia decided to go back to the river for a much-needed bath. Roslyn went along to keep guard. When she returned clean and refreshed, I suggested that we should stay put for the night.

"I'm tired, and we could all do with a rest. Have you worked out the whereabouts of the next jewel?" I asked, hoping that it wasn't the other side of the world.

"Yes, I agree, and I'm tired too," she said lying down on the dry grass. "The next two jewels are here in America, but I need to concentrate. I'll let you know this evening. Come, please lie down beside me, we'll sleep awhile."

I led down beside her, and while she held my hand, we fell asleep until a drop of rain woke me.

"Wake up Lucia," I said, giving her a poke. "We've been asleep for ages. It's going to rain. We had better get inside and quickly."

I was right, for no sooner than we were in our tent, it poured down. Later, after finishing a sandwich, Lucia told me that the next jewel was a fire opal and it was in the eye of a toad sitting on a rock. Cathedral Rock, somewhere in Sedona Arizona. That sounded like a long way away. So I said after looking it up on my map.

"I wonder if Roslyn can summon up those lovely tiger sharks again. If so, we could go down around the coast to Los Angeles. Sedona is about five hundred miles across the country from there."

The following morning, I was surprised to see that Roslyn looked tired after a night of watching over us. So we let her sleep for a couple of hours before packing up to head for the coast. However, before we went, I transformed Roslyn back into the lovely mare again. We didn't want anyone to see us riding a bear, a very large bear. Commanding my staff was so unreal that I worried about it sometimes.

We followed the river until we eventually came to Chelan Lake. By looking at the map, I could see that the lake carried on down to the sea. So, I tapped Roslyn on her neck, told Lucia to hang on, pointed my staff and asked the mare to take us to Los Angeles the best way she saw fit.

In a blink of an eye, we were now galloping across the lake on top of the water until we were sitting on board a small boat, sailing out of the lake, twisting our way down a winding river into the Pacific Ocean. In a jolt, we once again found ourselves back inside our small little ark. Lucia quickly ran to the bow of the boat wanting to see if the sharks were back.

"YES! Oh, yes Gwydion. They are there. Quick, come and take a look?"

They were there alright, and as we watched them swaying along in the calm clear water, Lucia gently held my arm.

In the afternoon, while we were led on the deck relaxing in the sun, Lucia wondered.

"How far did you say that it was to Los Angeles, Gwydion?"

"Well over a thousand miles," I replied. "And with our sharks travelling at least twenty-five miles an hour, we should be docking in about two days."

I wasn't far wrong, because, at eight o'clock on Saturday evening, we were galloping out of Los Angeles, into the woods to camp. Coincidently, other people were camped there too. So we went over to introduce ourselves. They were prospectors who had come from Kansas, a week ago. We found them friendly enough, though they seemed to be a little suspicious of us. Lucia asked them if it was safe to go into town and if there were any wild Indians still around.

"No!" replied a man smoking his pipe. "Not for a beautiful lady like you it ain't. As for Indians, most of them are in reservation camps, but there are plenty of outlaws around. So be careful on your travels. Butch Cassidy and the Sundance Kid, along with their gang, recently robbed a train in Wyoming. Where did you say you were going?"

"Sedona," I replied.

"Well, if you intend to travel by horse, you had better take plenty of water. From here to there are four or five hundred miles of barren land and mountains. It's a bad place for anyone son. Particularly for a lady."

We thanked everyone and went back to our camp, somewhat disillusioned.

"We are going to have to think of something, Lucia. Surely there's a railroad or stagecoach heading somewhere near Sedona?" I said after pondering.

"Why don't you ask your staff?" said Lucia, reminding me. "Ask for a stagecoach, a carriage, anything, but not now. Wait until after a good night's rest."

She was right, as always. I kept forgetting about my staff. So I asked Roslyn to watch over us while we retired to our tent.

In the morning, while looking at the map and after finding the road to Sedona, I came up with an idea. I thought we'd buy a buggy or a trap, something with a decent hood for cover and a few more things for the both of us. So we packed everything up and rode into Los Angeles just as the stores were opening. The first thing to do was buy more suitable clothes for our journey. I had plenty of money, so there was no need to keep our old ones. I had to laugh, for Lucia was so excited when I told her that she could have anything she liked. It was a great feeling knowing that I was rich and able to pay for it. It was funny though. Funny because the storekeeper kept looking at me each time Lucia picked the most expensive riding gear in the store. He also nearly fainted when I told him that I would have the same but in a man's size. I paid the flabbergasted storekeeper and asked where we could get a bath.

"With the money you've just spent, you are more than welcome to use ours," he replied. "I'll ask my wife to heat the water for you, right away. Pick up your things and come with me."

We followed him through the back of the store and into a brightly lit kitchen where he introduced us to his wife, who was sipping coffee. Within an hour, both of us had bathed and dressed ready to go. I gave Fred the storekeeper, two dollars for their kindness and we went away refreshed.

"I feel great now. How about you, Lucia?" I asked, skipping down the steps.

"Yes, I feel fantastic. Where are we going now?" She asked and laughed.

The town was bustling with parents bringing their children to school; others were collecting groceries. Across the street, I noticed a man standing outside the Sheriff's office. So we crossed over to him with Roslyn following behind. The badge on his waistcoat told us that he was the Sheriff.

"Excuse me, Sheriff. Could you direct me to the Livery stable, please?"

He looked at me, then turned his eyes to Roslyn and remarked, "That's a well-trained mare you have there son. Is she for sale?"

"No, Sheriff," was my reply. "I'm looking to buy a trap or buggy for her. We hope to be travelling on to Sedona this afternoon."

"Sedona!" he said, raising his voice. "Ah, you kids are too young to be travelling that road alone. It's a bad trail, son. You'll be lucky to get as far as the next town. Why those bandits would have you stripped and robbed before you had time to sneeze? Even if you were lucky enough to avoid them no good outlaws, there are also a few renegade Injuns out there too. And I can assure you son, they'll definitely love that mare of yours and your pretty wife. You'll be better off going on the wagon train, but that's not until the end of the month. What's your business out there anyway? Have you family, or are you going there to settle?"

"We have no family," I replied. "We are just touring around and would like to see Cathedral Rock."

He was inquisitive now, and his questions were becoming a little difficult to answer, making me wish I hadn't bothered talking to him. Then much to our relief, a lady from the other side of the street called out to him. With that and without even saying goodbye, the inquisitive sheriff began hurrying over to her. The very moment he turned his back, we quickly headed on up the street but were still none the wiser to the whereabouts of a livery stable. Eventually, thanks to a young boy, we were pointed in the right direction and arrived at the only one in town. I asked Oliver, the attendant, if he had any traps for sale. He did and showed me two large ones. They were nothing special, but they had hoods, and there was plenty of room for carrying barrels of water. I knew that one day we would have to ditch the trap, so I bought a saddle with bags and a long leather waterproof tube-like bag for our clothes etcetera.

After paying for them and some water barrels, he warned me.

"My advice to you, young Gwydion, is to get yourself a rifle. You shouldn't be going anywhere in this country without one. Not only are there outlaws, but there are also bears and mountain lions, even snakes."

I smiled at Lucia when he mentioned bears because little did he know we had the biggest one of all. I shook his hand and thanked him for his excellent advice. We then bade him goodbye and went our way until stopping for dinner a few miles out of town. With all the advice, I thought we had better prepare ourselves for unwanted visitors so I gave Lucia my cape to wear.

"Bleddwyn said the cape would protect me, so I suggest you wear it and keep your shield handy too."

"Don't worry," she replied, tapping her pocket.

After enjoying a few boiled potatoes, we headed out once again to the next town, Pomona. With the speed Roslyn travelled, we were in and out of the town in about two hours. I wasn't concerned about any bandits because I knew that in a chase, Roslyn would leave them for dust. It was during the night I was worried about, so I had to think of something before dark.

We travelled on for another eighty miles until we arrived at Palm Springs just before the sun went down. Palm Springs was a new settlement with no town to speak of, only ranches. As a result of no inns, we set up camp and enjoyed a full dish of beans and a chunk of bread each. It was a beautiful moonlight night and it seemed as if we could see every star in the Universe. The fire crackled and sparked as we chatted and it was well after midnight before we went to sleep. We slept okay, apart from a yelp, which must have come from a prairie dog being sent packing by Roslyn.

# Chapter 6

The morning we set off to Sedona, it began to rain, but the nice cool rain suited us fine until it began to pour down. Within minutes the desert road had turned into a muddy bumpy trail. So with my amazing staff, in a flash, we were soon skimming along on skis, both a foot wide.

"Oh, that's better," said Lucia and sighed. "If I'd have bounced anymore I'm sure I would have been sick. But, I do hope this rain hurries up and eases; otherwise we'll have to catch the boat again."

She laughed, and so did I. The storm soon eased and with the hot sun out again, the roads quickly dried, and we were back on wheels. I was thankful that we were because a mile further on, we were stopped by the United States Cavalry wanting to know our destination. The captain warned us that there were Indians up in the hills of Sedona. They hadn't surrendered yet and could possibly be around Cathedral Rock.

Early evening, we arrived in a city called Phoenix, a busy city with plenty of saloons and stores even a high school. Trotting through the bustling main street, I thought we should find a livery stable, then check out the Inn across the road alongside a small chapel.

"Thank goodness," said Lucia. "My head's in a daze now. I need to rest."

A lady directed us to Blackwood's livery stables and recommended the Cartwheel saloon for a room. The stables were run by a burly man called Jake and his daughter, Louise.

"Where are you thinking of staying the night?" Jake asked, after putting Roslyn in a stable.

"A lady recommended the Cartwheel Saloon," I replied. "What's it like there?"

"Oh, you don't want to be staying there, lad. You'll get fleeced in no time at all. Why, as sure as my name's Jake, those losing gamblers will rob you before you have time to speak. For an extra two dollars, you can stay here, both of you. I have a room above the stables. It has a couple of chairs and a nice bed."

I accepted his offer, and he showed us the room. It was as he mentioned, two rocking chairs and a bed.

Jake then left us, saying, "If you are thinking of going into town, be back before dark. There are trigger-happy cowhands in the city today, and they like making fools of visitors."

Lucia tried out the bed and was happy with it. There were only a couple of blankets, but we had our sleeping bags.

"Let's go and get a cup of coffee and a sandwich, shall we?" She suggested.

Off we went, holding hands down the busy dusty main street of Phoenix. It was a fascinating town but scary. Almost everyone was carrying a gun. After searching around, the only place to get a coffee was a Saloon. It sounded a little noisy, so I asked Lucia if we should go in.

"Why not, that's what we came out for, isn't it?" She replied, squeezing my hand

We went in, but as we made our way to the bar, silence fell, even the pianist stopped playing. I now wished we hadn't bothered until the barman welcomed us.

"Welcome, young uns. What are you having, whiskey or ale?"

"Just two coffees please," I replied as the piano began to play again.

"Two coffees it is then," said the happy barman. "Go sit yourselves down. Roisin will bring em over."

We picked a table in the corner out of the way of poker players. Across the room slumped over a table were a couple of drunks. I was hoping they'd stay that way because with us being strangers, there would probably be trouble. It wasn't long before Roisin came over with our order. She put the tray down and introduced herself as Roisin O'Donnell, then sat down for a chat. She was an attractive young lady with long dark hair, but not black like Lucia's. She was Irish, with a soft well-spoken accent that I instantly fell in love with. Roisin had only recently arrived in Phoenix from Clonmel, a little town in Ireland. She hadn't seen or heard from her brother since he left to work in America. She missed him dearly and was happy when he sent her a telegram. He had deposited a sum of money in an Irish bank to enable her to travel to Phoenix to be with him. Unfortunately, after arriving in Phoenix, Roisin found a letter from her brother saying that he had been summoned on urgent business to Alicante, southern Spain. He had left extra money for her to join him there.

"So, where are you pair heading?" she asked.

"We are just touring around, heading for Cathedral Rock," replied Lucia.

"You have a fair way to go then," said Roisin, rising from her seat. "Well, enjoy your coffee."

We did enjoy our coffee and watched as the poker players gambled away their money. Before we left, we wished Roisin good luck and headed back to the stable.

Now, before we go any further, Roisin is an Irish name and to pronounce it properly, it sounds like Roesheen.

No lady had ever held my hand, so it was a strange feeling, especially as we were the only couple on the street doing so. Still, although I felt kind of silly, I also felt really proud, for she was so pretty. We arrived at our room just before the last rays of the sun disappeared. Tired now, we led, fully dressed on top of the bed in our sleeping bags, and as usual, I had to hold her hand. The only way we could do that was to lie on our backs. Though it didn't seem to matter which way we slept, Lucia was still holding my hand in the morning. Sometimes it was embarrassing waking up face to face, especially if I had my mouth open, dribbling. As far as I know, I am a sound sleeper, Lucia was too, well, that's what she told me. So either she was telling fibs, or it's a mystery how we always woke up holding hands.

The wind must have whipped up overnight because it was a dusty windy trail we set out on. I felt sorry for Roslyn with all the dry, bleak desert dust flying around. Lucia and I were okay because we had wrapped cotton scarves around our faces. At about midday, we arrived and stopped in a town called Canon, known to some folks as Black Canyon. Lucia made sandwiches while I chatted and listened to a couple of interesting old-timers' fascinating stories. How they found gold in the mountains only to lose it all gambling with crooked card players and thieves. I mentioned our next destination, and once again, I was warned by these sad weather-beaten prospectors, that there had been sightings of renegade Indians around the Cathedral Rock area, also bandits. It was only a few days ago that a stagecoach carrying mail and a considerable amount of cash had been ambushed and robbed by outlaws who hide in the hills.

I was anxious about our safety now, but I didn't mention to Lucia my conversation with the old-timers, but I did insist she wore my cape before we moved on. It was a journey of about fifty miles through barren land, mountains and according to the old-timers, treacherous canyons.

We left Canon and were now on a trail that had fortunately been dampened by the earlier drizzle. Roslyn seemed happy enough and was travelling at a reasonable pace, meaning that we should be at the rock by nightfall. Everything was going fine until a narrow daunting-looking canyon came into view. We didn't like the look of it but trotted on regardless until we rounded a bend where riders on horseback were spread out, blocking our way.

"This looks like trouble Lucia. Whoa, Roslyn! I have to think a minute," I said, pulling on her reigns.

"They are probably robbers Gwydion. What are you going to do?"

They were a couple of hundred yards away, slowly trotting towards us and all looking as if they were holding guns. If it wasn't for their weapons, I would have headed directly at them. If I could have used my staff as a normal wizard, it would have been easy, but I could only use it for travel. So with something in mind, I took twelve dollars out of my pouch. I wasn't sure whether it was going to work, but I had to give it a try. If they are blocking our way, we need something to assist us in our travel. I threw the coins in front of Roslyn and held out my staff and cried. "Gofynnaf i chi,"

Immediately the twelve coins transformed into twelve long-horn steers, charging towards the bewildered horsemen. We followed close behind with our mouths covered, shielded from the dust. The nearer we rode, the more the riders panicked. They didn't know where to go or which way to turn. Bang, bang went their guns as we raced past and away out of the canyon. I looked back, but all I could see was dust. What happened to those bandits after that we didn't care nor were we stopping to find out.

"Yahoo!" Lucia shouted and laughed." Ha-ha, that was brilliant Gwydion, but scary. I bet they won't be so quick in holding us up again."

"Yeah. Ha-ha," I laughed. "I just love this staff. Ha-ha. I'm getting used to it now."

The steers headed off in another direction, disappearing in the distance. We slowed down to a canter and carried on for a few more miles until we tired. We had experienced enough excitement for one day. What we needed now was food, coffee and if possible, an afternoon nap.

Roslyn pulled off the road into a small wooded area out of the sun. I gathered wood and lit a fire to boil some water for a wash and some coffee. While sat by the fire, finishing our little snack, we heard a rattling behind us. Realising it must be a snake, I slowly turned to see a curled-up rattlesnake, looking at us from between some rocks. He was about twenty feet away, well out of harm's reach. So, we quietly rose to our feet, put out the fire, hitched up Roslyn and away we went, leaving the rattler in peace.

"I'm glad we didn't sit on those rocks, or have that nap you wanted," I said after thinking about it.

"Yes, me too," said Lucia, shaking her head in relief. "There's one good thing about Ireland; you don't have to worry about snakes; there aren't any."

The weather stayed fine until it clouded over about a mile from the unusual-looking Cathedral Rock. We could see how it got its name by the tall rocky steeples that were towering from a massive mountain of orange rock. We were there at last but were going to wait until morning before investigating the exciting-looking phenomenon.

"Look, Gwydion! There's the toad. He's sitting up there on top of that rock. Can you see him?"

Sure enough, one of the towering steeples of rock looked just like a toad sitting up, but how on earth was I going to get up there, is what I wondered.

"Well, at least, we know where he is now," said Lucia. "You'll think of something."

I had all night, but from there, it looked absolutely unclimbable. It was a warm night and with wolves and other animals howling and crying, we thought instead of pitching a tent it would be safer if we camped around a fire. Luckily, we had Roslyn to keep watch who woke us with a whinny just before dawn. We had slept all night, so if there were any renegade Indians around, they certainly weren't interested in us.

"Well, have you thought about how you are going to climb the rock yet?" Lucia asked after we had eaten.

"Yes, I've thought of something," I replied. "But you will have to come with me."

"Come with you!" she cried. "I can't climb up there, Gwydion!"

I couldn't leave her; she had to come. I assured her that there was no need to worry, for if my plan worked, none of us would have to climb.

"What! What are you saying? I thought you said we had to climb! Oh Gwydion, I'm worried now."

"Just trust me," I said and laughed. "It should be fun. Now, let's hide the trap because we can't take it with us."

We found a place under some trees, taking a chance it would be there when we came back. I mounted Roslyn, took hold of Lucia's hands and pulled her up behind me. I then leaned over and picked up my staff from beside a tree.

"Okay, let's check out that old toad of yours Lucia. Hold on," I said and laughed.

Making our way east towards Cathedral Rock, we could see the most brilliant orange sunrise emerging from behind it. There was no trail to follow, so we had to weave our way through bushes, shrubs and trees before finally reaching the base of the mountainous rock. As a guess; it must have been well over a thousand feet high. From where we were, the toad-shaped rock was nowhere to be seen, but I had a good idea where it was.

"How are we ever going to get up there Gwydion? It's impossible."

"Put your arms around my waist and hold on tight," I replied, holding out my staff.

I took a deep breath, and with my thoughts, I gave the command in the hope my idea was going to work. It did, and to my relief, but to Lucia's horror, we found ourselves sitting on the curled-up tail of a scorpion and as we began crawling up the face of the gigantic red rock, I tried to ignore the screams of fear coming from the petrified Lucia. Roslyn, now our incredible scorpion, seemed to know where she was going and inch by inch, she edged her way closer to the summit. It seemed an eternity and was such a relief when Roslyn placed her six hairy legs back on level ground. I was now looking up at another mass of rock. Although it didn't bear any resemblance to the toad we had seen from a mile away, I knew it was the one we were searching for. Thankfully, Lucia had stopped screaming now, either from being hoarse or speechless.

"Okay Roslyn," I said, giving her a tap. "Let's go and find that little fire opal. Hold on Lucia and try not to scream this time."

There was still no reply, but I felt her squeeze me twice, so I knew she was ready and must have lost her voice. On we climbed with Roslyn spiralling her way up and around the massive rock, searching for the elusive opal jewel until an orange flash momentarily dazzled me.

"Did you see that flash? Oh yes, there it is! We've found it Lucia," I shouted excitedly.

Yes, there it was, sitting two feet away from a small white marble stone.

"So these are the eyes of the toad," I said to Lucia, who was holding on for dear life.

"Hurry up Gwydion. Please hurry. I'm afraid I'm going to fall off," she croaked.

I slowly touched the twinkling jewel with the base of my staff and immediately a beautiful orange colour flowed up and down my staff until stopping above the red of the ruby that had brightened up. Both colours stayed glowing, dazzling me for some time until they faded.

"Phew! Thank goodness for that," I said. "Go on, Roslyn. Back down girl, but whatever you do, don't turn around. Go down backwards."

I didn't realise just how high we were until looking down. I closed my eyes in shock, thinking that I must be crazy doing this. If I thought going up seemed to take a long time, going down took even longer. It was such a good feeling reaching the bottom that we just slipped off the scorpion and collapsed on the ground.

"Oh, Gwydion, quick, change her back. I can't look at her," cried, Lucia.

In a flash, I had Roslyn back as our mare again, shaking herself down.

"Oh, that was terrible. I was sure we were going to fall," said Lucia, tearfully.

"Yes, it was scary alright?" I said, looking up. "By the way; I thought you had lost your voice from all that screaming?"

"No, I was too afraid to speak, but my throat feels really sore now," she replied, rubbing it.

"Ah, it's all over now," I said and held her hand. "Let's hope the next one is easier."

"It isn't," she sighed. "It's worse, but there's one consolation, it's not too far away."

Wherever it was, I said she could tell me later, for we had to go back to where we had camped. On our way, Lucia shuddered behind me.

"Ooh! I wonder what Roslyn thought of being one of those horrible, creepy crawling things?"

"She probably loved it," I replied, patting her hands around my waist.

Happily, our trap was where we left it, and with no sign of anyone wandering around, I lit a fire for some coffee. It was now midday, and while we were sipping our coffee, we had our first encounter with Brynmoroc. It began with a flash across the sky together with a gathering of clouds and a rumble of thunder.

"Quick! It must be Brynmoroc!" Said Lucia, alarmingly. "Use your shield. Your shield, Gwydion."

I quickly did, and as we stood against the trap with our gleaming shields in front of us, a soft, calm voice spoke out.

# Chapter 7

*L* ucia, I am Brynmoroc. What I am about to
tell you may come as a shock, but because
my time with you is limited, I can only be brief.
Lucia, I am your father. Sixteen years ago, you
were abducted by my cousin Bleddwyn, a devious,
power-hungry wizard. My darling child, please
listen while I try to explain the events of that
terrible day in our lives. Before I do, there is
something dear Gwydion that you should know.
Everything Bleddwyn told you about the
enchanted jewels and Vindaguar's prophecy was
said in truth, apart from one significant factor; that
being, it is Bleddwyn who violated the prophecy,
not I"

Before the wizard carried on, he paused for a
while as if waiting for a response. We couldn't see
him so as you can imagine, it was a weird and
worrying time wondering what next, and how
could we defend ourselves.

"My dear Lucia, Your so-called grandmother
is an imposter under the influence of Bleddwyn. I

can assure you that it is my blood flowing through your veins, not hers. Three years after you were born, your sweet mother and I found that you had extraordinary psychic powers. We knew then that you were to be the woman in the prophecy. Bleddwyn's intentions after hearing this were none other than to capture you by force. The reasons were, on one hand, you were a danger but on the other, an asset. Your mother and I fought desperately to prevent your abduction, but even with the aid of our colleagues, we were helpless against Bleddwyn's awesome power. Your grief-stricken mother collapsed and died, brokenhearted a week later. With you now in the hands of my devious cousin, all he had to do was to one day find the instigator of the prophecy, who happens to be you Gwydion. He aimed to trick and use you, along with Lucia's knowledge to seek out the jewels and absorb their energy. Unknown to you, your staff is also Bleddwyn's all-seeing-eye. Each time you locate and drain a jewel of its energy, Bleddwyn will know of its whereabouts. The crafty wizard will then reposition the empty gem somewhere else throughout the world where only he will know. On the very day, after you have accomplished draining the last gem, he will take the staff from you and transfer its energy back to each and every jewel. From that day on, Vindaguar's prophecy will be null and void, enabling Bleddwyn to carry on being the most powerful eternal master of wizardry throughout the entire world of magic. As for you, my lovely

Lucia and you dear Gwydion will become the tyrant's miserable pawns until the day you die."

Brynmoroc once again paused, but this time we could actually hear him sigh and as he carried on, his voice sounded saddened.

"I have been tormented ever since that terrible day you were taken from the arms of your weeping mother. I always knew that one day I would find you. As I already pointed out, this must come as a shock to you Lucia and I do not expect you to believe me. All I ask is to mull over my words, and I'll return here at the same time tomorrow. Then, if it is your wish, I'll take you both home to my castle where we can discuss the rest of the prophecy, an important factor you know nothing about. I must leave you now, but if by any chance you see an angry red sky tonight, Bleddwyn has heard of our meeting. It is inevitable that he will. Physically, my evil cousin cannot harm you, but we must fear his wrath. So, until tomorrow, sleep well tonight. I love you Lucia."

With those words, the clouds began to roll away to the east from where they came, and once more the birds began to sing. We waited to make sure he was gone before putting our shields away.

"Ooh, that was scary Gwydion. Wasn't it? Why didn't he attack us, was it our shields? And why did he say I was his daughter?"

I said that I wasn't sure, for as far as I could remember, Bleddwyn told me that wizards for fear of their own life, couldn't directly pioneer any source of energy to harm a human. They could, however, physically capture one. All I could think of was that after Brynmoroc spotted our shields, he chose not to appear. Instead, he fabricated a story about Lucia being his child and twisted the truth about the jewels to glorify himself.

"I think you are right, Gwydion, though you have to admit, he sounded very convincing, didn't he?"

"Ah! He's a wizard," I quickly said. "He can make up any old story in a flash. Don't be fooled by him. I have seen him in action, and he is nothing like the soft-spoken wizard we just heard. He's mean and nasty."

"We'll have to be on our guard then Gwydion, for he will be all out to stop us, even capture us. Oh! That will be terrible, won't it?"

I said that she was right and that from now on our lives would be in danger, especially hers.

"Oh Gwydion, you won't leave me, will you?" She asked in anguish.

I remember that day well because as she looked at me with her lovely pleading eyes, I could have kissed her.

"Well, as long as you are holding my hand, I won't be able to, will I?" I replied and smiled as she thanked me.

We stayed alongside Roslyn until about two o'clock. The weather was good, and with no sign of Brynmoroc returning, we lit a fire, and while having a bite to eat, discussed the location of the next jewel. It was in Oak Creek Canyon, way up on a sheer cliff, under a rock resembling the bow of a boat. After looking at my map, we had to travel through a gorge to as far as Sedona and from then on only a few miles away.

After working out our route, Lucia wondered how we were going to avoid Brynmoroc. I thought that if I played along with Brynmoroc by making him think that we believed in his fabricated story, I could then pretend that as soon as I had absorbed the energy from all the jewels, I'd hand the staff over to him. If he was happy with that, we could carry on with our quest. It will also give us enough time to plan our escape or battle strategy if that being the case. Lucia thought it a good idea but said that Brynmoroc was a wizard, an intelligent wizard who could play us at our own game. So even if he did agree, we would still have to be on our guard. Lucia was right; maybe he would try to trick us, but according to Bleddwyn, because Brynmoroc is one with the Sun Giant, we were safe until around midday. So between the times of eleven in the morning and two or three in the afternoon, I suggested that we should make that period a no-go zone. During that period, we could camp, have lunch and be ready to expect the unexpected.

Lucia agreed and decided that we should now head out, find the creek and camp there for the night. It didn't take us long to pack, and before setting out, Lucia laughed, for she had left a note on our trap saying, free to whoever finds it. We saddled up, mounted Roslyn and headed northwest across an orange, dusty, rocky, tree and shrub-ridden wilderness. It was such a lovely evening, and with the gorge only a few miles away, we weren't in any hurry. Roslyn took her time weaving her way across an eerie desolate-looking area, one you would never want to be stranded alone in.

Incidentally, you may well ask, why didn't I buy Lucia or conjure up a horse for her? The answer is; she didn't want to be on her own. She wasn't happy unless her arms were either around my waist or hugging my arm, but most of all, she loved holding my hand, something I found increasingly difficult to deal with, especially during the night.

With no trail to follow, we made our way through the rocky landscape the best way we could. After twisting, climbing and weaving, we eventually arrived at the edge of the gorge, looking down into the most incredible sight I had ever seen. It was like the beginning of time when the earth had split, leaving a deep, rocky, winding crack for miles. Looking over the sheer cliff, down through the trees and vegetation, I could see a lovely blue and white flowing river. The river was blue from the reflection of the clear blue sky and white from the rippling rapids.

"It's amazing," remarked Lucia. "Simply amazing. But now we had better make camp before the sun goes down."

I unhitched Roslyn, and while she trotted off to graze, we pitched our tent in amongst some trees, well away from the edge of the cliff. Later, we went for a stroll, and while taking in the fabulous scenery, Lucia spotted a pool down in the river below.

"If it's a nice day tomorrow I am going to have a bath in that lovely pool. You too Gwydion," she said meaningfully.

I just laughed and told her not to worry because I'd be the first in. She laughed too and gently punched my arm.

"Oh yeah, we'll soon see," she said. "The last time you were in the river; you were like a shivering whimpering pup."

"Oh, you little fibber you," I said as she rolled away laughing before I could tickle her.

"NO! NO!" She screamed. "Please don't tickle me Gwydion. I hate it. I'll die if you do."

She then jumped up and ran, laughing all the way back to the camp. I followed her, and when I got back, she was standing against a tree with one hand behind her back, and as I looked at her, she gave a gentle smile.

I thought to myself, "Dew! She's so pretty. What's she doing? Is she teasing me?"

She stood there saying nothing, but I could tell by her eyes and the way she parted her lips, that she wanted me to kiss her. So I slowly walked towards her, and just as I was about to kiss her, she put an apple between our lips and said, 'Peace offering.'

So I did tickle her after that until we both fell down aching from laughter.

After putting all romantic thoughts from my mind, we settled down for the night, but my last thought as she held my hand before I went to sleep was; "Never will I try to kiss her again."

We were up early, had our breakfast, and as the sun rose above the trees, we made our way down into the canyon to follow the river up to Sedona. It was a slow, tricky process, taking us about an hour before reaching the river that I was surprised to find, very shallow. The trees were tall and shaded us from the sun, but unfortunately, the ground cover was so full of brambles and weeds; it was impossible to find a path. So Roslyn quite happily trekked her way up the shallow river until we came to the pool Lucia spotted on our walk.

"There it is Gwydion" she shouted. "It's the pool we saw last night."

Roslyn climbed up onto the bank and with that, the excited Lucia slid down, saying, "Come on, I'm dying to wash."

She opened our bag, took out some soap and began taking her clothes off.

"Whoa!" I shouted, "Whoa! What are you doing?"

"It's okay," she said and burst out laughing. "Don't worry; I am only going as far as my underwear. Come on; I thought you were going to be first in. Ha, ha, last in and first out is more like it."

Before I could even take off my jacket and hide my staff, she had dived in, headfirst.

"Yahoo, it's lovely Gwydion, Come on in, you big baby," she urged.

"Yeah, I'll give you big baby," I said, jumping in and splashing her.

"Oh, Gwydion! That was a rotten trick," she said, rubbing her eyes. "I can't see now, and I've lost my soap."

"Ha, ha that'll teach you. Who's the baby now?" I said, splashing her again.

She laughed then scowled and splashed me back. "Just for that, you can give me your soap. I'll go over to the other side of the pool. You stay here, and I'll throw the soap over when I've finished."

I gave her my soap and she swam over to the other side and began washing her long black hair. I just swam around until she shouted, "Here's your soap; catch."

With a typical girls lobbing throw, it landed in the middle of the pool.

"Ha, ha," she laughed. "That's a shame; you'll have to find it now. Serve you right for splashing, making me lose mine,"

I dived down into the clear water, found the soap and stuffed it into the pocket of my long johns. I then stayed underwater, swam across the pool and came up behind her. She screamed as I picked her up and threw her into the middle. To my surprise, she loved it.

"Wee! That was great. Do it again Gwydion; I love it," she said, swimming over to me, giggling with excitement.

So I picked her up and as she squealed with delight, I threw her back into the middle.

"Again, again," she insisted.

This went on for a while until it got so funny that I couldn't do it anymore for laughing.

"Whoa, we had better get out now and dry before Brynmoroc finds us."

She then swam over to me and gently put her arms around my neck. She looked at me so lovingly that I knew she really wanted me to kiss her this time. So I quickly took the bar of soap out of my pocket and said, "Hey! Here's your soap."

"Why you little so and so," she blurted out. "I hope you get soap in your eye."

She swam out of the pool shouting something in Spanish but then burst out laughing, pretending to throw my clothes into the water. I too climbed out laughing and began pitching our tent to get changed. Lucia changed first and hung her wet things to dry while I changed mine. After a little food, we packed up to get ready for Brynmoroc. I found an ideal spot beside some rocks where we sat listening to the birds.

"I'm worried about Brynmoroc, Gwydion. Do you think he'll fall for your plan?"

"We'll soon find out," I replied. "But if he doesn't, we are in for a tough time."

"Oh, don't say that. It frightens me Gwydion," she said, hugging my arm.

As midday approached, the birds suddenly stopped singing, and apart from the sound of the rippling river, there was silence. At that point, we knew Brynmoroc had to be somewhere around. So with our shields on the ground beside us, we sat waiting for the tyrant. Our plan was not to use the shields unless he approached us. That was if we could see him. While waiting, a strange feeling came over me. I was thinking about the similarity of our mission being that of Welusa's. Because of his devotion and love for the most beautiful fairy queen that ever lived, he found himself on an incredible mission. I too found myself on a similar mission and like him, I was sitting next to the prettiest, most loving young lady I have ever seen or met in my life. Although it was actually happening, it was sometimes hard to believe. I then looked at Lucia, and as she gazed up at me, I suddenly asked myself why was I so lucky to have her hugging my arm right now. She was so lovely that I decided there and then that whatever the future held for us, just as long as it was with her I didn't care. I was lost now, deep in thought until the very moment we were dreading arrived. After a sudden force of wind that made the flowing river ripple backwards towards us, Lucia squeezed my arm and pressed her head against my shoulder and whispered: "It's Brynmoroc."

# Chapter 8

Hovering above the rippling river, with a long wooden staff in his hand, was Brynmoroc. Around his shoulders, a gold and black striped cloak flowed gently down to his bare feet. Like his cousin Bleddwyn, he had long wavy auburn hair, but his beard was shorter. He had a kind face and a loving smile and as he held his arms out towards us, his dress-like garment shimmered the colour of gold. We stayed still and were ready to grab our shields if he made a move towards us.

"Lucia, please don't be afraid of me," said the wizard in a compassionate voice. "I will never harm you. You are my flesh and blood; I love you. I have returned hoping that you believe in me and have decided to come home. Together, we can defeat my devious cousin."

He then stopped and beckoned with his hands as if waiting for our answer. For a moment, I had forgotten what I was going to say and had to shake my head.

"Good afternoon Sir," I said, remembering. "Lucia and I have been waiting for you. Firstly, I must tell you that I've been suspicious of Bleddwyn for some time now. Yesterday, after you informed us that you were Lucia's father, it made me think. When I first met Lucia, she told me that she had no recollection of her parents. I thought nothing of it at the time, until yesterday. We spent all night discussing the possibility that you may be telling the truth, but please Sir, you must understand and appreciate how confused we are. So is there any way you can prove that you are indeed Lucia's father?"

He smiled before replying, "Only fools would not have asked such a question."

He then slowly turned and pointed his staff towards some pine trees that began shaking vigorously. I could feel Lucia trembling as a cluster of pine needles headed towards us only to stop in mid-air about twenty feet away. They were now in the shape of a circle, and as we looked, a vision began slowly appearing. On a lawn in front of a castle was a lovely black-haired woman playing with a little girl, also with black hair. It was difficult to know how old the girl was, but according to Lucia, about three or four. I was now wondering what the wizard was playing at because the woman was now speaking to the little girl in Spanish. Lucia now looked confused, so I asked her what the woman was saying.

"Lucia, put that down, it's dirty she said, but then I heard another child shouting; she's always doing it, Mamma."

"What! What child?" I asked while blinking my watery eyes. "I can't see another."

"Neither can I," she replied. "But there is. A little girl I think."

I thought then that it couldn't be true. The wizard was tricking us. He had to be, but then, as the little girl smiled and ran away, she was running to Brynmoroc who stooped down to catch her as she jumped into his arms. To the girl's excitement, he put her up on his shoulders and walked off towards the castle while the woman called out to the other child.

"What's she saying now?" I asked.

Lucia still with that confused look, replied, "Come on, we are off back with papa now."

The vision then slowly faded away and so did all the pine needles. Lucia recognised the castle to be Lorca Castle.

"Well, is that proof enough for you? Or would you like to see more?" Asked the wizard.

At that moment, I honestly didn't know what to think. Like Lucia, I too was confused, totally disillusioned and was now wondering which wizard to believe.

"Take your time," said the encouraging wizard. "There is no rush. I am prepared to wait as long as it takes. I want you to wholeheartedly believe that I am your father and come to me of your own free will."

Lucia nudged me and whispered, "What do you think? He looks and sounds genuine."

"I don't know," I replied. "Because that dark-haired girl and the woman, definitely looked like you."

"Like me! Do you really think so? Well, what are we going to do? I'm worried now."

I couldn't think but we had to stick to our plan. So I took a few deep breaths, stood up and nervously looked at the beaming wizard. He wasn't the nasty twelve-foot gleaming giant I saw in Bleddwyn's vision. Instead, he was a kind-faced wizard, a little taller than me.

"Excuse me Sir," I said politely, "We are now completely overwhelmed and shocked. So please don't be offended when I ask for a little more time to think. As you know, Lucia never knew her parents and with you now claiming to be her father, comes as a shock to her. During the night, Lucia was ready to accept you as her father, but I thought we had better wait a while and think. I'm sorry to seem untrustworthy Sir, but for Lucia's sake, I have to be cautious."

Brynmoroc beamed broadly and replied, "I am pleased with you Gwydion and you are right not to believe in just a vision. So please, both of you, take your time and as the days go by, I will further prove and assure you that I am indeed Lucia's father. Now carry on with your mission, for the prophecy says; once started, it must be finished. But its fulfilment depends on the instigator."

He then slowly raised his eyes to the sky as if looking for something.

"I'll leave you now in peace and will return again tomorrow. By then, one way or the other, you might have made your decision. Goodbye for now."

With a smile and a wave, he was gone, disappearing into the trees. Lucia let go of my arm and as I looked into her bewildered eyes, we hugged.

"Oh Gwydion," she sighed. "I don't know what to believe now."

"Ah, we won't let him fool us," I said, just to encourage her. "He's a crafty old wizard who's probably afraid for his life. At least he told us to finish our mission. We are safe for another day, so let's pack and head up through the creek to Sedona then camp and think."

We chose to travel up the creek because it was a lot easier to find Sedona that way. Besides, it was only four miles and the only other way was through the dry desert and over its mountain. So we headed on up through the creek taking in its splendour. Roslyn sometimes walked in the river whenever it was shallow, but mostly we made our way along its banks through shady trees. It was fascinating but sometimes scary walking under high cliffs. Another scary moment was when a creature darted out in front of us and then ran away screaming. Roslyn swerved violently, throwing us headlong into a deep pool. I landed near the bank and was okay, but because the river was fast-flowing, Lucia was swept away into a beaver dam. I could just see her head and arms as she struggled to climb up onto it.

"Gwydion I'm stuck, help me," she screamed.

I shouted for her to hang on and that I was coming. I climbed out, slung off my jacket, grabbed the rope from my saddle and ran down the bank.

"It's my belt; it's caught Gwydion," she shouted.

I was so worried that she was going to drown that I dropped the rope and dived in. I swam over just as she was beginning to lose her grip. I held her up until she found a better hold.

"It's my belt. My belt Gwydion. Quickly, it's stuck, it's stuck," she cried, over and over

I put my arms around her waist, unbuckled the belt and she was free. After climbing up onto the dam, gasping for breath, she shouted, "Get my belt Gwydion, my pouch is on it."

I felt around and found the belt still caught up in the dam. It was actually her pouch that was jammed. I managed to free it easily enough and we swam over to the bank and climbed out to catch our breath.

"What happened? What was all that screaming?" Asked Lucia after we had recovered.

"I don't know. I've never heard anything like it," I replied.

I knew what it was but I didn't want to worry her. It was a strange short-haired naked scrawny kind of creature.

We were both soaking wet and before changing our clothes, Lucia wanted a towel.

"Will you rub my hair for me please Gwydion? My arms are aching now," she asked pitifully.

After drying it the best I could, I untied our bags from Roslyn's saddle and then found a place behind some rocks where we could change our clothes in private.

With dry clothes and our composure recovered, we mounted Roslyn and nervously carried on until we arrived in Sedona. It was another busy town, a very exciting town with interesting-looking stores, hotels and boarding houses. The first thing Lucia wanted was a bath, meaning, getting a room for the night. After finding a livery stable, a young lad there agreed to look after my riding gear for an extra fee and took Roslyn to a nice warm stable. There was a promising-looking boarding house further down the street, appropriately named Oak Creek House. I paid the prim-looking landlady for a room and a bath and as she happily led us to our room, she pointed out the bathroom. Our room was cosy enough and had a window facing out into the street.

"There's a Barber's shop opposite," said Lucia. "Tomorrow, you can shave and get your hair cut too."

That wasn't going to happen; I was quite happy with my hair and Lucia was doing an excellent job of trimming my beard. Besides, I didn't trust barbers; those long old razors gave me the creeps.

"Ah, this is lovely and soft, can you unpack please Gwydion?" Lucia asked, flopping onto the bed

I took out our sleeping bags, soap etcetera and lay them on the bed beside her.

"There you are your highness," I said, expecting a response, but she had fallen asleep. So I sat beside her, held her hand and watched as she lay there puffing every now and then. Although her hair was all messed up and frizzy and her face a little smudged with mud, she still made me sigh. I sat there watching her until a loud knock on the door made us jump.

"Your bath is ready, towels are hanging up behind the door," shouted the landlady. "Let me know when you've finished."

"My goodness! She gave me such a fright," said Lucia grabbing my arm. "Phew, come on I'm dying to get in that bath."

"You, you're what!! I stuttered, wondering what she was saying. "I can't come in there with you."

"Oh please, Gwydion, you'll have to," she begged. "I'm afraid to be in there alone. You can turn around, look out the window or something, I won't mind."

"Don't be silly, I can't do that," I said in disbelief. "I'll stand outside the door. You'll be okay, don't worry."

"No, no!" she implored. "You'll have to come in, please Gwydion. Brynmoroc will get me."

I had no choice but to give in. So as we made our way down the corridor into the bathroom, she held my hand. The room was relatively spacious, but there was no window. So I had to sit on a chair facing a painting of a lady who was also sitting on a chair. I thought that very uncanny, almost as if it was placed there purposely. I could hear Lucia splashing away and singing something in Spanish. She had a lovely voice and I enjoyed listening to her.

"It's okay, you can turn around now," she said after finishing.

I turned to find that she was fully dressed, with a towel wrapped around her head.

"You can jump in now if you like, I won't look," she said, to my astonishment.

Once again, as you can guess, that wasn't going to happen, but I did wash my hair. In our room, and after drying Lucia's hair, she suggested we go out for supper. The landlady recommended a saloon around the corner. I was never going anywhere without my staff again. So with everyone else walking around with guns in their holsters, I thought an old staff shouldn't bother them. Unfortunately, little did I know that it would, but I'll come to that shortly.

It was dusk, and as we walked down the street, heavy rain clouds darkened the sky. We found the saloon and after entering, noticed that the soup was indeed very popular. I spotted a free table and while making our way over to it, customers stopped and stared. I thought perhaps it had something to do with my staff. We sat down and as I looked towards the bar a pretty young landlady acknowledged me and came hurrying over.

"Hello there strangers. Welcome. I'm Dannon. Dannon Carrey. Now, what are you having?"

She had pure white teeth and a lovely smile. If I had not met Lucia, I would have said that she had the most beautiful smile I had ever seen. We ordered two bowls of soup and some extra bread; we were famished. Dannon told us that she had come to Sedona from Tipperary Ireland and had been there for some time. That was someone else from Ireland. I was beginning to think that America was full of them. While we were waiting, a curious lady came over and sat at our table, asking if we were travellers or new settlers. I told her that we were just passing through and were staying at Bridget Stanton's boarding house.

"You sound very Welsh. Are you from Wales?" she asked. "My grandmother was Welsh, but I have no idea what part of Wales she came from."

Before I could answer, she asked while looking at my staff, "Are you some kind of wizard? They say there are quite a lot of them in Wales."

I was anxious now and wanted her to go away. So I told her that I wasn't a wizard and if I were, I'd probably wouldn't be here right now. She stood up, gave me an awful look, swished her skirt and stormed off. Whatever I said had the desired effect; she was gone. The next lady that came to our table was the cheerful Landlady with our hot vegetable soup and some freshly baked rolls. Our meal smelt and tasted absolutely lovely but as we began to enjoy it, a mean-looking man, who had been staring at me, came over with the lady I was talking to earlier. He poked me in the arm, sat down beside Lucia, put his arm around her and glared at me. I thought, oh no, here we go again

"Hey you, Welshy. My lady says you're a wizard and that you didn't like her company. Well, I sure like this one's, so what are you going to say about it, boyo?"

I could feel the blood draining from my face now with contempt for this troublemaker. Then I remembered what my Granddad told me.

"Don't let someone belittle you Gwydion, and never back down from anyone, for if you do they'll walk all over you. You are a man now son, let them know it."

So I stayed calm and said to him that if his lady thought that I had offended her, I'll apologise to her. I did apologise and asked if there was anything I could do to make it up to her.

"Ha! Make it up he says!" roared the man. "How could a fool like you make it up to a lady like her?"

I turned to the man, who still had his arm around Lucia, and calmly spoke to him.

"Now, what I am going to say to you is; if you don't take your arm from around my lady's shoulders, maybe I'll break it taking it from there. Now, what do you say to that, fool?"

He jumped up, flinging his chair behind him and raged, "Fool, am I! Break my arm, will you? Well come on then, I'd like to see you try."

I calmly replied, "I will, but first, if you can manage to pick up that chair and sit back down, we'll do battle. You've heard of arm wrestling, haven't you? Well, let's see how good you are in front of the ladies."

When I mentioned arm wrestling, everyone in the room gathered around, urging him to take me on. Surprisingly enough, even Dannon the young Landlady offered to be the referee.

Now, I am no weakling, but back home in Wales, no one has ever beaten me at arm wrestling, not even lifting chairs by the leg with one hand. So with his pals cheering him on, this mean-looking character picked up his chair and slammed it down opposite me.

"Why I'll break both your arms and laugh while I'm doing it," he roared.

The look on Lucia's face now was one of anguish as if saying, are you crazy?

We took a firm grip, and as we locked our arms together, Dannon placed two full bottles of whiskey twelve inches away from our elbows.

"Whoever wins, gets to keep the bottle," she said, much to the delight of my mean-looking opponent."

I could hear gamblers shouting and taking bets. One of them hollered, "Go on Joe, break that wizard's arm and we'll drink ya toast in both them bottles."

Hearing that, Lucia pleaded with me, "Gwydion, forget it. Don't be silly. He didn't hurt me."

"No! But I'm going to hurt him. Hurt him real bad," said Joe, quick to respond.

I said nothing, only smiled and winked just as Dannon was about to begin the contest.

"Are you ready? One, two, three, BEGIN," she ordered.

We were stalemates for a few seconds or more until I slowly put the pressure on. I could feel that he was never going to beat me, so I thought I'd play with him for a while. To make it even more exciting, I let my arm go Joe's way making him think I was weakening.

"Go on Joe; you've got him. Look at his face. Ha, he's easy," his mates were shouting.

"Do you give up? Err um wizard, do you give up?" asked Dannon.

I pretended to grimace and shook my head. At that point, thinking that I was finished, they all began to shout.

"Yes, yes, finish him. Finish him, Joe. Break his arm, but not the bottle."

That was it; I wasn't going to play any longer. My grip was my biggest asset, and when I began to squeeze Joe's hand, he didn't look so mean anymore. He was a worried man now, and as I slowly moved his arm over to my side and down onto the bottle, he roared in pain.

Dannon declared me the winner, but I took no notice of her and carried on holding his arm down on the bottle.

"You did take your arm from around my lady friend's shoulders, so I am not going to break it. I apologised to your lady friend; now it's your turn to apologise to mine."

There was silence now, and as I let him go and stared at him, I asked, "Well?"

He held his painful arm for a moment, turned to Lucia, looked into her eyes and told her that he was sorry. Everyone began to clap and cheer, but before Joe rose to walk away, I stood up and handed him the bottle of whiskey and said, "This is mine, now it's yours."

He shook my hand and to everyone's applause, he shouted out, "The drinks are on me."

All but a few of the gamblers congratulated me and walked happily away back to their seats, chatting with one another.

"My goodness!!" Exclaimed Lucia. "You were amazing. I thought he was going to break your arm or even worse, kill you. If it wasn't for Dannon taking away his gun, he might have. Oh Gwydion, please don't do anything like that again. My heart won't stand it," she said, punching me in the arm.

"Well, you're my lady aren't you?" I said gently punching her back, "I always fight for my ladies."

She hit me again, only harder this time, "What ladies? How many do you have?"

"I'm only joking, there aren't any," I replied. "Never have been. In fact, you are the first lady I've been with for more than a day, and hopefully, the only one I will ever fight for."

She put her arms around my neck to kiss me, but as I staggered back onto my chair, the leg gave way and we tumbled to the floor, laughing.

"Hey wizard, I thought you had finished wrestling," joked Dannon placing fresh bowls of soup on the table.

I apologised for the chair and offered to pay and anything else that was broken.

"Ah, that's alright," she said, as I picked up the chair." There's more than that gets broken here, especially when them old cowboys comes in from the cattle run."

The fresh bowls of soup, for some reason, tasted even better. When finished, we spent another hour listening to the piano and a few singers. So all in all, apart from the angry confrontation, it was a good night. Dannon and a few others, including Joe, wished us luck as we left.

We walked back through the street, hand in hand and arrived at our boarding house feeling very happy with ourselves.

"I don't know about you Lucia, but I'm worn out," I said, after collecting the keys to our room.

"Yes, me too. I could sleep for a week," she said and began to yawn.

Our room was dark now, so we just climbed into our sleeping bags and led upon the bed. As we lay there thinking, she held my hand, gently squeezed it, sighed and said 'goodnight my hero' and fell asleep. I then lay there thinking about the fight until I too drifted off to sleep, knowing that she was happy.

# Chapter 9

Lucia was up early and before waking me, had already packed everything away into our bag. I washed, put on my boots and within an hour we were downstairs having breakfast. Generally, the guests usually sit around a large table, but we were lucky and had a table for two. After breakfast, I thought we had better head on for we only had until midday to find the jewel before Brynmoroc turned up. We settled up with the landlady, collected our belongings and headed off to the livery stable. To make life a lot easier, we decided to buy another horse to carry our bags etcetera. Lucia picked a lovely quiet chestnut-coloured mare and called her Hazel.

With everything packed and safely tied on our new companion, we mounted Roslyn and as Lucia wrapped her arms tightly around my waist, we waved goodbye to Sedona.

"Oh, it's so lovely without the bag and that tent sticking in my back. Thank you Gwydion," she said, squeezing me

Feeling her arms around me and how she chatted in her lovely Spanish accent, I did nothing but sigh with happiness. How many times I sighed that morning doesn't come to mind, only that I was falling in love with her.

"Look Gwydion, it's so beautiful," she remarked as we rode into the canyon.

It was, and the further up the canyon we went, the more incredible it became. The jagged, orange-coloured cliffs were enormous and over the years the steadily flowing river had cut into their base so much that we found ourselves walking through C-shaped tunnels at least ten feet wide in places. One of them must have been a quarter of a mile long and with the river reflecting the morning sun, the beautiful colours created an absolutely fabulous scene. Eventually, we came to a point where the canyon forked. According to Lucia, we were to go left and our next little gem was only a mile away.

Searching that part of the creek was equally mesmerising. We could have wandered for miles taking in the breathtaking beauty, but it was a bow of a ship we were looking for and as we rounded a small bend in the river, there it was. Above us now, overhanging a sheer cliff was a rock identical to the bow of a ship. A ship that looked as if it had come to rest there and fossilised over the centuries.

"Look at it Lucia. Perhaps it's Noah's Ark," I jokingly suggested.

"Well, no one has ever found the ark," said Lucia, studying it. "You never know, perhaps it is?"

She then pointed to the bow saying that the citrine was on the left-hand side of the keel and facing the sun. Almost all the canyon's awesome cliffs were hundreds of feet high, but this one seemed even higher and definitely sheerer.

I looked at Lucia and cringed, saying, "I'm sorry Lucia, but there is only one way we are going to climb up there."

"Oh no Gwydion!" was her quick response. "Not that creepy scorpion again. Oh, that was horrible. I didn't like her and I thought we were going to fall."

"Ah, it's only Roslyn, she'll not harm you," I said to console her. "Besides, if we do fall, we'll fall into the river. It's deep enough here."

"Don't say that Gwydion! You are frightening me now," she said, slapping my shoulder.

"I'm only joking," I said and laughed. "Don't worry. Roslyn won't let us fall."

We planned to reach the citrine before noon and then get far enough away before Brynmoroc found us. I looked at my watch and it was ten-twenty-five. As long as we didn't come across any problems, we had plenty of time to achieve what we came for and get well away from the jewel's secret hiding place. We tied Hazel to a tree, remounted Roslyn and sat there bracing ourselves for what lay ahead. Then, with Lucia almost squeezing the life out of me, I raised my staff, cried out my command and within seconds we were crawling up the jagged face of the cliff, sitting on the curled-up tail of a scorpion.

"Oh, please don't let us fall Roslyn?" Whimpered Lucia, as we slowly crept.

We made good steady progress until we came to the bow of the ship. That's when our hearts were in our mouths, for we now found ourselves almost in an upside-down position. Roslyn curled her tail a little tighter and lifted her back two legs for us to hold on to. Oh yes, boy o boy, as we searched around for that citrine jewel, not only were our hearts in our mouths, everything else must have been there too.

At last, much to our delight and relief, we found the citrine sitting in a hole that could have been where the anchor chain threaded through. It was so uncanny. I slowly slid my staff from across my knees and touched its base on the tiny yellow crinkly sparkling citrine. Immediately, there was a beautiful golden glow that raced up and down the staff until the golden colour settled underneath the brightly lit orange and red. With my staff now returned to its normal state, I asked Roslyn to make her way back down slowly, backwards, as before.

Once again, we were so happy reaching the bottom, Lucia collapsed on the bank of the river.

"Oh, I'll never, ever no matter what Gwydion, do anything like that again. I have never been so terrified in all my life."

I said that I felt the same way but was mystified by how smoothly everything was going. I remembered Bleddwyn telling me that it wouldn't be easy, possibly fatal, yet that was the third jewel I had drained without any trouble.

Lucia agreed, "Well if there is going to be trouble and there probably will be, we'll face it together."

I ordered Roslyn back to herself and waited for our fabulous mare to satisfy her thirst. We then set off back through the amazing canyon until we had climbed up and out, well away from the fantastic phenomenon. I found the perfect place to lie low out of the midday sun that would undoubtedly be bringing trouble in the shape of Brynmoroc. It was a nice little spot shaded by trees, and with large rocks that we could rest our backs against. The only way Brynmoroc could approach us now was from the front.

It was well past midday and while sitting by the rocks waiting for the wizard, Lucia, with her arm in mine, was quiet as if in thought, so I asked for them.

"I was thinking about Brynmoroc and the vision," she replied. "What if he's telling the truth and I am his daughter."

I thought perhaps he was just a crafty old wizard and that if he did turn up, I'd question him about his claim. She thanked me but said that there was one more thing. Who was the other child? One I had forgotten about. I was more wrapped up in the dark-haired girl looking so much like Lucia. The other child was a mystery, but we had to stay

focused for now and see what happens. If those
wizards were playing mind games with us for one
another's benefit, I would abandon the mission
and burn the staff. With that sorted and after
waiting for three long hours, for some reason,
Brynmoroc didn't appear. So happily, we packed
up and made our way back to Sedona. Jake, who
ran the livery stable, was surprised to see us again
and took the horses away to their stables. Bridget,
the landlady at the boarding house, was also
surprised to see us.

"You are just in time for tea. I have a lovely
roast on today's menu with my gorgeous apple pie
for dessert, will I set the table for you?"

"Yes, please," we replied almost together.

We were that hungry; it didn't take long to
wash and dust ourselves down and head
downstairs to the dining room. An hour later, we
were full after eating our lovely meal, but we still
had enough room for a few drinks at the bar. It
was midnight before we went to bed. It was a
chilly night, but we were nice and warm in our
sleeping bags covered with soft woollen blankets.
While we lay there nice and snug, I asked Lucia
the whereabouts of the next two jewels, but I
didn't like the way she sighed before replying.

"Well, the next, being the emerald, is almost
two thousand miles away in Kentucky. It's
situated in the crevice of a large heart-shaped
rock, either in or on the side of a small lake.
There's a gorge called Red River Gorge and the
river that runs through it feeds the lake. So, if we
follow it downstream, we should find the lake

easily enough. The other jewel being a blue Sapphire is in Switzerland."

Two thousand miles. No wonder Lucia sighed. As you know, our Roslyn wasn't any ordinary horse and could easily do well over a hundred miles a day. So providing the road was good, and with no upsets, we should make it in about three weeks. Knowing now the whereabouts of the next jewels, I lay there quietly, thinking until Lucia turned and faced me.

"I really think Brynmoroc is telling the truth and that Bleddwyn is deceiving us, but as for my grandmother, I just can't believe it. Can you?"

I had been thinking about the possibility of being deceived but didn't know by who, and why. The only answer I could give was that maybe Brynmoroc was her father, but he could also be playing with her mind, hoping to convince her into submitting to him. So until we find out otherwise, we still had to treat him as our enemy and be on guard at all times. She agreed, gave a huge sigh and it wasn't long before she was sound asleep, tightly holding my hand. With my other hand, I reached over to turn down the lamp, but as I did, there was a crash of glass, followed by a terrible scream. I jumped out of bed only to be knocked to the floor by the same kind of screaming creature I saw back in the canyon. It was on top of me and while doing all I could to stop it from biting me, out of the corner of my eye I saw another coming through the window.

Lucia was screaming, "Gwydion, I can't see, where are you? What's happening?"

"Get under the bed Lucia!" I managed to say as I caught hold of the creature's throat.

The very moment I had my hand around its skinny throat, he rolled backwards, roaring in pain holding his throat. I rose to my feet and rushed over to the other screaming creature who by now had hold of Lucia. I dragged the crazed thing away and forced it up against the wall by its throat. Once again, the same thing happened. It crumpled up, falling to the floor in pain clutching his throat. There was so much screaming going on I didn't know what was happening. Then thankfully, as both desperate creatures were struggling to get to their feet, there was banging on the door. At that point, a few men came bursting in just as the skinny creatures began climbing out the window, roaring in agony. Bang, bang went the men's guns as I ducked away.

"What the heck were they!!" Said one, rushing over to the window. Bang, bang went his gun again, but they were gone. Lucia grabbed hold of my arm just as the distressed landlady came in wanting to know what had happened. I explained everything and was thankful the men confirmed my explanation. I insisted that I would pay for the damages and gave her more than enough to replace the window.

It was obvious the creatures were an act of wizardry and it was probably not going to be the last we'd see of them either.

After cleaning up all the glass and covering the window with a blanket, we went back to bed.

Unable to sleep, Lucia shared her thoughts with me.

"According to Brynmoroc, Bleddwyn has since moved the two jewels that we had found and probably now, the third. So I, being the only one with the knowledge of how to find the jewels, what benefit would either wizard gain by moving them? Nothing. They would gain absolutely nothing unless both wizards know more than they are letting on. None of it makes any sense to me. What do you think?"

My answer was that it was baffling and had many theories to think about. Maybe the prophecy hadn't been violated until now and we were the culprits. We could speculate for a week and still wouldn't know for sure. What I did know was that we had just been attacked by some weird mystical creatures, either trying to kill or prevent us from carrying on with our mission. If it was the work of any wizard then yes, what would he gain from it? Regarding Bleddwyn; he told me that he and other wizards could only venture out at night, no further than their vicinity. If true, except for the birds, there was no way he or his colleagues could possibly see or know where we find the jewels. As for Brynmoroc, who has very conveniently told us his side of the story in broad daylight, he was the only one who could. This leaves us, with Brynmoroc still the favourite of being the violator.

"Yes," said Lucia squeezing my hand. "If that is the case, he will do all he can to lure us into his parlour and take your staff. What good it will do him I don't know, but alright Gwydion, we'll see how it goes, but I wish the sun would hurry up and rise."

Within an hour, the cock crowed and the sun she had wished for, began to filter through the side of the makeshift curtain. It made us feel a lot better, especially after the gong went for breakfast. During our toast, I heard one of the guests say that he was waiting for the nine o'clock stagecoach to Amarillo. I thought a coach might be a good idea for a change. So after thanking the landlady, we set off to the booking office and paid for our passage to Amarillo. Preparing ourselves mentally for such a journey was tough at first, but as Lucia would sometimes say, it will soon be tomorrow.

"What about Roslyn?" Lucia asked as we made our way to the livery stable.

"I thought you'd like a little dog for company," I replied. "Roslyn won't mind. What about you?"

She laughed, "Oh, you think of everything, don't you? Yes, that will be lovely."

I sold my saddle and hazel back to Jake, then when around a corner and out of sight, in a flash, Roslyn was now a happy tiny terrier with her head poking out of Lucia's bag.

For weeks we had been fortunate with good weather so we couldn't complain when it rained off and on for two days as the stagecoach rumbled across the bleak desert trail. After six days of continuous travel, stopping only for an overnight bed and many changes of horses, we finally, on a wet Saturday evening arrived in Amarillo. We could have carried on to Kentucky, but Amarillo was far enough. A boarding house was just down the street, but before booking in I had Roslyn back to herself and bedded down in the local livery stable. With her taken care of, we booked ourselves into the Brunswick boarding house. Not surprisingly, it didn't take Lucia long before she was enjoying herself, singing away in a tub. As usual, I was there, looking the other way, studying the patterns on the wallpaper.

"Okay, it's your turn now and better mind you do," she said, putting a handful of soap suds on my head. "Don't worry; I won't be looking. I'll be drying my hair."

I shook them off, turned around and laughed, "Watch it, or I won't be looking at the wall next time."

"Just you dare Gwydion, and the soap will be in your eye, not on your head," she said, waving her finger.

I thought okay, for I could do with a scrub and felt better for it. Later, when we were about to venture down for supper, Lucia happened to look out the window.

"Look, Gwydion! That young lady coming out of the Sheriff's Office, isn't she the lady from Phoenix? You know; the waitress who's looking for her brother."

It was her and she seemed upset, so we thought we had better go down to find out why. By the time we arrived out into the street, she was in tears and walking towards us.

"Roisin, what's the matter? Why are you crying?" I asked, taking hold of her arm. "Whoa, hold on, don't walk away. What's the matter? Are you hurt? Tell me?"

"I'm okay," she replied, wiping away her tears.

I held both her arms and while looking into her tearful eyes, I insisted she told me why she was so sad. Eventually, after much sighing and sobbing, she broke down. Roisin had been robbed of all her money, and now she would never be able to travel to Spain to be with her brother.

"That's terrible Roisin," said Lucia putting her arm around her. "You had better come with us and change those wet clothes."

A few miles out of town, the stagecoach Roisin was travelling in had been held up and robbed, but not only did the bandits rob everyone they also took the horses. As a result, coachmen and passengers had to walk in the pouring rain. The sheriff had been informed but said it was unlikely he would ever be able to find the bandits. I told her not to worry and paid for her to have a bath and room for the night. Lucia's nightwear and clothes fitted Roisin perfectly.

"Thank you. You are so kind, both of you," she said gratefully.

We were up simultaneously in the morning and were soon downstairs enjoying a bacon sandwich. I told Roisin that I would pay her way to the port of New York and her fare across the Atlantic. She was grateful and thanked me, but said she was a little frightened now of travelling on her own. New York happened to be where we were eventually heading. So, feeling sorry for

Roisin, we left her sipping coffee while Lucia and I went to our room for a discussion. Lucia suggested that because we were going to France later on, we could take Roisin along with us to the port. That settled, we packed our bags and went down to tell Roisin our decision and how we were travelling.

"If it isn't too much trouble," she said. "I'd like that very much. I can cook and make lovely sandwiches."

I told her to go to her room and collect what little possessions she had and to wait for us outside. Meanwhile, Lucia and I went to fetch Roslyn, and after collecting the excited mare, we walked her behind some buildings. With no one around, I threw two coins alongside Roslyn, lifted my staff and gave its command. After a bright flash and purple haze, stood precisely what I had summoned. It was a four-seater coach with another dark bay mare harnessed alongside Roslyn, eager to be on her way.

"Ha-ha, oh yes Gwydion, another one. We'll call her Sophia and look at the lovely coach, it's wonderful."

It was, but now we had to get away before the sheriff, or someone started asking questions. I helped Lucia up onto the driving seat and within five minutes, we had picked up the very surprised Roisin and were out of Amarillo, heading west on a dusty trail to Oklahoma, three hundred miles away. A few miles further on, I pulled up to check on Roisin. She didn't mind being on her own in the carriage, so that was fine with us and away we went just as the sun peeped through some puffy white clouds.

# Chapter 10

Fifty miles into our journey, I remembered about Brynmoroc. We had forgotten about him and it was almost noon. We had to find somewhere to hide. When we agreed to take Roisin, we hadn't thought about the wizard. So naturally, we were in a right predicament, wondering how we were going to explain him to her if he turned up. She'd be terrified.

"What are we going to do Gwydion? Please tell me you'll think of something?" Asked Lucia, shaking my arm.

We travelled on through a canyon until I spotted a secluded spot in an alcove where we could rest for a coffee and a sandwich. I searched around for some wood and at the same time, nervously kept an eye out for any signs of Brynmoroc. With enough wood collected and the coffee made and as we began to enjoy Roisin's lovely sandwiches, a force of wind whipped up, making Lucia grab hold of my arm. I quickly told Roisin to come and sit close to me. She looked a little worried but thankfully did as I asked. Then just as we were seated with our backs against the rock face, a small and thick fluffy white cloud dropped from out of the sky, settling down about thirty feet away.

"Okay, here we go," I muttered as the cloud slowly cleared, revealing a happy smiling Brynmoroc, with outstretched arms.

"Gwydion, Lucia my child, how are you both?" he lovingly asked.

"Gwydion! He's a wizard!" Said Roisin grabbing my other arm.

There was nothing I could say, only whisper, "Don't be afraid, he can't harm you."

Lucia had her hand in her pocket and if necessary, ready to take out her shield.

"Good day to you, Sir," I said, trying to look unconcerned and happy to see him. "We were waiting and hoping you'd call. Since our last meeting, Lucia and I have been discussing your version of events. However, Lucia is still a little sceptical and finding it all hard to believe, but despite that, we have decided to carry on with our mission as you suggested. When it's accomplished, and on the condition that we will not be harmed, you can have my staff and do whatever you want with it."

He was beaming with delight now and accepted my condition. He also assured me that he would do all he could to prevent Bleddwyn from trying to abort the mission. He then turned to Lucia and his face saddened.

"I understand just how sceptical you are of me Lucia, but I can assure you; I am who I say I am. I love you and in time if all goes well, you will know my heart is true."

He then waved his hand towards her, and a red and yellow coloured rose floated down onto her lap. With that, the cloud he had heralded his arrival on, surrounded him once more and with a gust of wind he was gone.

"Is he gone now, Gwydion?" asked Roisin, trembling beside me.

"Yes, he's gone and don't worry, he won't be back," I replied as she sighed.

"Who are you people? Are you some kind of magicians' or sorcerers'? Because that was a wizard. Something I've only ever seen in fairy tale books."

Explaining this supernatural event would leave Lucia and me wide open to being arrested for witchcraft or even worse, but I had to tell her.

"Roisin, back in Oklahoma when Lucia and I offered to take you to New York, we completely forgot about meeting the wizard you have now just witnessed. If we'd remembered, we would never have suggested you come with us. So you are welcome to take the carriage to the next town, the mares will come back to me. I will also give you more than enough money to get you safely over to Spain."

"No! Gwydion. I'm afraid now," she quickly replied. "I didn't like the way he looked at me and as for the wind, it was the same wind that startled the stagecoach horses. I remember it whipping up before those rough-spoken, hooded bandits robbed us. There was someone else there too. He was in the shadows, giving orders and that wizard's voice sounded very much like him. So no, I don't want to take your horses. You and Lucia seem so kind and I feel that I can trust you. So, please let me stay with you. All I want to do is to find my brother."

"Yes, Roisin. You can ride along with us for as long as you wish," said Lucia, sympathetically.

"Well, there's your answer Roisin. So welcome aboard again," I said and she hugged me.

I had to tell her that Brynmoroc could be revisiting us possibly every day. When she was happy with that and after understanding the complications that may arise, we headed out once more just as the rain began to fall.

Galloping along, a curious thought entered my head. Why didn't Brynmoroc acknowledge Roisin? She mentioned that she didn't like the way the wizard looked at her, but I was sure that he didn't. I was expecting him to acknowledge her, but his eyes never once looked towards her. I mentioned this to Lucia and that I had something else in mind too. According to Brynmoroc, Bleddwyn would try and abort the mission. Now to me, regardless of whether Bleddwyn is evil or not, I had every faith in him and would offer him my staff this very minute. Also, if it so happened that Bleddwyn was the evil wizard, then how could Brynmoroc who said he was inferior to his cousin, possibly prevent Bleddwyn from doing anything he so wished? When Brynmoroc talked about Bleddwyn aborting the mission, he meant himself. Although I offered him the staff after we had accomplished our mission, he probably still intended to make sure, by stealing it. Why, I didn't know, unless he could somehow replace the energy back into the jewels. If I was right, then things were going to get really grim and desperate from then on, especially, if those skinny creatures were anything to go by. So, from now on we were going to have to expect the unexpected. Lucia agreed with me but was worried about Roisin.

"There's something strange about her, isn't there Gwydion? You would have thought after seeing Brynmoroc, she would have ran away. Anyone else would have. We'll have to be careful what we say in front of her from now on."

We galloped on until we arrived at a strange town made up entirely of tents. According to Roisin, they were immigrant farmers waiting for the government to issue plots of land. Consequently, we didn't stop there; instead, we travelled on for about another fifty miles and camped under some trees alongside a large lake. Both girls helped one another make supper before the sun disappeared behind the mountain.

Sitting now around a fire, I thought I'd make up a half-truth story, telling Roisin that we were on an assignment for another wizard and while visiting America, we were suddenly pursued by Brynmoroc, the wizard she had foreseen claiming to be Lucia's father and that ever since we had been attacked several times by strange and weird-looking creatures.

"I know it's all hard to believe Roisin," stressed Lucia. "We couldn't believe it either, but Brynmoroc is real and with him being a wizard, from now on anything can happen. So, once again Roisin, we are very sorry for getting you mixed up in all this, but you can rest assured, Gwydion will make sure no harm comes to you."

"Well, in that case, I had better prepare myself," said Roisin, who stood up, calmly walked over to the carriage and came back with a tightly curled-up whip and a catapult.

"I hate guns, but I love these," she said and grinned, "So as you can see, and if it helps, I am well prepared to defend myself."

I kind of knew from the first day we met her in Phoenix that she was a girl with a fiery spirit. Up until she spoke those words, there was one thing that I wasn't sure about telling her. That being; the only way we could be warned of an attack while we slept, was to change Roslyn and Sophia into watchdogs. Now, because of Roisin's willingness to stay and even fight with us, I thought it only right to show her what I was capable of doing. Before I did, I asked her if she was still happy about travelling with us to New York.

"Yes, I'm sure," was her instant reply. "Yes, and even though this is like some kind of fantasy, I trust you Gwydion and I know you'll never harm me."

With that confirmed, I sat her down saying that there was something she should know about me, but for all our sakes, it had to be kept secret. She was okay with that, so I began.

"Lucia and I appreciate you trusting us but don't be offended when I say that we can't say the same about you. For that reason, after I show you something, we cannot afford to stop near any town folk until we reach Kentucky. After that, you are free to do as you like. Now, once again, I have to ask you, are you absolutely sure you want to travel with us?"

Again, without hesitation, she replied, "Yes, I've told you and as for secrets, my whole life has been one enormous one. So yes, you have my word that a secret will always stay secret with me. Although I have only known you a few days, you are both more of a friend to me than anyone I have ever known."

I thought perhaps I could trust her now and called Roslyn and Sophia over to me. Then, alongside the flickering flames of our lovely fire, I raised my staff above my head, and by giving my command followed by a blue flash of light, there were now two Great Danes on guard alongside our tent.

"Oh, good grief Gwydion. I don't believe it. You're a wizard too," said Roisin, breathing heavily. "Even if I did tell someone, they would never believe me."

Lucia laughed and said, "No, Roisin, he's not a wizard. If he were, you wouldn't be sleeping in a tent tonight; you'd be in Spain with your brother."

Roisin was stunned, still shaking her head in shock. So I put my arm around her in comfort.

"Don't worry. You are quite safe with us, and as I have already said, we will never harm you."

I was thinking now that she should sleep along with us in the tent and not in the carriage as initially planned. I wasn't going to leave her alone, but unfortunately, because of that, I had no choice but to give her my sleeping bag while I used the blankets.

So that night, as I lay on my back in the middle of two lovely girls, I knew I wasn't going to get much sleep. I was right because with Lucia holding my hand and Roisin hugging my arm, each time I tried to turn over I was pulled right back again, until sunrise. By that time, my back was painfully aching, my bottom definitely dead and with freezing cold feet from sticking out of the only blanket, I was stiff as a board trying to get up. Not only did the girls have sleeping bags they had also taken some of my blankets.

"Ah good morning all," wished Lucia, as she yawned.

"Yes, good morning," murmured Roisin.

"Good morning," I squeaked, still trying to straighten up.

"What's the matter? You look in pain Gwydion," asked Lucia.

I was, but as I painfully opened up the tent, I told her that I was okay, but my feet were a little cold.

Lucia mentioned that it looked as if it was going to rain. So with Roslyn and Sophia back as my mares, we headed out. Lucia was never wrong at predicting the weather, but the occasional showers didn't heed us any. We made good progress and arrived in Oklahoma late morning. After finding a store, we had the same old nosey questions about where did we come from, where we were going and why. This particular storekeeper even said how lucky I was to have two lovely ladies travelling with me. So after buying supplies, including a sleeping bag and new clothes for Roisin, I was glad to get out before he asked which lady was mine.

Coming out of the store, Roisin had to go back for her cotton handkerchief which she had somehow left in the store. To be on the safe side, we went with her and right enough her handkerchief was on the counter, but when Roisin went to retrieve it, the storekeeper, after looking at a piece of paper, quickly put it away under his counter. It could have been someone's receipt or a bill, but it seemed strange and a little suspicious making me think perhaps it was a note from Roisin.

We climbed aboard and carried on for another hundred miles across an open prairie with very few trees for shelter. With the lack of them to hide under we travelled on taking a chance Brynmoroc wouldn't turn up. Luck was with us for we arrived and passed through Tulsa at around seven o'clock without any sign of him.

"Yahoo!" Lucia shouted as we passed through. "Do you think he believed you Gwydion and he's going to leave us alone now?"

"We'd be so lucky if he did," I replied. "But I doubt it very much. So from now on, we had better have our shields out, visible to him."

By using our thoughts, we could actually make our shields as small or as large as we wished, even my staff. I didn't want to travel through the night, so we pulled into a small creek. By then we were all exhausted and looking forward to resting our jarred bodies. The wind had earlier whipped up, so the creek was an ideal sheltered place to set up camp. We did and were soon enjoying Roisin's sandwiches while sitting by a warm fire. I always looked forward to chatting with Lucia around a fire, but it was even more enjoyable now. I had another interesting companion to chat with. Perhaps the stories we told each other were not exactly true, but it made for a very entertaining evening with much laughter. As the embers died, we settled down for the night. A night, a lot more pleasurable as I snuggled into my lovely new sleeping bag. Cold feet were a thing of the past, though I couldn't say the same about my arms that were outside for the girls to hang on to.

"Where are we going next Gwydion?" asked Roisin, giving me a nudge.

"If things go well. We should be in St. Louis in time for tea," I replied. "We'll stop there and stock up with more provisions."

I didn't know whether to stay in St. Louis or not. I was still in two minds about trusting Roisin, but I decided to take a chance and said that we'd stay there a night.

With that settled, we drifted off to sleep though during my slumber, I woke many times dying to turn over but because of the girls, there was no way I could. Eventually, I got used to it and rose in the morning with my back feeling a little better than the day before and thanks to the sleeping bag, so were my feet.

We were up, fed and away by seven o'clock keen to make good time before it rained. We had another undisturbed night and were reasonably confident that we had fooled Brynmoroc. The rain had held off, but it was cold now. The winter was beginning to creep in. I asked Lucia many times to ride inside with Roisin out of the cold, but she always refused, so I gave her my sleeping bag to sit in.

"Oh, why are you so kind to me Gwydion?" she said, hugging my arm.

"Maybe it's because I'll have a nice warm sleeping bag tonight now," I replied and laughed.

She laughed too and said, "Well, in that case, maybe I'll keep it. You can have mine tonight."

Joking was fun and helped the time pass a lot quicker. It also made the journey less monotonous. At midday, long after passing through a town called Joplin, we pulled up and made camp in a canyon for something to eat. Then as we were about to wash up, Roisin pointed to the sky.

"Look! Look at that cloud! Is it the wizard?" she asked, grabbing hold of me.

"Quickly, behind us Roisin! Grab your shield Lucia," I said as a black, corkscrew-shaped cloud gathered speed and in a matter of seconds 'BOOM' went an almost deafening explosion.

# Chapter 11

The cloud had smashed into the side of the canyon, causing a roaring avalanche to come tumbling down into the creek. We stayed crouched behind our shields and watched as the whole road in front of us filled with massive rocks and earth. It took until the dust settled before we could see the full result of the devastation. The canyon was now completely blocked with rubble over a hundred feet high.

"It must be the wizard's doing," cried Lucia. "Do something, Gwydion."

I was about to concur when crawling out from between the rubble came a dozen or more of those skinny, screaming creatures again. Holding out our shields, Lucia and I faced up to them, but as they charged, they tumbled over themselves about twenty feet away from us. After regrouping, they spread out holding their hands to their eyes. Our shields were our only source of protection. We couldn't fight for we had no weapons, and neither did they, but they did have claw-like fingers and horrible sharp pointy teeth. I remembered Bleddwyn telling me that my staff was a weapon, but I had never tried to use it. Roisin, before I could stop her, dashed over to the carriage and shouted, "I need to get my weapons Gwydion."

For some reason or other, the creatures did nothing only watch Roisin as she quickly picked up her bag and race back.

"That was silly Roisin, they could have grabbed you," said Lucia.

"Well, something's for sure; they are not after me," said Roisin, opening her bag. "They are after you two."

Roisin took out her catapult and a bag full of round pebbles. She aimed, let fly and hit one square in the chest, making it stagger backwards screaming in pain until he fell to the ground crumbling into dust. She aimed once more and hit another, who also suffered the same fate.

"I think they'll be after all three of us now, don't you," said Roisin as the creatures screamed with contempt towards her.

They were furious now and making so much noise that it was hard to think. Regardless of Roisin's intervention, they continued with their approach, but slowly, and as they crept, I noticed their eyes were closed now, making our shields useless against them.

Knowing this, we quickly moved away, but unfortunately, even though their eyes were tightly closed, they knew exactly where we were. We crept close to the wall of the canyon until they trapped us in a crevice. So with our shields raised waiting for them to attack, Roisin aimed again, but they were wise to her and somehow avoided her shots. Then with one almighty terrifying scream, they blindly charged. All I could think of doing was to hold my staff over the top of our shields and ask it to defend us and as I did, I felt a tingling vibration in my hand. At that instant, a quivering blaze of colour flashed in front of the creatures sending them reeling back in shock. Knowing now what my staff could do, we advanced while they backed away making that horrible noise until a flash of lightning hit the wailing creatures, crumbling them all in to dust.

"That was incredible! You truly are a wizard Gwydion, aren't you? You must be?"

"No, Roisin, I'm no wizard. I'm just me, on a mission for a wizard, using his staff."

I let down my shield and was about to sit back against the rocks when Lucia shouted, "Look out Gwydion!"

I spun around in time to see one of the creatures creeping down the cliff, ready to pounce. I caught it by the throat as it sprang, but I was off balance and we fell to the ground. Its breath and screams were horrible. It wasn't heavy, only about four or five stone, but it was as lively and slippery as an eel. The slippery creature, just like the others, didn't like me holding its throat and its expression was one of pleading with me to let it go. I was in two minds and probably might have if I had not heard a roar of thunder and a deep voice, "BE GONE!" Be gone, I command you!"

With those words, the desperate creature crumpled up, leaving me coughing and spluttering holding a handful of dust. The owner of the deep commanding voice was none other than Brynmoroc, standing about thirty yards away. Lucia handed me my staff and we backed away against the rock.

"Are you all right my children? Are you hurt Lucia?" asked the concerned-looking wizard, holding his arms out to her. "Those creatures were the work of my cousin Bleddwyn."

At that moment, whether it was Bleddwyn or Brynmoroc I didn't care. The creatures had gone and we were safe. So, just to keep Brynmoroc happy I thought that I'd quickly thank him.

"Thank you Sir for saving me. I am so grateful that you came, but honestly, I am more than confused with it all. If it's Bleddwyn, then why?"

"You are very welcome Gwydion. I know this must seem strange and you are right to ask why Bleddwyn would want to stop you from accomplishing the very mission he assigned you. He doesn't. My cousin knows; the only way to beat the prophecy is to let it run its course. The creatures he sends are of no threat to your life, only to make you think it is I who sends them. Gwydion, once your staff is fully charged, Bleddwyn will ask you to offer it to him, knowing that you will. If you can remember, at our last meeting I informed you of the consequences once Bleddwyn has the staff in his hand. Take heed of what I say son for I am the truth and father of my Lucia."

He then looked over to the mountainous pile of rubble and said as he shook his head.

"I eliminated the creature, but unfortunately, I am unable to remove the destruction that lies in your path."

Then, with an anxious look on his face, he abruptly bade us farewell and waved disappearing like a puff of smoke.

Lucia wondered why Brynmoroc was helping us. I wasn't sure. It didn't make any sense. He told us earlier that Bleddwyn was trying to abort the mission, but now he was contradicting himself. As far as I was concerned, Brynmoroc, by destroying his creation, was playing the hero, saving the day to gain our trust. I then asked Roisin if she was hiding behind us the whole time.

"No, I was alongside you, holding your arm just as I'm doing now. Why?"

"I was just wondering why Brynmoroc didn't look at you, that's all," I replied.

"What do you mean? He did look at me. He looked at me a couple of times. You must have seen him, surely you did?" she replied anxiously and began to cry.

I apologised saying that I had so much dust in my eyes that I couldn't see for wiping them. I also said that when we arrive in Saint Louise, I'd buy her something nice. That cheered her up and she went over to the carriage. I wanted to follow but my lovely affectionate Lucia, with a cloth and some water, insisted on cleaning up my wounds.

All I had was a few small scratches. Normally I would have insisted that I was okay, but she was so caring and gentle, I loved it and let her carry on fussing over me.

"There we are. You can put your shirt back on now," she said when finished.

I put on my shirt, looked back down the trail and thought, we had better get away before riders or even a stagecoach turned up. I told the girls that we had to move on quickly and to get ready for the ride of their lives. Then after collecting our belongings and tying everything loosely on Sophia's back, I couldn't help laughing, to which Lucia responded.

"Why are you laughing Gwydion? What are you up to now?"

"Yes, why are you laughing?" Roisin also asked." And where's this ride of a lifetime we are supposed to be getting?"

I was laughing because I knew what our next mode of transport was going to be and how the girls would react.

"Ah, I just thought of something funny, that's all," I replied. "So if you ladies are ready, we had better be on our way."

I walked over to my mares and said apologetically, "Okay, you two, I'm sorry to have to do this to you, but I'm sure you won't mind."

I raised my staff and after a bright purple flash, much to the horror of both screaming girls, Sophia was a six or seven-foot-long giant centipede loaded with our baggage, and Roslyn a millipede the same size, waiting to be mounted. I must say, I couldn't blame the girls for screaming because Roslyn and Sophia did look a formidable sight. In fact, Sophia looked so horrible; I was happy we were going to ride Roslyn and not her.

"Well, are you coming or not?" I asked, climbing onto Roslyn. "Or will I just leave you here with Sophia?"

That made them move and it wasn't long before they were carefully, reluctantly climbing up behind me while I laughed.

"Stop laughing Gwydion? It's not funny, it's horrible," they both shouted.

"Oh, poor old Roslyn. What a terrible thing to say," I said giving her a pat

The girls were right, for it was bizarre sitting on a long black leathery crawly, creeping up over the enormous pile of rocks. But watching Sophia scuttling alongside us, was the most horrendous sight I had ever seen in my life. With the debris being scattered for over two or three hundred yards or so, it took us some time to climb. Still, eventually, after a long unforgettable and uncomfortable ride, we finally arrived on the other side. The very moment we were back safely on the road again, Lucia and Roisin quickly slid and fell off Roslyn without even giving her time to stop, but they should have waited. Sophia, who was passing by, did with her hairy long spindly legs, walk all over the poor screaming girls who had been struggling to get up. The horrified pair quickly rose to their feet, took one look at Sophia and ran away screaming, gasping for breath. I couldn't help it, but the sight of their terrified faces made me double up with laughter.

"Yes, you can laugh Gwydion, you are just as horrible," shouted Lucia. "We'll get you back for that. Just you wait and see."

I dissolved into laughter once more, which made Lucia so mad that her beautiful Spanish accent came out strong as she gesticulated with her hands like a true Spanish lady. But after much ranting and raving by both girls, it wasn't long before they saw the funny side and were laughing too, but that was not until after Roslyn and Sophia were back as themselves.

While Lucia was apologising to Roslyn for calling her horrible, I threw a coin in front of me and 'wham' we had another lovely carriage. Roisin, who looked absolutely stunned, flopped down on a rock.

"Gwydion, oh Gwydion will you ever cease to amaze me? I really can't believe this is all happening."

It was real alright. Sometimes I couldn't believe it myself, but now we had to go. So, with the mares hitched up and everything packed away, Roisin hopped up into the carriage and led down on the soft bench.

"Ah, this is lovely. Sorry everyone but I'm having a nap," she said.

I laughed and after jumping up alongside Lucia, I picked up the reigns saying that I'd be glad to get away from there.

"Yes, me too," said Lucia, but after turning around to look; she gave me such a fright that I almost lost the reigns.

"Look, Gwydion! Look! It's gone. Everything's gone. All gone. Look?"

Now when I say I couldn't believe it, I really mean, I couldn't believe it. The canyon was normal as if nothing had ever happened to it.

"Good gosh!" shouted Roisin, poking her head out of the carriage. "How can this be? Hurry up, let's get away from here before it crashes down again."

"Yeah, you're right. Go on Roslyn, Sophia, let's get the heck away from here," I shouted, jeering them up.

Ten to fifteen minutes later, we were out into the open plain, well away from the canyon. Safe now and sighing with relief, I pulled over to gather myself.

"Are you alright?" Asked Lucia patting my hand. "You look so worn out."

"I'm Alright," I replied. "But all that rubble disappearing was really weird, wasn't it?"

"Yes, weird alright, but Sophia walking all over me; that was horrible Gwydion," she replied, rubbing her legs.

The clouds were beginning to gather and looking as if it was about to rain. I wanted to reach St. Louis before nightfall, so we travelled on, passing through a town called Springfield. From there on, I couldn't help wondering about Roisin saying that Brynmoroc looked at her when he didn't. So I mentioned this to Lucia.

"I had my eyes open all the time Brynmoroc was talking to us, but not once did I see him look at Roisin. How about you?"

"I noticed that too," she replied. "Also, if you remember, Brynmoroc's first words were, are you alright my children? Well, I think I know who Roisin might be, but I'll say nothing now. I'll tell you later, in St Louis."

I was in even more of a hurry to reach St. Louis now and didn't stop until we arrived in the city just as it began to pour down. It was well past eight in the evening before we settled Roslyn and Sophia in Joshua's livery stable. There were several hotels, even boarding houses to choose from, so we picked one called Welcome. The name was very apt because we were made just that as we walked in. I was a little hesitant about Roisin having her own room. I knew that if I'd asked for one between us, the Landlord would have probably kicked us out. So I paid for two and once again, because I was under pressure, three baths. Roisin was so looking forward to the tub that we let her go first. While she was enjoying her bath, Lucia took the opportunity to reveal her thoughts about Roisin.

"Do you remember after Brynmoroc showed us that vision, you were sure that the woman and the little girl looked like me?"

"Yes I do and I think I know what you are about to say," I replied

"Well, I believe it's quite possible that the other child, who couldn't see, was Roisin. After seeing Brynmoroc today at the canyon, apart from her hair, I thought she looked so much like him. So if Brynmoroc is my father, that would mean that Roisin is my sister. Were you thinking that way too?"

I told her that I had my suspicions and was thinking it a possibility, but after remembering Lucia saying the girl spoke in Spanish; Roisin was Irish with an Irish accent, I had decided against it.

"Yes, but that doesn't mean she isn't my sister," said Lucia, quickly interrupting me. "I'm Spanish, but I also speak English."

She spoke English, yes, but with a Spanish accent, but it was something I had never thought of and trust her to think of it. I had no words now only that we shouldn't jump to conclusions. I thought Roisin was genuine and the vision an illusion conjured up by Brynmoroc. He must have known we would meet her at one point and the holding up of her stagecoach was probably his doing.

Lucia was reasonably happy with that until another tormenting thought entered her head.

"Supposing the vision is actually real and Roisin and I are truly sisters, then why doesn't Brynmoroc acknowledge her? She insists that he did, but we definitely know he didn't. Although I can't get to grips with it and hate the thoughts of Brynmoroc ever being my father, I have a sickly feeling that he is, and for some reason, although she helped us back at the creek, I think Roisin is conspiring with Brynmoroc against us. What do you think?"

I couldn't make any sense of what she was saying. To me, it was nothing but the wizard playing with her mind. Supposing the vision did happen to be true and Brynmoroc was her father, that, I could believe, but for Roisin being Lucia's sister; was something I couldn't. Brynmoroc had never mentioned Lucia as ever having a sister. A more feasible answer would be, perhaps the other girl was Lucia's friend, but there again, Lucia did say that the girl called the lady Mamma.

I was totally confused with it all and said that we had to carry on until we had more time to think. Then as we pondered, we heard a little tap on the door. In came Roisin with her hair all wrapped up in a white towel and wearing the green robe I bought her in Oklahoma.

"That was one of the nicest baths I've ever had," she remarked, beaming with delight. "I feel a new woman now. Is it alright if I stay here with you until bedtime?"

"Of course. Come and sit down by the fire and warm yourself and dry your hair," replied Lucia.

She sat down, warming herself, but as we chatted about the trauma we endured back in the canyon, it didn't seem to bother her. I was sure that if it were anyone else, they would have run away as far and as fast as they were able.

Ten minutes later, our baths were ready. We left Roisin drying her hair and I followed Lucia out the door, down the passage, passing by the men's washroom to sneak into the ladies.

There were no windows to look out, so once again, I had to do my schoolboy stunt, sit and face the wall. Fortunately, I found a newspaper to read, so that was handy. As I flicked through the paper, one of the articles was about how the city was still coping with the aftermath of a tornado, three years ago. I must have read through the paper at least three times and was beginning to wonder if Lucia was ever going to finish. That was when she plopped her usual big blob of soapsuds on my head.

"Okay paper boy, it's your turn now," she said and laughed.

After waiting all that time, I didn't feel like a bath, only a swill. Unfortunately, my very pretty companion blackmailed me. If I didn't take a bath, she'd tell Roisin that we were in the tub together. So in a way, I was glad she once again insisted, for I did feel better for it. While walking back to our room, I asked Lucia if she had read about the tornado and the devastation it caused.

"I didn't look at the newspaper I was watching you," she replied, bursting out with laughter.

"Why you little monkey. That's the last time I'll be facing any wall," I said, giving her a little push.

"Ah, I'm only kidding," she said and laughed. "Yes, I did read about it. It must have been dreadful."

I had earlier told Roisin to lock the door behind us. So we tapped and she let us in. Roisin always had her hair tied up under her scarf, but now with it all dry, it was hanging loosely down around her shoulders.

"Wow! You look completely different Roisin," I remarked, "Your hair is such a lovely colour."

"Ha, it's all thick and scraggly, you mean. I think I'll cut it all off," she said, pulling a jib.

"No, that's crazy. It's lovely Roisin," said Lucia, encouraging her not to.

"I probably never will, but sometimes I get really fed up with it," she said, looking as if she meant it

Lucia encouraged her even more by saying that she looked beautiful. After getting over the amazing transformation, we enjoyed a small snack before hitting our beds. We walked Roisin to her door, wished her goodnight and that we would see her in the morning, but after saying that, she sighed deeply.

"Oh, Gwydion, Lucia. I am so frightened to be on my own now. Can I sleep with you tonight, please?"

I hesitated, but before I could answer, Lucia told her that she could. I was happy really because now I didn't have to worry about her betraying us. Well, that was until I realised the bed was only wide enough for two. So we had to sleep across the width. Roisin brought in her sleeping bag, placed it alongside mine and climbed in. The girls were okay for they were only about five foot three. I could have done with about another foot or more, and because of it, it was one of the worst night's sleep I have ever had in my life. To give you an idea of what it was like; imagine lying on your back trapped between two ladies, not able to move or scratch. On top of that, you'll find your legs dangling over the edge of one side and your head drooping off the other. Then, in the morning, after crying all night, you'll find yourself stiff as a board, with your mouth wide open and a sore throat. Then, finally, after you have managed to speak and ask for help, they would tenderly ask,

"What's the matter? Did you sleep well? What are you doing hanging over the edge of the bed?"

Yes, and after all that and about ten minutes of massage by both girls, you'll manage to move and roll over, and if you are lucky, not like me, they'll catch you as you fall off the end of the bed. Yes, that's precisely what happened to me on that miserable night in Saint Louis, but I did see the funny side later and laughed along with the girls.

During breakfast, I reminded Lucia about the train station we saw on our way into the city, and because it looked like rain I thought it a good idea to check out where the trains were running. The station was within walking distance, so we all set off and were excited to find that we could go as far as Louisville. After buying three tickets for the nine o'clock train, we collected our bags and went along to the Livery stable. Joshua was surprised to hear that he could keep the carriage, so he didn't charge me for boarding the mares. Once around the back of the stables and out of sight, I had Roslyn and Sophia as two small terriers. Roisin was excited and cuddled Sophia.

"Oh, you are so lovely. I used to have one just like you," she said, nursing her.

Lucia picked up Roslyn and off we went to catch the train that was already in the station since eight o'clock. After putting poor Roslyn and Sophia in the Guards van, we boarded the train and found a seat just as the guard's whistle blew. Crossing the Eads Bridge was a little scary for Roisin; she didn't like heights. It was going to take about six hours to reach Louisville and that was after changing trains at Evansville. I didn't care how long it took because I was tired from that miserable, sleepless night. Both girls were happily chatting with one another while I was happily looking out the window. Lucia was alongside me, Roisin sitting opposite. It was lovely sitting there without worrying about which way to go next. So with the rickety rackety sound of the rails and the chugging of the train, I closed my eyes until I heard Roisin say, "Oh! Hello Papa."

# Chapter 12

I opened my eyes to see sitting alongside Roisin, was no other than the wizard Brynmoroc. She was holding his arm and looking lovingly up at him. I stared in surprise and as he looked at me, he smiled broadly.

"Gwydion, this is my daughter, Roisin. Lucia, this is Roisin, your sister."

I was in shock and could feel Lucia squeeze my hand a little, but never uttered a word. She must be in shock too, I thought.

"It's true Lucia," said Roisin and smiled. "I would have told you earlier, but Papa told me to wait. He knew that sooner or later, you would remember and realise that I was your sister. Last night after returning from my bath, I was outside the door and heard you talking to Gwydion about me. I knew then that Papa was right to wait."

"Gwydion, her words are true," said the wizard. "I have already explained to you about my devious cousin and myself. So now, apart from what you have just heard, there is no more I can tell you other than, it's up to you to do what you think is right."

A couple who were reading in the seat across from us were wondering about Brynmoroc's clothes and wanted to know if he was a circus act, or perhaps going to some kind of show.

He smiled at them and replied, "No, sir. I am a wizard, a real wizard."

They laughed, thinking he was joking and while they carried on reading, I once again, couldn't believe my eyes because Lucia was now reaching for Brynmoroc's hand.

"Oh, Papa, I remember you now, oh Papa, Papa," she said with tears in her eyes.

The smiling wizard took hold of her hand, leaned forward and kissed it.

"I love you, Lucia. All I want now is for you and Gwydion to come home with your sister and me. The whole of Murcia are eager to welcome you."

"Oh, Gwydion, I remember. I remember it all now," said Lucia excitedly. "I remember how I cried as a man wearing a cloak carried me away from my screaming mother, and how the noise and flashes were hurting my ears and eyes. Oh, Gwydion it's true, it actually happened, Brynmoroc is my father. Oh, Papa! Papa! I am so sorry I didn't believe you."

"It's alright my child. It is what I expected," replied Brynmoroc.

I didn't know what to say. I was speechless until Roisin leaned forward and held my hand.

"Please believe and trust us Gwydion. We are telling you the truth. Our father is kind and sincere. He has waited for this moment a long time now and would gladly embrace you as a friend, if not a son. All you have to do is believe in him and trust him with your staff."

"Yes, Gwydion," pleaded Lucia. "I am sure it's the right thing to do. We should trust my father."

Looking at her lovely pleading face, I thought, "Okay. She's happy, so what the heck. Whatever happens, happens."

So I faced the smiling wizard, "Well, if Lucia's happy, and as long as I can be with her for the rest of my life, then I'll be happy too."

"Oh Gwydion, that was lovely. I love you and we are going to be happy forever," said Lucia, hugging me.

With that, I handed Brynmoroc my staff. He gently took it from me, but as soon as he had it in his hand, his affectionate expression changed to a wicked grin. The wizard swiftly stood up, and with the staff in one hand, he grabbed Lucia with his other.

"Now, you little nuisance, I have you at last," he said and laughed as she struggled and screamed in his clutches.

The man opposite was appalled and stood up and in a meaningful voice, demanded.

"Hey, you! What are you doing to the young lady? Let go of her this instant or I will be forced to apprehend you sir."

Brynmoroc took no notice, only looked at him with an expression of wickedness.

"This is the last time that I will tell you sir. Let go of that girl or else," demanded the man.

By this time, more men came to offer their assistance, but to their horror, as they approached Brynmoroc, he began to gleam brightly and glared at them. Seeing this, they quickly backed away, terrified.

"He's a wizard! A real wizard," someone shouted. "Run, everyone! Run for your lives."

For some reason, I couldn't move. All I could do was watch in horror as Brynmoroc and Roisin walked down through the carriage with Lucia struggling, crying out for me. There was nothing I could do only shout back to her, "Lucia, Lucia, Lucia!"

I could still hear her in the distance calling Gwydion, Gwydion, oh Gwydion, wake up, please wake up."

"Wow!" I said as I opened my eyes to see my pretty Lucia's concerned face looking at me.

"I'm here, I'm here Gwydion," she said lovingly. "You were dreaming."

Roisin was leaning towards me and she too had a worried look on her face.

"Yes Gwydion, you were dreaming, desperately crying out for her. We couldn't wake you."

I shook my head and looked around to see that everyone was staring at me, but they probably realised that I had been dreaming.

"Dew, I'm glad you woke me. I had some bad old dream. How long was I asleep?" I asked as the train jolted to a stop.

I had slept for hours, and we were now at Evansville station and had to change trains. My head was spinning now from that dream. It was so realistic.

I sat at the station waiting for Lucia and Roisin while they went to the ladies. Thankfully, that was probably one of the very few places Lucia insisted she went alone. I asked her one time, for a laugh, if she was sure she didn't want me to come with her.

"I don't think so Gwydion," she scorned, hitting me with her bag.

The train came in on time, and we set off to Louisville. On the way, I could feel myself nodding off again but tried to fight it.

"You look so tired Gwydion. Why don't you put your head on my shoulder and go to sleep?" suggested Lucia. "I'll wake you when we get to Louisville.

So I did and was happy she suggested it because her perfume was simply wonderful. I remember feeling myself drifting peacefully off to sleep while she gently stroked my head.

"There now, wasn't that lovely?" She asked after waking me at Louisville. "Do you feel any better?"

At that moment, with her lovely face and lips drawing me in like a magnet, I honestly felt like kissing her.

"Yes, that was lovely Lucia," I replied. "And yes, I do feel better now and a lot fresher too. Where's Roisin?"

"She's down there, looking out the window. Look! She's waving to you."

"Yes, I see her now," I said in relief. "Well come on my lovely Spanish lady. Let's go and collect Roslyn and Sophia, and we'll be on our way."

I picked up my staff and pack, joined the happy Roisin, and we all headed off to the guard's van to collect our faithful pooches. They were glad to see us and enjoyed the cuddles that they so rightly deserved. By now, it was getting on for four o'clock, and I wanted to be on our way because there were still a hundred miles to the next jewel. I gave the girls money to buy new clothes and underwear for us all. We always threw or gave away our old ones. The less baggage we had, the better. I restored Roslyn and Sophia to their former glory then after hitching them to another fine-looking carriage, we were on our way out of Louisville into the open plain

During our journey, we met numerous wagons. Some were on their way home from cattle runs; others were settlers coming from abroad. They were all friendly and joked as we passed. So that was nice, and with the weather being good, it made our progress more enjoyable.

"Well Lucia," I said, tapping her on the knee. "Only about sixty miles before we are somewhere near Red River Gorge. According to my map, there's a town called Winchester not too far away from it. I suggest that while we go in search of the jewel, we should take a chance and find Roisin a room there for a couple of days. What do you think?"

"Yes, that's the only thing we can do," she replied and yawned. "It's out of the question to take her with us. Are you and I staying the night too?"

I already decided that we would, but just for fun, I replied but trying not to laugh, that we had to head-on and sleep rough in the forest because it was impossible to take the carriage.

"Oh no, Gwydion. I can't sleep rough in a forest! What about the creatures? I'm afraid."

I felt terrible then and put my arm around her, saying, "Of course, we are staying overnight ya dafty."

She was happy now, put her head on my chest and went to sleep slipping down onto my lap.

Arriving in Winchester, I was surprised to find just how big the town actually was, because on the map it was just a little dot. I found a livery stable open and left both mares and the carriage in the hands of Jade, the owner's young daughter. Next on our agenda was a room. There were a couple of hotels to choose from, so I asked Roisin to pick one.

Now because of the dream I had earlier on the train, I had already decided that Lucia and I should only stay for that night. I wasn't going to take a chance on Roisin betraying us before we had found the jewel.

Roisin had decided on the Steers Hotel. We went in and I introduced Lucia and Roisin to the receptionist as my sisters. I then asked if she had a room with a double and a single bed for a few days. I explained that my sisters had recently been through a traumatic experience and were now afraid to be on their own. The receptionist was very understanding and went away to ask the manager, who came with good news. They had a large double room facing the street and a couple of the lads would bring up a single bed. Before retiring to our beds, we took a stroll through the brightly lit main street. In the heart of the town was a well-structured town hall with a tall clock tower. There was even an opera house, and while walking passed, we could hear the singers performing.

"Oh, they sound so lovely," said Lucia, listening by the door. "I would love to see an opera. If it's on tomorrow night, do you think we can see it?"

"Uh um, not with me you won't," was my definite reply.

"Nor with me, either," said Roisin and laughed.

With the thoughts of Lucia wanting to go see an opera and with the sound of singers still ringing in my ear, I felt the sudden need for my bed. So with a loud exaggerated yawn, I told the girls that I was exhausted and we ought to head back. We did, and I was happy to be back in our room, nice and snug in our sleeping bags. Roisin was in her own bed, so I was looking forward to a reasonably good night's sleep.

Now, I know you must think it strange that Lucia could ever possibly hold my hand all through the night. Well, I was thinking that way myself, until one night after turning over, I found she had wrapped a ribbon around our wrists. But even before the ribbon, the very moment I moved she would wake and gently clasp my hand again.

After blowing out the candles, I felt good and drifted off to sleep listening to the town folk walking home, probably from the opera. I slept until hearing the town clock chime three, but as I moved to turn, I found I couldn't. Roisin was on our bed covered in a blanket hugging my arm, snivelling. I sat up and asked her what was wrong. Lucia woke too, asking the same.

"I'm afraid," she replied. "I don't know why. I'm just afraid that's all. You don't mind me lying here, do you Gwydion?"

My sleeve was soaking wet so she must have been beside me for some time.

"No, it's okay. Cwtch up and go to sleep," I replied, but not without a sigh.

The next morning, an hour before Lucia and I left, I gently broke the news to Roisin. Lucia and I were going somewhere for a few days but promised to return. I had already paid for her room and meals for the next four days. She wasn't very pleased and began to cry.

"You are going to leave me here, aren't you? You don't trust me, and this is just an excuse for you to run away. Isn't it?"

I said that it wasn't and once again promised that I would return and to prove it, I gave her my granddad's watch to mind. She knew how fond I was of it so with that now assured, I collected Roslyn and Sophia and paid for the coach to be stored another week. I loaded Sophia with our bags, and before Lucia and I left, I gave Roisin money to do with whatever she wanted. As a joke, I told her that if she wanted, she could visit the opera.

"Thank you, but no thanks Gwydion. I think I'll save the money and do my own singing; it's just as bad."

We laughed and said goodbye as she waved and blew kisses. The road was rough, so we took our time, and after passing through a town called Stanton, we ventured into logging country. With an enormous forestry in front of us now, things began to get a little scary. According to Lucia, the lake was another twenty miles away. So all we had to do was find the gorge and then decide whether the lake was up or downstream. We trekked on through the forest until we came to a trail to our right.

"This is the one we have to take, but look at the sun Gwydion. It must be getting on for midday. Don't forget about Brynmoroc."

I looked up through the branches, and yes, the hot sun was about noon position. We were lucky because the trail led us to a little alcove, an ideal place to be if the wizard turned up. Within half an hour, we were sitting on a log having a snack and a mug of coffee to help it down. We could hear men in the distance shouting, "Timber" and the cracking and thumping sound of trees as they toppled to the ground. We were reasonably happy until a loud deep roar gave us a terrible fright. Lucia put her coffee down and huddled up to me. I thought it had to be something to do with Brynmoroc. I ordered Roslyn and Sophia to go back up the trail and wait until I called them. We backed into the alcove just as another roar echoed through the forest. Lucia was shaking now with fear, I was too but tried not to show it.

"Don't worry," I said, summoning my shield. "I won't let anything harm you. Whatever happens, keep your shield in front of you and don't move from this spot."

I remembered my staff being a weapon. I had used it before, but what about now. All I could do was to hold it out, close my eyes and asked for a weapon to defend us from whatever materialised. I did, and in an instant, I felt my staff violently quiver in my hand, but now, instead of holding my black wooden staff, I was holding a black wooden sword.

"Whoa! What's this?" I asked myself. "A wooden sword. What can I do with this that I couldn't do with my staff?"

I was more than disappointed, but before I could ask for something else, there was another roar. I braced myself because whatever it was, it was slowly coming through the trees. I didn't know what to expect until it came into view. I knew then that it was definitely the work of a wizard because creeping towards us now was a male lion. An animal that only lives in Africa. I didn't really know how big they were, but right now, this one was big, too big.

The moment he caught sight of us, he crouched down like a cat stalking a bird. He was growling deeply, and as he crept menacingly towards us, he kept his evil yellow eyes permanently fixed on me. Within ten or fifteen yards of us, he suddenly caught sight of himself in our gleaming shields and immediately backed away snarling, shaking his head. He advanced twice more, but because of our shields, he couldn't get near us. He then paced around for a while as if thinking up some kind of strategy. Suddenly, the lion rushed towards us, roaring loudly only to dive to the ground about twenty feet away. As he lay there, growling, I could smell his foul breath and a horrid stench of urine, plus, all I could see of his eyes were two long slits. He was testing us now and stayed there growling not moving an inch until slowly retreating into the trees. Lucia thought we had won, and he had gone, but I somehow knew that he hadn't. I was right because the cunning lion had slyly crept through the forest and was now charging from the side. His fearful roar made me lose my balance, but as he leapt I managed to turn my shield towards him and there was a flash causing the beast to be deflected away from me. In an instant, my reflexes made me strike out with my wooden sword. I hit him, but where I didn't know. To my bewilderment, the lion fell writhing to the ground, falling onto his side in pain. Then after struggling to his feet, he keeled over once again onto his side. It seemed that I had managed to hit his leg which was now crumbling into dust. Unfortunately, that was only momentarily for another one quickly grew in its place. Before I had time to think, he charged and leapt once more only to be sent sprawling into a hawthorn bush by my flashing shield. I struck out as he passed, but missed him. He gathered himself and crouched down, but this time, his contemptuous eyes were looking towards Lucia. I stood in front of her, saying to stay still. The lion, with his eyes closed again to slits, slowly advanced in his crouched position towards us. I wasn't going to let him think that I was afraid of him, so I waved my shield and moved towards him.

"Come on!! Come on then, you monstrous animal?" I shouted as loud as I could.

He just roared back and charged but once again, dived to the ground in front of me. The force of the impact sent a pile of leaves and debris into the air. In the next instance, the massive beast was leaping over me, knocking me to the ground in the process. A painful roar ripped through the air, and as I rose, I saw that the lion had been deflected by the force of Lucia's shield. The stunned beast was now lying prostrate on the ground at the base of the alcove. Before the sickened creature could gather himself, I rushed forward and thrust my sword into the lion's heaving chest, making him roar in pain. Then just as I was about to retrieve my sword to thrust again, I was bowled over backwards by a force, knocking the wind out of me. As I staggered to my feet, gasping for air, I found that I had no shield or sword to protect me. My thoughts now were that I was finished, I'm dead, when suddenly the stricken lion, who was desperately struggling to get to his feet, crumpled into a heap of black and orange dust that was blown away by a gust of wind. I made haste to retrieve my sword, but as I ran, a desperate wizard with his staring eyes fixed on my sword was rushing towards it. I lunged and managed to dive onto it in time, but when I stood up to face the wizard, he was gone.

"Oh, you were so brave Gwydion," said Lucia, hugging me like a bear. "That thing was so mean and terrifying. I thought we were going to die."

She then buried her head in my chest and began to cry. I held her there while I looked around and waited. As soon as the birds began singing again, I lifted her chin and wiped away the tears from her pretty face.

"Why are you crying?" I asked. "It's all over now; we are safe."

"I don't know why I am crying; I'm just so happy that you are not hurt and that horrid lion is gone."

That moment was very emotional, so once again, how I refrained from kissing her, I will never know. It may have been, either I was afraid to, or I had remembered the warning Bleddwyn gave me.

"Yes, he's gone now," I said quietly. "But we have to stay here a while longer just in case Brynmoroc turns up."

She took her handkerchief out of her pocket and as she began wiping her face, I suddenly remembered about the mares and called out to them. In a couple of minutes, they came trotting down the trail to be greeted with a couple of pats from me and a kiss from Lucia. My throat was dry, so I lit another fire to boil the kettle for a coffee. While waiting for it to boil, there was a sudden hush; the whole forest was silent again. We quickly withdrew back into the alcove just as Brynmoroc came riding out from the forest on a snow-white stallion. I wasn't going to give him time to speak so before he said anything I quickly greeted him.

"Greetings Sir. We are so happy to see you. We have been subjected to a horrendous battle with a fierce lion type of animal. Fortunately, after enduring and overcoming the beast, he disappeared in a gust of wind. Strangely though, the moment he vanished, I thought I saw Bleddwyn, but I could have been mistaken."

"What?" whispered Lucia, but I nudged her with my elbow just as the wizard solemnly replied.

"Yes, it was indeed, Bleddwyn. You have succeeded in finding three of the enchanted jewels and absorbed their energy. He has since moved the empty jewels and relocated them to a place where only he knows. You are of no use to him now Gwydion, and neither is my daughter. All he wants now is your staff to enable him to disrupt the prophecy. I will repeat myself by saying that once he has it in his hands, you will both be at his mercy. Mercy, unfortunately, is something Bleddwyn does not possess."

"What do you recommend we do now, Sir? Shall we carry on?" I asked.

Out of the corner of my eye, I saw Lucia turn her head to look at me. I knew what she was thinking.

"You have a good heart Gwydion but do not let it rule your head. Remember this; if the love for a bird makes you yearn to capture it, the bird will die overnight. You must do whatever you know is right and not how you feel."

That didn't make a lot of sense to me, but that was all he said before turning his eyes to Lucia.

"This is Diablo the son of Mario. Mario was your mother's stallion. He is yours whenever you are ready to come home. Please keep her safe Gwydion. She is all I have now."

Brynmoroc said no more only bade us goodbye and a safe journey before riding away, disappearing in among a swirl of leaves.

"Did you really see Bleddwyn?" Asked Lucia. "And what were you doing asking Brynmoroc's advice?"

"Yes, it certainly looked like Bleddwyn," I replied. "He was after my staff, but I grabbed it in time. I thought I'd mention it to Brynmoroc, just to hear what he'd say. It was for the same reason I asked him for his advice. No matter what answer he had given, we would have still carried on regardless."

"This is getting more and more complicated every day isn't it?" she said, shaking her head.

I agreed, but I still thought Brynmoroc was behind it all. It was crazy to think it was Bleddwyn, for he knew I would give him the staff any time he asked, but then I thought, that once the battle with the lion was over, Brynmoroc was quick to appear, meaning he must have been there all along. So he, of both wizards, had ample time to snatch my staff while it lay on the ground. So why didn't he? This now made me wonder if it really was Bleddwyn I saw.

"Perhaps it was Bleddwyn Gwydion," said Lucia. "If you remember, Brynmoroc told us that he was powerless against Bleddwyn, so in that case, he was probably unable to do anything. Does that make any sense?"

After her suggestion, I was regretting ever asking, for I was completely baffled now. I didn't know and told her so. Nothing made sense to me anymore. Perhaps Brynmoroc was cleverly contradicting himself to confuse us. But there was one thing that I was sure of, and that was, no one was taking my staff and I wasn't giving it to anyone either.

"The emerald is not too far from here," said Lucia after we thought it safe to move out. "If we make haste, we should be nearing the lake before sundown."

After another half hour of trotting through a magnificent forest full of unusual trees, incredible alcoves, rivers and cliffs, we arrived at the Red River Gorge. If I thought the scenery on the trail we had just travelled was amazing, the Red River Gorge was something else. It was fabulous, utterly indescribable. Lucia was in awe of it all.

# Chapter 13

"Isn't this place just beautiful? Could you ever imagine living here, Gwydion?"

I picked up a stone and threw it down into the gorge, and as I watched it splash into a large pool, Lucia gave a loud cry.

"Oh, Gwydion! You might have hurt a poor little fish with that stone."

I gave a sigh of relief, knowing that it was just a fish that had caused her stress. So just for a laugh, I apologised.

"I'm sorry, I wasn't thinking, but he's okay. I missed him and hit that big one, come on, let's go down and get him."

I couldn't help laughing even after she caught hold of my arm and slapped it.

"It isn't funny Gwydion and better mind you haven't hit any fish, big or small."

"I'm only kidding, ya dafty," I said, tapping her back on the shoulder.

"Oh you, you. You and your teasing Gwydion. I'll get you back for that, don't you worry."

We made our way down to the river and then trekked along its banks for a while. It was wide and murky, but every now and then a waterfall gave us the sight of clear water tumbling down over red rocks. For much of our trek, we were able to follow trails that were probably forged by animals, possibly natives too, for there were strange markings on some of the trees. The trees were huge and looked as if they had been growing there since time began. Every now and then, during breaks in the trees, we were able to see the high rocky ridges that occasionally swept down across the river, forming beautiful natural bridges. It was amazing, but a little worrying as we passed under these impressive wonders of nature. We eventually reached a point in the river, where there was a distinct sound of a waterfall. Approaching it, Lucia shouted excitedly.

"This is where the emerald's hidden. Down there in what I thought was a lake."

The small lake Lucia had foreseen, turned out to be none other than a massive pool at the base of a waterfall. Whether it was a lake or not, Lucia was adamant the jewel was somewhere in the water, sitting in the middle of a heart-shaped rock. I asked if the rock was above or below the water

She replied with her hand to her eyes, shading them from the sun.

"I'm not sure but look Gwydion I think that's it over there, can you see it?"

I could, and urged Roslyn forward. With no trail to follow, we had to weave our way through the trees and undergrowth before we reached the large pool.

"That doesn't look much like a heart to me," I said after we arrived. "In fact, it doesn't look anything like one. Are you sure it's the one?"

She confirmed that it was, but like me, was disappointed that it had no resemblance to a heart at all. It was the only protruding rock in the pool. We were baffled and sat down to think. Lucia, when she had visualised the heart-shaped rock, she was looking down from above the trees.

"What if I climb a tree and take a look?" I said. "It might be over on the far side where we can't see."

She was adamant that it wouldn't be, but just to satisfy my curiosity, she replied, "Well, if it will make you happy then okay, go on, but mind you don't fall."

I wasn't going to leave Lucia on her own, so I had Roslyn and Sophia changed into two fierce-looking Great Danes, guarding her while I took a look. The trees were tall, so I picked a horse chestnut tree with lots of branches. I climbed almost to the top, only to find that Lucia was right. There was only one rock in that pool and it was the one she had predicted.

"You are right Lucia," I shouted. "That's the only rock in the pool."

"I told you so. Now come on down before you fall. You look very shaky up there."

Shaky! I'll give you shaky," I said to myself and was in two minds about dropping a pile of prickly chestnuts down on her. I didn't, just carried on down witnessing a fabulous setting sun filtering through beautiful autumn-coloured trees. I climbed down safely, and while that glorious sun drifted down behind the ridge, we made camp thinking we'd look for the rock in the morning.

It had been a tiring day, and while lying in our tent, knowing that we had two mean-looking hounds watching over us, we listened to the sound of night birds. All I recognised was the hoot and screech of a couple of owls and a quack of a duck. Lucia named a few others, but I can't remember what she said they were. Maybe it was her Spanish accent.

"Goodnight Gwydion. Sleep well and don't worry, we'll find the emerald in the morning," she said, pulling my arm around her.

With that day over, and with my arm around the prettiest girl I had ever known, I happily drifted off to sleep until I pleasantly felt her warm lips kiss mine. Surprised, I opened my eyes to hear her say, "I love you."

She had turned over and was facing me now, so I quietly asked, "What? What did you say?"

I waited for a second or two, and with no reply, I realised that she was asleep. If I felt that I was falling in love with her back in Sedona, I was definitely in love with her now. So I leaned forward, gently kissed her lovely lips and whispered, "Me too."

She never stirred; in fact, she stayed that way all night until I woke her in the morning.

"Come on pretty face, it's time we were up," I said, giving her a little shake.

"What? What did you say? Oh yes. It's morning, come on then," she said, yawned, and stretched.

It was a cold, cloudy morning, and after a brisk walk to wake up, we were sitting around a nice warm fire having coffee and dry toast. The weather stayed dull until the bright sun rose above the trees. During that time, I was thinking about how I was going to reach that solitary rock to take a look at it. My first thought was to swim over until Lucia said that there might be crocodiles or even snakes in there. That quickly put me right off. So I paced up and down the bank and after studying the rock, I was beginning to doubt it ever being the one. Yes, doubtful until I saw Roslyn taking a drink from the river. Her reflection in the water was very clear.

"Yes! That's it! That's it Lucia," I shouted. "It's the right rock. Look! Look at its shape. It's only half a heart. The other half is its reflection."

I was excited and just to prove it, I climbed the tree again and found that I was right. The next step now was how to get over to it. I couldn't see any sign of crocodiles, but there could be snakes, so I wasn't going to risk swimming.

"Trust you to mention crocodiles and snakes," I said after climbing down.

"What about a boat?" she suggested. "A boat is a form of transport, isn't it?"

I hadn't thought of that so with my staff in hand, I threw a coin into the water and said out loud, 'Gofynnaf i chi' and there it was, a small canoe with two paddles.

"Come on, let's do it," I said, wading in to pull our canoe into the side.

The canoe was very wobbly, so we were careful about climbing in. The rock was only thirty or forty yards away, but it must have taken us half an hour to reach it. We were hopeless paddlers. I mastered it eventually, but Lucia was useless. Every time I managed to straighten up the canoe she would somehow manage to spin us around again. But I have to say, it was hilarious and the more she laughed, the more I did too. When we finally reached the rock, I found it larger than I initially thought, and for a rock, in the middle of a pond it was not only sticky, it was full of small holes. If the emerald was there at all, it was going to be hard to find. According to Lucia, it was small, about the same size as the holes, but definitely visible. I wasn't all that confident about finding it but after something like an hour of searching, I finally found it. It was while we were trying to steady our wobbly boat to study the rock, I noticed a flash as the ripples lapped against it. We rowed over to investigate and found that the emerald had been strategically placed at water level, making it look, from the reflection, as if it was in the middle of a heart's crevice. It was sitting proudly on the rock, slightly above the waterline. The ripples lapping against the emerald prevented us from noticing it

I waited for a clear opportunity before I picked up my staff and placed it on the emerald's sparkling face. The reaction this time was immense. The moment my staff touched the jewel, there was a flash, and the whole pool lit up a sparkling colour of green. I held on to the rock and managed to stand still while the dazzling colour raced up and down my staff until it stopped next to the citrine. I was okay and was just about to sit down when a piece of the rock I was holding, came away and stuck to my hand. This sudden action caused me to lose my balance; as a result, both of us landed spluttering in the freezing cold water. What a panic this caused. Lucia and I were in the water and didn't she say there may be crocodiles and snakes in this river? I had lost my staff, but I didn't care. I was more worried about Lucia and of course, crocodiles.

"Are you okay Lucia," I quickly asked as she began to swim.

"Yes, I'm alright," she replied. "Come on, let's get out of here!"

With those words, I can tell you, that that day, as we swam hell for leather over to the bank, I must have broken my own record. We both arrived together and flopped down on the leaves exhausted, but now worrying about my staff. There was no need because as I looked towards the river, Roslyn had my staff retrieved and was bringing it back in her mouth. It was only after I had it back in my hand, did Lucia tell me that there weren't crocodiles in this part of America.

"What!" I said, facing her. "You mean to tell me that I did the fastest swim of my life, for nothing?"

"Swim!" She replied before bursting out laughing, "That was more like a desperate dog paddle. I couldn't swim for laughing."

I thought that was funny and said, "Well, that makes two of us, but your paddling was worse than mine."

"How would you know what I was like?" she said in between her laughter. "You couldn't see me for all the splashing you did."

It was a good feeling lying there laughing, which was probably the reason why I rolled over and without thinking, kissed her.

"And about time too," she said as I looked into her beautiful eyes.

Hearing her saying that and after realising what I had done, I began thinking. For Lucia's sake, Bleddwyn warned me about my emotions towards her. Remembering this, I had to apologise for kissing her.

"Why?" She softly asked. "I liked it, didn't you?"

"Yes but, we..."

"But we what?" she replied, demanding an answer.

I didn't know what to say, so I said something stupid, saying that we were all covered in weeds and she could have swallowed some.

"Rubbish!" she said alarmingly. "Weeds, covered in weeds, why I..."

Thankfully, much to my relief, she burst out laughing and so did I. All I can remember after that is that we were soaking wet but happy lying there drying in the sun.

Later, while sat up talking, I noticed the piece of rock that was stuck to my hand had fallen off and was now lying on the side of the bank. I picked it up and found that it wasn't sticky anymore, so I thought I'd keep it. While placing it into my pocket, Roslyn nudged me in the back. I turned, and as I did, a roar bellowed out in the distance. We stood up and looked anxiously in the direction of another roar ripping through the air. Both dogs were beside us now facing the trees, snarling and growling, ferociously.

"Oh no, here we go again," I said as a large brown bear came charging through the trees.

We reached into our pockets for our shields and held them firmly out towards the bear who wasn't very pleased to see us. Roslyn and Sophia, with their heads slightly lowered, began advancing slowly towards it and snarling. The bear stopped and began gnashing his jaws and shaking its head. Roslyn rushed in to attack, and as she did, the bear made a snap and a swipe at her. Within an instant, Sophia joined in from the side, but the bear spun around to meet her. As the bear rose, I could see that it was a female, probably after the fish that were jumping up the waterfall. Both dogs kept their distance, which I was happy about because that mean female's claws looked lethal. While the dogs stood there snarling, the encounter turned into a ferocious, noisy standoff until the bear retreated into the woods and was gone.

We didn't bother changing our clothes for fear of the bear deciding to come back. I quickly had the hounds back into mares and within five minutes of the bear running away, we were running away too, a lot faster than her. We didn't stop until out of the gorge and back onto the road that ran through the massive forestry. By that time, we were ready for a rest and stopped at the roadside. We were only there ten minutes before we were once again running away, leaving a gang of wild hogs behind in our dust.

That was it; we were not going to stop anymore and kept on until we arrived in Stanton for a well-deserved rest. After popping into a store for a sandwich and some milk, we sat outside on a bench. While watching the townsfolk of Stanton going about their daily business, Lucia began worrying, hoping that Roisin hadn't betrayed us. I didn't think so because what would she profit from it? If she was trying to get to Spain to meet her brother, she had no money, no means of transport, no friends only us. To betray us now would be ludicrous. We were her only way out of America. Besides, who would ever believe her, I thought. Maybe they would, but we had to take a chance because I had given my word that I'd go back for her.

It was getting on for midday, making us think of Brynmoroc. So I tethered Roslyn and Sophia to the rails outside a hotel and paid for a room where we could lie down for a few hours. We were happy to rest and even more delighted when four o'clock came without any sign of the wizard. After a quick cup of milk, we set off to Winchester. The weather was good, and because we were a little sore from riding, I bought a small trap from an old travelling salesman trading on the side of the road. It was only ten miles to Winchester but sitting on a soft seat again made the journey seem a lot quicker. When we arrived back at our hotel, Roisin was delighted to see us.

"I knew you would come back for me. I have been worrying about you all day, wondering if those horrid creatures had attacked you again. You must be tired, come and sit down and rest."

While we were away in the gorge, Roisin bought a few items of clothing for her journey. One such purchase was an emerald green dress which she had been trying on just before we came in. As she twirled, the green of the dress complimented her lovely dark hair gently bouncing on her shoulders.

"Wow, Roisin, you look amazing," I remarked. "Your brother will be really proud to have such a lovely sister."

After going through the same ritual in the bathroom, Roisin had a round of tender beef sandwiches and a jug of hot milk waiting for us.

"Oh, by the way, Gwydion," said Roisin walking over to a draw. "Here's your watch. Quick, take it for I've been worried to death I'd lose it."

I had forgotten about my watch and kissed it as she handed it back to me.

"Don't I get one too for looking after it?" she asked with a smile.

I stuttered yeah okay, but not just now for I had soap in my eyes and I couldn't see a thing. She laughed and sat down by the fire, waiting for me to dry Lucia's hair.

While enjoying our supper, we described the beautiful Red River Gorge to Roisin. A while later, our conversation turned to our next destination, New York.

"What form of transportation are we using this time?" Asked Roisin.

"Why don't we go by train? It will be a lot comfier," suggested Lucia. "New York is supposed to be one of the main shipping docks in America, so surely there has to be a train running there. We'll find out in the morning, but now it's time for bed."

I was relieved when Roisin told me that she wasn't afraid to sleep on her own anymore. Whether she stayed in her own bed that night I didn't know because I didn't wake until I felt something crawling on my nose. I jumped up to the delight of both girls who were in fits of laughter. They were up, dressed and tickling me with a feather.

"Ha-ha. I told you I'd get you back," said Lucia as she tickled me again.

I laughed, grabbed a pillow and threw it at them as they ran away laughing. I felt so happy that it made me think again of how fortunate I was to have two lovely girls as companions. I was pleased, yes, but suddenly a strange feeling of sadness came over me. I realised that I was probably going to miss the lovely Roisin when we say goodbye in New York. That feeling dampened my appetite, so I skipped breakfast, saying that I wasn't hungry and had a cup of coffee instead.

We returned to our room, packed our bags and headed off to enquire about trains to New York and where we could get one. A clerk at the stagecoach office said we could get a train at Charleston, and the next coach there was outside ready to go in an hour.

Knowing this, we went along to the stables where much to Jade's astonishment, I sold her our coach for a dollar, even signed a piece of paper for proof. She couldn't believe her luck and was delighted until she went to fetch the mares.

"They are gone Sir," she said, running back in distress. "Someone has taken them and left two terriers."

"Oh, that's okay," I said to console her. "The little dogs are lovely, and I'm sure my lady friends will love them. There is no need to worry. I'll take the terriers instead."

Lucia and Roisin picked up the terriers and we went away, leaving Jade staring at another five dollars I had given her. With that sorted, we made our way down the busy street and into the waiting stagecoach. Two elegant-looking ladies sat opposite us both chatting while fiddling with their handkerchiefs. Though later, much to their dismay, our travelling companion's handkerchiefs now seemed to be permanently over their nose. I had a distinct feeling that they didn't like dogs.

After two hours of travelling, I was regretting missing breakfast. Horrible gurgling noises were howling around the carriage, much to the disgust of our lady friends. How the girls kept a straight face, I'll never know. Eventually, after arriving in Moorhead to change horses, we heard one of the ladies mutter as they stepped down from the coach, "Thank goodness we're not going any further."

There was to be half an hour wait, and with it raining, we stayed in our seats, put the dogs on the floor and had a much-needed bite to eat. With the howling wolf fed, I sat back in my seat and relaxed. While waiting, Lucia and Roisin nodded off for a nap. With them asleep, I sat quietly thinking until just as the coach was ready to move off, I heard someone shout, "Stop!"

The door opened and in came a man wearing a hooded cape. I had a bad feeling that it might be Brynmoroc, and as he pushed back his hood, my feelings were confirmed.

"Good afternoon Gwydion," he wished, with a smirk on his face.

Sitting up in disbelief, I heard the coachman crack his whip, and we slowly moved off.

"Good afternoon to you Sir," I said, giving Lucia a nudge. "We were just thinking about you, weren't we Lucia."

There was no response, and when I looked, I found her still asleep, but Roisin was wide awake. Now, because I still wasn't sure about Brynmoroc,

I held on to my staff with one hand and slowly reached into my pocket for the other.

"Oh Gwydion, Gwydion," said the wizard and laughed. "Even if you take out your shield, it would be useless against me. Tell him, Roisin!"

"It's true Gwydion," she said. "Your shield is useless against my father or any other wizard and so too is your staff. My father has been very patient with you and my sister for some time now. But, unfortunately, his patience is now overdrawn."

"Roisin's right Gwydion and now I have come for Lucia," said the evil-eyed wizard.

"Never!" I said as I shook Lucia to wake her.

"You are wasting your time son. Lucia will not wake; she's coming home with me."

I caught hold of Lucia with both hands and shook her violently but there was still no response. In the meantime, my staff had fallen to the floor.

"Now do you believe me Gwydion? Asked Brynmoroc, after picking up my staff and handing it to Roisin.

The coach jolted to a stop, but before I could make a move towards him, he snatched Lucia up in his arms. I made a grab for her, but the powerful wizard just knocked me down and everything went black until I heard Lucia shouting.

"Gwydion! Gwydion! What's the matter with you, wake up. Get off us."

I opened my eyes to find myself on the floor, lying on top of the girls.

"Yes, get off Gwydion, you were dreaming again," said the laughing Roisin

"No, not again!" I said, jumping up. I couldn't believe it. Perhaps I'm going crazy, I thought

"You were shaking me and shouting in your sleep again. I grabbed hold of Roisin, and we all fell to the floor."

I was devastated now for that was the second bad dream I'd had in a week. Roisin said that I had been asleep for ages and sure enough after looking at my watch, it was fifteen minutes to twelve. I slept right through the rest of the journey.

When we arrived in Charleston, the coach driver let us off outside a hotel. There was no train until nine in the morning. We didn't mind for we'd had just about enough travelling for one day. So once again, I booked a family room for me and my pretend sisters. Roslyn and Sophia had to stay outside in the kennel. We slept well and it was eight in the morning before we were awakened by a wrap on the door.

"The train is due in shortly Sir," shouted a lady. "Your breakfast is ready, so if you want to catch that train you had better hurry?"

We hadn't bothered undressing that night, so we were all ready to go and arrived at the train station in plenty of time. We were happy to have decided to take the train, for within ten minutes of sitting in our seats, there was a mighty crack of thunder, followed by a downpour of hail and rain, lasting thirty minutes.

It was a long old journey, but thankfully after the tiring ordeal of changing trains three times, we finally arrived in New York at midnight. Although midnight, the main street was lit up as if it were noon. Across the street was the hotel Normandie but the number of busy people milling around, made crossing the road a nightmare. Not only did we endure dodging our way around iron trams, we also had to avoid being knocked down by fast-running horses pulling carts and carriages. The hotel Normandie was enormous, unlike any building I had ever seen and as we walked through its large grand doors, Roisin said as she grabbed my arm.

"As this will be our last night together, can we please all stay in the same room? I'm afraid and really don't want to be on my own in this strange place."

I replied, "In such a place as this, the manager probably doesn't care who sleeps with who, and besides, you are both my sisters, ain't ya?"

She squeezed my arm and kissed my shoulder, saying, "Of course we are, brother!"

It was late, but there was no problem getting a room with a double and single bed. Roslyn and Sophia were taken off to the kennels while we were shown to our deluxe-looking room. I led on the bed, letting the girls change behind the screen but there was no way I was undressing that night; I was too tired.

Lucia unpacked her sleeping bag and gently lay beside me and as usual, I had to endure the same ritual of her wrapping a ribbon around our wrists. Holding Lucia's hand through most of every day and all night was second nature to me now. You may well ask, why sleep in sleeping bags on top of a bed? Well, with Lucia being a respectable lady, I thought it the most honourable thing to do. Though, I could have done with a rest from both activities.

Within five minutes of Lucia being asleep, Roisin called out to me in a sad kind of voice saying that she was frightened. She sounded choked up and of all things, began to snivel. Hearing this, I reluctantly had to tell her not to be afraid and that if it would make her feel any better, she could sleep alongside us.

She came with her blanket and led beside me. It was a large bed and with Lucia and Roisin being quite slim, there was plenty of room. She was still crying, but before I could ask her why, she whispered.

"Please don't leave me, Gwydion. I don't know what I'll do without you."

I had to sigh now because one, I was feeling sorry for her and two, we couldn't take her with us. It was crazy; we had only known her a few days. So once again, I reluctantly had to tell her to stop crying, go to sleep and we'd think of something in the morning."

"Thank you," she said, kissing my cheek. "Thank you."

Not only had I found myself in the middle of two battling wizards, but I had also found myself amid two lovely but emotional ladies.

"Who's who? Why? Why? Why?" I asked myself. "Who are these lovely girls? Who are these crazy wizards and which one is the villain?

Perhaps there is no villain, and I'm involved in some kind of conspiracy, a plot to take over the world of wizardry. Or are they using me as a pawn to be sacrificed for some unknown cause?"

If it were not for pinching myself a thousand times, I would have sworn that I had gone loopy after falling off Mad Luke. It all seemed so unreal, especially after that landslide disappearing without leaving a speck of dust to show it ever existed. It was real alright, and so was my growing love for Lucia.

After my sleepless night, we all went off in search of a booking office. As luck would have it, the new cruise ship Oceanic, was about to sail. It was due to return to Liverpool and was heading out the following morning. I paid for three first-class tickets, a double and a single cabin. I had told Roisin that Lucia and I decided that she could only travel with us to as far as Liverpool. After that, she would have to travel alone.

My pouch was simply wonderful, making me feel like an important rich millionaire. I could literally have anything I wanted. The trip was going to take about ten days, so we bought new clothes for the journey. In the afternoon we spent our time mingling with the crowd of shoppers, hoping Brynmoroc wouldn't turn up because of them. Maybe it worked, for come four o'clock there had been no sign of him.

We were up at six a.m. and caught the next train to the port. Arriving there, passengers were already boarding the massive brand-new cruiser. Standing on the dockside were at least a hundred well-wishers waving and shouting, goodbye and don't forget to write. Others were onlookers probably there admiring the fabulous-looking ship. All animals had to be caged down in the hold. I didn't like the thought of that, so we took Roslyn and Sophia to a quiet part of the dock and released them as averaged size orca whales to go on in front.

Eventually, after booking in and being given the keys to our cabins, we boarded the ship and made our way to our deluxe quarters.

"Wow, this is exciting, isn't it?" said Lucia, looking out the porthole.

Roisin was in the cabin next door and had already unpacked and had a cup of coffee waiting when we popped in. So we stayed until the ship's whistle sounded.

"We must be ready to sail. Come on, let's go up and check it out," said Roisin excitedly.

There was a mixed atmosphere on deck. Some passengers were crying, waving to their friends and family while others were frantically waving with excitement. The loud cheering, weeping and wailing as the ship's anchor went up was something I have never forgotten. Then as we sailed out of port, we went around to the ship's bow to look for Roslyn and Sophia. They must have seen us for they thrashed their tails, letting us know that they were there.

Lunchtime soon came around, and while we were in the dining hall, Captain Cameron announced that at eight o'clock there would be a celebration ball in honour of the cruisers' second return journey. The announcement was received with a loud cheer from all the diners, including Lucia and Roisin but not me. Although I was a fair dancer, I wasn't fussy about it, plus my head was in a daze from thinking all night. I had a lot to worry about now and was not going to let Lucia out of my sight, even for a second; if that was ever possible.

Thinking it was a cold wind up on deck, we didn't bother going there; instead, we browsed around the vast shopping area until retiring to our rooms. Opening the door to ours we found that all our clothes and furniture were strewn around the cabin. We knew this could only be the wizards doing, but before we could retreat, one of those horrible slimy creatures dropped off the ceiling onto the screaming Lucia. I put my arm around its throat and somehow managed to drag it off. The beast was of human-like form, just like the others, but this time, its skin was that of an eel. It was so slippery that it quickly wriggled itself out of my grip. I was just about to hit it with my staff when it screamed and spat slime at me. He rushed again at Lucia, but by this time she was behind the table, screaming even louder than the creature. I went after him with my staff and caught him square on its back, but the blow didn't affect him. He just turned, snarled, and spat again at me before turning once more to Lucia who was making her way to the corner. I managed to grab him with my staff around his chest only to lose him again as he slid to the floor. He was fuming now, and as he rose showing his gruesome teeth, he came at me. I managed to grab his skinny neck with both hands and as I did, he gave out a terrible scream and dissolved into a lump of smelly jelly that turned to dust. I rushed over to Lucia, asking if she was okay and that the creature hadn't hurt her. Apart from the horrible smelly slime all over her, she was fine; just a little shaken up.

With all the screaming going on, I was amazed no one came to investigate. I wiped my hands and arms and tidied up the room. Next was to wash, but where was the washroom? With us being covered in slime we couldn't ask a steward, only Roisin. She was surprised to hear what had happened and couldn't understand why she didn't hear anything. The bathroom happened to be just across the corridor, so while we were away washing, Roisin cleaned up as much of the slime and dust as she could.

Having to watch over Lucia every single day and night was beginning to take its toll on me. She didn't seem to mind, but I found it uncomfortable and embarrassing, especially in the bathroom. After the attack by that skinny slimy creature, I knew now why Bleddwyn told me not to let her out of my sight. Unfortunately, I had to put up with the whole protection business even though it meant her insisting I hold her hand almost twenty-four hours of every day. But after saying that, I couldn't have wished for a lovelier girl to hold hands with.

I wasn't looking forward to the Captain's ball that night until I saw both Lucia and Roisin in their lovely dresses. Lucia's was red, edged with black lace while Roisin's was green, also edged with the same black lace. Lucia had her beautiful black hair tied up with a ribbon on top of her head with ringlets trickling down. Roisin had hers flowing down around her shoulders. They looked sensational, making me joke, "Are you sure you want to go to this party with me?"

I had already dressed and wanted somewhere to hide my staff. So I took the knob off one of the bedposts and slipped it down inside.

"Okay, ladies. Let's go and check out this party," I said while opening the door.

Walking along the corridor to the function room, there was nothing I could say to stop both girls from holding my arms. It was embarrassing, especially entering the hall and being shown to our table. I felt like a rich show-off and couldn't believe Roisin was asking a waiter for a bottle of champagne. It was eight o'clock and by then the room was full of important-looking people. The captain made a little speech about the ship and its maiden journey to New York and back again to Liverpool. When he had finished, and after the applause died down, he declared the ball open and the band began to play. Roisin was well away dancing, but it took me two glasses of champagne before I set out to dance with Lucia. As you know, she wouldn't leave my side, so there were quite a lot of disappointed young men turned away. We were having a good night until Roisin wanted to dance with me. She had probably danced with every young man in the room, so I suggested she sat down for a while. I then made up an excuse, saying that I had hurt my ankle and couldn't dance anymore. This didn't go down too well; she immediately accused me of not wanting to dance with her. Consequently, she swished her skirt and stormed out of the room.

"Ah, just let her be Gwydion, she'll be alright after she's cooled down," said Lucia.

Lucia's feet were sore after all the dancing, so we stayed there enjoying the music until midnight. On our way back, we called in to Roisin's cabin only to find that she wasn't there. Lucia was tired, and with it being such a massive ship, Roisin could be anywhere. My top priority was Lucia and although Roisin was like family now, we couldn't go looking for her. It was just as well we didn't for as we opened our cabin door, Roisin was sitting in an armchair, looking very solemn.

"I am sorry for being so childish Gwydion," she said. "I don't know what came over me. Will you forgive me?"

There wasn't anything to forgive her for, but just to make her happy, I said that I would. She then apologised to Lucia and went back to her cabin.

From that night on and throughout most of our journey, we only saw her at mealtimes and the occasional time she popped in to say goodnight. She had confined herself to her cabin, writing letters to post to her brother as soon as we arrived in Liverpool. That suited Lucia and me for we had our privacy back.

Lucia was fun to be with, and as our voyage progressed, I became more and more besotted with her. So I made up my mind to forget about Bleddwyn's warning and on my birthday, two days before we were to dock, I was going to declare my love for her. So the twentieth of October was going to be one of the best days of my life, but it wasn't to be, for on that very morning my heart was dealt a devastating blow.

# Chapter 14

"Good morning, Gwydion," said Lucia as she hurried out of her sleeping bag. "It's my birthday today."

"It's your what! Did you say your birthday?" I asked, hoping that she knew it was mine and was joking.

"Yes, I am nineteen today," she replied, skipping across the room to the washbasin.

"Why didn't you tell me yesterday? Or even before?" I asked in disbelief.

"I was keeping it a secret," she replied.

"Well happy birthday pretty one," I said, trying to be happy for her.

With her hands and face washed, she went behind the screen to dress. I dressed too but with tormenting thoughts racing through my mind. Her birthday was the same day as mine, and she was the same age too. Strangely enough, we were also the same age when losing our parents. I began wondering about the child we couldn't see in Brynmoroc's vision. Then there was the castle that

Lucia said was Lorca Castle. My mind then flashed back to Wales and the painting of a castle on my bedroom wall. I always knew there was something strange about it. Granddad said it was from my parent's house and that was all he knew about it. But does he, I thought. Was he really my Granddad? That crazy old dragon, Ohibronoeler, told me in one of his rants that he wasn't; and then there was Bleddwyn, how he addressed me as Gwydion my son. If that was just a figure of speech, then why did he say that I was his body and soul, his equity of blood? I wasn't sure if that was his exact words, but I was devastated now. The more I thought, the more I began to believe that Lucia and I were probably his son and daughter, or even Brynmoroc's.

"Are they hiding this from me," I whispered, slumping down in the chair. "If so, then why?"

I had never felt so low in my life. It was as if my heart was sinking, down, down and down, taking the blood from my overworked brain along with it. My head was numb and my chest heaved with pain like I had never felt before. No matter how hard I wished it wasn't true, the truth was right there inside me. Had I possibly fallen in love with my beautiful twin sister? We had very similar kinds of skin and black hair, but we definitely didn't look alike.

"Well, what do you think?" asked Lucia, coming out from behind the screen.

She was standing there, wearing a lovely green and lemon dress. Then as she flicked her long wavy black hair around her shoulders, my heart sunk even further. I just didn't know what to think, say or even do. I was still in a daze from the fact of knowing that she was possibly my sister.

"You look lovely Lucia," I eventually managed to say. "When did you buy the dress?"

"I bought it in New York," she replied along with the other. "You said we could have anything we wanted. I have another one for tonight too."

At breakfast, Roisin was also surprised to hear Lucia's secret and was quick to wish her a happy birthday.

That afternoon, although still in a dream, Lucia and I went for a stroll around the bow of the ship. While looking out across the ocean, Roslyn and Sophia would pop up now and then as if to let us know they were still there. Lucia laughed every time, but not me. I couldn't, because deep down I was searching for the happy heart that I once had, but it was gone; gone because of some selfish old wizard. Yes, lost to a lovely Spanish girl that I could now, never share it with. I was sad, yes, but I wasn't going to show it or even say anything to Lucia about my assumption. There were two reasons why, and that was; although I wasn't very happy with Bleddwyn, I promised him that I wouldn't and secondly, I wasn't entirely sure if the whole birthday thing was just a coincidence. Either way, at that moment in time, the thought of me ever being the son of one of the wizards, depressed me even more.

"What's the matter love? Why are you so sad?" Asked Lucia, slipping her arm into mine.

It was so ironic, for she had never called me love until that day. I felt cheated and was beginning to hate those wizards now.

"I'm okay," I replied. "But now I think we should go tell the captain it's your birthday, maybe he'll have the musicians play for you tonight."

Captain Cameron was delighted for Lucia and promised to reserve a table in the dining room and would arrange to have the musicians play for her. Lucia was happy, but that evening, while waiting for her to change into her new dress, I remember sitting on the bed dreading seeing her in it.

"What am I going to do?" I muttered. It was so cruel and when she finally came from behind the screen, my heart skipped. I just knew she was going to look amazing.

"Well, what do you think? Does it suit me?" She asked and twirled.

I sighed, and as she delicately twirled once more in front of me, you can just imagine what I was thinking.

"Well, do you like it or not?" she asked again. "Why don't you answer me?"

Of course I liked it. The reason why I didn't answer was; I couldn't speak. Her dress was royal blue with gold frills; her hair was tied up with a gold ribbon in a fashion that let ringlets hang down to her shoulders. Whether it was because I knew that I had lost her, she looked the loveliest girl that I had ever seen.

"Yes, you look beautiful Lucia," I replied as she walked towards me. "I have never seen anyone so lovely."

I then thought, "Oh no, please don't kiss me." But before I could stop her, she softly kissed me on the lips and said, "Thank you Gwydion."

Well, that was it for me. My insides were in a right state now, and I was glad when the musicians turned up outside our cabin. When they heard about Lucia's birthday, they came and serenaded her outside the door and all the way into the dining room. It was embarrassing, but both ladies loved it. I suppose that's what the power of money can do for you. They knew I would tip them, and had been all week. Even the cooks knew it because after we arrived at our table, they came in with a cake singing happy birthday. It was a lovely fruit cake with just a thin layer of icing on top and of course, nineteen flickering candles. As Lucia leaned over to blow out the candles, they all went out except for one. It was funny but at the same time very strange, because each time she blew, it wouldn't go out. Then to my surprise, she wanted me to try. It was as if that candle was waiting for me, for as I blew, out it went. Then much to Lucia's delight, the band began to play.

It turned out to be an enjoyable night of dancing and playing all kinds of silly games. Lucia was the star, of course, not only because it was her birthday, but because they were amazed at her card tricks. Roisin too enjoyed herself immensely and joined in all the games. At midnight, and after the band played the last waltz, we happily headed back to our cabins, worn out and ready for bed. I took off my jacket and waited for Lucia to change. We slipped into our sleeping bags, and as Lucia handcuffed us together with her ribbon, she sighed.

"It was the loveliest birthday I have ever had in my life. Thank you Gwydion, I love you," she said, kissed my cheek and quietly drifted off to sleep.

During the party, I pretended to be happy, but the heartbreaking thought of us possibly being brother and sister kept flashing through my mind, then after hearing her say that she loved me; my misery deepened. I fell asleep that night hating those wizards even more. I was even dreaming about them until I woke to the sound of the ship's fog horn.

It was early morning and just about daylight. I gently untied our handcuff, stretched and went to turn out the lamp. Lucia didn't like sleeping in the dark, so I would leave it on for her. Then, as I turned it out, there was an explosion of breaking glass, a shower of water and a thud. I quickly got off the bed to see that a large white snake-like creature had slithered in through the porthole window.

"Wake up, Lucia!" I shouted.

"What's the matter? What's happening? What's that?" She said and screamed in fright.

"Quickly, get up and stand on the bed, the creatures are back," I said as the slithery thing hissed at me.

Lucia screamed again when she heard it hiss and quickly stood up on the bed. It was a strange giant snake with one eye that shone like the moon. It had a tapered shape body. How long it was, I couldn't tell, because only half of it was in with us. I had no staff. It was still inside the bedpost where my jacket was hanging. My shield was the only thing I could use to protect us, but that was in my jacket. The snake just led there, watching me with its one eye as if waiting for me to make a move. I did, but slowly towards my jacket, but as I grabbed it, the hissing snake rose and spat at me. The force of its spit sent me flying across the bed, knocking Lucia off and onto the floor. The snake was struggling now, and just as it was trying to get the rest of itself into the cabin, the door burst open and in came Roisin in her nightdress, holding her whip. By this time, I had taken out my shield. The snake quickly turned to Roisin and rose up, but before it could do anything, Roisin lashed it across its neck. The writhing snake was hurt and thrashed about smashing up the furniture. Roisin tried desperately to slash again, but with the snake thrashing around, she couldn't. Fortunately, because of its shape, the snake couldn't come in any farther. The creature was writhing and thrashing about so much that Roisin couldn't hit it, but when she did manage to thrash it, the leather-wrapped around its neck. Instantly, the savage-looking thing reared backwards dragging Roisin towards it. I rushed the creature with my shield, making it give out an awful cry, something like a desperate goat. Roisin was led on top of it now, and as I forced its ugly head against the wall, it hurled me across the room. Thankfully, Roisin was up again with her whip and we moved back away to Lucia. The horrid predator had now risen, showing us its teeth like a snarling dog. It didn't like my shield and kept moving its head from side to side, blinking its bright eye as it did so. Roisin was fearless, and before I could stop her, she stepped forward, raised her whip and caught the snake across its eye. It went berserk after that, thrashing around again, spitting green slime everywhere. The only thing I could think of was to advance and hope somehow the snake would go back through the porthole, but it knocked the shield out of my hand and managed to pin me down. I could have sworn then that the snake said something that sounded like, 'You're finished.' Then suddenly, the horrid thing shot back out of the porthole, leaving behind a pile of skin on the jagged glass. I rose to my feet, looked out the window and saw the snake thrashing about until it disappeared down into the ocean. Although there was no sign of Roslyn and Sophia, I took it that they had seen the snake and had come to our rescue by dragging it out and killing it. Then as I turned around to check on the girls, I found that the cabin was as if nothing had ever happened. Everything was as it was when we went to bed. Lucia and Roisin stood there flabbergasted saying that all the destruction and mess vanished before their eyes. I turned to the porthole and that too was intact, even our clothes were clean. There was absolutely no evidence to suggest that it happened, but I can assure you that it did.

"Roisin, you were simply magnificent," said Lucia hugging her.

"Yes, if it wasn't for you Roisin, goodness knows what would have happened," I added, also giving her a hug. "We are in your debt now. So after breakfast, we'll go to the store and you can buy anything you want."

"Well, what about taking me to Spain instead?" She quickly suggested.

"Ah Roisin, that, as you know I can't do," I replied and smiled at her crafty move. "I told you that we have an important assignment. But, if all things go well and when Lucia and I have accomplished our mission, I'll take you anywhere in the world. How is that?"

"You Promise?" she asked, but sadly.

I promised, and with that, she went away making us laugh by cracking her whip.

All we seemed to talk about that morning, was the snake and how courageous Roisin was. In the afternoon, while up on deck, we heard great laughter coming from the front of the ship. We went to investigate and found that passengers were excited about two orca whales jumping out of the water, showing off. They were having a lovely time.

"Look!" Said Lucia shaking my arm. "What's that coming across the water? It looks like a small whirlwind. It's Brynmoroc; I know it is."

She was right, for not only did the whirlwind come directly towards us it also drifted through the crowd of people and settled down twirling on top of the rails before us. As we watched, it blew up like a balloon and burst, leaving a serious-looking Brynmoroc, standing on a small cloud about ten feet away.

"Gwydion, Lucia my child, you are in grave danger," said the wizard, shaking his head. "As you already know, you were attacked this morning by a Taperlite snake. The snake was a cruel wizard, transformed and banished to the depths of the Atlantic Ocean by the great Vindaguar. Since Bleddwyn obtained the sole power of wizardry, he released and commanded the snake to attack you. The snake, because of its excitement at being free, had forgotten about Vindaguar's law, 'He that attacks a human will be a victim of himself.' I dragged the creature away, leaving him to die in the ocean."

I was sceptical about this, so I asked why Bleddwyn would want us dead.

"I have already told you, Son! Were you not listening? I have come here to warn you that I may not be able to help you anymore. Bleddwyn probably knows that you believe in me and will take away what little freedom I have. Now I must go for I feel his presence. I have faith in you and your promise Gwydion and will be waiting for you in Spain. Until then, goodbye now my children."

Brynmoroc drifted away, disappearing like a wave smashing against a rock. The length of time he was standing there, not one other person saw him, but there again; he is a wizard, isn't he?

"Gwydion, why does Brynmoroc keep calling you, Son?" asked Lucia.

I didn't know, but it was probably just a figure of speech, was all I could say.

"Who called you Son?" Asked Roisin in bewilderment.

"Brynmoroc! Didn't you hear him?" I asked, looking at her puzzled face.

"No! All I heard and saw were you talking to a seagull, perched up on that rail."

I didn't say anymore, only that I must have been dreaming again.

Back in our cabin, Lucia and I asked ourselves many questions without any positive answers. Why did he call me, son? Why did he call us children and why didn't Roisin see him? There again, perhaps she did? Also, it was eight in the morning when the snake attacked us, by then; most passengers were up and heading for the breakfast room. The passageway was busy, so why was it only Roisin heard our ordeal? We didn't know, and that's how we eventually fell asleep, all muddled up.

# Chapter 15

On the morning, everyone was now very excited. Our long journey was coming to an end and soon we'd be sailing up the estuary into Liverpool harbour. My thoughts turned to Roslyn and Sophia. Back in New York, I had commanded them to be waiting and ready, hitched to a carriage when we arrived. Just to make sure, we went on deck to look for them. They were there, and as usual, popped up to acknowledge us. We waved and then went back to our cabin only to find Roisin in tears saying that she was going to miss us. There was nothing I could say that I hadn't said before. So Lucia comforted her until she cheered up after a nice cup of tea.

After disembarking at the harbour, we made our way through a crowd of people who were greeting their loved ones and family. Once out of the port and into the street, our mares stood waiting at the back of the buildings. The main thing now was to get Roisin checked into a hotel and to find out the train times for her. That was easier said than done because almost half the ship's passengers were doing the same thing, but we managed to find her a room and left her there while Lucia and I checked out the whereabouts of the train station. There was a train to Southampton going out that afternoon at five o'clock. I bought Roisin a ticket, but unfortunately, she had to change trains three times on the way. We went back and gave her the news. I had never seen anyone so upset. She didn't expect to be leaving so soon and was thinking we could all spend one more night together. I couldn't understand why she was so upset; for once again, we had only known her a couple of weeks. I thought she'd be happy that she was on her way to see her brother.

"Oh Gwydion, I'm sorry, I am so sorry," she sobbed.

"Please don't cry," I said, sitting down beside her. "I thought you were excited about meeting your brother."

"That's the trouble; I'm not anymore, I hate him," she replied, holding tightly onto my arm. "Oh, Gwydion, I'm sorry."

I was baffled now and asked as I looked deeply into her flooded eyes.

"Up until now you were keen to be with him, but now you say you're not. On top of that, you are even saying that you hate him. Why? What has your brother done? What could he have possibly done since yesterday to make you change your mind? I don't understand and why are you saying sorry to me, anyway?"

"Oh, I don't know," she replied. "But I'm alright, don't worry about me. I'll be out of your way soon and you'll never see me again."

Before I could ask once more what she was so sorry about, she ran out of the room crying. Lucia wanted us to follow her, but I said to let her be for a while, she was just upset because we were leaving her.

Around lunchtime, we went looking for her, but she was nowhere to be found. That was, until around about a quarter to five when we found her sitting on a bench at the railway station, looking really solemn.

"It's okay; there is no need to worry. I'm going to see my brother. Thank you both for your kindness and your generosity. I am going to miss you terribly and I am so sorry for what I did, but I'll make it up to you."

"Now don't be saying that Roisin," I said, sitting beside her. "Of course we'll see you again; I promised you, didn't I? Also, you keep telling us that you are sorry about something you have done. I want you to know that whatever it is, I don't care. You have apologised, so it's in the past. I'll be back for you, I promise. So go on now, your train is coming. Lucia gave you her address so you can write to her, can't you?"

I was happy that we could now carry on with our mission but sad as we helped Roisin board the train. She gently kissed us, and as she tried to hold back her tears, she managed to say, "Goodbye and please be careful. I'll be writing to you, Lucia."

We stepped back off the train and stood there talking to her through the open window of the door until the guard's whistle blew. The train slowly moved off, and as we waved, Roisin shouted, "Gwydion my…."

I couldn't hear anymore because the train's whistle blew drowning out the rest of whatever she was saying. With that, we headed back to the hotel where we sat saying nothing, only thinking until Lucia broke the silence.

"What was Roisin so sorry about and why was she going to make it up to us? She has nothing to do with our mission. She's just a stranger."

"I'm like you. I don't know," I replied. "She's a strange one. Perhaps she's just another clever illusion and doesn't even exist. I don't know what's going on Lucia; it's a complete mystery. One day I think I know what's happening, the next I'm no wiser than the day I started out in Wales. I'm worried now and have been thinking. Do you still want to carry on and finish what we started? Or shall we quit and leave these wizards to fight their own battles? It seems to me that they are using us as pawns, or at least one of them is."

"I think we should carry on and finish what we were destined to do," was her quick response. "Strange as it may be, somehow and for some reason, Roisin seems to be a part of it too. How and why we'll have to wait and see. You know as well as I do that once the prophecy has started it has to be finished. Goodness knows what will happen to us if it isn't."

"That's what I was hoping you'd say," I said, tapping her knee. "But I am still worried about you. Whichever wizard wants us dead, and I am pretty sure it's Brynmoroc, will be desperate now knowing that we have only three jewels left to find. So I think a good idea is to go down and sneak Roslyn and Sophia up to stand guard for us."

Lucia agreed and we went around the back of the hotel where they were waiting. With no one around, I had them back as two little terriers under my jacket.

We felt safer bedding down that night, knowing that there were now, not two wee terriers, but two savage-looking hounds at the foot of our bed.

We rose early the next morning, hitched up the mares to another carriage and set off on a wet miserable day. Within an hour we were heading down the beach and ploughing into the English Channel. A few minutes later, we were back in our cosy little ark, on our way to France.

"Oh yes! There they are again Gwydion. Can you see them?" Shouted Lucia.

The tiger sharks were back, about twenty of them gracefully pulling us along. We left them to it and went below. While having breakfast, Lucia told me that the jewel, being a blue sapphire, was going to be a difficult one to reach. It was on an enormous rock jutting out from the middle of a towering waterfall called Saut du Doubs. How I could reach it, she didn't know.

"Well, that doesn't sound very promising," I said and laughed. "Maybe I'll turn myself into a salmon and jump up."

"Oh no! You smell bad enough already," she said and also laughed

"Oh yeah!" I said and joked. "Well in that case Senorita, I had better not sleep with you tonight nor any other night."

She thought I was serious and grabbed my arm. "Ah, don't be silly; I was only kidding. Don't say that to me Gwydion, you know I can't sleep on my own."

As she looked at me with sad, but lovely eyes, I laughed and said that I was also kidding. Then moved away before she poked me.

"Oh you old rotter Gwydion," she said, joining me in my laughter.

It rained all morning up until the late afternoon, by that time the sharks had gone and we were sailing down the coast of France approaching a sandy shore near Sainte-Adresse. Sainte Adresse was the home town of the famous artist, Monet. The very moment we hit the beach, we were back in our carriage, passing through the town and out into the country until we came to another town, Rouen. Travelling over sixty miles called for a much-needed rest and refreshments. This we surely did, but walking into a late-night café, caused us to be overcome with curious looks.

"We had better get out of here Gwydion before they start asking questions," said Lucia anxiously. "We are dressed differently from them and I don't like the way those men are looking at us."

I had never thought of that and it was too late to buy new clothes.

"You're right," I said. "And by the way, did you see that plaque on the way in? This is the town where Saint Joan of Arc was executed."

As I mentioned that, a few of those hostile-looking men were getting up, making me think that we had better clear off and sharpish.

We turned around and were out of that café and gone before those men even had time to sneeze from the dust we left behind. Safe and far enough away, we pulled into a forest and made camp for the night. I collected water from a stream and made a small fire sufficient to boil the kettle for we didn't want to attract any unwanted attention. Not only were we dressed differently; we couldn't speak French either. That was another thing I didn't think of. I was stumped, but Lucia informed me that there were plenty of English, even Spanish people living in France and many of the French spoke English. I told her that we'd soon find out because once in Paris, we had to buy a change of clothes.

"Perhaps you should buy a couple of diamond necklaces and rings just in case you lose that purse of yours," she joked.

"Yeah, good idea. Maybe I'll buy myself a couple and a gold watch too," I said for a laugh.

She looked at me to see if I was serious, "Are you, really?"

"Why not?" I replied. "I have never seen a diamond ring or a gold watch."

"What about me?" she then asked, expectantly

"You can choose it for me if you like," I replied, but couldn't hold my laughter.

"Oh, you! You are only teasing me again, aren't you?" she said, pushing me.

I said that I was and that it was a good idea, but unfortunately, if we did buy them, we'd be quickly robbed and thrown into a ditch, probably the next day.

We slept well, not worrying too much about any bandits. Well, would you, with two fierce-looking bull mastiffs outside your tent?

In the morning we found that it must have rained all night. It had stopped, but we were getting wet from all the dripping trees. So after hitching Roslyn and Sophia to our new four-wheeled carriage, we made our way out into the open. Looking at the rough road ahead, I thought of something. On our way to Rouen, we had crossed the River Seine many times. According to my map, it flowed into Paris, and as we noticed, many boats were sailing up it. One of them being a large steamboat. So I wondered what Roslyn would come up with.

The river ran alongside a village about a couple of miles from where we were, so I thought we'd join it there. It was about nine in the morning before we passed through the small village and after finding a nice quiet spot, we entered the river unnoticed. Although we had experienced it many times, it was still exciting as we ploughed into the wide River Seine. Surprisingly though, this time we found ourselves in a small sailing boat, with a cabin just big enough for two to sit in. There was no sign of Roslyn or Sophia until we saw them blasting water into the air in front of the boat. Lucia laughed, for they were now dolphins, happily towing us along but well below the surface. It was fun for a while until early afternoon when after meeting a couple of congested spots, we had to abandon the river and carry on by coach. Unfortunately and devastatingly, as we approached our first signpost, it stated, sixty miles to Paris. That meant, due to all the meandering of the mighty River Seine, we had only travelled about twenty miles. I hadn't realised the time until Lucia reminded me about Brynmoroc. It was beginning to rain, so we quickly pulled off the road and took shelter in an old disused mill. It was an excellent time to have some lunch. So we did and then sat, waiting for Brynmoroc to arrive. Frustratingly, because of the false promise we made to him, it was now difficult to know what to do with our shields. If we held them in front of us, he would think it strange and that we were still afraid of him and if we didn't, we'd be vulnerable. All we could do was keep our hands in our pockets, ready with our shields.

As it turned out, Brynmoroc never appeared. So with it being four o'clock and still pouring rain, we headed on to Paris. I gave Lucia my cape to keep her dry and to physically protect her. Later, I was thanking my lucky stars that I did because a few miles outside Paris, we were held up by two bandits. It happened while we were pulled over for a rest. With the bright setting sun dazzling us, we didn't notice them creeping up alongside our carriage. What they said, I couldn't tell you, but going by their aggressive attitude, we had an idea of what they wanted. But unfortunately for them, they didn't get it. I refused to comply with their demands, resulting in one of them pointing his pistol and bang, he fired. By that time, my shield was out ricocheting the bullet hitting his accomplice in the leg. While he went hopping about, the gunman tried to grab Lucia, but as he lunged towards her, a force from my staff sent him hurtling backwards, thumping into his wounded friend. I then took that opportunity to advance towards the squealing pair and with my shield afore me, and my staff held high, I spoke to them in the deepest voice I could manage.

"Go now, before I turn you into hogs or a couple of flea-ridden rats."

Whether they understood me or were just terrified, it did the trick and they were up and gone, hobbling away before I could even think of anything else to say. It wasn't a very pleasant experience, but it turned out funny in the end.

"That put pay to them," Lucia said and laughed. "But I think we had better wait until Paris before stopping again."

With that said, we were up and away travelling on until tired eyes got the better of us. Unable to keep our eyes open, we were soon knocking on the door of a little bed and breakfast cottage on the outskirts of Paris. A skinny-looking ginger-haired man answered and with us not able to speak a word of French, Lucia pointed to the sign portraying a bed. He understood and took the mares around to the stables while his wife happily showed us to our room. Before she left, and while gesturing with her hand, she asked, "Soup, bread to which Lucia replied, "Oui s'il vous plaît."

I was surprised and looked at my smiling companion.

"It's French for yes please. Well, I think it is?" she replied, shrugging her shoulders.

The lady's husband was a weird-looking chap and I mentioned it to Lucia. She laughed and said that he just needed fattening up. It wasn't long before the Landlady called us to the kitchen table for our meal, leaving us alone to tuck into our delicious supper. We hadn't eaten much that day and our tummies were now rumbling, so the soup and bread were very much appreciated. We saw no one after that and went back to our room wondering what kind of people were running the place. I was wishing now that we had Roslyn and Sophia as guard dogs again. So I opened the window and hoping the mares would hear me I quietly ordered them to listen and keep watch over us. I closed the window and as usual, took out my journals to write about the day's events. Lucia would sometimes go over them with me just in case I had forgotten something. When finished, we didn't bother to undress just led on top of the bed for a while.

"There's something very strange about this place," said Lucia as we lay listening for any kind of movement.

There was no sound to be heard, not a sneeze, a cough, or even a door creek to break the silence. We had a notion that something was going to happen and were now wishing we had kept on going to Paris. To give us peace of mind, I jammed a chair underneath the door handle. It was a cold night, so I lit a few extra candles. Lucia slipped into her sleeping pouch to keep warm; I did the same but made sure my staff was in with me. We lay there quietly talking to each other for a while until there was a terrible smell.

"Where's that smell coming from?" Lucia asked, sitting up smartly.

It smelt like sewage. So with my staff and shield, I went to investigate and saw white mist creeping in under the door.

"Quickly, get up Lucia," I said. "We have another visitor. Hurry, get your shield."

With our backs against the wall, we watched as the mist rose into two columns twisting around each other.

Lucia began to shiver and whispered, "It's so cold. What is that stuff?"

Then as the columns split into two, I was thinking, oh no; not more snakes. They weren't, for as they separated, they were now the landlord and his wife, but they certainly weren't human anymore, they were walking figures of dry ice. They moved well away from each other, and as the two fiends began advancing, they brought the perishing cold with them.

"Hand over the staff and you'll live to see your Granddad again. Refuse and you'll die a terrible death," said the man of ice.

I didn't know how I was going to battle with these creatures. I had been in contact with dry ice before and was severely burned. We were trapped with no way out. The only thing to do was to step forward and bluff them.

"Okay, tell my Granddad that I am ever so sorry to disappoint him, but I don't want to see him today. So come on! Let's get it over with."

They said nothing, only stood there grinning as the room began to get colder and colder. I realised that we had to do something quickly before they either froze us to death or we'd die horribly stuck to them, which was obviously their intention. They kept coming until our shields flashed, dazzling them. At the sight of this, they backed away with their hands covering their blinded eyes to protect them. I knew from my school days, that dry ice when in contact with warm air, would absorb it, giving out gas. Our room was small, and the creatures were big. So even if we could keep them at bay without freezing to death, we would surely die from lack of oxygen.

"Lucia, open the window while I hold them back," I said as they stumbled blindly, trying to advance.

"No! I can't! I can't, Gwydion! I'm afraid," she said, grabbing hold of my belt.

I then backed towards the window saying that we'd do it together. Lucia opened it only to find that it was barred. The only thing I could think of now was to throw some coins on the floor in front of the stinking creatures, hoping my staff would do something to help. So with my staff outstretched, I threw a handful down in front of them. To my surprise, as the ice creatures walked onto them, they began to vibrate and shake violently, so I threw some more. This rendered them completely disorientated, resulting in them backing away, squealing, into the corner of the room. In their retreat, pieces of them were spitting out like sparks from a fire. One of them landed behind the collar of my shirt, burning my neck. We grabbed our belongings and quickly made a dash for the door, throwing more coins in their path as we made our escape.

We ran out of that house, up the garden path, and out onto the road like a pair of bolting rabbits. Then as we paused to check if we were being followed, we were astonished to see that the guest house had vanished. Of all the crazy things, it was gone. With just the moonlight, all we could make out were our beautiful mares hitched up to the carriage at the side of the road.

"Was that place ever there at all?" said Lucia trying to catch her breath.

If it wasn't, then how did I burn my neck? Also, it was nine-thirty when we arrived there and now it was one in the morning. So yes, it was real alright, just like the avalanche. Now it was time to get away before it came back. That we did, and as we headed on into Paris, I asked Lucia what she thought about those odd icy creatures not putting up much of a fight. It was as if they had planned the whole outcome of it.

"I'm not really sure," she replied. "But I remember a boy putting a coin into dry ice, and like those creatures, it began vibrating. So as those creatures trod on those coins, they couldn't walk. The only thing they could do was to back away from them."

I tapped her on the knee and said, "You are probably right, my clever little Spanish bambino."

She laughed, kissed my arm and said, "You are the dafty now. Bambino is Spanish for baby."

"Yes, that's what I meant," I said, then flinched as she dug me in the ribs.

We travelled on and after arriving in the busy city of Paris, I knew it a waste of time asking Lucia what she wanted. I knew too well her reply. So at the first hotel, I reluctantly paid for her traditional annoying bath but was happy to pay for a much-needed room for the night. That's what we did and didn't rise until ten in the morning.

It was almost noon before we started trotting our way through Paris. With there being so much traffic and so many busy people hurrying across the streets, it was well after four in the afternoon before we were out into the country. Lucia, while holding her tummy, said that she was hungry. I pulled over, and while we were having a snack, I heard a train whistle in the distance. Earlier, I had noticed a railway running alongside the road. I hadn't thought about taking a train. I also remembered seeing a signpost saying four miles to Evry. Then as I heard the train whistle again, I stood up telling Lucia that we should see if we could catch that train in the next town. She then surprised me, saying that she would like to ride Sophia, but for one time only. I agreed, though only if she wore my cape. I raised my staff, and both mares were saddled up and rearing to go. We left the carriage on the side of the road and after quickly tying our bags behind the saddles, we mounted up and were soon racing away like the wind.

I let Lucia stay in front so that I could keep an eye on her. I was amazed to see just how competent a rider she was, probably better than me. She was having a great time and laughed all the way into Evry. We beat the train easily enough and had plenty of time to have the mares back as two wee terriers again.

Happily, after boarding the train, we made our way through the carriages until we found an empty seat. We had only been seated for a few minutes when we were joined by two well-dressed elderly sisters who sat opposite us. It was a pleasant surprise to find them both speaking English. They were heading to a country retreat in Southern France for the winter. The damp weather in England didn't agree with them. Their grandmother was French, so they were also fluent in the language.

It was to be a four-hour journey to Dijon, but listening to those fascinating ladies telling their childhood tales, passed the time away very quickly and we arrived in Dijon at precisely nine o'clock.

"Where are you staying tonight?" asked one of the ladies as we walked along the platform together.

"We are not sure yet, but we'll find a hotel somewhere," replied Lucia."

The lady then suggested, "Well, in that case, the Hotel de Ville where we always stay, is lovely. So if you like, you can come along with us. We are well known there and will make sure you get a nice room. Also, the receptionist and one of the maids speak English which will make your stay more pleasurable."

Her sister concurred and gave a little chuckle. We didn't care where we stayed as long as it wasn't too far away. We thanked the sisters and joined them in their carriage.

"Wow, it's more like a stately home than a hotel," remarked Lucia when we arrived.

Walking up to the entrance, one of the sisters said as she patted Lucia's arm.

"Don't you be worrying about expense now? Just leave everything to us."

"Bonsoir, Lady Michelle, Lady Anne," said the receptionist to the sisters.

"Bonsoir, Catherine," was their reply. "Our two friends would like a room for the night and whatever they wish for breakfast."

Lady Michelle then leaned over and whispered something to Catherine.

"I told you we are well known here," said Lady Anne. "Now go on; the maid will show you to your room and the bathroom. Goodnight now, we'll see you at breakfast."

We followed the maid up the broad stairway, but when we turned to give a little wave, the sisters were gone, and so too had the receptionist. I sighed, for there was something strange about those happy-go-lucky generous ladies, and now, I had a bad feeling that more trouble was on its way again.

The room was as the Lady predicted and was one of the nicest we had been in so far. Lucia was happy and walked around the room saying that it was lovely, but there was no double bed. This made me wonder. The sisters must have noticed Lucia had no ring on her finger, which was probably what Lady Michelle was whispering about and why she booked a room with two beds.

"I don't trust those Sisters Lucia. Do you?" I asked, hoping she'd agree.

"I think I do," she replied. "But it does seem strange they insisted on paying for our room. After all, we don't know them from Adam. I do hope they are genuine?"

I was hoping too, but thank goodness we had Roslyn and Sophia. They were there with us, settling down on a rug.

After joining the two beds together and changing into our nightwear, we settled down for the night, though I hardly slept from worrying about those suspicious ladies.

In the morning, we woke to someone outside our room, trying to get in. After shaking the door a few times, a woman called out in French, then went away shouting to someone who was probably downstairs. Wondering what all the fuss was about, I went out onto the landing to take a look. I was glad I did, for an anxious-looking man was talking to two Policemen and at the same time, pointing towards the stairs. All I could understand was, "trente," which was the number thirty of our room. Looking as if there was going to be trouble, I told Lucia to get dressed, opened the window, dropped our bags down into the backyard, dressed and put on my cape. Immediately I felt a surge of energy rushing through my whole body. I picked up my staff and commanded Roslyn and Sophia to be saddled up and outside waiting.

"Okay Lucia," I said, taking a deep breath. "Let's see what it's all about, but hold my staff and stay behind me."

I opened the door, and as we began to walk across the landing, two policemen were coming up the stairs along with the man shouting, "Payer, Payer!"

One of the policemen quickly walked across the landing towards me while the other blocked our escape from down the stairs. The grinning officer caught hold of me, saying, "Ok!"

I grabbed hold of his jacket, and as incredibly as you may think, I lifted him up above my head and held him there as I looked at the other policeman

"Now, back away! Or else!" I roared in a loud and deep voice as I pretended to throw the struggling policeman over the balcony.

"Non, non, non!" Screamed the policeman, and so too did his colleague and the manager.

I turned to our room and pointed towards the door with my foot and shouted, "Back away in there, pronto, pronto before I throw him over,"

They knew what I wanted and quickly backed into the bedroom. I put the distressed policeman down and after pushing him in along with them, I snapped off the inner knob and slammed the door. With it tightly shut, I stooped down, asking Lucia to quickly get onto my back for we had to get out of there. She did, and as we raced outside, I must have run around to the back of that hotel quicker than any man that ever lived. We picked up the bags, mounted our waiting steeds and galloped away out into the country, even faster. When we were far enough away, we stopped and hid behind some rocks. I didn't know where that deep voice came from, but I had a sore throat from it.

"Do you think we are safe now?" Lucia asked, struggling to sit up.

I didn't know if we were or not, but to stop her worrying, I said that we were. It was a hundred and twenty miles or so to the Swiss border and a few more to the falls of Saut du Doubs. We'd had enough of horseback riding, so after summoning up a small black coach, we were on our way with Roslyn and Sophia swiftly galloping along the cold and blustery trail. We made good progress up until midday when it was time to prepare for the wizard. We were only a couple of miles from Dole so we pulled over and hid, hoping the menace wouldn't turn up.

Hiding under some trees, I remembered learning in school about the Chemist, Louise Pasteur. I told Lucia that he was born in Dole and was the very chemist who discovered a vaccine to prevent rabies and anthrax. He also came up with a system to make milk and beer safe; and loads of other discoveries.

"That's interesting, perhaps we'll see him then?" she said excitedly.

I told her, hardly, for he died four years ago, but the house where he was born and lived should still be there. I wasn't sure where he was buried, perhaps in Lilli where he worked. Lucia was disappointed; she would have loved to have met someone famous.

At that moment, the wind whipped up, bringing a cloud that loomed menacingly above us.

"Okay, here he comes! Keep your hand on your shield Lucia, I said, putting my hand in my pocket. "I'm going to ask him something he may not like, but whatever I say, just go along with it."

Then, like a hawk diving onto its prey, Brynmoroc dropped out of the dark and eerie-looking cloud, onto a rock before us.

"Lucia, I fear for your life. Bleddwyn has succeeded in achieving all he needs to stay the most powerful wizard that will ever be. Knowing the whereabouts of the achieved sacred jewels, the rest of your mission matters not to him. All he needs now is your staff to return the energy back into the rearranged jewels. Gwydion, to save you both from a terrible death, you must willingly give me the staff and come home with me before it is too late."

At that moment, I remembered him saying all this before. Why tell us again? Also, back on the boat, he said that he wouldn't see us until after the mission was finished. So I put a question to him.

"Excuse me, Sir. Lucia is almost convinced now that you are her father. So to prove to her once and for all, could we ask you one question?"

"Certainly," he said and smiled. "I am only too happy to prove myself."

I took a deep breath and calmly asked, "Lucia has a black birthmark on her shoulder. Can you tell us which shoulder?"

"Gwydion! Do you think I can remember that far back? I know she has one on her shoulder, which one I cannot remember. Is there anything else you would like to ask?"

"Only one more please, Sir? During your visits, we had a friend along with us; her name was Roisin. Roisin told me that you knew she was there, but I noticed that you did not acknowledge her. Can you explain why?"

Brynmoroc frowned and with a look of anger, he raised his voice, "Gwydion! I know not of this Roisin. Are you trying to trick me, Son? Not at any one time, was there anyone else with you during my visits!"

I had infuriated him now, so I had to think of something quickly.

"I'm sorry Sir; I don't know what came over me. It was like someone told me to ask you that. I have been saying a lot of silly things lately. Perhaps it was Bleddwyn?"

"Maybe! Maybe not!" He said with the same expression. "Make up your mind son about the staff. I will leave you now and be back in half an hour for your decision."

He then swished his cloak, turned, soared into the sky and was gone.

"Did you hear what he said Gwydion? It's you that has the beauty spot on your shoulder, not me!"

"Yes, I know," I replied.

"How do you know that I haven't got one, anyway?" she asked, looking into my eyes.

"I dry your hair, don't I? So I knew you didn't have one on your shoulders. This means, we now know for sure that he isn't your father, but what about Roisin? He was adamant that he didn't know her, but how could she be present without him noticing? Roisin, once again, is a mystery to us. Either she is some kind of sorceress or Brynmoroc is a very convincing liar."

Lucia then reminded me about Brynmoroc asking for my staff and what I was going to say when he returns. There was only one thing I could say, and that was no, then see what happens. I had a feeling that he was desperate now, and because of it, we should have our shields out in full, regardless of what he may think. A moment later, Lucia quickly grabbed my arm, saying that Brynmoroc was here amongst the trees and had probably been listening. Uttering those words, a rush of wind forced us back against the tree we were sitting by. She was right; the wizard was coming from the very trees she had pointed to. Brynmoroc, frowning now, walked slowly up to us, only this time closer.

"Why the shields Gwydion?" he asked. "Are you afraid of me again?"

"Okay here goes," I said to myself as I nervously cleared my throat. "I'm sorry Sir, but we have decided to carry on and finish what we started. To do otherwise would be a total waste of time. Also, we are a little sceptical of you now since you were wrong about Lucia's birthmark. She hasn't got one on either of her shoulders. We think you could be mistaken about her being your daughter….."

Before I had time to finish, he raised his voice, "Do you mean to tell me that I don't know my own daughter? What do you think I am? A fool! Maybe?"

"No, no," I replied, "We don't think you are a fool, Sir. Just someone who's mistaken, that's all."

We held on to our shields for dear life as he flew into a rage and hollered.

"Argh! Who on earth would ever want such a miserable, pathetic, wimp of a daughter the likes of her anyway? No wonder her old winkle-picking parents left her to a witch. And you, Gwydion, a sloppy Welsh shovelling son of a no good tramp, why would anyone ever give you a crust of bread? Even the name Gwydion makes me laugh. Ha! What a silly name. My patience is now lost with the pair of you. All you had to do son, was give me your staff. I would have given you riches and let you live. But now, I'll just take it from your dead body that I'll leave to scavenging crows!!!"

What happened next made us thankful we had our shields because after disappearing, he returned, showing his true colours. A twelve or thirteen-foot-tall giant, gleaming, sparkling like crystal in the sun. We held our shields high as he rushed towards us roaring like a mad bear only to be sent hurtling backwards, crashing into the trees. He rose and came back from another angle, but once again, the same thing happened.

"You'll pay for this Lucia! Now you'll die too" he roared, pointing his staff towards the trees.

In a gleaming flash, the trees came to life and arched their branches to the ground, completely surrounding us. There was no way out.

"Welcome, both of you, to the last place you will ever see," roared Brynmoroc. "But at least, you won't die alone now Gwydion. I'll be back tomorrow to feed my dogs on your bones."

We now found ourselves trapped, helplessly inside a cage of impenetrable branches.

"Oh, no! Look, Gwydion! They are moving!" Exclaimed Lucia, squeezing my arm.

Yes, they were moving, moving slowly towards us. I had to think of something quickly before we were crushed to death.

"Quick, Gwydion! Think of something! They are going to crush us."

"I am trying! I'm trying!" I replied. Then I remembered my Granddad telling me that the only way to kill weeds was to burn them.

"Yes, fire!" I shouted. "The only way to drive them back is with fire. Quick Roslyn, Sophia, I'm sorry to tell you, but you're going to be fire-breathing dragons for a while."

I lifted my staff above my head saying, "Gofynna i chi" but nothing happened. In the panic, I had held my staff in the wrong hand. Without hesitation, I quickly swopped hands and in a bright flash, both mares had changed, though not as dragons, they were gigantic savage-looking tree creatures that ripped into the creeping trees, engaging in a fierce battle. There were branches, leaves and sods of earth flying everywhere, making us run for the carriage. We climbed inside just in time as a branch crashed down on the spot where we were standing. There was a terrifying, ferocious and deafening battle going on around us. All we could do was cover our ears and hope for the best. It was incredible and how we didn't get crushed, I'll never know. Roslyn and Sophia tore into those thrashing trees like crazed animals fighting for their lives. It seemed as if it went on for hours before there was silence. The battle was over, and we were outside amongst a mass of chopped-up branches, broken trees and leaves floating everywhere.

"Wow! That was immense!" said Lucia, looking up at our massive, ugly-looking saviours who had fearlessly cleared a way through. Within minutes, I had my mares back and we were riding away into Dole looking for a place to stay. We didn't bother picking and choosing, we just booked into the first lodge we came to. Lucia, as usual, had her bath but this time I was defiant and refused. Bath times were becoming increasingly annoying. One, I had never washed so much in my entire life and two, I was looking forward to the day when I could have a nice hot bath on my own. Up to then, all I had was leftover chilly ones and by the time I massaged my stiff neck from looking at the wall, I was all shrivelled up with the cold.

"I feel better now, knowing Brynmoroc is not my father," said Lucia, getting into her sleeping pouch. "What about you?"

I was happy too. All we needed now was a peaceful night's sleep.

"Why do you think Roslyn and Sophia turned into those tree creatures instead of fire-throwing dragons?" She then asked.

I had no idea only that perhaps there was no such thing as fire-throwing dragons. But there again, fire was a silly thing to ask for. We'd have been burned alive. The mares knew what they were doing and did a magnificent job of it too.

"Wasn't it a terrible noise," said Lucia, holding her ears. "All that cracking and crashing. We were lucky to get out from there in one piece and by the way Gwydion, did you hear what Brynmoroc called me? A miserable, pathetic wimp. That's what he said, and that my parents were old winkle pickers and grandmother a witch. The cheek of him! Why I wish I could have given him a right good slap."

With her lovely Spanish accent, she sounded so angry that I had to laugh and say something funny to calm her.

"Yeah, and I'm the son of a tramp. It was a terrible thing to say. I even felt like slapping the cheeky twerp myself."

That did the trick, and just like she usually did, burst out laughing.

"Oh Gwydion, I love you," she said and rolled over and kissed me.

I quickly jumped up, pretending I'd heard something, not to kiss her back.

"Ah, it's okay. It's just next door, that's all," I said, lying back down.

"Oh, you gave me such a fright then, Gwydion. I thought it was Brynmoroc. What do you think he'll do when he finds that we have escaped?"

"Nothing tonight," I replied. "But I've asked Roslyn and Sophia to keep all eyes open just in case."

"Well, at least we know he's not my father Gwydion, but what about the woman in the vision?"

The only explanation I could come up with was that part of the vision may have been true with the little girl being Lucia and the woman her mother. The rest, Brynmoroc cleverly conjured up to deceive us. We both agreed my theory was probably right and wished each other goodnight. Lucia slowly drifted off to sleep, but not so for me. I was tormented all night again, unable to sleep. Not so much from worrying about Brynmoroc, but thinking of Lucia. At that moment in time, going by Brynmoroc's outburst, if being true, not only did I now know that Lucia wasn't his daughter, I also knew by his ridiculing descriptions, our parents were not the same. This told me that we couldn't be brother and sister, but I was still baffled, baffled, because we were born on the same day and also happened to be on the same mission. The whole thing was just a mess, and it was killing me. To make matters worse, she was in love with me and I, with her.

The promise I made to Bleddwyn was the only promise in my entire life that I wished I had never agreed to. I was now thinking that the mission was looking more and more like a rotten conspiracy. Once again, I felt we were being conned by both wizards conspiring together, using us not as pawns, but knights, zigzagging around the world seeking out the dead king's hidden treasure. The dead king being the all-powerful Vindaguar; his treasure, the enchanted jewels. There again, if they were conspiring to gain possession of the gems, then why were they trying to prevent us from finishing the mission? Another thing puzzling me was, if a wizard cannot directly use his energy to harm us, then conjuring up creatures to attack us is the same thing, isn't it? If Bleddwyn is in with Brynmoroc, then why have Roslyn and Sophia saved our lives, numerous times?

All these questions and more ran through my mind for ages, none of them making any sense. I was so mixed up; it made my head hurt. So, before I eventually dropped off to sleep, I made up my mind that I was going to ask Lucia a little more about her family.

# Chapter 16

The next day we took a stroll around the town and found the house where Luis Pasteur was born and lived. It was a strange feeling peeping through the windows, thinking that such a genius once lived there.

"Ah well, perhaps we'll be famous one day too!" said Lucia with a laugh.

I said being arrested would be more than likely if those policemen caught up with us. It was time we cleared off from there and quickly too. There was a train running to Valdahon, which was handy, so we bought tickets. It was a cold, draughty old boneshaker, but we didn't mind. It was a change from riding the range.

"Okay, let's find out a bit more about Lucia's parents," I thought as we settled down.

"Lucia, you say you were reared by your grandmother in a mansion somewhere around Murcia. Do you know anything about your parents at all? Did your grandmother ever speak of them?

Were there any memoirs or portraits around the house?"

"All I know is that my mother married a Spanish Admiral, and it was on their fourth anniversary that during a terrible storm, they were lost at sea."

"What about your grandfather, did you ever know him?" I then asked.

"Why are you asking me all these questions, Gwydion? Are you testing me, thinking that I am hiding something from you?"

"No, no!" I quickly replied. "I just wondered if you knew your grandfather because you have never mentioned him, that's all."

"That's alright then," she said sadly. "I don't want you thinking that I have been lying to you. No, I didn't know my grandfather either, but I have seen his portrait. My grandmother keeps it in her bedroom. She met him in the local hospital of Murcia where she was a nurse. He came in as a patient with a broken leg from an accident up in the mountains. They were married three years later, but he died from ill health ten years after. That's all I know except that he didn't look as if he was Spanish, more like an American or an Englishman. When I queried my grandmother about him, all she would say was, "Oh, he was just my knight in shining armour."

I didn't learn a lot, only that her grandfather sounded suspicious. Suspicious because my Granddad had a slight limp, but that was something I quickly dismissed as ridiculous to even think they were one and the same.

"You can tell me more about your parents now?" She asked, shaking my arm.

I was about to make up a story but got lucky; the train stopped to let some cattle cross the line. They were not in any hurry, so it was at least fifteen minutes before we set off again.

It was a sunny, late autumn day and with the warm sun shining in through the window, we both fell asleep and didn't wake until the train jolted and stopped. We had now reached the small town of Valdahon where we bought more clothes and camping gear. With that done, we were soon hitched up to a new trap, leaving Valdahon behind us.

It was way past mid-afternoon and with no sign of Brynmoroc, we stayed up in the hills overlooking a town called Morteau. There were vast amounts of burnt-out tree stumps in the area, indicating that there must have been a raging fire sometime in the past. After discussing our next move, we camped a little closer to the town, spending the night alongside a river with our two hounds watching over us.

It rained most of the night and it was still raining when the hounds woke us in the morning. They were probably worried about the river that had risen considerably during the storm. Breakfast was the first thing on our minds now. So after feeding the mares, we set off into town, found a small cosy little café and enjoyed a lovely couple of rounds of toast. The owner was pleasant and spoke English. When I asked about Saut Du Doubs, I was warned that at that time of year, the falls could be raging from floods further on up country. Other than that, the beautiful colours of late autumn in that area would be spectacular.

We knew that the quickest way to the falls would be off-road, across country. The rain had eased, so we gave the trap to an elderly woman and headed out on horseback. Lucia was happily riding Sophia, making my ride more comfortable. I was keen to get to the falls before midday because after recently upsetting Brynmoroc, we were expecting a whole load of trouble from him now.

After three hours of tracking over hills and wide rivers, we finally arrived on top of the falls well before noon. Standing alongside the waterfall, Lucia pointed out the rock where the jewel was situated. The rock wasn't as large as she first thought, but big enough to see a thundering fall of water crashing its way down over it. Even more intimidating was the frightening drop of death into the pool below.

"How am I ever going to get over there, without flying?" I thought.

It looked like a truly formidable task. In fact, once again, it seemed impossible. We planned to wait until early the following morning and hopefully by then I would have thought of a way to reach it. I was doubtful, for it was right in the middle of a thunderous waterfall. Our first objective was to find somewhere to protect our backs from Brynmoroc. The only place was where an oak tree had fallen across smaller trees. I didn't know how my cape could help us against

Brynmoroc, but I put it on. So with our two hounds beside us, we sat against the tree, shields out, waiting for something to happen.

"What's that noise?" Lucia asked as I was going to ask the same question.

I wasn't sure, but it sounded like a whole lot of birds, and they were getting closer, too close. Within minutes, the sky was black with crows, and we were under attack by hundreds of them. All we could do was cover ourselves as they bounced off our shields, lying dead on the ground. They were suicidal, dive-bombing us, trying to make us drop our guard. Others were pecking our legs and arms while the hounds tore at the crazed birds. This went on for ages and was becoming unbearable until the sound of gunfire rang out. With that, the birds took off and disappeared back to where they came from.

"Good grief, Lucia, are you alright?" I asked, looking at her terrified face.

"I'm okay, but my legs are sore from those horrible things pecking me. What were those bangs that scared them away?"

"They were guns shots, look?" I replied as two men came running towards us.

I didn't know what they were saying but going by their expressions, they were asking if we were okay. When they realised that we were foreign, both men shook their heads and made signs as if they were saying that they had never seen anything like it before. After moving well away from all the dead birds, I thanked them by shaking their hands and offered to make them coffee. They said non, shook our hands again and walked away, talking to themselves.

"What are we going to do now?" asked Lucia, rubbing her legs and ankles.

It looked as if more rain was coming and probably Brynmoroc too. I quickly conjured up another carriage alongside the oak tree and had our hounds on guard. I was dying for a coffee, but it was too wet to make a fire. Then, looking out of the window, I saw a huge flash and heard a crack of thunder, followed by a familiar voice in the distance.

"Gwydion, my son, Brynmoroc is giving you a chance to save yourselves. Give him the staff, forget the mission. It was selfish of me to involve you in such a life-threatening ordeal. Once he has the staff, he will leave you in peace."

It sounded like Bleddwyn, but I thought it was probably Brynmoroc, so we stayed put, saying nothing, waiting to see what happened next. Nothing did until an enormous dark cloud turned the sky black. Then, 'boom' went a massive explosion directly above us. Another boom' and down came thunderous rain. It was so intense that it sent us, carriage and all, hurtling over the top of the waterfall down into the pool below. The force with which we hit the water, stunned me for a moment. I was groggy but conscious enough to know that our carriage was bobbing around with water coming in fast. I looked for Lucia and saw that she had been thrown out and was now floating face down in the water. I was almost out of the window when the carriage tipped upside down;

sinking to the bottom with a bump. I was struggling to hold my breath but managed to swim out and up to the surface. Without hesitation, I swam over to Lucia, turned her over and managed to get her out onto the bank. I led her on her stomach and began pumping her back until she started coughing and spluttering.

"Thank Goodness," I said as she began to breathe. She was breathing okay but unconscious. Sophia swam over to me, holding my staff in her mouth with Roslyn following behind carrying my bag. Lucia was wet, cold and white as a sheet. I needed to warm her until she regained consciousness. My immediate thought was to have Roslyn as a small bear inside a large stagecoach. That's what I did and gently led Lucia beside Roslyn on the bench seat. It was about fifteen minutes before she woke screaming, pushing Roslyn away.

"It's okay. It's only Roslyn," I said and she hugged me. She was groggy but still managed to ask if I was alright.

"Am I alright!" I replied in disbelief. I'm okay, but what about you? How do you feel, because you were knocked unconscious for a while."

"I'm alright, but my head hurts. Where's Soph…?" Was all she could say before closing her eyes.

I let her sleep while I broke off the back luggage compartment and the roof rack to make a fire. Everything we had, except my leather bag, was at the bottom of the pool; clothes, food, oil, and even the matches were down there. It was a stroke of luck that Lucia told me always to keep a flint handy in my pocket; otherwise, I wouldn't have been able to light a fire. To start the fire, I snipped off a clump of Roslyn's fur, and after a few attempts, I got a nice little fire going. Lucia was still asleep, so I stripped down to my long johns and dried my clothes the best I could. My journals were okay because my leather bag was tied up and waterproof. The next thing now was Lucia's clothes.

"Gwydion, where are your clothes?" said Lucia, in shock after waking.

"Here they are," I replied, handing them to her. "If you change into them, I'll dry yours before we run out of wood."

I went outside to let her change while I put on my cape. I had forgotten how strong I was when wearing it. Amazingly, this enabled me to break up the driving shafts with ease. Lucia handed me her wet things and within an hour, we were back in our dry clothes, but hungry.

"Oh, my head is aching and I'm hungry, Gwydion, Do you think there are nut trees around here?"

The sky had cleared, so with Roslyn back as a hound, we went off in search of food. It was tough climbing back up the side of that steep waterfall until Lucia suggested holding onto Roslyn and Sophia's tails. Ha-ha, they didn't mind and we thought it hilarious, but a lot easier. After reaching the top and as the sun beamed through the trees warming us, the birds began to sing. We searched around and collected a few wild mushrooms and some watercress on the side of a stream.

"That will do us nicely, said Lucia. "There is no need to cook mushrooms, but if you want to make a fire, we can bake them on the cinders?"

The wood was too damp to make a fire, which meant, that we had to sit down and eat our makeshift meal raw which surprisingly turned out to be okay. It was much needed to stop our tummies from rumbling.

With nowhere to sleep now and no sleeping bags to keep us warm, I suggested asking for one of those covered wagons and two large cuddly teddy bears to cuddle up to. Lucia laughed, then held her aching head.

"You mean Roslyn and Sophia, don't you? Yes, that sounds like a good idea, as long as they don't have fleas. I don't want to be scratching all night."

That made me laugh, and after summoning up a cosy wagon with the two brown bears' sound asleep inside, we joined them.

At about six o'clock, before the sun went down, I brought my journals up to date. The corners were a little damp, but they were okay. Of all the things we lost in the pool, I was happy we didn't lose my bag. The bag wasn't one hundred percent waterproof as I thought, but I had it wrapped so tight that everything stayed dry enough. Roslyn must have known how vital it was to me and Sophia also knew how much we needed my staff.

It was getting dark now, and without fire and food, we decided to bed down and think about reaching that sapphire. So, while lying up against two soft, warm bears, we covered ourselves with my cape. Although they were to be our bed, they were also staying awake, keeping guard. Thinking of a plan was just a waste of time for whatever we came up with was so ridiculous, we ended up in fits of laughter. In the end, we cuddled up and fell asleep, gently rocked by the rhythmic breathing of the bears.

In my slumber, I had a dream that awakened me. I now had an idea of how to reach the jewel. It was a crazy one, but one that just might work. I went back to sleep chuckling to myself, wondering what Lucia would think of it.

"What! An octopus," she exclaimed when I told her in the morning. "Oh Gwydion, that's crazy. It was bad enough with a scorpion, never mind an octopus. I don't know if I'll be brave enough."

"You don't have to come with me," I replied. "I'll use Sophia, Roslyn can stay with you."

She sighed with relief, "Well, that's okay then, but do you think it will work?"

"Well if it doesn't, I'll be in for another dip in the pool. So be ready to fish me out, won't you," I replied and laughed.

"That's not funny, Gwydion," she said, slapping my arm. "Don't say things like that. I'm worried enough about you now."

"Oh, you know me," I said. "I was only joking to make you laugh. Sophia will never let me fall. Don't worry about me. I'll die when you do. We'll die together."

"Oh, that's a creepy thing to say, Gwydion!" She retorted and frowned.

"Yeah, I suppose it was?" I said. "I don't know what made me say that, but it was a nice thought, eh? Besides, I couldn't imagine life without you now."

"Do you really mean that?" She asked, looking lovingly into my eyes.

I did, but after realising what I said and as she was about to kiss me, I pretended that I heard something, which made her grab my arm.

"What! Where? What was it? Is it more creatures? Oh, no, not again!"

"It's okay. Just the trees creaking," I replied, but under my breath, I was saying, you fool Gwydion, think boy, will you?

It was eight o'clock and not a soul in sight, so I decided to go ahead with my plan because noon would come around quickly enough. Roslyn and Sophia were now back as hounds, and as you know, although they couldn't speak, they were able to understand me. I told Roslyn to stay and look after Lucia while Sophia and I searched for the sapphire.

I didn't want to lose my staff, so I secured it to my arm with my belt.

"Okay, Lucia let's do it," I said, raising my staff. Then as Sophia shook herself excitedly, probably with the thought of being an octopus, in a moment, she was one. She was enormous, at least fifty or maybe sixty feet radius and her body, was easily seven feet tall. Yes, Sophia was awesome, but I must admit, she was also a terrifying sight, not only for Lucia but for anyone else who was to meet her. She was the same dark bay colour, but her eyes were now red and bright, and as she rose, her mouth was a horrible sight, one you wouldn't want to get too close to.

"Thank goodness she's mine," I said to myself.

Yes, she truly was a mean-looking creature, and as she crawled her way into the river, holding me high in the air, it was such an incredible and weird feeling.

"Be careful Gwydion! You might drown. Oh please don't drown Gwydion," shouted Lucia as Sophia crept along the riverbed to the falls.

"There she goes again," I said as we crawled even closer to the edge.

I looked over at her once more and waved. She was still shouting, but with all the noise I couldn't hear a thing. It was just as well for she was only making me nervous.

"Grief!" I shouted as Sophia began to lower me down over the raging falls.

Down, down, down I went as she uncurled her long tentacle. I was clear of the water but soaking wet from the spray, making it difficult for me to see, but I could just about see Sophia's eyes above me. When I reached the rock, she stopped and held me out a few feet away from it. I stayed there studying the rock for quite some time, but once again, the spray of water was making it so hard for me to focus. It was only after the sun came out from behind a cloud that I finally saw a flash of blue light. It was the sapphire, set in the very point of the jutting rock. It was big, larger than all the other jewels. With a bit of a struggle, I managed to place the base of my staff onto the sparkling gem. The moment I did, a huge and almost blinding flash lit up the whole waterfall for many seconds. As I watched the colours race up and down my staff and stop, I sighed with joy and signalled to Sophia to pull me up. I was happy now and looking up at Lucia, who was standing on the rocks above, waving like mad. Then, as Sophia slowly began to crawl her way back up, I suddenly felt her grip on me loosen, and as I began slipping from her grasp, I shouted, "Sophia!"

I managed to hold on to her, but it was of no use because we were both falling through the pounding water. I remember hitting the pool below but nothing more until I found myself looking up at the same hunter who saved us from the crows. Then BANG, a shot rang out, and as I sat up, I saw Sophia. She was semi-submerged. Then, as I watched her eyes slowly closing, she raised one of her tentacles as if to wave goodbye, then spread out, lifeless across the side of the pool. The hunter and his partner had shot poor Sophia, thinking she was going to kill me. The man pointed up to Lucia, who was desperately waving. He then made signs with his hands, rubbing them together as if he was excited about his catch. He uttered something and quickly ran over to his pal who by this time, was poking poor Sophia, making sure that she was dead.

I was shattered, and as I looked up at Lucia, who now seemed to be on her knees, I shook my head in disbelief. It was terrible, and the sight of those rotten men laughing at Sophia sickened me. I still had my staff tied to my arm, so I thought I had better get away quickly, back up to Lucia. I was a little wobbly standing but managed to make my way into the woods, out of sight. I looked around and saw that the men were now busy with the impossible task of roping Sophia into the side of the pool, which had now turned black.

I turned away and made my way up the side of the cliff to Lucia, who was also devastated.

"Oh, Gwydion! Gwydion! Oh, Gwydion!" She sobbed, putting her arms around me.

I gave her a little hug saying that we had to get away before more people came. I had Roslyn back as herself and lifted poor sad Lucia onto her back, picked up my bag, climbed up behind her and away we went, back the way we came.

Far enough away, we took shelter in the woods and sat down on a large rock, shaking our heads, still in a state of disbelief.

"Ah, poor Sophia, that was terrible Gwydion, wasn't it?" Lucia said sadly.

I shook my head again, and as she squeezed my arm, I tapped her hand saying that, yes, it was a shame, but we couldn't blame the men. They probably thought the octopus was going to swallow me up. It was sad, and we were going to miss her, but we couldn't afford to dwell on her any longer. Right now, we needed food supplies to enable us to venture on with our mission, which was the next thing I asked.

"I meant to tell you last night," she replied. "But I thought I would wait until you collected the sapphire. We are off up into the mountains of Austria next. Somewhere way up in Johannesburg Mountain is where the tanzanite jewel sits. I'm not sure where the amethyst is, but as soon as we find the tanzanite, the knowledge will come to me."

I was happy with Austria because it wasn't too far away. Remembering my geography from school, I knew that Johannesburg, especially at that time of year, would be covered in snow. Unfortunately, I had no map now and was going to rely on Lucia to guide us until I bought one. I had no watch either, and as there was a storm brewing, I couldn't tell the time from the sun, but it was probably way past noon and we had to get ourselves ready for the wizard. He was bound to be crazed with rage now and would do everything he could to capture Lucia and of course, my staff, being his main objective. I put on my cape, and with Lucia staying close beside me, I began snapping off branches to make a small barricade on both sides of us. We had not long finished when, with our backs against a large oak tree, there was a mighty roar and a loud thumping noise not too far away. We grabbed our shields in time to see a black hairy gorilla, well over six feet tall, charging through the trees, stopping a few yards away from us, beating his chest. I held my shield towards him, but it appeared only to make him angrier. Maybe it was because he could see his reflection, thinking it was another gorilla or he just didn't like the look of himself. Either way, this time the shield wasn't holding him back because he charged towards me. With my cape, thankfully on, I was hoping that I could match his strength. So I braced myself, and as I stood fast against the tree, the gorilla ploughed into me. In the collision, my shield and staff were knocked out of my hands. For some reason, the gorilla was disorientated now and staggered back groaning. Realising my shield was of no use to me, I looked for my staff, but it was in our barricade of branches, out of reach. The gorilla backed further away, shaking his head to regain his senses. I felt that we were probably matched for strength, but in a physical battle, he would rip off my cloak, leaving me weak. My staff was my only hope, but unfortunately, as I was moving the branch it was lying under, the beast was ready to charge again. I swung around with the branch and advanced towards him. The branch was big and strong, so at that moment in time, all I could think of was to poke and try to keep him away from me. This was a waste of time because the raging animal caught hold of the branch, and I found myself involved in a tug of war. Eventually, I managed to ram him against a tree, making him let go.

Lucia, who was crying behind me, wasn't helping much. I was worried about her and couldn't think straight. In an unexpected battle with no prepared strategy in mind, all I could do was mindlessly thrash and poke the gorilla continuously. I manage to keep him at bay, but he wasn't showing any signs of giving up. Then out of the corner of my eye, I saw a flash and as I glanced I saw the tall gleaming figure of Brynmoroc. By now Lucia had picked up my shield and had both of them in front of her. Unfortunately, because I had taken my eye off the giant ape, he was on me like a flash, knocking me to the ground. In his eagerness, he stumbled over me and fell. This enabled me to quickly get to my feet and face him. I had lost my branch in the impact, so as he rose, I swung a punch and caught him on the side of his jaw then kicked him square in the chest. The blow didn't affect him much, but the kick made him reel backwards into the barricade groaning as if trying to catch his breath. The kick had probably winded him.

My concern now was for Lucia, but there was nothing I could do for her. I had my own safety to think of and the only way I was going to stop this gorilla, gruesome as it may sound, was to kill him because he had vice versa on his mind. I had no weapon and no time to look for one. The only weapons I had were my hands and feet, but that was just as long as I had my cape on. I remembered reading that gorillas' were afraid of lizards, but without my staff, I couldn't change Roslyn into one. The savage-looking gorilla soon recovered and sprang at me, showing his greenish-brown stained teeth. I caught him as he leapt and fell backwards with him on top of me and as we rolled over and over, I tried to stop him from biting me, this being his main objective. So with my cape getting wrapped around my neck, I knew

I had to get up and rearrange it before I lost it. I was a dead man if I didn't. Luckily enough as I poked my finger in his eye it made him lose his grip and I rolled him off me. He gave out a painful cry, and I quickly got to my feet. The gorilla had rolled over onto a splintered branch which I could see had pierced his side. My cape was hanging off me now, and I could feel my strength beginning to drain. In the middle of me trying to adjust it, the ape made another rush towards me only to stop as the heavens opened and it began to pour down with rain. He took one more look at me, turned and hobbled his way back into the woods. At first, I thought the gorilla had left because he was in so much pain, but to my bewilderment, it looked as if he didn't like the rain because as he scuttled away, he was covering his head with his hands, vigorously shaking himself. Either way, I didn't care just as long as he didn't come back. All through my battle with the gorilla, I was constantly aware of flashing and loud cracking all around me. I could only assume that it was Brynmoroc attempting to abduct Lucia and grab my staff. I spun around to see her surrounded by rocks and all kinds of objects. Then I caught sight of Brynmoroc throwing a large rock that landed alongside her. I grabbed my staff, and once in my hand, Lucia desperately handed me my shield.

It was all about Brynmoroc now and how long he would continue with his bombardment of rubble. His plan was probably to terrify Lucia into dropping her shield to enable him to snatch her like he did Eluciana, but with the gorilla out of the way now, he had to deal with both of us. This he knew was to no avail and roared out, "You fools, what dull miserable fools you are. Why I'll…

Brynmoroc hesitated before saying, "Ah, I'm just wasting my time and energy with a couple of kids. Kiss her goodbye Gwydion, for very soon the day will come when you'll never see her again. Your silly old stick means nothing to me."

It was strange Brynmoroc saying that because he could have easily grabbed my staff. So why didn't he? Or could he? I wondered.

Then as he stood there in the pouring rain, without even getting wet, he gave a deep wicked laugh and in amongst a huge flash and a ball of flames, he was gone.

Lucia collapsed, passing out with exhaustion. I gently picked her up and sat her against a rock until she came to her senses.

"Thank goodness. Is he gone and that old gorilla thing? He was horrible?"

"Well, we are still here, aren't we? So they must be," I joked, wiping her muddy forehead.

We were soaking wet and had no way of drying ourselves until the sun came out. I was confident that Brynmoroc wouldn't be coming back, but I wasn't sure about the gorilla. As soon as Lucia felt better and the rain had stopped, we headed out into the open as quickly as we could.

"I feel a lot safer now, but I wish I had a change of clothes," said Lucia, looking at them.

I asked her where we were heading next and how far the next town was. It was west through Switzerland, and it wasn't a town, it was a city, not too far away. So, we headed west, taking it easy until we arrived in the city of La Chaux de Fonds. What we needed now was new clothes, etcetera and there were plenty of stores to choose from. Once kitted out, we found a livery stable for Roslyn and a hotel for us. We were weary and exhausted from travelling and because of it, Lucia wanted to stay a few days. I didn't see why not, it would give us time to plan our route, and besides, if we stayed among company, there would be less chance of Brynmoroc turning up. I paid for a week, and as soon as our heads hit the pillow, we didn't wake until noon the next day.

With no sign of our menacing pursuer, we spent the rest of the day exploring the city, eyeing up different shops. Trying to find someone who spoke either of our languages wasn't easy, but we found a few. La Chaux de Fonds was famous for wristwatches invented by Leon L. Gallet. Leon had passed away over six months ago on the eighth of May, but his factory was still thriving. I needed a watch because my dear Granddad's pocket watch had been ruined back in the waterfall. I took a look at one of the wristwatches and probably would have bought one, but after looking at it, I thought it would only get damaged on my wrist. So I bought a small pocket watch on a chain with a pouch to put it in. The next precious thing I purchased was a map of Switzerland and Austria. After studying, I realised that we were probably in for a challenging and cold time. Knowing this, Lucia thought we should stock up on winter clothing. I agreed, but not until we reached the city of Bern.

# Chapter 17

For the next couple of days, we strolled around the fabulous buildings, lovely cafes' and monuments. We even visited the cemetery and grave of Leon L Gallet. As for his large factory, it was a fascinating sight, but we were not allowed inside.

Everything was going fine, and we were enjoying the rest until one afternoon, disaster struck. While Lucia and I were walking back to our hotel, a riderless horse came bolting down the street. Lucia jumped up onto the sidewalk while I waved frantically in front of the frightened horse, trying to stop it. The horse stopped okay but knocked me down and in the process, trampled on my left ankle. Immediately, I knew something terrible had happened to my leg that made me quickly sit up only to look down at a sickening sight. My foot was now jutting out at an awkward angle. Suddenly the pain set in making me bite my teeth to stop myself from crying out. Lucia didn't help matters either.

"Oh, no! Gwydion! Your foot, look at your foot. It's fallen off," she said in anguish."

If she were anyone else, I would have shouted, shut up, shut up, you idiot. She was at my side in a flash calling for someone to please get a doctor. Then I heard a lady's apologetic` voice.

"Oh, I'm so sorry. It was my horse that knocked you down. Are you alright? Oh no! Good lord! Look at your foot; it's terrible."

That didn't help either, only made me think the worst. The pain was excruciating now, but lucky enough, it wasn't long before a doctor came and had me lying on a table in his surgery. I couldn't understand a word he was saying, but the English-speaking lady, whose horse had knocked me down, could speak his language.

"He's asking if you like whiskey. It will dull the pain," she said with a distraught expression.

I must have swigged half the bottle before Lucia, and the lady held me down for the doctor to put my foot back in place. I couldn't remember much about it until the young lady repeated what the Doctor said after he had finished. It wasn't as bad as he first thought, but there was no walking for me. Not for at least three weeks and then another three or four before I would be able to ride again. I also had to place my foot in a bucket of icy water to bring the swelling down. Lucia asked the lady to thank the doctor and to tell him where we were staying. The distressed lady relayed the message and once again apologised to me.

"Oh, please forgive me. It was all my fault; I should have known better than to bring my young mare into town. I live nearby, so please come and stay with me, both of you. Please, Sir, I beg you. Let me make amends. My name is Cynthia, Cynthia Witney. I live alone, so come stay with me until you are better."

I was grimacing with pain now, and with slurred speech, that was probably difficult to understand, I replied.

"Don't call me, Sir. I'm no Sir, my name is Gwydion, and there is no reason to apologise. It was an accident, no more than that. I'll be alright, don't worry. Take no notice of the doctor I'll be up in a couple of days."

"Uh-uh. Not if I can help it," said Lucia. "And yes, we will accept your kind offer, Cynthia."

"Good, I'll just go and fetch my carriage," said Cynthia. "It will not take me long."

So that was that. I was in no position to argue. Having never drunk so much whiskey in my life, my head was swimming, and I was overcome with the most horrible feeling of sickness. Despite the copious ingestion of whiskey, I could still feel the pain.

Cynthia returned within an hour, and when we were about to leave, I paid the doc, and he gave me two wooden crutches. So with great difficulty, we mounted the carriage and made our way to the hotel. Lucia collected our belongings, and after picking up Roslyn, we headed off to Cynthia's smallholding, outside the city border.

Her home was the most beautiful wooden Swiss cottage surrounded by a veranda from where one could see green fields and craggy snow-topped mountains. Dismounting from the carriage, we could hear the jingle of a bell around the neck of Cynthia's cow. She was coming over to greet us. It's amazing how large a cow's nose looks when you've been drinking whiskey.

It took a while to get me up the steps into this beautiful pristine cottage. Red check curtains and sparkling white nets adorned the windows, and the sunlight illuminated the polished wooden furniture. It was a shame the walls seemed to be going in and out; another problem caused by whiskey drinking. The cottage was surprisingly large with a kitchen, a living room, two sizable bedrooms and one small one.

"I hope you don't mind me asking, but are you married or are you just a couple?" Asked Cynthia.

With all the whiskey intake, I had completely forgotten about our sleeping arrangements. As you know, Lucia wouldn't sleep alone, and because of my commitment, I wasn't going to let her either.

"No, we are not married, not even a couple," I replied. "I've been employed by someone to accompany Lucia across France and down to her grandmother's place in Spain."

"Spain!! And you're in Switzerland. I thought you were going to Austria," said Cynthia, confused and squinting.

"Austria!" I exclaimed. "Who told you that?"

"You did, at the doctor's surgery when he was putting your foot back in place."

"Did I?" I asked, looking at Lucia.

She jested with her hands, nodded her head and said, "Yes, Cynthia's right."

So I had to make up another story that I can tell you was more than ridiculous.

"Oh yeah, I'm sorry about that. It's just that my head's going around at the moment. Yes, you are right. We have to collect something there before we move on to Spain."

Cynthia just shrugged her shoulders saying not to worry and that Lucia could take the large room; I could have the smaller one. My first thought was, why did I come here? I had to get away and was on the verge of making up an excuse to go back to the hotel when Lucia responded.

"It's kind of you Cynthia, but I'd prefer to be in with Gwydion. I can keep an eye on him and his injury. I wouldn't be able to sleep otherwise."

"Well, in that case, both of you should sleep in the large room," suggested Cynthia, much to my relief.

Later, after having time to think, I explained to Cynthia that for security reasons and because Lucia was afraid of the dark, we always slept in the same room, though not together. She just swished her hand, saying that our business was our own and how we slept was entirely up to us. With that solved, the girls, before sorting out our sleeping arrangements, sat me down in a comfy chair with my leg up on a stool, staring into the fire, feeling very sorry for myself until Lucia returned.

"Never mind, Gwydion," said Lucia, trying to lift my mood. "You'll soon be back on your feet, but you have to be patient, and besides, we could both do with a rest. It's November, and there are only two more jewels to reach, and we have five more months to find them."

For supper, Cynthia brought in a lovely meal, but with my sickly gurgling tummy I couldn't eat a thing. I was disappointed because it looked so lovely. To add to my misery, before we retired to our beds, Cynthia brought in a bowl of ice-cold water. The agony I went through placing my foot in that bowl was unbelievable, but I had to put up with it. Lucia, with her hands on my knee, keeping my foot in the water, made sure that I did.

"Behave yourself now and don't be such a baby," she said as I suffered.

I remember crying out in pain, "I'll get you for that, you, you hypocrite you."

She just laughed, "It's what the doctor ordered. It will be alright in a minute or two."

It was more than a minute or two. More like ten before she let go of my knee.

"There now, that wasn't too bad, was it?" she said, kissing my head.

My foot felt better now, but that was only because it was out of that bucket of icy water. It was absolute torture, and it was the one time in my life that I could have cried.

We said goodnight to Cynthia, and she went to her bed. We had already bought new sleeping bags, so after pushing the two single beds together, we settled down. My lovely young

Spanish lady soon drifted off to sleep and slept well, as for me, if I did sleep, it was only for an hour because my tormenting foot pained all night. It was only after Lucia woke and released me from our nightly bondage, did I nod off. Sadly, that didn't last, for no sooner than I closed my eyes, my face was splashed with cold water.

"Okay, wake up Gwydion, it's time for the doctor's orders," said Lucia, flicking me once more.

"Boy, oh, boy! She can look out when I'm better," I said to myself.

My unbearable ice bucket treatment went on three times a day for a week until eventually and thankfully, the swelling went down. For that miserable long week, we got on well with Cynthia as if we had known her all our lives. Although she felt obligated towards me, I still insisted on paying for our keep and filling her barn with dry logs.

I couldn't do anything only sit chatting with Lucia, who stayed fussing over me with the odd teasing joke. There was the occasional odd poke in the ribs too. I got them from watching Cynthia schooling her two young mares. She would smile and wave to me as I watched from the window. This didn't go down too well with my Spanish Senorita, hence the dig in the ribs as she jokingly warned me.

"I wouldn't be smiling back too much if I were you, dear Gwydion, or you might get a kick in the other ankle."

All I knew about Cynthia was that she was selling up her place to live near her sister in Vienna. Why her sister left America, I didn't ask.

It was another two weeks before I could hobble around without crutches, but I wasn't allowed outside. When I complained, Lucia would say, "You'll do as you are told. I don't want you tripping over and hurting your ankle again. Besides, the doctor said you are to stay in for another week."

So now, instead of sitting in the living room all day, I spent time out on the veranda looking at the mountains and sometimes witling away at a stick with my knife.

It was out on that veranda, early one evening that I got a shock, which quickly turned into a pleasant surprise. It happened while Lucia was taking a bath, something she had to do on her own now. Our usual bathing ritual would have been unacceptable. So, as I walked out onto the veranda to watch the sun go down, I saw a pretty young lady, standing there, leaning against the railings, smiling at me. She looked familiar, and as I was thinking about where I might have seen the lady, I recognised her. It was Cynthia. Instead of being in her usual working clothes, she was wearing a red dress with a white flowery cardigan around her shoulders. Her dark hair, which had always been tied up on top of her head, was now loosely hanging down.

"Wow," I said, shaking my head. "I didn't recognise you for a moment. My, you look so pretty standing there."

She smiled and as she walked slowly over to me, softly said, "Do you mean to say that I don't look pretty any other time?"

"No, I didn't mean that," I quickly replied. "Of course, you do. It's just that I haven't seen you dressed like that, especially with your hair down. Anyway, what are you doing dressed up? Are you going somewhere?"

"No, I am not going anywhere," she replied. "I'm waiting for my husband."

"Husband!" I said, in bewilderment. "I didn't know you had a husband, Cynthia."

She came closer, gave a lovely smile, kissed me and said, "I haven't. I'm waiting for one."

That tender kiss took me by surprise, making my legs weak, and causing them to buckle. Before I could do or even say anything, she was kissing me again, but this time, I was kissing her back.

"Wow," I said, finding my arms around her waist. "You are so lovely, but I'm not the one for you. I'm no one, and besides, I have a mission to accomplish."

"I'm in love with you, Gwydion, like no one I have ever loved before," she said, again to my surprise.

I was overwhelmed and couldn't believe what I was hearing. I didn't know what to say, but as I tried to think, I heard a little cry and a door quietly closing. My immediate thought was that Lucia had seen or heard us talking.

"Oh no," I muttered. "I'm in for it now."

Cynthia heard me, and after noticing my reaction, asked, "What's the matter? Is it Lucia? I thought you told me that you were not a couple."

"We are not," I replied, and stuttered. "It's just that I uh, I've made a pledge with my employer not to get involved in a relationship with anyone. Now, if she saw us kissing, she might be thinking I'm going to leave and let her find her own way."

It was a pathetic excuse, I know, but it was the only one I could think of.

Cynthia wasn't very pleased, "Oh well, you had better go and see her then, hadn't you?"

I couldn't believe it, and as I hobbled over to the bedroom door, I kept asking myself, "What am I going to tell her? Whatever I say, she'll never believe me anyway?"

"Are you okay Lucia?" I asked, opening the door. "Did you enjoy your bath?"

She was sat on the edge of the bed with a towel covering her head, gently rubbing her hair. I asked once more if she was okay and did she want me to dry her hair.

Underneath her towel, I could hear a little snivel as she replied, "I'm okay, Gwydion. It's almost dry now."

I wasn't having any of that, so I lifted the towel, and as I expected, she was crying. I looked into her saddened red eyes and could have died. Although I knew what she was probably crying about, I asked her why?

"I heard her Gwydion," she said as she cried. "I heard Cynthia say that she loves you."

I'm not really one for telling lies, but I felt then that I had to. So I pretended to laugh just to find out if that was all she heard and whether or not she had seen anything.

"Oh, is that all!" I said as I sat down beside her. "Well, didn't you hear me tell her that I wasn't interested and that I already have a girlfriend back home?"

"No, I didn't. All I heard was that she loved you," she replied, then frowned. "What girlfriend? You've never mentioned any girlfriend to me!"

I felt a lot better knowing that she hadn't seen anything, so I replied, "Yeah, I know I haven't. That's because I haven't got one, but I've already told you that you were the only lady in my life and the only one I will ever fight for. Surely you remember that, ay?"

She sighed, "Yes, I remember, and I'm sorry, Gwydion. It's just that you know how much I care for you and what you mean to me. I don't know what I'd do if you left me. But you wouldn't do that to me, would you?"

"No," I quickly replied. "I'll never leave you, never. You're my lady, ain't ya?"

I couldn't imagine life without her, either. So I thought of something and said, "Come on, cheer up. I'll tell you what."

She sighed and looked at me. I gave her a little squeeze, stood up and reached into my pocket. I took out that old green and black coloured rock that was stuck to my hand after collecting the emerald.

"This rock," I said as I faced her. "For some reason stuck to my hand and I have kept it in my pocket ever since. Now all of a sudden I think I know the reason why it stuck to me. When you look at it, it looks as if there are two stones in one."

After showing her the rock, I placed it on the floor, picked up a poker and struck it, firmly. What happened then was as I had predicted, it broke into two smooth, odd-shaped green and black rocks. I picked them up and looked at her.

"To prove that I'll never leave you, we'll use these stones and pledge ourselves together. How is that?"

"Well, that sounds nice," she replied but still looked a little baffled.

I picked up my staff and was just about to think up a command when she asked, "What are these stones anyway?"

"I don't know," I replied. "But, what if we call them 'Promesa?' That's what you call a pledge in Spanish, isn't it? So, how about this?"

After placing the base of my staff on the stones, I looked into her lovely Spanish eyes and said,

'A rock that was one, looked to be two
I broke it in pieces and find that it's true
I now ask these stones to bond us together
So we can be as one, forever and ever.'

I suggested that we should now pick one each. Lucia picked hers, and I took the other.

"Now what?" she asked. "Oh no Gwydion! My hand, it's bleeding!"

Mine was too, but I wasn't expecting anything to happen. I was making it all up. I was puzzled, but I didn't let her know it. Instead, I asked her to exchange stones, but as we did, another amazing thing happened. Our blood was quickly absorbed into each of the stones which suddenly disappeared, leaving their impressions in the palms of our hands.

"Gwydion, did you see that?" she asked, looking at her hand. "What have you done? What does it mean?"

I was as baffled as her, probably more so. All I could think of saying was; "It means that we could now look forward to the future and our unbreakable bond of friendship."

I didn't know what it meant. I just said that not for her to worry. The whole thing was beyond me. Nothing was making any sense; in fact, it never did. I was wishing the mission was all over so that we could disappear somewhere, anywhere away from wizardry.

She then lovingly looked at me, and asked, "So we are together now, forever. Does that mean we are kind of married now?"

That made me splutter and cough, pretending that I had something in my throat.

"Ah no, no, it just means that um, well I don't know what it means, only by the looks of it, we are bonded in blood and stone now."

Looking at my hand, I noticed that the pattern the stone had left in my hand was a strange one and mentioned it to Lucia.

"Mine's weird too! But Isn't it strange how mine is on my right hand and yours on your left? That's how we hold hands Gwydion."

Lucia was right, but then, as she beamed a lovely smile, she went into some kind of trance and fainted. With a struggle, I picked her up, sat her in the chair and put her head between her knees.

"What happened?" She asked, after coming around. "Hold me Gwydion; my eyesight is not so good now."

I asked if she wanted the curtains opened, but her instant reply was, "No, no! Just hold me. Don't leave me alone. Let's just go to bed. I'll be alright in the morning."

I agreed but was worried about her and what I had done. I wasn't going to leave and told her so, then for a joke I added, "Besides, how can I? I'll be handcuffed to you anyway, won't I?"

She gave a little laugh and said, "Gracias." I had learned a fair bit of Spanish during our time together and was getting better every day. So I replied, "De nada, bonita." Which means; 'You are welcome, pretty one.'

We slept well that night and didn't wake until Cynthia called us for breakfast. We always looked forward to her tasty cereal with yoghurt and fresh creamy milk straight from her cow. I was happy to see Cynthia carrying on as if nothing had happened. Lucia was happy too and kept looking at her hand studying the impression left by the rock. My hand also had a curious impression, but it was worrying. Worrying, because of something being absorbed inside our bodies. "What's going to happen to us?" I thought.

We endured everything wizardry had thrown at us, but I didn't like the thought of it messing around with our bodies. As lovely as Lucia thought it was, it didn't have the same effect on me. We felt okay with no ill effects, but I was feeling as if Bleddwyn and his staff were maybe taking over us and it was frightening me. However, I had to accept it and get on with my healing process so that we could head on and finish what we had started. Lucia didn't mind staying on with Cynthia, saying that it was the doctor's orders. I had no choice but to stay another couple of weeks though I was worried about the weather. Snow was going to be a big problem, and the longer we stayed, the colder it was getting.

Those next couple of weeks brought us into December, and during that time, for some reason, there was no sign of Brynmoroc. My damaged ankle healed back as good as new, and all three of us enjoyed ourselves together. The only problem was; the more we enjoyed ourselves, the more we bonded. Each time Lucia took a bath, Cynthia would sit beside me to chat and read stories. I used to wonder; how was such a lovely lady living here on her own. I grew really fond of her, but when she moved a little closer, I would keep calm and think about my mission, but, it wasn't easy. You could probably say that I definitely deserved a medal. I would lie in bed thinking that my life now seemed to be revolved around beautiful ladies.

"Who am I?" I asked myself one night. Not long ago I was back home shovelling iron ore and looking after Granddad's sheep. I was wishing that I was back there now. Those beautiful ladies were getting too much for me to handle. Bleddwyn warned me about sweet loving ladies, but he didn't say beautiful.

The day came when it was time to move on and say goodbye to Cynthia. She was extremely emotional, not bringing herself to accept that we were leaving and before breaking down in tears, she blurted out.

"Gwydion, Lucia, don't leave me, please don't leave me here alone. Take me with you, please. I hate it here now. I don't want to live here anymore. I have a buyer for my place and can move out at any time, even tomorrow. I want to go to my sister's in Vienna, but I'm afraid to travel on my own. Oh, please take me with you. I won't be any trouble, I promise?"

"Ah, no!" I said to myself. "Not again. Not another Roisin. I don't believe this."

I looked into her eyes and could see that they were genuine, but was wishing they weren't. I felt so sorry for her, and because of her kindness to me, I felt that I owed her. So I thought for a while and came up with an excuse that might make her change her mind.

"Cynthia, you have put me in an awkward spot. Firstly, we are not going anywhere near

Vienna. Secondly, I've told you that I have an obligation to Lucia and her safety. Ever since we started our journey, we have travelled through many countries and their borders. To avoid lengthy delays and complicated explanations of where why, what and how we have had to bypass their border checkpoint is too complex to explain, plus it's too dangerous for you, anyway. When I say dangerous, what I mean is; if we are caught, we'll be arrested, locked up and probably treated as spies and you know what happens to them. So for your sake, we can't risk taking you with us. I'm sorry, but if there is anything else I can do, anything at all, I will?"

That seemed to do the trick with her, but not without a long, sad face.

# Chapter 18

Setting out with Roslyn hitched to a new hooded buggy purchased from a livery stable, we said our sad goodbyes. I hate goodbyes because I get so choked up. So with both girls crying and hugging one another, it was a good hour out on the trail before I cheered up enough to give Lucia's hand a little squeeze and said although I felt terrible leaving Cynthia behind, it was for the best.

"Yes," she replied. "But it's natural to be sad when leaving someone, especially someone who has been so kind to us."

We carried on heading west to the city of Bern, admiring the scenery as we went. What I had told Cynthia about avoiding border checkpoints etcetera was true. To do this meant travelling over rough territory and running across many rivers and bogs. It wasn't too bad going through France for with the population being so huge, the Parisians didn't take much notice of us, even though we were strangers. That wasn't the case for the many Swiss folks we met on the way. They were extremely curious and didn't seem to like strangers. The only thing to do was to sometimes get off the highway and travel overland for a while. As you know, our incredible transport can develop legs whenever needed, even without me asking. So that was how we reached Bern, fifty miles away.

Arriving in Bern, Lucia wasn't feeling too good and thought it was from the journey. We were not stopping only to buy more suitable clothing for our trek up into the Austrian Alps, but there was a problem. The first store we entered, only had some of the clothing items on display, the rest was out at the back of the shop. Neither of us could speak their language, so it was impossible to explain what we wanted, which seemed to upset the storekeeper. My thought then was to get out of there pretty quick, but before I could say thank you and go, we heard someone behind us.

"You'll never get anywhere without me."

It was Cynthia. Despite my wishes, she had followed without us knowing.

"Cynthia, what are you doing here?" Lucia asked.

"I'm willing to take the risk you were worried about. I sold my place the minute you were gone."

I wasn't happy with the way the storekeeper was looking at us now, so we took Cynthia outside.

"Cynthia," I said, shaking my head. "I told you that we couldn't bring you along. Besides, there are things you don't know about us, and you wouldn't want to, either. Please, Cynthia, I know you were good to us, and I feel that I owe you, but try and understand."

Just then, Lucia cried out, "Gwydion! There is something on my neck. Oh no, what is it? Quick, Gwydion!"

It was only an old tick, so I told her to hold still while I took the thing off.

"NO! NO! Whatever you do, don't pull it off! Shouted Cynthia. "They are poisonous."

Hearing this, Lucia screamed and just before fainting again, cried out, "Get it off?"

I caught her before she fell and sat her down on the porch steps.

"Poisonous!! I said, looking at the tick.

"Yes, Gwydion," Cynthia replied. "Do you see the red ring around the tick? That means there is an infection. We will have to take her to the doctor immediately. Quickly now."

Before Lucia even came properly to her senses, I had her in the buggy and away to the doctor, a street away. We were lucky, for as Cynthia said, the tick was poisonous, and there would have been severe consequences if I had pulled it off. It was a different species of tick from the ones I used to pull off granddad's sheep. This sadly meant that Lucia and I were now, once again, in debt to Cynthia. It was unbelievable, as if it was all planned. I was grateful that she turned up when she did, but now, I had no alternative other than to bring her along with us. How I was going to, I didn't know.

Within an hour, Lucia had developed a fever and was to be confined to bed for at least three days. Cynthia was our spokeslady and booked two rooms in the nearby hotel. When I accepted this mission, the thought hadn't entered my head about other countries speaking different languages. So once again we were lucky Cynthia was there to save the day.

For the next few days, Lucia needed twenty-four hours of care until the fever left her. Those three days were a worrying time for me, and I would always be thinking.

"Surely she's not going to die? She couldn't. I've never heard of anyone dying from a little old tick before."

Finally, thanks to the loving care of Cynthia and a maid, Lucia came through the fever okay. We were now anxious to move on before the snow. So Cynthia had her wish, but with her ability to speak several languages, we thought would come in handy, but Brynmoroc was going to be our biggest problem. It was inevitable that the wizard would be turning up in some shape or form. How Cynthia would react to him and his wizardry, was a worry. Maybe she'd run like a scared rabbit to the nearest Police station, but it was a chance we had to take, though I wasn't looking forward to it. A day earlier, I had told Cynthia that we were heading somewhere near Johannisberg Mountain. Knowing this, and just to give Lucia another day of rest, she suggested taking the Monday train to Zurich. She knew of an all-weather store there with all the equipment we needed for our journey.

The following day, being Sunday, and every other Sunday if we were near a town or city, Lucia would have to attend Mass. Being her guardian, I had to tag along. Cynthia was also a Catholic and went to Mass every Sunday, so on this particular Sunday morning, all three of us went. The rest of the day we spent at the hotel.

Monday morning, we arrived at the train station to take the eleven o'clock train to Zurich. After seeing Roslyn safely loaded into the guard's carriage, we boarded a train packed with passengers who were heading to a music festival. We didn't mind the company, the more people around us, the less chance of Brynmoroc turning up, but that was no guarantee. It was going to take a good two hours to get to Zurich and for most of the way, because it was a music festival, we were unfortunately serenaded by singing enthusiasts. They started okay until a few whiskey drinkers joined in thinking they were better. That's when the fighting began, and it carried on until they all fell over one another as the train stopped suddenly in Zurich.

We were quickly off that train, picked up Roslyn and in the same haste, headed into the busy city streets where it was a whole lot safer. The few stores that were there quickly became swamped with shoppers. Most looking for cold steaks and bandages. We thought we'd stay put for a while until it calmed down. It did, and eventually, the crowd headed off to wherever the festival was.

Cynthia led us to the all-weather store where we kitted ourselves out ready for the wintry weather.

There were no more trains that day, but there was a stagecoach travelling out to St. Gallen at four o'clock. St Gallen was fifty miles away, and further on was the Austrian and German border. Needing to press on, we decided to take the coach, stay overnight in St, Gallen and have an early start in the morning. There was one problem though; with Cynthia along, I was unable to change our Roslyn, so I asked the coach driver if it would be okay to tie her to the back of the coach. I was only going to pretend to tie her, of course. With it being a fifty-mile journey, he wasn't too happy, until I flashed a few coins in front of him.

"Okay, it's your horse, but I won't be responsible for it," he replied, taking the money.

Away we went with Roslyn galloping happily behind, much to the coachman and Cynthia's amazement, especially with her looking so fresh after stopping twice to change horses.

St.Gallen was another lovely city. Every country, city, town and village that we had been through had its own style of houses, buildings and churches, all of them fabulous. I was lucky being rich, for we could stay in all their exceptional hotels, like the one we were now staying in.

That night, while Lucia and I were sitting in our room studying the map, we decided that Innsbruck was as far as we could take Cynthia. From then on, our journey was to be across rough ground, through and over the Alps. We told Cynthia that whether we could even take her to

Innsbruck depended on there being a train or stagecoach to take us. If there wasn't, then we would have to say goodbye, for bad weather was closing in.

Fortunately for Cynthia, stagecoaches were going that way, stopping overnight in St Anton, seventy miles away. Although Roslyn could probably run forever I wasn't going to bring any more attention to us by having her run behind again. So later that morning, without telling a lie, I told Cynthia that just to cheer Lucia up I had exchanged Roslyn for a terrier.

"That was crazy!" She said, with an exasperated expression. "Sell her, yes, but exchange her for a terrier, that was madness."

The coach pulled out at eleven o'clock, and after a couple of stops, we arrived in the town of Feldkirch to change horses. Lucia was still feeling the effects of her fever and was glad to have the hours of rest. While on our way again, I couldn't help thinking once more about Brynmoroc. For weeks we hadn't seen hide nor hair of him and his wizardry. Back when I was injured, we were at his mercy, but he let us be. It was strange, and I was wondering why.

"He's up to something, or someone is, and that's for sure, but what?" I asked myself.

It had me thinking again about the Wizards conspiring together, especially after seeing those rocks being absorbed into our bodies. I felt now that we were trapped and were more like prisoners than missionaries. Were they up to something? I wasn't sure, and as I looked at Lucia, who looked so lovely and innocent sitting there smiling with Roslyn on her lap, I thought, how could I protect her? I couldn't compete with wizards; it was impossible.

My head was in its usual spin, and with my thoughts running away with me, we were pulling up in St Anton before I knew it.

"Wake up Gwydion," said Lucia, shaking me. "You've been asleep for ages. I thought perhaps you were going to start shouting again."

It was well into the afternoon and still no sign of the shimmering giant. It was good in one way, but we still had to be on our guard; sleeping with one eye open, so to speak. Also, there were a lot of hostile-looking characters around. Lucia didn't feel like browsing, so we checked into the nearest boarding house. Cynthia went off for a wander and came back with news of snowfalls in the Alps. That didn't go down too well, but it wasn't going to deter us.

Cynthia was curious and asked, "Where exactly are you two going? I think you are hiding something."

To satisfy her curiosity, I said that we were off somewhere up in the Alps, but if it snows, we'd probably turn around and head on to Spain.

In our room, I reminded Lucia that after sending Cynthia on her way, our journey from then on would be tough going. The only way we could travel; was with Roslyn, but not as a horse.

"Oh no! Not again Gwydionj!" She sighed, "What do you have in mind now?"

I said that wasn't sure yet, but whatever it was we'd have to travel in the dead of night.

"Dear me Gwydion, what a crazy life we are living," she said, holding her head. "My grandmother said that it wouldn't be easy, but we would succeed. I believe in her, so whatever happens, we mustn't lose faith because that's just what Brynmoroc wants us to do."

Yes, we had to keep the faith, and now I had to think of our next form of transport. It was always an incredible feeling knowing that I wasn't a wizard, but I had the power to do amazing things with my staff. Something I was quite happy to perform.

The next day, it took the long journey to Innsbruck before I finally thought up something ridiculously crazy.

"What were you laughing at?" asked the girls, after stepping down from the coach

"Oh, I must have been dreaming again," I said, trying not to laugh.

All the hotels were full of people on skiing holidays, but we managed to find one in a quiet part of the city. Cynthia by now knew that from Innsbruck, she was to find her own way to Vienna. She wasn't very happy, but she eventually accepted it. So after settling in and during a traditional Austrian meal, and because it was our last night together, Cynthia wanted to go out for a farewell drink. We thought it a good idea, but unfortunately, it turned out to be one I was going to regret. Cynthia had been asking around and knew of a quiet saloon, a street away. We left

Roslyn curled up on our bed and off we went, for that farewell drink.

The saloon was a cosy little place and because we were early, picked a table not far away from a crackling fire. A pianist was playing away on a stage, accompanied by a lady singer. Cynthia knew their language, so she went to the bar and ordered a jug of the local Austrian beer. It was smooth and tasty, and we enjoyed it. We were having a good time laughing and joking until, sad to relate, our little happy get-together came to an abrupt halt. A mean-looking chap came over to us, scowled at me and said something that Cynthia reluctantly interpreted.

"Don't you think someone else would like to sit by the fire? Move away, I want to sit there, and why can't you buy your own drinks, stranger?"

He made me feel guilty as if I was hogging the fire, but we weren't. We didn't want trouble, so we moved to a table by the window. Apparently, according to this trouble-making gent, it wasn't far enough. This he made clear as he came over, trod on my foot and pointed to the door. I cringed but said nothing only looked at him and moved my foot away. He then half-stamped on my other, but still I said nothing. It wasn't until he kicked my staff, now a walking stick, that I decided I'd had enough. I remembered my Granddad telling me.

"If you have turned both cheeks Gwydion, then that's enough. You've done your bit, just make sure he does his."

I made sure alright, and he knew all about it, but only after the landlord woke him up with a jug of water. By this time, folk were not looking very friendly. So for the sake of us all, I was wishing instead of thumping him, we should have gone back to our rooms.

"Ah well, it's time for my cape," I thought as half a dozen mean-looking men moved towards us. Luckily, an average size man with black hair and cropped beard stepped in between the men and spoke to them. According to Cynthia, he was saying, "Leave them! They are with me."

The men were still not happy but went away back to the bar and their seats. Lucia said that she had noticed this black-haired gent watching us. She thought he looked familiar but shrugged it off as a coincidental likeness to someone she knew.

"Good evening," said the gent who spoke English. "I am Lord Steiner. I happened to hear and recognise the lovely lady's Spanish accent. My grandmother is Spanish, and I speak the language fluently."

Lucia was quick to thank him, "Thank you, my Lord. We are truly in your debt."

"No, no Senorita. It was nothing. If there's anything else I can do for you, my home is Steiner Mansion, two miles east of the city."

He was very friendly, and Lucia clearly enjoyed their Spanish conversation and his attention.

"What are they talking about?" asked Cynthia pulling at my sleeve.

Of all the languages, she couldn't speak Spanish, so it was my turn to be the interpreter. From what I could gather, they were talking about Spain, and very coincidentally, the Lord's grandmother was born somewhere near Murcia, where Lucia lived. Also, because Lucia was holding my hand, the Lord was asking if we were married or a couple.

"Why is she always holding your hand, anyway?" asked Cynthia tapping my arm.

"I am not sure really," I replied in pretence. "But sometimes I wish she wouldn't."

"Ha-ha, Gwydion," she laughed. "You two are the funniest pair I have ever met."

The Lord stood up, saying that he had to collect someone from the theatre. He shook hands with me, kissed both the girl's hands and bid us goodnight. With his departure, the landlord came over to order us out. We were not welcome there anymore. So we finished our drinks and left.

Walking up the street, Cynthia mentioned that apart from the pest, it was a lovely evening.

"Yes, and the Lord was nice too," added Lucia. "That pest and most of those men in the club work for him on his estate, so we were lucky he was there."

We arrived back at the lodge only to find that we were not welcome there either. Our bags, together with Roslyn, were in the hall alongside the manager who was waiting. If it were not for Cynthia, I would have had a carriage and been away out into the country for the night. We were stumped until a carriage pulled up alongside us. It was Lord Steiner on his way home with his daughter.

"Is there a problem, Lucia? Can I be of any service to you all?" he asked in English.

She told him of our predicament, and he seemed quite concerned.

"You are all welcome to stay with me for the duration of your stay here. I live alone with my daughter Emily."

I wasn't happy, but Lucia and Cynthia seemed to think it alright. So, for their sake, I accepted his kind offer, and we climbed into his large carriage, and within ten minutes, we were driving through an estate to his mansion. The butler was there to greet his Lordship and opened the carriage door. It was too dark to see the outside of the mansion, but inside, I found it fascinating, though creepy looking. There was unusual furniture, similar to inside Bleddwyn's cellar and to add to my eyrie feeling, a long and winding wooden staircase seemed to go up forever. The Lord informed the maid that we were his guests, and to show us to our rooms. Once again, I had to explain to Lord Steiner why Lucia and I slept in the same room. It was challenging and took a lot of explaining before he finally accepted but in separate beds. The maid showed us to the appropriate rooms saying, breakfast at eight. Cynthia was in the room next door and tapped the wall for fun.

The single beds were up against the walls and were big enough for two people. Lucia and I had one, Roslyn, the other. Sleeping side by side in sleeping bags, holdings hands tied with a ribbon was the most frustrating and tiresome thing that I had ever done. Many times while Lucia slept, I would let go, but within seconds, she had hold of it again. It was crazy, and I was once again longing for the day I could be free from my annoying bondage.

"There's something strange about Lord Steiner," said Lucia with a puzzled look. "He told me his name is Morados. Morados is Spanish for purple, and Steiner I'm sure is German for stone. Our last stone as you know is an amethyst, which is purple."

"Yes, strange is right," I said. "Purple Stones! Who would name a future Lord, purple? This is suspiciously like it has something to do with Brynmoroc."

Lucia seemed to think that I was jumping to conclusions and that the meeting with Lord Steiner could have something to do with finding the last jewel. I didn't see it that way simply because for well over a month, for some reason, we had no visits from the wizard. So to me, this coincidental meeting with the so-called Lord Purple Stones had to have something to do with the wizard or even both wizards, probably even back from the time I was knocked down by Cynthia's crazy mare. Whether Cynthia was involved, I wasn't sure, but I was hoping she wasn't. Between those thoughts and worrying about our safety, I didn't sleep well at all, but that wasn't unusual.

In the morning, all I wanted to do was to be on our way as soon as possible, but Lucia had other ideas. She was sure Lord Steiner was genuine and insisted we should stay

"My mind's a blur at the moment," was her frustrating reply. "I need to know if his name has anything to do with finding the amethyst or not."

In my mind, with him being half Spanish, she was just infatuated with him. Either that or he had some kind of hold over her. I noticed that each time I looked into his eyes, my head felt light and I had to look away. As usual, I was worried and tried to persuade her differently.

"We should go now before the bad weather and snowstorms," I begged. "How can I look after you without being constantly at your side? I can't be walking around the house with you holding my hand almost every minute of the day, can I? It's ridiculous; the Lord will think so too. He'll feel uncomfortable, and so will I. Also, if you intend to ask him questions, he's not going to speak freely in front of me now, is he? I wish you would change your mind and let's get away from here."

"I'll be alright," she said and smiled. "As long as you are in the room with me, we don't have to hold hands. Don't worry Gwydion; he's not going to hurt me."

She wasn't to be swayed, only all the more adamant we should stay. Cynthia didn't mind either, so against my advice, Lucia told the strange Lord that we would be happy to accept his kind offer and stay for a week.

Throughout most of the afternoon, Lucia and the Lord sat on the seats in the bay window of the living room, chatting and laughing among themselves. Cynthia, Roslyn and I were there too, but on the other side of the room. I can't remember what we were talking about because I was far away, keeping an eye on Lucia.

"Are you listening to me or not?" Asked Cynthia, punching my arm. "What's the matter with you? Why are you constantly watching her? You said you're not a couple, but if you ask me, it looks as if you are jealous. So come on, speak to me. Tell me the truth, are you a couple or not?"

She was right; it must have looked that way, so I apologised, saying that I was only worried about her.

"Worried about her? Whatever for? Do you think he is going to run off with her or something?"

All I could say was, "No, no! I told you back at your place that I'm responsible for her safety. I'm obligated to take her to where ever she wants to go. As for being a couple, once again, I have also told you that we are not. Now come on, what were you saying?"

"I have forgotten now," she replied crossly. "But what I am now asking is; are you in love with her?"

Without telling a lie, I thought of a roundabout way of answering, but incredibly, instead of saying what I intended, something else came out.

"That's silly. I hardly know Lucia. Besides, how can I be in love with her when I am in love with you?"

"You are what?" She said softly. "Tell me that you are joking, and I'll slap your face."

I was flabbergasted because that wasn't what I was going to say. It was as if someone else uttered those words, not me. What could I say or do now? I just sat there like a dummy with my mouth open waiting for her to either slap or kiss me, but I was saved. Lucia had finished talking and was asking if I was ready to take Roslyn for a walk. That brought sweet music to my ears and my saviour all at the same time.

"Yes. Okay," was my immediate response. "Are you coming, Cynthia?"

"Of course I am," was her frustrated answer, but at the same time, kicked my ankle.

I tried my best to avoid being alone with Cynthia after that, but it wasn't easy. Before we retired to our rooms, Lucia noticed Cynthia looked a little sad saying goodnight.

I felt terrible and was hating who or whatever it was that made me say those fateful words. I wanted to console her, but how could I? On top of that, for some reason, Lucia had decided to sleep on her own in the other bed. Well, that was it for me. Between the misunderstanding with Cynthia and the now strange uncharacteristic behaviour of Lucia, I really felt like taking off back home to Blaenafon.

# Chapter 19

The day after was worse than the day before. At breakfast, Lucia sat on the opposite side of the table alongside Lord Steiner and his daughter Emily. As a result, the now-delighted Cynthia came and sat beside me.

All during the afternoon, the strange Lord and Lucia sat in the same window, chatting and laughing while Emily brought them tea and biscuits. I was just someone sitting by the fire, throwing a few logs on now and then. Cynthia had gone into the city with Lord Steiner's coachman.

During tea, once again, we were all sat in the same arrangement. Finishing off our meal with a glass of wine, Cynthia whispered to me.

"I've bought you something today. If you come to my room tonight, I'll give it to you. I promise not to keep you long. So please come."

I had to think awhile before saying that I would, but for no more than five minutes. She smiled, put her hand on my knee and kept it there while we sipped our wine.

Going to our rooms that night, I noticed Lucia's eyes were weary-looking, so I asked if she felt alright.

"Yes, I feel fine, better now than I have ever been," she replied, slipping into the other bed.

That wasn't how it looked to me. I was almost sure now that the Lord had some kind of hypnotic power over her, trying to get into her mind. I knew he wasn't Brynmoroc in disguise because he would have snatched her by now. Even so, I was still thinking that whatever was going on between the lord and Lucia, the crafty wizard could have something to do with it.

Within a very short time, I could tell by Lucia's breathing that she was asleep. I felt then that I had to keep my promise to Cynthia. So I hid my staff, had Roslyn on guard of Lucia and crept out of the bedroom, locking the door behind me.

"What's she up to?" I asked myself.

Cynthia must have heard me coming because she opened the door before I even knocked. She was wearing a long blue dressing gown, and her dark hair flowed down over her shoulders. I sighed, and she noticed.

"It's alright Gwydion. I am not going to jump on you. Come in."

It was a small room with a comfy-looking bed and lovely furniture, much the same as ours. She had two glasses of white wine on a small round table by her bed.

"Come, sit beside me," she said after sitting on the bed. So I nervously did and took a sip of the wine.

"Now Gwydion, before I give you my little gift, answer me one question. Why did you say you love me when you clearly don't?"

I knew she was going to ask me something like that, but right then, I was afraid to answer for fear of what I might say and what she would do. It was as if I was struck dumb and couldn't answer until she held my hand and asked, "Well, why did you?"

I had to answer her, but once again, I couldn't believe what came out.

"I do love you Cynthia. I really do and have done ever since you kissed me. I love you and want to be with you forever."

I could have died, especially when she looked more surprised than me. I wanted to run away, somewhere, anywhere. Then to add to my amazement, she said as she caught hold of my hand.

"Yes, I know you do Gwydion. I have seen it in your eyes, but you are too wrapped up with Lucia to believe it. You are now telling me how you feel without even knowing it, but the day Lucia leaves you, your mind will be your own again. So, until then, I want you to have this."

She gave me a little red box and when I opened it I saw a three-stoned, sparkling diamond gold ring. In complete bewilderment at what was happening, I managed to say that it was beautiful but was puzzled as to what it was for.

"Well, go on then. Put it on, and then I'll tell you," she said excitedly

I took it out and tried it on all my fingers. The only one it fitted was the third finger of my left hand.

"I can't put it on there," I said to myself. So I pretended that it fitted my little finger and showed her.

"Not that one Gwydion, the next one," she said, pointing to it.

"I can't put it on there," I said, but softly. "That's a special finger."

"Well, am I not special then?" she asked and smiled. "Put it on."

In fear of the wrong words coming out again, I reluctantly replied.

"Yes, of course, you are special. It's just that if I wear it on this finger, it means, it means, well I don't know what it means. But anyway, men don't wear diamond rings like this. It's only women who wear such a ring."

She was quick in saying, "It simply means that I love you; that's all."

So, not to cause an upset, I put the ring on my third finger, but I had no intention of keeping it.

"Now you can put mine on," she said, taking another box out of her pocket.

I had a bad feeling about this and said to myself, "Don't panic; it will soon be tomorrow."

I opened the box to find another lovely three-stoned diamond ring inside.

"Don't worry, I didn't pay for it," she said, holding out her hand. "You did, with the money you gave me."

I then said to myself, "I didn't give her enough money to buy one ring, never mind two. Where did she get them from?"

Trying not to look as if I wanted to throw it away and skedaddle out of there, I gently slipped it on her finger. She looked at it, smiled, leaned forward and softly kissed me, saying, "You can go now if you want. I'll see you in the morning."

There was something about her now that made me want to stay, but I had Lucia to think about. So I tapped her hand and said that I had better go, but as I walked to the door, she reminded me.

"I know you have an obligation to fulfil, and I respect it, but just remember what I said about when she leaves you."

I was relieved to be back in my room and to find Lucia still asleep. I flopped down on my bed, covered myself with a blanket and dropped off to sleep, thinking of Cynthia.

"Wow, she's beautiful, but she must be crazy. Bleddwyn warned me about ladies, and I bet she's one of them. As soon as we get out of here and drop her off, I'll be getting rid of this ring."

It was eight in the morning before I woke, happy to find that once again there had been no interruptions, meaning the wizard's horrible creatures' and such. Lucia was still sound asleep. I gently shook her until she slowly stretched and wide awake. Her eyes were still odd-looking, but she insisted there was nothing wrong with her.

Once again, our breakfast sitting arrangements were exactly the same. So too were the Lord and Lucia's little chats, only this time we were in the study. I was reading a book with Roslyn sitting on my lap; both of us keeping an eye on Lucia. While there, I heard Lord Steiner quietly asking Lucia.

"Why does he constantly follow you around? Does he ever leave you alone? And why does he always wear a cape and have that walking stick with him? His legs seem okay to me."

Lucia's reply made me sit up in disbelief, "Oh, he can be a bit of a nuisance sometimes. He thinks I can't look after myself but don't worry; I'll be getting rid of him, relatively soon."

I knew then that I had to get her away from him and the house, for that wasn't her speaking. I had only known her a few months, and that certainly wasn't the loving, kind character I had come to know and love. I was one hundred percent sure now that she was under some sort of spell.

In the afternoon, we were back in the living room, but this time all four of us were sitting beside the fire. While Lucia sat next to Lord Steiner, Cynthia came and sat by me and of all things caught hold of my hand. Lucia noticed this but didn't seem bothered. Although I didn't want to, I had no choice but to join in their conversations and laughter until the gong sounded for tea.

That evening, I was determined to get Lucia to go for a walk. I wanted to talk to her in private. She eventually agreed, but that was only because the Lord had to go somewhere. Unfortunately, Cynthia came too. It was well after eleven before the Lord came home, and by that time we were walking through the hall ready for bed.

"Did things go well Morados?" Asked Lucia as Lord Steiner came up to her.

He looked at her with an expression that said; she shouldn't have asked him in front of me.

"I enjoyed myself immensely, now goodnight to you all," he replied.

We wished him the same and went to our rooms. Before opening her bedroom door, Cynthia kissed me and said in front of Lucia.

"Good night. If you feel like a nightcap, I'll leave the door unlocked."

"That's just great," I said to myself looking for Lucia's reaction, but once again, it didn't seem to bother her; she just walked on into our room.

"Go on dear, before she locks you out," said Cynthia and laughed. "But you know where to come if she does."

Lucia didn't lock me out; she had collapsed fully dressed on the bed and went sound asleep. I tried to wake her to discuss leaving in the morning, but she wouldn't stir. So I covered her with a blanket and put the lamp on her bedside table. I then led on my bed thinking about my mates and the wizard Bleddwyn.

"Why did I ever let my curiosity get the better of me and go back to that wizard's cellar, and why did I ever agree to take on his crazy mission?"

I was sick of women, and the problems they were heaping on me. Back home roaming the mountains of Wales, I had no such worries. I was free as a bird. With these thoughts running through my mind, I dropped off to sleep until I woke from my slumber by a flash. I was dreaming of Bleddwyn, and it was a flash from his staff that woke me. A sudden fear came over me, making me jump out of bed and quickly put on my cape. I turned up the lamp in time to see what I can only describe as a monster walking through the closed door. He was white and about my size. He had three short arms, a tail, two legs, no hair and his face was all screwed up and ugly. Even more frightening was; I could almost see right through him. He was semi-transparent, so how I was going to battle with a ghost-like figure, I didn't know. I stood my ground, faced the growling creature and called out to Lucia, but she didn't respond. I had no time to call her again because the thing was advancing. I told Roslyn to stay and held out my staff towards the creature, and as I did, I could actually see the force from my staff go right through him, blowing the door off its hinges. By that time he had two hands around my throat and the other holding my arm. Strangely enough, although he was kind of transparent, I could physically feel him and was able to grab hold of his wrists to squeeze them. He let go, and as he cried out, I quickly hurled him back against the wall. I picked up my staff and threw it over onto Lucia's bed. Then in a whirl, he knocked me to the floor, desperately trying to strangle me with one hand while holding my arms with his other two. I could feel the pressure building up in my head now, but I managed to wriggle away and flip him over. By forcing my hands up, I was able to grab the arm he was holding my throat with and squeezed it. He hollered out, and as he let go I wrenched myself free of him and stood up. Before he could make another move, I grabbed one of his spindly legs and slung him against the wall. He was furious now; so was I. I adjusted my cape and rushed at him only to be kicked back against Lucia's bed. I rose to my feet to see that he had now turned a ghastly colour yellow. Then to my horror, he opened his mouth and spat out a snake-like creature that wrapped itself around my neck. I caught hold of the snake, and just as I was about to rip it away, the beast came at me again. I held on to the snake and ran with my head down into the weird monstrosity, sending him out through the broken doorway onto the landing. I managed to unravel the snake from around my neck and crushed the wriggling creature's head. The monster was once again back in my room, pinning me against the wall, strangling me. For some reason, I felt weak and helpless and could do nothing about it. My only advantage was that my arms were longer than his. So I reached up and managed to grab his throat to push him back, and as I did, he cried out and let me go, but this time, desperately clutching his throat. In his agonising state, he gave out a terrible scream and crumpled up into a yellowy-coloured dust, which drifted away, disappearing out the doorway.

The reason I felt so weak was; my cape had come undone and was lying on the floor. I quickly put it on and picked up my staff. Lucia was still asleep. My main concern now was to get us away from there and fast. I was expecting the Lord or someone to arrive at any moment, so I shook Lucia until she eventually woke.

"What's the matter Gwydion?" Leave me alone; I want to sleep," she retorted.

"We have to get away from here now and quickly," I said, pulling back her blanket. "Brynmoroc is active again. Quick Lucia, let's go."

"Are you crazy? I'm not going anywhere," she snapped, pulling the blanket back over her.

I wasn't going to stay another night, so I picked her up saying that we were going whether she liked it or not.

"Put me down, put me down Gwydion. I hate you," she screamed and bit my arm.

"Okay, okay," I said, putting her down. "But we must go and go now."

She pushed me away and ran towards the doorway, shouting, "I'm not going anywhere. Lord Steiner, Lord Steiner, help me, help me Lord."

I caught hold of her hand to stop her, but as she turned to slap me, a pain went through my hand and arm as if being stung by a bee. Lucia dropped like a stone to the floor and lay there unconscious, shaking violently. I staggered back and with my left hand paining like crazy; I looked at it to find that I was now holding the black and green rock that we were bonded with. I dropped the rock and went to pick up Lucia who was now groaning.

"Oh, Gwydion! What's happening? Why was I on the floor? I feel terrible. Oh, my hand, my hand, it's …. What!! Look Gwydion? It's the rock," she exclaimed, looking at her hand. "Oh what's wrong? What's happening? Where are we? I'm frightened now Gwydion."

"We haven't time to explain," I replied. "But our lives are in danger. Grab my bag, leave the rest, but hurry for we have to get Cynthia."

Thankfully, Cynthia did leave her door unlocked, so we rushed in, only to find that she too was on the floor and groaning. We quickly shook her, and as she came around wondering what was going on. I said we were in danger and that we had to leave immediately, even dressed the way she was. Cynthia grabbed her dressing gown, picked up her handbag and followed us out onto the landing and down the stairs. By that time, Lord Steiner, his butler and the coachman were on their way up, talking in Spanish. I gave Lucia my staff and told both girls to stay behind me. I stood on the stairs, facing the Lord who scowled as he spoke.

"Where do you think you are going? Are you running away? You are not going anywhere with the girls Gwydion. They are staying with me."

"Stand aside, Sir? Let us pass, and I'll do you no harm," I said, loud and clear.

"Now listen to me, you little sheepherding fool," demanded the insulting Lord. "The only place I'll be standing aside is your coffin. Those girls are with me now."

I ordered him once more. "Stand aside Sir, or you'll suffer my wrath."

He laughed, "Suffer my wrath, he says. Well, what do you know; he thinks he's a wizard."

He then spoke in Spanish, telling the men to throw me over the bannister. Both men rushed me, and as they tried to grab my arms, I kicked the coachman down the stairs into the Lord then lifted the butler high above my head and shouted.

"Throw me over the bannister, will you? Well, how about I throw you instead?"

He was terrified and screamed. No! No! No! But I just held him there, looking at the Lord, rising to his feet.

"Now, O Mister Lord Purple Stones, let us pass, or the same thing will happen to you."

He took another look at the screaming butler and backed away down the stairs to join the coachman who was running away, shouting in Spanish, "Get him yourself."

I let the butler down but held onto him until we were safely out of the house and grounds. I let the petrified man go and watched him scarper up the moonlit drive and out of sight. I had no choice now but to lift my staff and cry out my command. With that and before Cynthia's startled face, we had ourselves a small coach, lit up with lanterns along with a new pal for Roslyn, ready to go. I told Cynthia to get in and that I would explain later, but she just stood there, stunned and couldn't move. So, I lifted her in and sat her opposite Lucia.

"On you go Roslyn. Head on to the next town," I shouted and climbed in alongside Lucia.

There were the usual blankets in the carriage, so I covered poor stunned Cynthia who was now lying down on the seat in shock. Lucia cwtched up to me, sighed, and as her head slowly slipped down onto my lap, she fell asleep. I gently stroked her hair and began to wonder; why was it that every time I grab one of those creatures' throats, they either crumple up or run away clutching their throats and screaming. In my mind, I was going over and over the battles until through sheer exhaustion, I fell asleep until Roslyn woke us with a whinny. I looked out and saw that we were alongside a river with a signpost saying, Wattens. How long we were parked there I didn't know, but it was now eight-thirty in the morning.

"Where are we?" I'm thirsty. Are we near a town?" Lucia asked, looking out the window."

Cynthia was saying nothing and looked now as if she was afraid of me. So I looked into her frightened eyes and said to assure her.

"I'm sorry that you had to see what you did. I know what you are thinking, but I'm not a wizard, I'm just working for one. Please don't be afraid of me; I will never harm you. Besides, Lucia and I have grown to love you as a friend. Come on, let's go into town. I'll buy you anything you want."

She sighed, wrapped the blanket around her and quietly said okay. Then as the colour began creeping back into her face, I knew that her fear of me had left and I was happy. Lucia, stepping out from the coach, noticed the signpost saying Wattens three miles away. We needed clothes and a few things, and with Wattens not too far down the road, that's where we headed

On the outskirts of the town, we passed by a few large buildings. One of them was a crystal jewellery-producing factory that Lucia thought looked interesting. We rode on into town and pulled up outside a store. Cynthia wrote down what she wanted, and Lucia showed it to the storekeeper. We got everything off her list and added a nice warm coat for the cold weather. As for Lucia and I, we once again rigged ourselves out for our exertions into the Alps. Cynthia was delighted with her clothes and quickly changed into something a lot warmer than her nightwear. Following that, we found an outdoor store and bought a load of camping gear. The last thing on our agenda was to stock up on food from the grocer next door. Being happy with our purchases we headed out of town into the woods where after making up a fire, the girls made something to eat. I could tell by the expression of disbelief on Cynthia's face that she wasn't over the shock of witnessing such an ordeal. So, while we were sat enjoying our fried egg sandwiches, I thought I'd try and explain myself to her, but she wouldn't hear of it.

"I told you before Gwydion; your business is your own. All I know is that you can perform some kind of magic. Something I thought to be nonsense. I have given my word to Lucia and now to you that I will not give your secret away. Besides, apart from silly witch hunters, no one would ever believe me. Now finish your breakfast before it gets cold."

She then noticed the ring on my finger, "You have the same ring as me! It was on my finger when I woke up this morning. Did you give it to me Gwydion because I can't remember?"

I had forgotten about the ring and didn't know how to explain it other than the truth, but before I could, Lucia joined in.

"What did happen back there with Lord Steiner? Why did we have to rush away, anyway?"

They couldn't believe it when I told them all about how Lord Steiner had them both under some kind of spell or hypnotism. It took a while before it sunk in, especially after telling Cynthia that it was her idea with the rings and we should take them off. I was happy and probably sighed more times than her. Also, with her loss of memory, I didn't mention my promise and definitely not any of the crazy things I said to her.

Cynthia, as she struggled, said that her ring wouldn't come off and to my disappointment, mine wouldn't budge either. It looked loose enough, and I could spin it around, but it just wouldn't come off. I suggested perhaps the rings would come off later in some hot soapy water, but

Cynthia, looking at hers, said she liked the ring and was keeping it on. I certainly wasn't happy keeping mine, so I gave it another few twists and off it came. I then handed it to Cynthia and told her that she now had two. She didn't look too pleased, but Lucia didn't mind. So that was that, and now it was time to tell her that after Worgl we had to part company. I thought because of all that had happened, she'd be glad to be free of us, but like Roisin, it was quite the opposite. She was all the more eager to come with us across Switzerland.

"I can speak their language. It will be handy for you. The Swiss, just like the Austrians don't like strangers," she said as she pleaded.

She was so persuasive that if it wasn't for the fact that it was a mission for Lucia and me alone, I probably might have taken her along. So, sadly but firmly, I said it was impossible, but promised that if she gave me her address, I would call in on her the following year. With that, but only after a lot of tears, she apologised.

"Okay and I'm sorry Gwydion, but it's just that ever since I met you both I have grown to love you."

We then packed up and headed on towards Worgl, our last journey together. Travelling along, Lucia reminded me of the time, and Brynmoroc. I looked at my watch, and yes, it was almost noon. I thought we were okay for an hour or two, but how wrong I was. Not having seen the wizard for nearly two months, I had forgotten the positioning of the sun. With it now being winter, the duration of the sun in the sky was shorter, even the time zone. Instead of it being at its peak around two o'clock, it was now hovering around twelve. Then, no sooner than I had told Lucia that we were safe, I saw what looked to be a sandstorm heading towards us.

# Chapter 20

"Surely that can't be a sandstorm in this country," said Lucia alarmingly.

Snowstorms maybe, but never sandstorms. It was bound to be the wizard. I called out to Roslyn to pull over, but she took no notice of me. Both mares were now galloping on even faster towards the oncoming storm. Knowing Roslyn, it was pointless shouting again. Instead, we braced ourselves behind our shields for the impact. As the mares raced on, I could now see that it wasn't a sandstorm, but an army of sand-like creatures. They were all shapes and sizes, running suicidally towards us, waving flashing swords. Then as the mares ploughed into the creatures, they shattered into smithereens. Others leapt onto the carriage only to be deflected by our shields and blasted off by my staff. Snake-like reptiles also suffered the same fate as they ferociously tried to bite us. Lucia hid behind her shield while I battled with the crazed beasties. It was an exhausting battle and to describe the whole devastating encounter, is impossible. Eventually and thankfully, after we were through the mass of nasty screeching non-anthropoids, we stayed going, full speed ahead until well out of danger. I pulled over to check on Cynthia. Surprisingly, she was sound asleep and had slept through the whole confrontation. Before waking her, we dusted ourselves down the best we could.

"Oh no. We are not there already, are we?" She asked disappointedly. "Why are you both covered in sand and dust? And look at you, you're bleeding Gwydion. What happened to you?"

Yes, I was bleeding. The reptiles had bitten my arms and leg. As a result, the blood had run down my hands and over one of my boots. I couldn't be bothered to explain, I just told her not to worry and that I was okay.

"No, you are not," she replied sharply. "Take off that ripped jacket and shirt and those pants."

With Lucia agreeing, I had to do what I was told and stripped down, but no way my pants. After rolling up one of the legs, the girls were horrified.

"You have been bitten Gwydion! What on earth happened? Tell me?" Demanded Cynthia.

"Now don't start asking me what, how and where because it's all over now," I replied. "You can clean me up if you want, but after that, we'll have to be on our way."

The girls cleaned up my wounds and made some temporary bandages. When they had finished fussing over me, they popped outside while I changed. Within an hour, we were away again and arrived in Worgl, pulling up outside the chemist. Cynthia bought enough supplies to stock up our medicine bag and a bottle of spirits for my nasty-looking bites. Lucia insisted that it was foolish for me to travel on without seeing a doctor. Reluctantly, only to keep her happy, we went along to see the doctor who happened to be a lady. She examined me, but before giving Cynthia a bottle of ointment, she dowsed my wounds with spirits, making me clench my teeth in agony. Her diagnosis was that I had to get myself a bath, clean up the wounds again with the spirits and apply the ointment with clean bandages three times a day. I was also ordered to stay put for twenty-four hours and go back for another visit. That suited Lucia more than me. She had already said that she felt terrible, and with her hair full of sand and dust, you can guess what she wanted.

We found the nearest hotel and booked in while Cynthia took the mares and carriage to the livery stable.

In the morning, I felt okay. My aches and pains had eased, and I was rearing to go. There had been talking of snow on its way, so moving on was a must. I wasn't going to call in on any doctor, even though Lucia insisted I did. I felt okay and stayed adamant about my decision.

That afternoon, there was no sign of the Brynmoroc or his creatures, but it was a miserable occasion for us all. We had to say goodbye to Cynthia. She had already paid her train fare to Vienna and now we were saying our sad farewells.

"Well, this is it," I said to her at the train station. "Thank you once again for everything you have done for us, especially me and my broken ankle. I know we are saying goodbye now, but as I promised, we'll see you again, soon."

The train was getting ready to head out, so I helped the sorrowful Cynthia onto the train. She dropped down the door window, and just as the guard's whistle blew, she reached out to me, and I held her hand. Then as the train began to move slowly away, Cynthia softly told me that she would never take her ring off. She then let go of my hand, and as the train chugged out of the station, we heard her shout, "I'll never forget you."

That was another sad farewell, but at the same time I was kind of happy, because we could now continue our journey through the Alps, but we were going to miss her. Lucia, while wiping her eyes, asked me what was next on the gender. I thought we should stay another night. My ankle was okay, but my leg wounds were still a little sore; besides, I needed more time to study our map. I knew Roslyn would surely know her way, but I wanted to see what the route entailed. Lucia thought it a good idea, and we went back to the hotel, not bothering going out for the rest of the day. We stayed in for two reasons, one, we couldn't speak their language and two, we didn't want any more trouble from unsociable people. Although we always dressed accordingly to the custom of every country we travelled through, there were always a few wise guys who somehow didn't like the way we looked. The only time we did venture out was to collect our mares from the stables. I patted Roslyn's pal on the neck and set her free to go back to her world or wherever she wanted to go. Roslyn knew what was happening next and was happy being back as a terrier, curled up on our bed.

After studying the map and before bedding down for the night, I gave Lucia some news she didn't want to hear. In the morning, we would go as far as Kitzbuhel in a carriage. After that, the only way to reach Johannisberg was across country, up and over the Alps, but by night. Before I could say another word, she held her ears.

"No, don't tell me! I don't want to know how we are getting there. It's bound to be something weird and horrid."

In the morning after swapping our dual horse carriage for a single, we headed out for Kitzbuhel, thirty miles away. It was a cold day, but we were well wrapped up as we galloped on through beautiful mountainous valleys. By the time we reached Kitzbuhel, it began to snow, but it was just a shower and didn't last long. So, as the valley roads weren't as bad as I thought, we carried on.

We were now only about thirty miles from Johannisberg and after every mile, the whiter the mountains were. The snow was kind to us and held off until we were approaching a large town called Mittersill, where we stopped under some arches to recuperate. The snow turned out to be just another shower lasting no more than half an hour before the sun came out, making us feel a little better.

We moved on and pulled up opposite a café and went in. The town was very busy with dozens of excited people carrying skis. The café owner, who happened to be Portuguese, said that most of them were tourists on a skiing holiday from Switzerland. Lucia couldn't speak Portuguese but managed to figure out a few of her words. It was now one o'clock, and up to then there had been no sign of our pursuer, so I thought we'd find a room for the day. I told Lucia that we needed to rest until midnight because our next plight was to be in the dead of night.

"Oh, you do say some awful creepy things, Gwydion," said Lucia, after slapping my arm. "It's bad enough waiting for whatever kind of thing you are conjuring up, never mind saying things like the dead of night. That's made me feel cold all over."

With the number of times, she slapped or poked my arms and ribs; I probably had more bruises than I had from all the battles I endured. It wasn't easy finding a room, but eventually, we found a lodge with one left. I wasn't taking any chances, so I made sure Roslyn was on guard at our bedside. We were tired and slept soundly until I felt Roslyn's cold wet nose touching my eye. It was midnight. We rose smartly, and after looking out the window, the town now white with snow. If it wasn't for the fact that it had completely spoiled my plan, you could say that the snow looked quite spectacular. The sky was clear, and the snow glistened as it reflected the flickering light from the street lamps. I turned away disappointedly and led back down on the bed, staring up at the ceiling. I was expecting snow alright and knew the Alps and Johannisberg would be covered in it, but fresh snow I had completely forgotten about.

"Never mind, Gwydion," said Lucia lying down beside me. "You'll think of something."

I didn't know if I could, but what I did know, was that if we had not gone out that night we met old Lord purple stones, we would have probably been on our way to the last jewel by now.

She sighed, then cuddled up to me while I led there thinking. My first plan back in Switzerland was to use Roslyn as a polar bear to cross the Alps until we reached Johannisberg. My choice of travelling by night was to give us less chance of being seen, but because of the soft snow, my plan was of no use. I lay there thinking, but just when I couldn't think anymore, I saw something crawling across the ceiling.

"That's it!" I said to myself, sitting up. "A spider, it has to be a spider."

I knew spiders were cold-blooded creatures and would have a better chance of walking on soft snow than a bear.

"Yes, a good idea," I said to myself again. "Even better if I can give her flat feet. If we get into trouble, I can always use my fly once opportunity."

"Lucia, I've had an idea," I said, gently waking her. "Quickly, let's get dressed, we are off."

We quickly dressed into our nice and warm severe weather clothes. We were not taking a tent. If we needed shelter, I could always have a carriage in a flash; besides, I wasn't planning on stopping long. I just packed a bag with our sleeping bags and two blankets. I carried them while Lucia carried the bag containing our personal belongings and a little food. Creeping out the back, and with Roslyn now back as herself, we slowly made our way out of town. Once in the clear and on our own, it was time to notify Lucia.

"Okay, I am going to ask for something now, but don't be afraid, because whatever it is, it will only be Roslyn."

So, with her hood covering her head and face, and her arms tightly around me, I held my staff over Roslyn. Then, after crying out 'Gofynnaf i chi,' a dazzling blue flash lit up the whole area.

I was in shock for a moment, but at the same time, excited. We were still sitting on Roslyn, but now she was a pure white, long-bodied thick hairy spider. She was enormous with her body about fifteen feet long, and her eight spiky legs were even longer. I looked down, expecting her to have feet, but she hadn't any. She was standing, twitching on the snow without making any impression at all. I felt strange as if I was as light as a feather and had to hang on thinking that I was going to blow away in the breeze.

"Are you okay Lucia?" I asked, after hearing her mumbling.

"Yes," she murmured. "But I feel funny, and I'm not looking, so don't ask me."

I gazed up into the starry quarter-moonlit sky and said, "Go on girl. You know where you're going."

With that said, our amazing spider set off through the quiet and deep snow-covered valley, heading for the impressive Alps. We were travelling at about the same speed as Roslyn normally runs, but it felt as if we were gliding along on a sleigh. My main concern was not to be seen and to reach Johannisberg before the skiers woke in the morning.

Roslyn made her way through the valley of snow, across fields and sides of mountains. There was one incredible moment when she had to walk over the top of a mansion before she could cross a river. That was amazing but worrying because animals were running around like crazy, frightened to death. Looking back, I saw bedroom windows lighting up, but we were travelling so fast, we were away and gone before they probably opened their curtains. After spotting our giant, even a pack of wolves scampered away like rabbits. Yes, we were going so fast that along with the bitter wind and us being so light, we had to hang on for dear life. Strangely, although Roslyn was a cold-blooded spider, her body was actually warm.

Our ordeal went on for an hour until Roslyn finally stopped at the base of Johannisberg Mountain. By then it was four-thirty in the morning, and the sky had already clouded over. It was too dark to look around, so we dismounted; well actually, we both fell off. The reason why we fell was; Lucia wouldn't open her eyes. So as I tried to dismount to help her down, she clung on to me, fell and dragged me with her, but she was soon up pretty sharpish with an immediate request.

"Oh Quickly Gwydion, change her back to herself again. I hate spiders?"

I did, but as a Saint Bernard. She was happy with that and Roslyn didn't mind either. With another command, we had ourselves a lovely little carriage to shelter and sleep until dawn. After brushing ourselves down, we were soon sound asleep with our faithful Roslyn on guard.

Roslyn woke us at dawn with a deep bark making us jump, but it was better than a wet cold nose. The sky was clear, but it had snowed another six inches while we slept. I thought we had better get going before another fall. So we stepped out into about a foot of snow and faced up to a cold and bitter wind. We were now looking up at what I thought was a cold daunting task to accomplish. From what we could see, apart from a cloud sitting way on top, was a mountain covered in snow.

How were we supposed to find the tanzanite or any jewel up there in all that snow? It was impossible. It dispirited me into complete dejection and I told Lucia so.

"You say that every time. Yet we always find them," she replied, holding my arm. "Besides, it's not on this side of the mountain; it's on the southwest side. I wasn't sure until now, but the tanzanite is facing the sun under a line of overhanging ledges where no snow falls. You'll recognise the shape of the ledge by its profile of a wizard, though this profile will only be visible from a certain point."

I looked around, scanning the area, wondering if there were any signs of human life. There wasn't, it was all clear, and with all the fresh snow, there was no way any skiers were coming that day. If they did, they had to be crazy.

"Okay Lucia. Let's get this over with before we freeze to death," I said, holding out my staff.

Roslyn was now back as the snowy white spider and much to Lucia's reluctance; we eventually climbed aboard. Well, that was after carrying her on my back with her eyes shut.

"What's the matter with you? It's only our Roslyn," I said laughing.

"I don't care, she's horrible Gwydion," she replied, covering her head.

I had to laugh because I thought she was fantastic. So with Lucia safely clinging on for dear life, our spider slowly made her way against a perishing wind, around the other side of the mountain into the sun. The sun was lovely, and we could feel its heat until a nasty-looking cloud sailed across it. Compared to the north side, which was completely covered in snow, on the south side there were patches that there weren't, only treacherous-looking rock faces. When I thought finding the tanzanite on the north side looked somewhat hopeless, this side didn't look too bad except for the treacherous-looking rock faces. Johannisberg looked an easy enough mountain for Roslyn to climb, but I had my doubts about the over ninety degrees rocky inclines. It was above these inclines that the overhangs were. Naturally, that's where I assumed the jewel was going to be and more than likely, somewhere near the summit. I needed help now, and because of the wind, I had to shout on Lucia.

"You'll have to open your eyes and help me out. Can you point out the part of this mountain where you think the jewel could be?"

She eventually let down her hood, and after scanning the vast southwest side of the mountain, she shouted, "I'm unable to pinpoint it, but looking at the mountain from here it's somewhere way above that dry patch of rocks."

I asked Roslyn to get a move on before that looming snow cloud breaks. With that, my incredible spider crept her way up towards the rocks Lucia had pointed to. Everyone knows what a spider looks like so when I say we were sat snug in the middle of Roslyn's body, you'll know what I'm talking about. As long as I held on to her hair and Lucia hung on to me, there was no way we were ever going to fall off. Up and up we went with me constantly scanning all the ridges for the profile of a wizard. The snow by now had begun to fall again, severely impairing my vision. We couldn't go on, so Roslyn crept into an alcove where we sheltered underneath her warm body for a while. Lucia by now had gotten used to our awesome spider, and was happy to pat her.

It took until eleven o'clock before the storm eased and blew over. I was now worrying about Brynmoroc and was hoping we'd find the jewel before the midday sun, otherwise we were at his mercy with nowhere to hide. With this in mind, we set out once more towards the ledges looking for the profile of a wizard that could only be seen from a certain position. The cloud sitting on top of the mountain had lifted, but the bright sun still didn't reveal the elusive rock face we were looking for. We searched every ledge, rock face and probably every rock in sight, but to no avail. I was thinking now that if we did find it, it would only be by luck.

"It's hopeless, Lucia. Are you sure it's on this side of the mountain?" I asked.

"Yes. I'm positive Gwydion," she replied. "But we need to stop and think."

We found shelter out of the wind and sat there without dismounting, thinking. We were perished with the cold, and although I had gloves, my fingers felt like icicles. Earlier I had tied a rope to my staff and attached it to my wrist. I was thankful that I did for at that point and time, I wouldn't have been able to. After about half an hour, thanks to Roslyn's warm body, my fingers were coming back to life. I asked Lucia what she thought about calling it a day and maybe call back tomorrow.

"No," was her definite answer. "I think we should stay until we find it. It's up there. I know it is and it's on this side."

"Okay, okay we will," I said. "But when you see this vision of a wizard's profile, what side of his face do you see? Is it his left or right side?"

She closed her eyes for a while, then said, "It's his left side. I see his left side."

"That's it then!" I shouted after thinking. "We should be approaching those rock faces and overhangs from the right. All this time we have been scanning from the left. Go on Roslyn, head on around to the south side, and we'll work our way back from there."

It was freezing now, and with no sign of another storm, we excitedly scuttled across to the south side of the mountain and stopped. Lucia was adamant that the jewel was somewhere here, where there was no snow. So we began our search from about halfway and started crawling up and down creeping more and more, over to the west until we finally saw it. The wizard's profile was as clear as day now. I was happy that we had found it, but that was until Lucia said that the jewel was underneath the precarious-looking overhang. After arriving above the rock face, I found that the overhang was at least ten feet and underneath was a sheer drop of another hundred or more. I remember saying that Roslyn could probably crawl under there, but even though she could, we'd be upside down and wouldn't want to be sitting on her."

Roslyn must have heard me because she began to pace around. It was as if she was making a web or something similar. Then as I was about to dismount, Roslyn reached up with two of her legs, lifted me into the air and threw me over the ledge.

"ROSLYN!!" I shouted as I dangled in mid-air with her sticky thread around me. My heart was in my mouth until I realised what she was doing. She was slowly swinging me from side to side so that I could search for the jewel. I could hear Lucia screaming my name. I shouted back that I was okay. I felt secure now and trusted my spider, but I couldn't help thinking about Brynmoroc. This made me all the more determined to quickly find that tanzanite and get away from there.

"Yes, there it is," I shouted as I swung past it. "I've seen it Roslyn. Take me back, but slowly."

She slowly brought me back until I yelled to stop. It was about the size of a teacup and was underneath the ledge in a crevice on the rock face. It was well over ten feet away, too far for my staff to reach. So, I shouted up to her once more.

"I see it clearly now, but it's in the rock face, and I can't reach it."

As I dangled there pondering, the wind whipped up even stronger.

"Oh, no! Not Brynmoroc! Please, not him," I said, looking around.

Saying that, I saw Roslyn's leg loop down behind my back and she began pushing me under the ledge towards the jewel. I quickly slipped my staff out from my belt but making sure it was still tied to me. Roslyn pushed me in until I was about two feet away from the rock face but not close enough to the jewel. There was no way I was going to ask Roslyn to move me over. If I did, the thread would more than likely rub against the sharp ledge, snap, and that was me falling a hundred feet onto a pile of rocks. So, by poking my staff in different cracks, I eventually pulled myself over enough to grab a jagged piece of rock with my feet. In this position, I could just about reach the dazzling Tanzanite with the base of my staff and as I did, WHAM, a massive flash sent me hurtling backwards. At that point, I thought I was going to die until I felt myself swinging again with my sparkling staff and its glorious colours flashing up and down, lighting up the rock face until it settled. The wind was howling now and I couldn't see a thing from being dazzled by the flash and my staff.

"Okay Roslyn. Haul away; I have it," I shouted at the top of my voice.

How relieved I was feeling her gently pulling me up. Then just as quickly as she threw me down over the ledge, she had me once again sitting on her wet, but warm furry back. Lucia, with her arms now wrapped around my waist, almost squeezed the life out of me as she cried and repeated

"Oh, Gwydion, Gwydion. I thought you were going to die. Oh, Gwydion."

"So did I," I sighed after getting my breath back. "So did I, but I didn't. Now let's get away from here before we do finish up dead. Go on Roslyn, back to the carriage, quickly as you can?"

"Oh Gwydion, I'm freezing, freezing. My hands and feet, I can't feel them," cried Lucia pitifully.

We were both perishing cold and were relieved to be arriving back at our snow-covered carriage. Sadly, because of the blustery storm, it hadn't been an easy task for our faithful Roslyn.

Our hands, fingers and toes were numb now, and we couldn't stop shivering, not even inside our sleeping bags. It took a couple of hours, but after having Roslyn as a small warm and cuddly bear squashed in between us, we were reasonably warm. By now, the storm had passed, the wind had dropped considerably, and the sun was bright in the sky, which was a warmth we eagerly stepped out to enjoy.

"When are we heading back to Mittersill? Soon, I hope?" Asked Lucia.

It was going to be dark in a couple of hours, so I thought we'd wait until then. In the meantime, we would just have to hang around and try to keep warm.

"Okay," said Lucia, throwing a snowball at me.

"Hey, what are you doing?" I asked and scowled at her.

"Keeping warm. That's what you said, wasn't it?" She replied, throwing another and laughing after catching me in the ear.

"Right, if that's the way you want it, take that," I said as I caught her a good one on the bottom as she turned away.

After that a full-scale battle broke out, blasting one another into fits of laughter. Compared to me, Lucia was a good shot. As a result, I was the one mostly splattered, making it even more hilarious for her. We bombarded each other so much we couldn't even throw another flake. With the battle over, the victorious Lucia, with tears rolling down her pretty face from laughing, staggered away to collapse in the carriage. It was great fun, and it certainly warmed us up, even though we were covered in snow.

After recovering from Lucia's victorious battle, we brushed ourselves down and had something to eat. By this time, the sun had set, and it was time to go. Roslyn was ready, and once again, we were up riding our fabulous white spider. It wasn't the dead of night, so to stay out of sight, Roslyn quickly and quietly crept her way up over the Alps and through uninhabited land. Within a mile or two from Mittersill, we were back riding our lovely mare, trudging down the semi-cleared road into town.

# Chapter 21

Back at our lodgings, I paid for a week to give us time to relax and think. After freshening up and leaving Roslyn curled up on the foot of our bed, we went downstairs for a nice hot meal. When finished, realising how tired we were, especially after our exhausting snowball fight, we retired to our room. Lucia went behind the screen to change while I sat on a chair, but as I did, I soon jumped up. I looked, thinking I had sat on something, but I hadn't. It was only after putting my hand in my back pocket that I knew what I had been sitting on. It was my little green and black promesa-rock. After Lucia had finished dressing, I showed it to her and asked if she had put it into my pocket, because I had left mine at the Lord's house.

"No, I didn't, and no it's not mine," she replied. "I have mine in my jacket pocket. I'll show you if you like. I've kept it on me ever since that night. "

I laughed and said. "Oh well, It must be mine then, but I thought it was gone forever."

"What does it mean?" she asked, looking at her hand. "Why did the rocks disappear into our hands and now all of a sudden reappear? And what about this impression in my hand?"

They were unusual stones, probably more like a jewel. I had also been studying the impression left in my hand and had kind of worked out what it was. If Lucia's was anything like mine, it would represent an image. I looked at her hand, and it was just as I had expected. I then asked her to show me her rock and found that the stone had the same image as the impression in the middle of her palm. My stone and impression were also identical, but the image was slightly different to hers, so I mentioned it. Lucia looked at hers and suggested comparing them, but as we did, WHOOSH, our hands joined together like magnets. Instantly we both felt a warm sensation in our hands that flowed up our arms and down to our chests. The stones had once again, been absorbed into our bodies.

"Gwydion they have disappeared again. That warm sensation went straight to my heart. What's it all about?" she asked with a worried expression.

She was asking me something that I had already told her I had no answer to. I thought for a while and came up with something that I thought was nonsense, but it was all I could think of to pacify her.

"Well, it could be that if we are ever separated, the rocks will somehow always reunite us just as they did back at Lord Steiner's. So, if I'm right, you could safely say that it's as we pledged, we'll always be as one, in our red blood and stone."

She put her arms around me and lovingly said, after giving me the softest kiss, "I love you Gwydion,"

She felt so warm and soft that my instinct was to draw her into me, but as I did, Roslyn barked loudly making us quickly let go of each other, only to find her settling back down again. It was as if she was reminding me of my promise to Bleddwyn.

"Did you see that?" said Lucia. "I think she's jealous of me Gwydion. Look at her, lying back down as if nothing had happened."

Although unhappy at being disturbed, I soon realised it was for the best and took the opportunity to laugh and shake my finger at Roslyn.

"You naughty little girl. Or are you telling me you want to go out?"

Lucia slipped on her overcoat and boots, and we headed out into the cold night air for a walk, but only far enough for me to cool down. Back in our room, we slipped into our sleeping bags, and while waiting for my pretty companion to tie us together, she didn't. She was fast asleep with the ribbon still in her hand. I gently took it from her and wrapped it around our wrists, sighing, "Oh, Granddad, She's so lovely."

This promise of mine was really tough, and if it wasn't for Roslyn, goodness knows what would have happened. I turned down the lamp and lay there thinking about my heart-stopping moment when Roslyn threw me over the ledge. It was the most terrifying experience I've ever had in my life and wouldn't wish it on anyone. I then turned, put my arm around Lucia and went to sleep and didn't wake until I heard the clock tower strike and a lot of excited children shouting. I didn't know what they were saying, but I had a very good idea of what it was all about. I looked at my watch and found that it was just past eight in the morning. Lucia was still sound asleep, and as I faced her, she looked so lovely lying there with her lips slightly parted that I just had to kiss her.

"Gwydion!" You kissed me!" She said, opening her surprised eyes.

"Yes, I know I did," I said and smiled. "Merry Christmas pretty one."

"Oh Gwydion, it's Christmas," she said, sitting up. "It's Christmas, and I haven't got you anything."

"Neither have I," I said. "The only thing I had, I just gave you."

She then untied the ribbon, dived on me and said, "Well, here's mine then, Merry Christmas," and kissed me.

I put my arms around her only to be interrupted again by Roslyn.

That made us both sit up, shouting, "ROSLYN." Then as we looked at her and ourselves, we burst out laughing.

"Hurry now, Gwydion, we'll have our breakfast and then we are off to church," said Lucia, excitedly.

All I had to wear was my ordinary riding clothes. Lucia had one blue dress and a shawl that took ages to iron the creases out of. She had no proper shoes, only her riding boots, but her dress was long enough to hide them. So with Lucia dressed, we were soon downstairs enjoying a traditional Christmas breakfast of muesli. Six other guests were staying at the lodge. Two of them were husband and wife from America, and the other four were two French couples, all on a festive skiing holiday. They were looking forward to Christmas dinner at 3 o'clock, but most of all, heading up the Alps on St Stephen's day.

Finishing our breakfast, we followed a crowd of excited people down the road to the Christmas service. The church had been beautifully decorated with bounteous amounts of holly and pine. The smell of pine was so wonderful that along with the service and carols it made it a Christmas to remember. With us now warm, happy and glad to be alive, we headed back to our lodgings looking forward to our Christmas feast. When the gong finally went for dinner, we went down to the dining room. Lucia, compared to the other ladies, felt a little undressed, but she was a whole lot prettier.

After the best Christmas dinner that I have ever had, we all joined in playing different card games, skittles and wooden puzzles. It was great fun, but I couldn't help wondering about poor old

Granddad. I was hoping he was down at the tavern with his pals. Lucia also had her grandmother on her mind, but then remembered that she would probably be over at her friend's villa.

It was passed seven before we went to our rooms, both full of Christmas pudding, etcetera.

"That was a lovely day Gwydion, wasn't it?" said Lucia as she sat in the chair.

"Yes, one I'll always remember," I replied, lighting an old oil lamp.

There was no fire grate in the room, so we climbed into our sleeping bags to keep warm. I was wondering now where we were heading next and when to head out.

"I don't know yet," said Lucia. "I thought after finding the tanzanite, I would be able to see it more clearly, but every time I try, my vision disappears. My grandmother told me that the last jewel would be the most difficult. I'm sorry Gwydion, but there must be a reason why. We'll just have to wait and see what happens."

I lay there for ages thinking about Brynmoroc and his wizardry. For the past two months, we had no more than a few confrontations with him. Perhaps he doesn't like snow, I thought. Although possible, it was highly unlikely. Maybe he was just pretending that he didn't care. If that were the case, he would be hoping to catch us off our guard and pounce. The more I thought, the more I sided towards the snow theory. With a limited amount of sun in the winter and with no snow in their one-dimensional world, that possibility was now looking a lot more feasible.

The following morning we found that it had snowed another few inches overnight. It didn't seem to bother the skiers, for after breakfast they were away to the Alps like excited school children. During the afternoon, there were the traditional Saint Stephen's Day fun and games. We didn't take part but laughed and cheered watching their funny antics. In the evening, much to everyone's delight, all skiers arrived back safely. They joined us for supper where our newfound friends, the Americans, gave us the run-down of their enjoyable time in the Alps.

"Why don't you join us tomorrow?" They asked. "We'll kit you out."

With our experience up on the snow-ridden mount of Johannisberg, especially with my life hanging by a thread, we kindly thanked them and said, "No. No, thanks."

That was another delightful day over, but it didn't end there, we had a few more. Lucia still didn't have any inclination as to where our next and final venture was going to be. I thought it better if we moved on out of the country away from the cold, but Lucia thought otherwise.

"I think we should at least stay another week; it's bound to come to me by then. Perhaps it's somewhere in this area? We have to be patient, Gwydion."

I accepted her advice and paid for another week. I was happy really, for it meant we would be staying for the new centenary year celebrations. There was to be a lot going on with parties, games etcetera. Some folk mentioned that there would also be a show of fireworks. I had heard about fireworks and how spectacular they were, but I hadn't seen them. So I was excited and looking forward to the display in two days.

Those two days were not long coming, and with a buzz of anticipation in the air, we participated in the games and partook of the glorious food on offer. As midnight approached and with the snow sparkling in the occasional light from the moon, the chimes from the town clock along with the glorious sound of church bells could be heard. Not only was it the beginning of a new year, it was also the turn of the century. Everyone was so excited, and as the firework display lit up the night sky with colours of every description, their shouts of pure joy could be heard probably in the next village. It was the most spectacular sight we had ever seen, and undeniably, a night we will never forget.

By the end of our extra week and after the New Year Centenary celebrations, the skiers had gone and we were the only customers left at the lodge. Lucia was still unable to locate the amethyst, but I was determined to move on to somewhere away from the snow.

"Why don't we go to the south of France?" I asked one morning. "I heard it's warm there. Even if it isn't, it certainly won't be snowing."

She couldn't answer and was getting very depressed. I then remembered that during our long week, I had been thinking about the two worlds Bleddwyn told me about. We would be travelling through two worlds at the same time, but wouldn't know it. That's what he said, and the more I thought about the fact that no snow ever falls in their one-dimensional world, I suddenly realised that at that present time, we couldn't be in it. After supper, I mentioned this to Lucia, asking if it would make a difference.

"That's it! That's it Gwydion!" she said, jumping up. "That's the answer. All the jewels have been in the wizards' dimensional. We are in our world with the snow, and that's why I can't see it."

I was puzzled because if it doesn't snow in the wizard's dimensional, how could Vindaguar place the tanzanite here, but then again it wasn't snowing at that point and Blethwyn did say that wizards' also live along with us. Nothing made sense to me anyway, but if Lucia knew what she was saying, it was okay by me.

"Well, at least we know now," I said in relief. "Tomorrow, we'll head back to France or somewhere, anywhere out of the snow."

I felt better now, bought a bottle of wine from the bar and we went to our room to celebrate. We toasted one another with a glass each, then happily settled down to bed with one of Lucia's Spanish lullabies. As she sang herself to sleep, my thoughts went back to the impressions on our hands. I was almost sure what mine looked like, and after seeing Lucia's, it confirmed it for me. Both our images were that of a baby curled up in a womb. I wasn't going to let it upset me because as you can imagine, I could come up with a dozen theories. I put it at the back of my mind and eventually dropped off to sleep, but for all the luck, for the first time, since we slept there, the tower clock woke me every single hour. So just because I had gone to sleep looking forward to the morning, it took a long time coming.

Finally, it was eight o'clock, and we were up, dressed, packed and ready to go. We said goodbye to our landlord Abraham, and his wife Hannah, and made our way down to the river out of sight. With my command, I had Roslyn harnessed up to a new sleigh with a canopy for shelter. The next stage was to head back to St Gallen and once there, we could hopefully take the train through Switzerland to as far as Bern.

It was a cold day, and as we made our way across the country, we had the occasional light snow shower. This didn't bother Roslyn as she galloped along taking many shortcuts. As a result of her cross-country running activities, we arrived in the city of Innsbruck at midday. With still no sign of the wizard, we took that opportunity to stop at a café to have our lunch, but I wouldn't say that I enjoyed it. We had never had goat's cheese before, and the smell of it always reminded me of my pal Brent William's old goat. Even worse, Lucia's face had turned a funny greyish colour. So without hesitation, I gave my lump to the café owner's dog, who must have been waiting, knowing what I was going to do with it.

It was some time after lunch before we could get the taste of that old goat out of our mouths. If it wasn't for Lucia's suggestion of gargling a glass of wine, it would have undoubtedly taken all day.

"That's better," I said. "Now if we are lucky, it's only going to take another three or four hours to reach St. Gallen. We'll be able to rest there for the night, and in the morning we can check out the trains to Bern."

"I'm happy with that," she replied. "The sooner we are in France, the better."

With that decided, we were up and way again but from then on sleeping with our shields inside our sleeping bags. Brynmoroc was bound to wake soon. The roads were clear enough now, so we were back in a carriage. Each time Roslyn took a shortcut the carriage wheels turned into legs. Watching this peculiar sight, I remember sitting there shaking my head in disbelief. The whole mystical and magical experience of being part of something only children would believe, was sometimes frightening.

Our long haul to Innsbruck went without any mishaps, and after finding a room for the night, we were soon sound asleep and didn't wake until the morning sun peeped through the bedroom window. Following a quick wash and a piece of toast, we were up and away again travelling through the Alps. Eventually, after avoiding the Swiss border checkpoints, we arrived in St. Gallen by mid-afternoon. As luck would have it, the last train to Bern was due at five o'clock, giving us enough time to buy fresh clothes and have a meal before boarding. With it being the last one out of the city, we were lucky to get a seat. It was a three-hour journey, so by the time we arrived in Bern, we were glad to stretch our legs. That was it for the day, and with the same hotel we had stayed in earlier being just up the street, we headed for it. The receptionist recognised Lucia and asked, what sounded like, "Better now?"

After a toasted sandwich, it was straight to bed for us but not without Roslyn for security. I think she enjoyed being a mean-looking hound rather than a terrier led on the bed. She would strut quietly around the room as if hoping that something might move so she could attack, and sure enough, she had her wish. We were awakened to the sound of savage animals fighting. It was Roslyn. She was locked together with a hairy wolf-like animal, only much bigger. I quickly got out of bed, turned up the lamp, put on my cape and grabbed my staff ready for anything else that might appear. There was nothing I could do to help Roslyn; it would have been suicidal to even try. I had seen dog fights before, but this fight was the most savage I had ever seen. It was fast and furious, and as they savaged one another, furniture went crashing everywhere. At one point, when the wolf-like beast had Roslyn pinned down, I tried pointing my staff to drive it back

but Roslyn flipped him over, so I couldn't. All through the battle, I had one eye on the door that was shaking and banging. Although I didn't have a clue how to defend myself, I stood there expecting another creature to enter or even Brynmoroc, but as the door opened, it was neither. It was the landlord and his son carrying a rifle. As soon as they entered the room, the creature ran headlong towards the door, roaring as he leapt through them like a ghost and was gone. It was obvious to me that they didn't see the wolf because all they did was point the rifle at Roslyn. I quickly stood in front of her, and as she began shaking herself, I shouted.

"No, no! Don't shoot her. I'm sorry. I'll pay for the damages and more. Please don't shoot her," I said, hoping they knew what I was saying.

The only thing they understood was, "No, no," but it made no difference, for all they must have seen was Roslyn rolling and snarling like a rabid dog. I had no choice, but to grab the barrel of the rifle just as the landlord's son aimed. BANG went the rifle which ripped a hole in the ceiling. I snatched the gun away from him and to their amazement, I bent the barrel right there in front of them. They were afraid of me now and cried out, "Non-non!"

Pointing to the bed, I instructed the frightened pair to lie on it and ordered Roslyn to guard them while we collected our things. When ready to leave, I threw down more than enough money to pay for the damages and quickly left, locking the door behind us. Once out in the street, I had our courageous Roslyn back as herself, and we were racing away out of the city, heading for the French border. To avoid the border involved crossing over a large lake and a few rivers before finally passed through St Brenets into France.

It was six o'clock, and after hiding away in a forest, we had a bite to eat and slept until eleven. Lucia was shivering with the cold now, so naturally, I was worried for her. With Dijon being a hundred miles away, I thought another train ride would suit us better. I checked my map and suggested that because Morteau was only a few miles away, we should go there in the hope that there was a train station. Arriving at Morteau, much to our relief we found that there was one. I paid our fare to Dijon, found a café for a coffee and we warmed by their fire. We had a couple of hours to wait, giving us once again, enough time to buy new clothes, sleeping bags, boots etcetera.

It was lovely being back on a train, sitting down and relaxing. Lucia sat near the window and with her arm locked in mine, Roslyn lay asleep on her lap. We were tired, and with the rhythmic sound of the train's wheels rackety tacketing on the iron rails, we soon nodded off to sleep.

When we arrived in Dijon, because of what happened the last time we were there, we had no intention of stopping. So with a brisk walk around a corner, we were once again away on the back of our faithful mare heading into the hills to camp overnight. Finding a nice quiet and secluded spot to pitch our tent, we were not long bedding ourselves down.

"Tomorrow, I'll concentrate on the amethyst," said Lucia as we lay quietly in the silence of the night. "I am almost positive of its whereabouts, but I'll let you know in the morning."

I was looking forward to knowing, but a little apprehensive of how and what it entailed to reach it.

Morning came without any trouble, and we were not going to wait around for any either. We quickly packed and were soon back on the road heading south until I pulled off the road to ask where our last journey was taking us.

She sighed and replied, "Oh Gwydion, this has been so hard to work out and I'm sure that you are not going to like it. Our route now is through the jungles of Peru in South America. I see the amethyst in a rock of granite somewhere in the mountains, not far from Cuzco."

"Peru! Are you sure?" I asked. "That's on the other side of the world, and I can only fly once. How will we ever get back?"

"You'll think of something, I'm sure," she replied. "One good thing about going to Peru is that the Peruvians have been speaking Spanish ever since sixteen hundred. The amethyst, apart from the ultimate destruction of Brynmoroc in my homeland of Murcia, is our last one and then it's all over."

I needed time to think and sat staring at the fire for a while before I came up with something. Undoubtedly, the all-powerful wizard Vindaguar must have known that one day some wizard would be tempted to steal the power of the stones; otherwise, he wouldn't have set out his prophecy. Thinking this, he obviously knew how difficult the amethyst would be to reach, but what he couldn't have known was, how long it would take the instigator to reach the point where we were now. So, with him being all-wise and powerful and with that in mind, he wouldn't have been taking a chance that I had months to spare in locating the amethyst. This was telling me that he had something else planned once we had found it. So we had no other choice but to fly to Peru and hope my theory was right. Perhaps when and after we arrive there, Lucia may be enlightened further. Lucia thought it feasible but was wondering how we were going to fly. We sat there in silence for a while, until I thought I'd leave the decision to the will of my staff and if we were going to fly, Lucia would be on my back and Roslyn a mouse in my pocket. Suggesting a mouse, made us laugh.

Decision made, and with Lucia on my back and poor lovely Roslyn a mouse in my jacket pocket; we headed out from the trees into an open space where I gave out my command. Suddenly, a swirling wind whipped up, and we were swept high up into the sky.

"Yahoo," I shouted as we found ourselves gliding through the air just as I had envisaged. I was flying, arms outstretched holding on to my staff, with Lucia lying on my back. We were now sailing across France towards the vast Atlantic Ocean, making our way to South America and ultimately, Peru. There was no wind; and the air at that high altitude, was warm and pleasant, not freezing cold as I thought. It was so quiet, not a sound to be heard except for Lucia's mumbling.

"Oh no, Gwydion. Don't let me fall off, will you? Oh, please don't Gwydion."

"Don't worry," I shouted. "Just relax and enjoy it. It's brilliant."

After realising she wasn't going to fall off, she too began shouting at the top of her voice,

"Yahoo Gwydion. Yahoo, we are flying. Oh, Gwydion this is amazing."

As we flew under a clear blue sky, all I can remember us saying to one another was, "Yahoo, yahoo."

We were travelling at such a tremendous speed that as we fled over France, it was almost a blur, but as for flying over the vast ocean, we thought it was never going to end. Though after saying that, at least we were warm and dry, even when we were caught up in a severe storm, it didn't matter, for we were enjoying it. You may ask, how could we breathe up there while travelling at such speed? I asked myself that question, but we just did.

It took five sensational hours before we finally reached Peru and Cuzco. From the sky, South America was just a blanket of trees and mountains, with no sign of any life.

"There's Cuzco," shouted Lucia, as she pointed.

Yes, there in the distance was Cuzco, a large town made up of fantastic stone buildings with red rooves. I was astonished for I thought the inhabitants of that part of the world would have been living in mud huts with thatched roofs. I wasn't going to land too close to Cuzco; instead, we swooped down like a bird and landed alongside a small lake in a valley of tall trees. Once down and undercover, we sat between some bushes, speechless stunned and exhausted from our experience.

The climate was warm, and as I looked at the sun, I found it in exactly the same position as when we started out. It was strange because we were flying for more than five hours.

"Peru must be five hours behind France," said Lucia, stretching her arms above her head.

I agreed, and then after putting my watch back five hours, I put on my cape. I had decided that from then on, I was never going to take it off, even sleep in it. I asked Lucia if she was sure they spoke Spanish in Cuzco because we needed a change of clothes to suit the country. We didn't want to be walking around dressed like Austrian climbers.

She replied, "As far as I know they do, and by the way, it's not a town, it's a city."

With Roslyn back to herself, we were on a dirt-track road, in the midst of a forest heading for Cuzco, another fascinating City, nothing like I expected. Lucia recognised the buildings as being typical Spanish. There was a restaurant across the street next to a store. That was great because we were dying for something to eat and drink. Locals, who were shopping around, took no notice of us as we pulled up outside the clothes store, but we did get a few strange looks as we walked in. The strange look the lady attendant gave us, soon changed to a lovely smile when she heard Lucia speak in Spanish. My Spanish was passible, but the lady had a different accent from Lucia. Lucia could understand her perfectly, but I had to listen very carefully. We bought a completely new outfit of clothes an extra pair of long leather boots and a spare pair of trousers each. The lady didn't mind us changing our clothes in the back of the shop. The next step was to stock up on food supplies and then next door to feed our hungry stomachs. We packed our supplies onto Roslyn and left her munching in her nosebag. In the restaurant, we were a little apprehensive about what to order, so the local fish dish was a safe option. It was delicious, like nothing we had ever tasted and were soon full and contented. We felt as if we could quite happily stay in the city forever, but then remembered why we were there, which quickly brought us back to reality.

It was five-thirty in the afternoon, but to our bodies, it was ten-thirty at night. So with this time difference, we were tired and needed sleep. The nearest hotel with a stable was a street away, so we eagerly made our way to it. Lucia did the ordering, which included her traditional bath and a stable for Roslyn.

"What do you want another bath for? It's only been twenty-four hours since your last one," I asked.

"It might be our last one for ages," was her annoying answer.

"Well, in that case, you can have one, but I'm not," I said, shaking my head.

It was no use trying to get out of another scrub because she would say as she always did.

"I can't sleep by you if you are smelly, it makes me cough all night, and I can't stop my nose from running."

I had never heard such nonsense, but it was pointless arguing. Pointless because; has any man ever won an argument with a lady, especially a pretty insistent one? I don't think so!

As you can guess, that was me, well-scrubbed, dressed again and ready for bed. It was so warm there wasn't any need to get inside my sleeping bag. I just lay there, wrapped in my incredible cape, fully armed with my shield and staff beside me though I was wishing Roslyn was also with us, but there were too many people around to change her. Even in the back streets, traders were selling local products and trinkets. There was no need to worry, for we had a peaceful night and were up early enjoying poached eggs, bread and butter.

We picked up our bags, collected Roslyn and trotted out of the fascinating city back through the forest to where we landed the day before. Dismounting, I asked Lucia if she had any idea how far and in what direction we had to go to reach the amethyst.

She replied, "The rock is about forty miles north of here, high upon a mountain. Below this mountain once stood a thriving city, probably wiped out by smallpox or some other disease. It is now a ruin, and because of its dense surroundings, it has never been discovered."

That meant that if we did ever manage to find this place, we'd be the first, but after looking at the dense forest before us, it was going to be some task finding it. Our one-time flying spell had been used up, so our journey from now had to be on foot. I told my Spanish lady that my biggest fear was snakes, so trekking on foot or by horse wasn't an option. So, while I pondered, I remembered that a mongoose was immune to snake bites and could smell a snake from a great distance.

"That's it, Lucia," I said out loud. "A mongoose! We'll ride a mongoose."

She didn't mind, just as long as it wasn't any more of those old creepy crawling things. So, with my staff stretched out over Roslyn, I asked with my thoughts. Then 'wham' after the usual incredible transformation, we were up and away on Roslyn, an eight-foot-long-five-foot-high, dark brown mongoose making our way through the forest. The paths through the trees looked as if they were man-made and because they were not overgrown, it was telling us that there was human civilisation around.

"What kind of people could possibly live in a jungle like this?" asked Lucia. "Oh no, Gwydion! What if they see us riding an eight-foot monster?"

"They'll probably run for their lives. Wouldn't you?" I replied jokingly.

All that day we slowly and carefully trekked on, weaving our way through a tall and dark forest until we came out halfway up a small rocky mountain. It was seven o'clock, and the sun had not long set.

"That's enough for today," said Lucia as we slipped off Roslyn to rest.

The sky had clouded over, but it was still warm. I found a nice grassy patch in-between some large weird-looking rocks to camp. Roslyn was back as herself, grazing away while we pitched our tent. There was plenty of dry wood around, so after lighting a small fire, we sat waiting for the kettle to boil.

"I have a bad feeling about this place," whispered Lucia. "This last jewel is not going to be easy. The mountain of rock where the amethyst is hidden was once considered sacred and was guarded by the tribal civilisation living in the city below it. Although smallpox or whatever epidemic wiped out the whole city, the rock is still being worshipped by another tribe. I didn't know this until now. My grandmother was right. The last one is going to be the most enduring."

"Ah, don't worry, we'll be alright," I said, putting my arm around her. "I'll think of something. We didn't come all this way just to fail at the last jewel now, did we?"

With this tribe and Brynmoroc in mind, we didn't sleep in the tent that night. Roslyn became our giant mongoose again, and as she curled up for the night, we settled down in the middle of her furry coat. It was safer there and a lot easier on our worried minds.

# Chapter 22

A t sunrise, it was our eight-foot-long giant who woke us just before it absolutely poured down with rain. Instead of diving for cover in our tent, I thought we would take advantage of the rain and head onward. If there were any hostile tribes ahead of us, they surely wouldn't be out in such a storm. So we climbed on up, over and down the other side of that rocky tree-covered mountain until we entered another massive forest. Roslyn eventually found a path she could weave through, but with the rain showing no sign of stopping it was going to be a slow process. During our journey, we came across many strange-looking animals, but none more than Roslyn. It was funny, for once they caught sight of our giant they were gone, hell for leather, flying or crashing their way through the trees.

Eventually, after travelling all morning and up until two in the afternoon, we came out of the jungle alongside a frightening raging river. Even with Roslyn, there was no way we could ever cross it. There was nothing we could do but stay put inside the hollow of a massive tree. We were soaking wet from the waist down. Our capes kept the rest of us reasonably dry, but poor old Roslyn, our giant mongoose, was a dripping wet soggy mass of fur, vigorously shaking herself down.

It was another hour before the rain stopped and the much-appreciated sun came out from behind the clouds. We changed and hung our wet clothes out to dry but well away from a terrifying, raging muddy river, tearing its way down through the valley of trees. We had no choice other than to wait a few days until the river subsided. The wood lying around was far too wet to start a fire, but our clothes were drying nicely in the sun. After setting up camp, we took an apple each and stood on the river bank watching small trees, large logs and broken branches bouncing and smashing their way downstream. Then, as we watched the raging river, four sturdy bouncing logs and a large broken branch, rose out of the water, joined together and began running across the river towards us. Lucia quickly ran back into the hollow of the tree while Roslyn and I faced the oncoming savage-looking abnormality. In other words, it was a large ugly tree monster with long slimy-looking tentacles waving around from the top of its head down to the ground. His mouth was round and hollow, and its green and red eyes were horribly sticking out and wiggling. The monstrous thing had jumped out of the river and was standing there staring until he lifted his tentacles and rushed us. I drove him back towards the river with a blast from my staff, but his tentacles prevented him from going over the bank. The weirdest thing about him was that he was totally silent. Not one single sound did he make as he recoiled, and by using his tentacles, thrust himself forward with tremendous force only to be met by Roslyn, who went tearing into him, but to my horror, the creature wrapped its slimy tentacles around her. Roslyn was now locked into a ferocious battle with bits of tentacles flying everywhere. They were rolling over and over until to my horror, both of them tumbled into the river.

"Roslyn, leave him, leave him Roslyn. Let him go," I shouted anxiously.

She wasn't listening and carried on fighting down the river, around the bend and out of sight.

"Oh no! Not again! Not Roslyn please not Roslyn?" I said turning to Lucia who was hiding in the tree.

"Where is she? What happened?" she asked, crawling out.

"She's gone. Roslyn's gone Lucia," I replied, shaking my head. "There was nothing I could do. She wouldn't listen to me."

"She's gone? What do you mean, gone? She couldn't be. Where is she?" she cried.

Before I could tell her where she had gone, the monster came running back up the river towards us.

"Go back into the tree, quickly," I shouted.

I was in the right mood now and felt nothing but contempt towards the oncoming creature who was now leaping out onto the bank. I immediately blasted him back into the middle of the rapids, but he just came back at me. I blasted him again, but it was of no use because he kept coming back, time after time. I then realised that my staff was just playing ball games with him. So the next time I sent him flying into the river, I asked Lucia to hold my staff. I was fired up now and as I waited for him, the more I thought about poor Roslyn, the more hatred I had for him. The very moment the creature jumped back onto the bank, I ran so fast into him that I managed to penetrate his tentacles. I aimed to go for his throat, but I couldn't reach it. He drew in his tentacles and pinned me up against his body, facing him. As I struggled to get free, the monster was not only trying to crush me; he was dragging me towards the river. If I didn't do something quickly, he was surely going to drown me. The only thing I could do as I looked up into his horrid wobbling eyes, was to wrap my arms around him and squeeze. I was lucky the creature hadn't thought of ripping off my cloak because as I squeezed, I slowly began to feel its bark crumble. Then as my arms and fingers sunk into its body, I lifted him enough to stop him from heading for the river. The monster then tried to drag me by using his tentacles, but it was to no avail. I was winning, and for the first time, the creature broke its silence and began to groan and bellowed. He was now feeling the pain of my arms crushing him. The most horrible thing about the whole ordeal was as he bellowed, I was face to face with his hollow mouth and stinking breath. This went on for some time, making me think that the creature would never give up until suddenly, he gave out a painful deafening roar, making him spew out stinking slimy jelly into my face and all over me. I didn't flinch; it only made me squeeze even harder until he gave out an unforgettable scream, collapsing to the ground in a heap of jelly with me in the middle of it.

I waded out and quickly went to check on Lucia. Thankfully she was okay, still there hiding behind her shield. She screamed a little when she saw me, but after realising that I wasn't one of Brynmoroc's creatures, she sighed in relief.

"He's gone, isn't he?" she asked. "He must be. Look at the state of you. Oh my goodness, you smell and look terrible."

"Well, thanks for that," I replied, flicking some jelly on her.

"Don't, Gwydion," she screamed and jumped up. "Oh poo Gwydion, you smell terrible. Take those smelly things off and throw them away. Your other clothes should be dry by now. I'll get you a towel or something. Oh poo, poo. Go on, hurry up."

If it had been anyone else, after all I had been through, I would have dumped them in the creature's pile of jelly. Instead, I just laughed and changed, but once I had, I picked Lucia up and pretended that I was going to dump her in the jelly.

"Don't you dare!" she screamed. "I'll never forgive you. Oh, Gwydion, don't, don't. I'll hate you forever."

I put her down and slapped her on the behind as she ran away, laughing, and saying, "I knew you wouldn't."

Her laughter soon changed to sorrow. Poor Roslyn had given her life, trying to save us.

"Oh, I hate Brynmoroc. I hate him even more now. He's horrible," said Lucia, with tears in her eyes.

My feelings were the same but said nothing only that we had to pack and carry on in the hope of finding a bridge further on down the river. It didn't take long to pack, but as we were doing so, I realised that my shield was missing. I hurried to where I had left it and with it safely back in my pocket, we made our way down alongside that hateful river. When I say hateful, it's because it took our lovely faithful Roslyn away from us.

Finding an ideal spot just inside the forest, we set up camp and waited for over a week until the river subsided enough for us to cross. Our supply of water came from a nearby spring, but we had very little food. We searched around in the hope of finding a few nuts or even berries. It was a waste of time; there wasn't any. We were now hoping and praying that the other side would be more fruitful.

We were not ready for another Roslyn. The only transport I could have now was, of course, a boat. What kind of boat was another thing? I noticed that because of the right-hand bend, the rapids were forcing debris over to the bank on the opposite side. With that in mind, I thought it would help us cross without too much effort. A rowing boat was the only boat I could think of and we were soon sitting in one, rowing steadily away downriver. Just as I suspected, the rapids sent us over to the side into the shallow where we were quickly able to clamber out onto the bank.

"That was nerve-wracking, wasn't it, Gwydion? We have never been without poor dear Roslyn to aid us before," said Lucia sadly, sitting on a log.

Hearing her reminding me of Roslyn, saddened me so much that it made my chest heave. I was missing her, and as I looked at Lucia, I thought that if anything happened to her, I wouldn't know if I could bear it. While I was thinking, Lucia stood up saying that she had spotted cones looking very much like coconuts under giant trees. So we gathered a few and sat down cracking them open like a couple of monkeys until furry seeds fell out.

"Yes! Oh yes!" Said Lucia, excitedly. "These are Brazil nuts. They are lovely."

They were, and they suppressed our appetite nicely. After cramming as many as we could into our bags, we sat down to decide on our next form of travel. Although we needed something to carry our baggage, the thought of having another mare just yet, was unthinkable. I thought we'd wait until we reach the mountain.

"Yes," said Lucia, agreeing with me. "Just a few more miles through this forest and we'll be close to the ruined city. We'll decide then, but with this last jewel being up on that sacred rock, we are going to have a whole lot of trouble, and it will not only be from Brynmoroc, either."

So, with Lucia carrying one bag and me the other two, we took a chance and headed out on foot. To walk, probably wasn't the best plan of action, but that's what we had decided and made our way through a forest of huge trees and undergrowth. Deeper into the forest, there were loads more of those coconut size balls. Most of them were broken open, with the nuts all gone.

"We are lucky that they have all fallen," said Lucia looking upwards. "Otherwise, we would have never been able to walk through here."

Looking at the balls, I could see that they had been split open by a sharp blade. This was telling me that they were definitely not opened by animals. Further on, I found out who it was that had opened them. A long arrow, shot from somewhere, landed in front of us and we found ourselves surrounded by dark-skinned natives who were half-dressed in animal skins. Suddenly, I felt a sharp stinging pain in the side of my neck. Within seconds of pulling out a small dart, I became groggy and began to stagger. Then, as my eyes were starting to blur, I saw something big coming through the trees behind the natives. All I can remember after that was saying, it's Brynmoroc, and Lucia calling out, "Gwydion! Gwydion!"

She was shaking and splashing me with water saying "Look Gwydion? Look?"

At that moment, as I opened my eyes, whatever it was that knocked me out I didn't care, because standing over me now, was my lovely Roslyn. It was her I saw coming through the trees before I passed out. Lucia said that after crashing through the trees, Roslyn stood over me, hissing and snarling. The natives seeing this, ran away terrified, with Roslyn chasing them through the forest.

"Ha-ha, good for you Roslyn," I said while rubbing her furry nose. "And thank you once again my friend for saving me. You are the best pal I could ever wish for."

"Hey, and what about me?" asked Lucia, giving me a poke.

I just laughed, looked at Roslyn and said, "But not before my pretty companion, of course."

It was about an hour before my head cleared enough to carry on, but I needed time to think. Then while we were sitting on a fallen tree, Lucia softly asked.

"You said earlier that I was just your companion. Is that all I am to you, a companion?"

"No, no," I replied. "You know I like you and you mean more to me than a companion. My head was groggy then; I just forgot to put you first, that's all."

"Oh you and your likes, that's all you ever say Gwydion. You know I love you, but you completely ignore me, don't you?"

I didn't know how to reply without telling lies. I was in love with her too, but as you know, I couldn't tell her. Luckily I didn't have to say a word because Roslyn nudged me off the tree as if she was once again, coming to my aid.

"Hey Roslyn, what was that for?" I asked, clambering to my feet.

I then noticed bits of fishing net tangled around one of her hind legs. So I took my knife and cut them away.

"What do you think happened to her?" Lucia asked. "Do you think that tribe trapped her in a net?"

My theory was, that during her scrap with the horrible tree monster, she must have got tangled up in a fishing net, and floated on down the river until she gnawed herself free."

My neck was sore to the touch, but my head felt okay now. Lucia thought that the dart must have contained some kind of drug to put me to sleep.

"They are the natives from the protective tribe of the rock mountain," she said, wetting a cloth to wipe the blood from my neck.

Cleaned up now and with our packs on our backs, we mounted Roslyn and set off once more, but this time, a lot happier knowing we had our faithful friend back to protect us. Roslyn hurried along, weaving her way through the trees with me constantly looking around for those dark-skinned natives.

"We are bound to meet up with them again," warned Lucia, tapping my shoulder. "They are very protective of their sacred rock."

As always, she was right, for as we came out of the forest they were there waiting only this time, more friendly with their approach. They were walking towards us with baskets of fruit and drink and bowed as they lay them down before us.

"I think they like us now," whispered Lucia. "Either that or afraid of us."

I thought, one or the other was pretty obvious, but unless they spoke English or Spanish, we'd never know. Then to our surprise, a lady came from behind the bearers and said "Bienvenida O lospoderosos."

She was speaking in Spanish, which meant, "Welcome, O powerful ones."

She went on to say, "We humbly beg your forgiveness and wish you no more harm. Our home is your home for as long as you wish. Come, we will lead you to our village."

I suddenly had a brainwave. To secure our safety, if they thought we were all-powerful having a giant mongoose, I'd show them something to convince them even further. I raised my staff towards Roslyn and cried out my enchanted words. Then, to the awe of every native, we were back on our lovely bay mare again. They were astonished and dropped face down to the ground mumbling some kind of chant. Lucia called out to the lady, telling her not to be afraid and that we were happy to follow them to their village. The bearers picked up their gifts, and we followed the band of about twenty through a valley of sheer cliffs and the jagged rocky mountains of the Andes.

I remember thinking to myself that Andes, must be a Peruvian word for 'Awesome,' because that's just what they were.

Once again, we found ourselves alongside the same wide and murky river that had meandered its way through the towering gorge of granite. At that point, the band of Natives veered to the right and began climbing up and around a winding path until we arrived, looking down at a fantastic village.

"Incredible!" said Lucia excitedly.

The lady called it a village, but to me, it was more of a small city because in the middle, towering above this grey-stoned village, were the turrets of what looked like a small castle. After descending into the village, most of our native guides went off to their homes; the rest stood around watching us. The lady, who had skin a lot lighter than the rest, led us to one of their dwellings and then spoke in Spanish.

"Welcome to Las Rocas Del Sol. My name is Milaniah, and this is my home."

Although we were a little apprehensive, Lucia introduced us, and Milaniah carried on.

"My father was Spanish, so I speak your language. It is because of this, I have been asked to share my home with you. So please, enter, and I will show you your room."

Before entering, to the amazement of Milaniah, I had Roslyn back as our guardian hound. I wasn't taking any chances, and by doing that, it boosted our status even more, for once again, the remaining spectators fell to the ground, chanting.

The inside of her house was very colourful with different coloured furs lying loosely on lovely wooden furniture. There was a large fire grate with pots and pans sitting on the hearth. Our bedroom was plain and simple with a straw bed, making me scratch to even look at it. The solitary window was just a round hole with some kind of animal skin lying on the sill to cover it. The speckled granite walls sparkled as a beam of light flickered through the window. It was an unusual house, to say the least, but at the same time, fascinating.

"You can rest if you wish. I'll make something to eat and call you when it's ready," said Milaniah, drawing the curtain across the doorway as she left.

My Spanish wasn't one hundred percent, but she talked nice and slow, making it easier to understand.

We were not going to stay, well not if I could help it, but after thinking, we probably had no choice. Also, the amethyst was on their sacred rock, so perhaps we could persuade them to let us climb it.

Lucia agreed to say that it would be better if we could persuade them, for without their permission, the next time, they could fill those darts with deadly poison. I had forgotten about those darts. With that settled, we unpacked and after laying our sleeping bags out on the dry straw, a lovely smell of something cooking made our tummies rumble. It was a large pot of stew that was the most delicious bowl of stew I had ever tasted in my life. It was so filling that it was hard work finishing off the last piece of bread.

"Come, sit beside the fire, I have something to tell you both," said Milaniah after we had finished.

Lucia sat beside me and held my hand while we listened to what Milaniah slowly had to say. So with me understanding a fair bit of Spanish and with Milaniah allowing Lucia to fill me in while she rested, this is what she told us that day.

She was twenty-nine years old; born in Cuzco to a Peruvian Indian mother, and her father, a Spanish doctor. Their names were Marian and Pedro. In 1863, during another outbreak of yellow fever, the Cuzco Indians, who had left this present village in the early eighteen hundreds, moved back here to escape the latest outbreak. Marian, being sixteen and the oldest daughter, stayed in Cusco to care for her dying mother and by doing so, developed the horrible disease. That was when she met Pedro, who happened to be the doctor there. He treated Marian, and after saving her life they fell in love and married four years later. Unfortunately, Marian died three years after giving birth to Milaniah, their only child. From that day on, Milaniah was raised by her father and Marian's sister who returned to Cusco to help. They lived a comfortable life until at the age of thirteen, Milaniah's father died. Following his death, Milaniah and her auntie were evicted from their home, leaving them with no choice but to come to this mountainous region. Milaniah's auntie has now since married and lives next door.

I remember her pausing for a moment, and before carrying on, she looked sternly at us, saying that we were probably wondering what all this had to do with us and why I was shot with a dart. Apparently, their warriors, ever since my battle with the tree monster, had been watching us. They recognised me as the grandson of a wizard who had been a vision in the sky every May since 1881. The warriors were also meant to shoot Lucia in order to bring us both here to their village. Luckily, Lucia's shield blocked the dart meant for her and she, along with our giant mongoose chased the warriors away.

Of course I wasn't a wizard, but I was curious to know about this so-called vision. So I thought I'd say nothing and carefully listened to her as she carried on.

In fifteen thirty three, the Spaniard Pizarro Gonzalez ransacked the city of Cuzco. Thousands of Cuzco Indians lost their lives in the battle, save for three hundred who managed to escape and took refuge in the vast Amazon forest. After setting up home in the forest, they grew in numbers forcing half the tribe to move up into the mountains. The year was sixteen seventy five and the new tribe, under the appointed Chief Malumbah, searched relentlessly for a suitable place to settle until one day, they came across a small abandoned settlement situated halfway up a mountain on a large level area surrounded by trees, an ideal place to live. Malumbah claimed the empty dwellings for his people. They all worked tirelessly, felling trees, collecting rocks and stones to rebuild this village we were now at. Now, unknown to them, on another nearby mountain

was an ancient city called Machu Picchu, also
abandoned. Machu Picchu means Old Mountain.
The Indians had heard of the city, but no one knew
where it was until Malumbah's son after following
tiny arrow markings scratched on several rocks,
discovered a scroll and a quipu in a gold casket
buried beside an old oak tree. The casket and the
two items were left by Malamchu, the Emperor of
Machu Picchu. Along with the scrolls' drawings
and the reading of the quipu, it explained the
history of the abandoned city. Malumbah sent a
search party to seek out this city that they
eventually found hidden by clouds on top of a
mountain not too far from their village. I didn't
know what a quipu was, so I stopped Milaniah and
asked. It was a group of knotted ropes, something
the Incas used to communicate with, like a letter
or a book. Down through the ages, the scroll and
quipu had been interpreted by Milaniah's people
who now had a much better understanding of its
content than when first read. When the searchers
found the city of Machu Picchu, it was intact apart
from some of the roofs. Over the years they had
rotted and blown away in the wind. The dwellings
were empty, but smashed pottery was scattered
everywhere. According to the Emperor's scroll
and quipu, the city of Machu Picchu didn't exist
until ten sixty eight. Before that, it was a place on
a mountain where during every autumn equinox,
Inca people came with gifts of flowers in honour
of the sun. In the year ten-sixty-six, while the
Incas were honouring the sun, a powerful wizard
appeared before them. He requested that the

natives declare the tall rock mountain towering up beside their place of worship, sacred; and enforce the law that no one be allowed access to it. In return, he promised to help build a city on their mountain of worship that would be guarded by the Sun Giant who would also provide them with his energy. The Incas agreed, and the wizard kept his promise. He helped them build a city that was accessed by narrow roads twisting up and around the mountain from the Amazon forest. With the city finished, the powerful wizard was never seen again, leaving the Incas to live in peace under the protection of the Sun Giant. For over two and a half centuries the city of Machu Picchu thrived from the Sun Giant's energy until one day it ceased. For some reason, their faithful Giant had disappeared. Without his enchanted energy and protection, they grew weak and were vulnerable to attacks from jealous tribes in the area. Also, for some reason, clouds would drift down covering the city with a blanket of cold, damp fog that after lifting, rained for days on end. The constant drinking water supply increased to such a level that eventually, along with the tormenting rain, it caused flooding throughout the city. Machu Picchu was then deemed uninhabitable, causing the Incas to move out and built the village we were now in, 'Rocas Del Sol' meaning Rocks of the Sun. The new Emperor, Tonalula, thinking that the wizard lived on the sacred rock mountain, decided to send out a search party of youths to find him. Sadly, only one returned; the others had unfortunately fallen to their deaths. The only survivor told the Emperor that the Sun Giant had called down to him, saying that he had been captured by a spirit and was now chained to rocks on top of the mountain. After hearing this, Tonalula ordered the Inca people to build steps and footpaths up the sacred mountain to free the stricken Sun Giant. From that day on and because of the loss of so many young lives, they called the mountain Wayna Picchu, meaning Young Peak. It took many years, but sadly, after hundreds of lives were lost, they finally reached the top only to find no sign of the Sun Giant. All they found were huge boulders in an area no wider than a native's dwelling house. The Inca's High Priest told the Emperor that the sun unchained the giant and had taken him back. Knowing this, the Emperor ordered the High Priest to offer flowers every day to the sun for the Giant's return. However, on one of these offerings, during an autumn equinox, the High Priest told Tonalula that he had seen a vision of a youth riding a goat up Wayna Picchu with an offering to the sun. It was this young man's offering that the sun would favour and return the Sun Giant to Machu Picchu. So, every autumn equinox for two hundred years, an Inca youth would attempt to fulfil the prophecy, but with each and every effort, the goat refused to carry them. Then in 1524, due to the plague of smallpox that devastated their village and most of Peru, the new Emperor, Cazuraloo, proclaimed Rocas Del Sol cursed. The Incas then abandoned the village leaving behind their quipu. Now, as I have already said, the Inca tribe found and rebuilt Rocas Del

Sol, but after reading the quipu, no one ever attempted to fulfil the prophecy of Wayna Picchu. They had been waiting for me.

I believed and knew that the wizard and the Sun Giant were true, but not how the giant disappeared. The time he disappeared was the same time Brynmoroc had absorbed him. The sole survivor's story must have been fabricated by the youth who had returned afraid after watching his friends fall to their deaths. The High Priest's vision was also fabricated for self-establishment. As for the wizard; being Vindaguar, he was probably long dead by then.

After being filled in, I sat up, shook my head, gave a little laugh and asked, "Why me? I'm no wizard's grandson. I'm the grandson of a Welsh sheep farmer, but I must admit, that I do know a wizard and I am on a mission for him, but it has nothing to do with making any offering to the sun. If you say your people have been waiting for me, then they must be mistaken."

Milaniah was adamant and replied, "It is you Gwydion. I myself have seen your very image in the sky. You are standing alone in triumph with the Sun Giant smiling above you, but, we don't see Lucia."

That shook my whole body. Although I knew this couldn't be true, when she mentioned Lucia wasn't there, it made a cold shiver come over me. I could feel Lucia's grip on my hand getting tighter. I looked at her worried face, shook my head and smiled to let her know that I didn't believe it. I then asked Milaniah how just going by my image she could possibly know that I was this grandson of a wizard. Her reply was that on the first sighting of my image, a few more knots appeared in the quipu proclaiming it.

Before Milaniah went, she informed us that at three o'clock the next day, their Chief Wabulamba was holding a feast in our honour. We would learn more then. She lit a lamp for herself, one for us, wished us a restful night, went away to her bedroom and we went to ours.

"That was a long story. I don't know what to make of it. What about you?" Asked Lucia to which I quickly gave her my thoughts. Although the tribe had never seen the Sun Giant or the powerful wizard, they seemed to know about their existence. So, that part of the story I believed. As far as I could work out, the Sun Giant disappeared from Machu Picchu at the same time Brynmoroc absorbed him. What happened after that was surely fabricated by the sole surviving youth and the power-seeking High Priest. As for their vision of me and this quipu thing, whatever they claim to have seen and read, as far as I was concerned, it was never going to happen. Lucia thought it made sense but seemed to believe it was a good idea to stay and find out what the chief had to say. She then reminded me about those poisonous darts of theirs and that they constantly watch Wayna Picchu Mountain, the one we had to climb. We were more than uncertain now, and with being so high up in the clouds, the air was hard to breathe. We couldn't think anymore and fell asleep, not waking until Milaniah woke us in the morning.

# Chapter 23

It was seven in the morning, and although feeling better from our night's sleep, it was still difficult to breathe. Milaniah said it would take a couple of weeks to get used to the mountain air, but I wasn't planning on staying that long.

After a lump of Milaniah's bread and a drink of some kind of herbs, she took us on a tour of her village. Their dwellings and outbuildings were single-storeys, built with large square and oblong stones, laid with absolute precision without any cement to hold them. To think they were created by those native Indians centuries ago was incredible. Although the village was up in the mountains, we were fascinated to find that it had stores selling almost all the clothes you could ever want, if you were a native Indian, of course. Other than that, there were food stores with supplies that had been brought in from Cuzco and shared out evenly. There was also an abundance of gold in their mountains, and that too was distributed equally.

Walking back to her home, Milaniah told us that no one in the village wanted for anything, except protection. They were constantly in battle with envious tribes trying to take over their village.

We had a few hours of rest which we needed to get our breath back in time for the feast at three o'clock. We had nothing fancy to wear, only what we had on. So while sitting down waiting, Milaniah came in saying that if we were ready, our lift was waiting outside. We were prepared, and when we stepped outside to what we thought to be a horse and carriage, it turned out to be a sedan type of chair. There were twelve natives, six on each side waiting for us to climb aboard. At first, I was reluctant to be treated in such a royal manner, but we were not allowed to walk. We had no option but to sit side by side in the chair as our bearers made their way to the castle.

Arriving at our destination, we found that it wasn't a castle, it was more like a palace with tall lookout turrets.

Wabulamba, along with his wife, was there to greet us at the door. The bearers set us down, and I bowed.

"Welcome, both of you, this is my wife, Lisuella," said the chief, in Spanish.

I told him my name and introduced Lucia as my companion and she curtsied and said, "Nice to meet you, your highnesses."

Lisuella smiled and beckoned us in and we followed them into a hallway full of gold figurines and trinkets. The floor was made from slabs of granite that were as smooth as marble. The doors opening into the dining room were a deep red colour and so too was the long wooden table in the middle of this spectacular room. Milaniah said that the wood was from a red tree called cambara. Everything was made from gold, silver, bronze, red cambara and granite. Whatever the linen was made from, it was certainly bright and colourful. Milaniah also introduced us to six other important-looking people. With the introductions finished and while we stood taking in all the opulence and splendour, a gong sounded. It was time to take our places at the enormous red table.

We had been invited to a feast and a feast it was. The centre of the table was piled high with meat, fruit, and vegetables the likes of which I had never seen. Lucia, who had a better knowledge of what was there, filled me in as we began the meal. There were duck, guinea fowl and peacock, accompanied by corn on the cob in a variety of colours. There were also fish with amazing cheesy sauce. Then to finish off the meal we had mangoes and pineapples with nuts and berries, all washed down with the local red wine.

With the meal and everything cleared away, we went into the sitting room. Once again, this room was equally impressive. The only thing strange about it was; there were no seats, only large feather cushions to sit on. We found them extremely comfortable a lot more than Granddad's old armchairs. There were twelve of us; all sitting around in a circle with wine and trinkets in the middle. Chief Wabulamba, who had difficulty pronouncing my name and understanding my not-so-good Spanish, eventually spoke.

"Milaniah tells me that both of you knew nothing about the vision and the high priest's prophecy," said the chief, looking into my eyes. "You can rest assured that it is you we Inca people have been waiting for. Centuries ago, the High Priest Minandoo, saw in a vision that every month of May, a youth's image would appear in the sky. This youth on a certain day, while riding a goat, will climb Wayna Picchu Mountain to make an offering the sun will favour. In return, the sun will send back the Sun Giant to watch over us."

Lisuella, who could also speak Spanish, asked, "If you knew nothing about the prophecy, then why, why were you both here in our forest?"

After Lucia reminded me of the consequences of climbing Wayna Picchu without permission, I had been thinking and had already prepared an answer to her question, but it meant hanging around until the equinox in March.

"I was just testing Milaniah, that's all," I replied. "I had to do this to make sure she was genuine because I knew nothing about having to ride a goat. In my vision, I didn't see it that way."

That went down well with everyone, especially the Chief, who then asked us to venture outside with him. He had arranged for us to be entertained by their colourful tribal dancers. The red sun that was about to go down was enhancing the dancers as they jumped up and down. They must have been incredibly fit. The ladies wore grass skirts and feathers while the men wore animal skins and had their faces painted. The dance was a mock courting ritual with the young men showing off their warrior and dancing skills while the young ladies danced, always teasing them. They danced opposite one another, facing the same partner throughout the ritual. At the end of the dance, if any of the young ladies were impressed by their partner, they would give him a small feather. The young men, if they liked what they saw, gave the girl back her feather, meaning that he accepted her offer of marriage. It was obviously going to be a big decision, for once he gave the feather back, he had pledged something that couldn't be broken. If he didn't give the young lady her feather back, she would have one more chance to win his favour. It was vice versa for the men. If a warrior wasn't offered a feather, then he too would get another chance, but by then he would have probably been worn out.

"How do they jump around like that? I can hardly breathe and walk, never mind dance," said Lucia.

During the offering of feathers, one of the young ladies gave Lucia a feather and pointed to me. Lucia then gave me the feather and smiled. I smiled back and put it into my pocket. She immediately scowled at me, much to the laughter of everyone. Well, it was only a mock ceremony; none of the others gave them back.

With the ceremony over, we went back inside where we were offered more wine and food, but we were full and ready for bed. After saying goodbye and thank you to Wabulamba and

Lisuella, we were carried off to Milaniah's house, in style.

It was only eight o clock, but being tired from the lack of air, we said goodnight to Milaniah and went to our room where we collapsed on the bed. It was so warm and stuffy that we just lay there until drifting off to sleep. I was so tired; I can't even remember what time it was when Roslyn woke us growling and barking. She was over by the door, so I unwrapped our wrists, turned up the lamp and went over to her.

"What's the matter?" I asked, as she growled and sniffed under the door.

It was Milaniah, asking me to let her in. I told Roslyn to go and lie down. I opened the door to find Milaniah in tears, trying to tell me something. Frustratingly, along with her crying and talking so fast, I didn't have a clue what she was saying.

"Come in, Milaniah. Let her in Gwydion," said Lucia as she sat up.

Milaniah was halfway in already, so I closed the door behind her. Roslyn was still growling, so I put her outside the door. Then as I did, I heard Lucia's muffled scream. I quickly turned to find Milaniah had Lucia on the bed, choking her. I rushed over to drag Milaniah away, but she was incredibly strong. I was now thankful that I decided never to take my cloak off because I caught hold of Milaniah's wrists and squeezed. This made her release her grip enough for me to fling her across the room.

"What the heck's wrong with you, Milaniah?" I hollered as she picked herself up.

Then, as she snarled and leapt at me, her eyes were red, and her face all screwed up. It was Milaniah, but, it was as if someone else was inside her. Nevertheless, I caught hold of her and half-heartedly threw her backwards. She was like a mad dog now with rabies, snarling and frothing at the mouth. She rushed me again, savaging my arm with her teeth as I grabbed her. So this time, I'm sorry to say, I smashed her against the wall so hard she slumped to the floor and stayed there. I spun around to Lucia, who was lying still, her face a terrible colour. I was raging now, and as I picked up Milaniah by her throat, she crumpled into dust, covering me in the process. Lucia wasn't breathing, so I shook and shouted at her to wake up until I remembered reviving a stillborn lamb. So I opened Lucia's mouth, held her tongue, and after blowing into her mouth a dozen times, I shook her vigorously. To my relief, she drew in a big gulp of air clutched her throat and began slapping me.

"Whoa! Whoa, it's okay. It's okay. You are alright now. Sit up and breathe," I said as she opened her eyes.

I lifted her up, sat her on the edge of the bed and told her to take in deep breaths.

"Where is she? Is she in with Brynmoroc? Oh, Gwydion, we had better get from this place. The whole tribe must be on Brynmoroc's side," insisted Lucia, holding her throat.

Her throat was bright red and getting darker every second. Milaniah was no threat now, just a pile of dust, as Lucia could see. I was covered in it. Brynmoroc must have created a creature in Milaniah's form, and if I was right, she'd still be there in the morning.

I had forgotten about Roslyn, who was scratching the door whimpering wanting to get in. I let her in and jokingly asked where she had been? She just wagged her tail and led down. The sun was beginning to rise, so before the attack we must have slept for a good six hours. I had Roslyn stay on guard while I went to the kitchen, soaked a cloth in cold water and wrapped it around Lucia's bruised neck.

"Dew, I love this girl," I said to myself while looking at her pretty little face. She was so delicate and innocent looking that I could have put my arms around her and told her how I felt. I would have, but for some silly promise.

"Ah well, just a few months to go and then I will," is what I remember saying to myself. My only worry was; Lucia might get fed up with me not reciprocating her loving gestures and hate me. That was the rotten chance I had to take. Besides that, I was also worried about how I was going to explain Lucia's bruised neck to everyone.

"I'll use a scarf," she replied when I mentioned it. So, that's what she did when we went to the kitchen for breakfast.

Milaniah was nowhere to be seen, making us kind of suspicious about her now. The fire was alight so she had either gone back to bed, gone out for something, or maybe she really was last night's creature. I didn't like to knock on her bedroom door, so I dropped a pan on the floor outside it. Alas, with no response, we boiled the kettle and made toast. We had only just finished when in came Milaniah, with a few eggs.

"Buenos dias," she said, with a smile. "I see you've already had toast, would you like an egg each too? I've been out feeding the hens."

I was waiting for her to say something about the noise during the night. She didn't, so I thought I'd apologise just to find out whether she had heard anything or not.

"What noise? I heard nothing," she said with a puzzled expression.

I said that I had knocked something against the wall and was worried I might have woken her. I said no more, but I did wonder how she hadn't heard anything because there was a whole lot of noise going on. We stayed puzzled all afternoon until Lucia remembered something that put us at ease.

"We have forgotten that we are in both worlds at the same time. In that case, you must have been battling with the creature in their one-dimensional world, which accounts for her not hearing anything."

She was right and remembering this and knowing the villagers were genuine, we decided to stay. The only thing we were worried about was Brynmoroc and his evil wizardry turning up in both worlds. That, we were soon to find out, because every single night for the next week, we were up battling some kind of creature or other, but thankfully in their own world. Brynmoroc, if it was him, sent creatures of all shapes and sizes, even the tapered head snake again. By the end of the week, we were exhausted. The only time we slept was in the morning, causing Milaniah to worry about us not having breakfast. Then with great relief, a few days after that tiring week, for some reason, the wizard and his wizardry left us in peace.

It was well into February now, and with a few months left before the eclipse, we were talking about Brynmoroc. I confided in Lucia something that I had been wondering about for some time. All through our assignment, we had been careful never to mention the jewels during the midday sun. We had done this simply because although we couldn't see the wizard, he obviously knew where we were and possibly listening. So I had been thinking; if he knows where we are and where we are looking, then why doesn't he, or why can't he find the jewels himself. We were able to locate them, so why couldn't he? Lucia had no answer. So that was the two of us falling to sleep thinking of what seemed to be another unfathomable puzzle.

The following morning, Lucia had a feeling that Brynmoroc was planning something significant to upset the villagers. So, because of her intuitions, we decided that from then on we would spend every midday in the woods. That way, if the wizard or any of his creatures did turn up in our world, we would be alone confronting them.

Within two days, we were thankful we made that decision because swooping down out of the clear blue sky was the menacing Brynmoroc. Instead of his usual appearance, he looked quite drawn and thin, his eyes weary and sad.

"My children. Oh, Lucia, my heart leaps with joy to see you alive and well. I haven't been able to see or protect you for some months now. Bleddwyn, that devious power-hungry cousin of mine, imprisoned me in my castle. I thought you were dead and lost forever. That terrible ordeal you had before the Swiss border was the work of my crafty cousin. He impersonated me. By using my image, he revealed to you his true identity, this being the gleaming giant wizard that he is. He intended to eliminate you, but if somehow you managed to escape, you would go away thinking that I, Brynmoroc was the culprit."

At that point, I interrupted to ask him if he would mind answering a few questions.

"Gwydion my son, I am so pleased with you. You must have guarded my little girl with your life. I only hope I can make it up to you one day and yes, go ahead, ask me anything you like."

The first question I asked was; if Bleddwyn had imprisoned him, then why did he let him go?

His answer, "Bleddwyn's centenary supply of enchanted energy is nearing its end and needs to be replenished. As you are well aware, the next centenary supply is due in May of this year. So, with him being in a weaker state now, my colleagues managed to overpower him enough to free me. But it will not last, so I haven't much time. Is there anything else you want to ask?"

I thought I would play crafty now and pretended that we still had faith in him.

"Just one more please, Sir. Lucia and I agreed that what happened before the Swiss border, was more than likely Bleddwyn's doing. So now, after listening to you, I feel we were correct. So, I am going to give you the benefit of the doubt. However, as you have already told us that Bleddwyn is capable of impersonating you, we will have to take precautions. This means until our mission is over, Lucia and I will still defend ourselves against you. Is that fair enough?"

"Gwydion my son," he said and smiled. "How happy I am to have such an intelligent boy at my daughter's side, and yes, that's fair enough. I wouldn't want it any other way."

He then looked at Lucia, who was shaking, peering over her shield.

"Gwydion will make you a good husband my child. I can see he loves you dearly and that you love him. Yes, and the day I walk you down the aisle, I will be the proudest father in both worlds."

I interrupted him before he got too sloppy and once again, craftily questioned him.

"Excuse me again, Sir, but I was wondering. After accomplishing our mission, how and when will I hand the staff over to you without Bleddwyn knowing and taking it from me?"

"Bleddwyn will be weak by then and will be no match for my colleagues and I. Besides, I have already told you that as long as the staff is in your possession, he cannot take it from you by force. The only way he can obtain it is by your hand or stealing it. When you have located the last jewel, hold out your staff to the sun and call my name. Then, as long as I'm able, I will be at your side within minutes. Now with that, I must leave you."

"Just one more question before you go please Sir," I quickly asked. "If you were incarcerated, how did you know about the Swiss border incident?"

"The birds Gwydion, it was the birds," he replied. "Goodbye for now Lucia. Look after her for me, son."

I could see tears in his weary eyes now, and his voice sounded choked up as he said, "I love you both."

Then, as he drifted back through the trees, he sadly waved until out of sight.

"Oh, I just don't know what to believe with him. What do you think?" Asked Lucia, squeezing my arm. "Is he telling the truth? You seemed to think so, or were you pretending again?"

I told her that I didn't believe a word he said and that he was just a crafty old liar. I was playing him at his own game, hoping to convince him enough that he might leave us in peace.

"Well, I hope so," she said and sighed. "I'm so tired from the lack of sleep lately; I could sleep for a week."

She had her wish because, throughout the rest of February, we had restful nights.

Incidentally, I have forgotten to mention that in that part of the world, it was autumn, so all that month of February, as we walked through the forest, we were enjoying the brilliance of its autumn colours. At night, we would join in with the many tribal games, but guess who the star player was? Yep, it was Lucia with her incredible hide-and-seek talent. I declined from performing any of my staff's abilities, simply because it wasn't for showing off purposes. Instead, we had great fun after I showed the men how to arm wrestle. I didn't want to cheat, so Lucia held my cape as I wrestled six times. It was tough, but at the finish, I still came away with my unbeaten record. Every night after that, Lucia and I were the judges at their newfound game of arm wrestling. I also taught a few of the young lads how to play jackstones, but arm wrestling was their favourite. In return, they taught us many of their tribal dances. I can tell you, with all that bouncing up and down, jiggling to and fro, it didn't do much for your belly. Especially after all the fruit they gave us to eat. So, after the first night of running back and forth the ditch every ten minutes, we waited until after dance practice before we had a meal, ha-ha.

Everything was going well, and despite our anxiety about wanting to get on with our assignment, we were having fun. That was, until one afternoon in March while we were strolling through the forest. A slithering length of creeping ivy wrapped itself around Lucia's ankles, dragging her back into a young holly tree which the ivy had been growing around. Fortunately, because we were always holding hands, she pulled me in with her. I drew out my knife, and after slicing away the creeping ivy, Lucia quickly rose to her feet in time before more slithering ivy wrapped itself around both of us. I pulled her hood up to protect her from the holly, then once again, slashed away at the ivy with my knife. The more I sliced them in half, the more they grew. Inch by inch they were drawing us further into the holly towards the trunk. I told Lucia to hold her arms up in front of her face to prevent the ivy from completely wrapping around her neck. As we were drawn into the holly tree, it was like being stabbed with a thousand needles. I knew there was only one way to stop the ivy, and that was to rip it up, but it was impossible to see anything. I couldn't see because we were in the middle of a thousand prickly holly leaves. So, I forced myself into the tree and felt around its trunk for the main ivy vine. The moment I found it, I ripped it away, breaking it as I did. Instantly, the vine withered and died.

"Ouch, ouch, oh Gwydion, I'm stuck and prickled all over. Help me down," she cried.

The ivy had pulled her up into the tree to about three feet off the ground. I looked around, it was all clear, so I joked with her, "Yeah okay, I'll go and fetch someone to give me a hand."

"Don't you dare Gwydion!" She screamed. "Get me down now. Right now, Gwydion."

I laughed, helped her down and got a slap for teasing her. We were both stinging something terrible as if we had fallen into a pile of nettles.

"Look at your face and hands Gwydion," said Lucia alarmingly. "They are covered in blood. We had better hurry back and wash it off so I can take a look at them."

Lucia, apart from the stinging prickles, was okay. She was wearing gloves and had covered her face. I was fine, just stinging that was all, but I had to do what I was told. I didn't mind; I loved her fussing over me, especially when she would kiss everything better after she had finished.

From that night and for another eight days after, we were constantly bombarded by howling, screeching noises sounding like wolves and a flock of parrots. We barely had an hour's sleep between us. Then one night, when we thought they had left us, another wolf-like creature, forced its way through our barricaded window and once again Roslyn was engaged in another fierce battle sounding as if it was a fight to the death. Although I was worried about her, I was glad the wolf thing didn't jump on me. As strong as I was, I would have been torn to pieces by that savage-looking thing. There was nothing I could do only block the window with my shield as more were trying to get in. The fight went on and on, and as they savaged one another, they knocked over the oil lamp which burst into flames. Lucia threw a blanket over it and put it out. We were now plunged into darkness, listening to a frightening savage battle until a sickening cry rendered us in silence. The wolves that were persistently trying to get in stopped and I could hear them yelping.

"What's happening?" whispered Lucia in a shaky-sounding voice.

I didn't know, but I could still hear growling. So I took my shield away from the window, and as I felt my way over to Lucia, I got a shock. Something touched me, but it was only Roslyn's nose, nudging me.

"Aw, well done girl," I said, patting her head. "Are you okay? I hope you are?"

I had no candles to light, so we had to wait until daylight to find that she had been victorious. The wolf was lying dead on the floor. Amazingly, Roslyn had only a few minor wounds which Lucia soon cleaned up. As for the wolf, I was surprised to find that he was real and not one of Brynmoroc's products. After tidying our room and telling the astounded Milaniah what had happened, we buried the wolf in the woods.

There were only two weeks to go before the equinox and to fulfil the Inca's prophecy of me climbing Wayna Picchu. We planned to have Roslyn as the goat that I was supposed to be riding, but we were not sure if the chief would allow Lucia to come with me. Not taking her wasn't an option, so I had to think of something to make sure I did. What I came up with was; I had a vision and in that vision, Lucia, with her all-seeing powers, was along with me. She was to make sure we took the safest route up the mountain. Chief Wabulamba knew that climbing Wayna Picchu was a hazardous task and that many had fallen to their death in doing so, even High Priests. He was reluctant at first then agreed, but only if I was on my own for the offering. That suited us fine, although I wasn't going to let it happen. Our main objective was to find the amethyst and get away as fast as we possibly could. We had to, because, as you know, the Incas' were expecting the immediate return of the Sun Giant. Something we knew was never going to happen.

Throughout the next week, we had no more unwanted visitors which we were pleased about. It also gave us time to come up with another plan, something that would enable us to stay in the village without running away. So, one morning, I told Chief Wabulamba that I had another vision. In my vision, the Sun after having accepted my offering, stated that the Sun Giant would return in May during the centenary eclipse of the sun. Wabulamba was pleased with my fabricated news and to our surprise told us that it was already written in the prophecy. We were relieved, for we were both a little apprehensive about what was going to happen after finding the amethyst. So now, whatever happens, we could either run or stay and leave amicably? Spain was where we were heading after that and the only way we were going to reach there was by sea, a daunting task to say the least. Be that as it may, we had two months to make the journey, so with that in mind, it gave us hope.

Finally, after another week of torment, the morning of the equinox arrived, and I was standing before Chief Wabulamba. I decided to make an early start because I wanted to find the amethyst before the midday sun, plus the actual equinox was going to happen around that time. As Wabulamba presented me with an offering of a wreath of flowers by placing them on my head, the sun began to rise. I had already changed Roslyn into a large nanny goat, the size of a horse. So, with a roar from the whole village, Lucia, Roslyn and I, were on our way down the mountain heading for Wayna Picchu.

# Chapter 24

We travelled south, following the river until we came to the foot of the precarious-looking tree and shrub-covered rocky mountain. I had told Chief Wabulamba that no one was allowed to follow me. The reason was; as soon as we were so far up the mountain, we were not going to be riding any goat. Though, after deciding that, I was impressed by the way Roslyn was climbing. She was like a cat on a mission. I knew goats were incredibly sure-footed and could run up and down mountains with ease. So I thought we'd stay riding her.

It was a slippery, tricky climb, sometimes terrifying. On one occasion, we had to scale across a path cut into the side of a sheer cliff. It was impossible for Roslyn; she was too big. The only way to cross was on foot. It took us a while to decide whether we should, or whether we shouldn't, but in the end, off we went. Roslyn walked on in front, not as a goat, but as our terrier. The path was more like a ledge, about fifty yards long and only two feet wide in places. It was the most terrifying thing we had done so far. One slip and we would have plummeted down a couple of hundred feet to our deaths. The safest way to walk was side-wards. So, with our backs against the rock face, without looking down, we slowly made our way across a ledge that made our legs wobble like jelly. Making it even worst, was when a sudden breeze whipped up. At that point, we just froze and hung on to each-others hand. Thankfully, the breeze stayed a breeze. So it was inch by inch from then on until we reached the end and onto a decent path again.

"Wow, I'll tell you one thing, Lucia. We are not going back that way again," I said as we lay down to rest.

"Thank goodness for that," she said while catching her breath. "That path must have been where those young lads lost their lives, and I would imagine, many more since."

We didn't have far to go now, so from then on we stayed on foot, zig-zagging our way up the rest of the mountain's tricky paths and steps until we finally reached the top. It was just as Milaniah described. The whole area was no larger than fifteen yards square with a few large rocks, nothing else. We were exhausted now and had to lie down. We led there for a good thirty minutes to recover before I placed my wreath on the stone where the chief had instructed me. Next was the jewel and where to find it before Brynmoroc found us.

"I was hoping I was wrong," said Lucia with a sigh. "But during our rest, it gave me time to think more clearly. The amethyst is exactly where I was hoping it wasn't going to be."

"Well! Where is it?" I eagerly asked.

Her devastating reply was, "Firstly; the amethyst is only the size of a small cherry, and secondly, it's sitting in a rock of granite, but now I see it's among hundreds of shiny stones and sadly, thirdly, it's high above that horrible ledge we walked across."

"Oh, no! Are you sure?" I asked, hoping she was only joking.

"Yes, I'm sure. I am sure Gwydion," she sighed, sadly looking at me.

"Okay, that settles it," I said. "Come on Roslyn, it's Scorpion time again."

"I just knew you were going to say that," said Lucia after a long groan. "Oh, I don't know. Oh Gwydion. Gwydion."

Before we set off down the mountain, I had to apologise to our poor Roslyn.

"I'm sorry girl, but it's for the last time. You probably don't mind, but I feel awful about doing it to you."

"Yes, and so do I," interrupted Lucia. "He's horrible to you Roslyn, isn't he?"

Roslyn just shook herself down as if she was saying, "I don't care."

I told Lucia that Roslyn was telling her to behave herself and not to be such a baby. As usual, she slapped me on the arm, saying, "Yes, you are horrible. And I hate you for saying that."

I laughed and said that I was joking and that she was the bravest girl I had ever known.

"I don't care," she replied with another slap. "I still hate you for saying that."

Going down was even trickier. Climbing up, we could use our hands and crawl, but going down was a matter of keeping our balance. By the time we reached the ledge, I was anxious. Time was ticking by super-fast. So with Roslyn standing before me, I raised my staff, and with my thoughts, she was once again the lovely creature Lucia was horrified by. Though I must say, when she wiggled her long spindly legs, if she were not mine, I would have felt the same way.

The cliff was not only sheer; it also looked as if some parts were ready to fall away. That made my stomach turn over a lot more than once. My cape was going to be too awkward for me to manoeuvre in, so I took it off and tied it behind me.

"Lucia, open your eyes," I said, lifting her onto the base of Roslyn's tail. "How far up this cliff do we have to go and in which direction?"

Pointing towards the part of the cliff that I had already thought unstable, she replied, "We must head up in that direction until we come to a small cave. The amethyst is inside."

"I thought you told me that it was in a rock of granite!" I asked, thinking she was mistaken.

"It is! That's how I saw it at first, but now I see that the rock is inside a cave."

I didn't want to worry her about that dodgy-looking part of the mountain, so I asked if we had to go in that particular direction.

"Yes," she replied, much to my disappointment. "That's the direction we have to take."

So off we went, slowly climbing at about sixty degrees, northeast across the rock face. Even Roslyn must have thought the precarious-looking area was chancy because she was testing it by tapping away firmly as she went. We were at such an awkward angle that it was difficult for me to hold on, especially with Lucia's arms wrapped around me. It was tough, but I was doing okay until some loose stones gave way from under us. My heart was in my mouth now, and it stayed there until long after we were well away from that treacherous part of the cliff.

We searched on, until Lucia shouted, "It should be somewhere around here."

Then all of a sudden, as Roslyn's action changed, my heart was back in my mouth again. She had found the cave and was clambering into it. The entrance was round about twice the size of a cartwheel. Inside was spacious, like any other cave, except the wall facing us was covered with glistening stones, lighting up the whole cave. The stones were glistening, yes, but they were not reflecting any sunlight; there wasn't any.

We slipped off our fantastic Roslyn, and even though she didn't look very appealing, I gave her a kiss on her face where I thought her nose would be. Lucia shook her head in disgust, but I didn't care. I just carried on patting and thanking her.

"Are you sure this is where the amethyst is?" I asked, looking at the wall. "If it is, we'll be forever finding it."

She was upset with me now, "I wish you wouldn't keep asking me if I'm sure. I said it's here and it is. We'll just have to look for it."

With me being told off, we set about the most tedious task imaginable. There were thousands of different coloured stones, pebbles and even jewels on that wall. All of them were glistening as if the sun was dancing upon them. After a while, our eyes began playing tricks, seeing things that were not there. One time, when I thought I had found the jewel, it turned out to be a beetle that wasn't even purple, it was white. It was as if we were being hypnotised, I even fell over twice from dropping off to sleep standing up. We must have gone over that wall a dozen times. Making it even more challenging, there were numerous amounts of blue-coloured stones, probably a few hundred, none of them purple.

"Ah, this is hopeless," I said after we sat down to rest. "We need a better system than random looking. Let's try again; only this time we'll work towards each other."

We did and must have scanned every inch of that wall over and over, but still, no amethyst could we find. Then, just as we were about to give up and come back another day, the sun shone into the cave. We were so dazzled by the reflection of the stones that we had to cover our eyes. At that moment, I felt a tingling sensation on the back of my neck, making me clasp it.

"There it is Gwydion! It's behind you!" Shouted Lucia, excitedly.

Sure enough, there it was, sitting in the middle of the wall behind us. The wall of sparkling stones was there to reflect the sun onto the amethyst at certain times of the day.

"Ingenious," I said to myself.

"Thank goodness. We've found it Gwydion. Who would have ever thought of looking there?" she said, shading her eyes from the bright light.

With no time to lose, I quickly told her and Roslyn to stand away to the side as I prepared myself for something I wasn't expecting. The moment I placed my staff on the jewel, there was no flash, only a burst of colour that lit up the cave with all the colours of the wizard's rainbow. Then as we watched, a stream of colour formed in the shape of an arrow, shot out of the cave heading for the sun. Within seconds the coloured arrow was back, sizzling up and down my illuminated staff in a mass of coloured flames until slowly fizzling out. Although I was holding the staff the whole time, my hand didn't burn. The entire ordeal lasted no more than thirty seconds, and while it was happening, I heard a man's voice call my name.

It was way past noon, and the sun had just past its peak. All our jewels were collected and we were happy, but now we had to get away. Knowing this, we quickly mounted Roslyn and started back down the cliff, only backwards this time but at ninety degrees. We didn't want to go anywhere near that dodgy patch again. Down, down, down we went, worrying all the time about Brynmoroc and his wizardry. If any of his creatures were to turn up now, we were at their mercy, meaning done for. Thankfully, we arrived safely on solid ground and with Roslyn back as the goat again, I sat on a rock and laughed with joy.

"Oh Gwydion, I don't know what you are laughing at," said Lucia after pushing me off the rock. "It wasn't funny. I will never do anything like that again. If I never see another creepy, crawly, horrible creature ever again, it wouldn't be long enough."

"That's why I'm laughing," I said, picking myself up. "We don't have to do it again. Come on, let's go."

I put on my cape, mounted Roslyn, pulled Lucia up behind me and away we went, down the mountain's tricky narrow paths and steps until we reached the river.

Our journey back to the village went trouble-free, and when we arrived, we were met with a loud cheer. The whole community were waiting, cheering away, jumping up and down. The chief and Milaniah were there to greet us as we dismounted.

"The great sun was pleased with you Gwydion. You and Lucia will be honoured forever more," said Wabulamba.

Milaniah said that after seeing the sun turn many colours, they knew we had been successful.

Knowing that they were happy was a relief. It now meant that we could carry on to Spain without any trouble.

For the rest of that day, up until the early hours of the morning, the whole village celebrated by singing and dancing. We happily joined in with their celebrations, but it wasn't for the return of the Sun Giant, it was because we had found all the jewels. Over the weeks, we had learned most of their dances, so it was great fun, but we were stiff as boards by the time we collapsed in bed. We said goodnight to our hound dog, Roslyn, and that's all I can remember until the cock crowed. He must have crowed a dozen times before we were up having a late breakfast, chatting to Milaniah.

When we announced that we were leaving, there was great sorrow in the village. Both Lucia and I felt the same way, but that's what happens when you leave friends.

"Ah, they'll get over it and so will we," I said, packing our bags.

There was a long way to go now and I was in a hurry to get started. Chief Wabulamba was waiting to thank us once again, wished us a safe journey and said that their home was our home anytime we wanted to return. Milaniah didn't help Lucia's saddened feelings, for she too was crying. So, with heavy hearts, we mounted our faithful Roslyn and headed out of that pleasant village full of lovely people.

Before entering the jungle, I had Roslyn back as a mongoose. It was the safest way to travel; we didn't want to be trotting over any snakes' etcetera. We made our way through the massive forest and its tall trees until we came to the river. It was flowing naturally now, so crossing was easier this time. Our amazing Roslyn simply ran across with ease.

We needed food supplies and plenty of them. By the time we reached Cusco, we were back on horseback and stopped at the first food store there. After stocking up and having something to eat, Lucia heard a lady say that a train was pulling in and it was going to Juliaca that very afternoon.

That was good news. The very thought of another four hundred miles to the ocean on horseback wasn't going down too well. So we made our way to the station where we heard even more good news. The train, after stopping overnight in Juliaca, would be going all the way to the port of Mollendo at seven o'clock the following morning.

"What a stroke of luck I overheard that lady," said Lucia, plonking herself down on the station bench.

Yes, it was a stroke of luck, for it was now going to save us a long tedious journey across rough open land, something we had just about enough of.

The train pulled out of Cuzco at two o'clock, and we arrived in Juliaca sometime after eight. The station master pointed us in the direction of a hotel, and within an hour we were lying on our bed with Roslyn led on a blanket by the door. I wasn't all that tired, but to be honest, I was afraid to close my eyes. I had a bad feeling that sooner or later, we were going to have a visitor. So I just lay there thinking and listening to the town hall clock strike every hour until I couldn't keep my eyes open any longer. I must have only been asleep a short while when Roslyn barked to wake me up. She was quietly growling and staring at the wall across the room. I gave Lucia a shake to wake her, then turned up the lamp in time to see a vision appear on the wall. There was a beautiful lady in the distance walking down a mountainside. She was wearing a long purple dress and walking towards us with her arms outstretched as if greeting us. The closer she came, the more realistic she looked. Her hair was dark, and her long dress seemed to flow and bounce as she walked between the heather. We were both sitting on the edge of the bed, holding our shields afore us. Roslyn was watching the lady and quietly growling to herself.

"Come here girl, and be quiet," I said as the lady stopped and looked down at her.

Roslyn came over, and as we watched, the strange lady smiled and as we expected, walked out of the vision, and into our room.

"Lucia, Gwydion. You have good reason to be afraid of me for as you know, during your ordeal you have encountered many false illusions. The road you took to overcome them is much to be commended. Your wisdom has surpassed any of our expectations. However, you have chosen to sail the vast Atlantic Ocean, a formidable task. One, deeper than the very ocean itself, further than you could ever see. During your voyage, you will be challenged by the merciless violator of Vindaguar's prophecy. This heartless wizard will haunt and drive you to the very limit of your endurance, leaving you desperate and in a life-threatening situation. If and when this occasion capitulates, you must cast your staff into the leaping waves before the ocean swallows you up."

I was tired now, and my patience was about to snap. I was sick of prophecies and visions, so I questioned the lady.

"You come here talking about some heartless, merciless, violating wizard, but I didn't hear you mention any names. Who is this merciless wizard? How many are there? We know there are at least two. You also come here, talking about life-threatening situations. Well, let me tell you now misses, whoever you are, we have already experienced more than enough death-defying stunts thank you very much. So you have come here wasting your time telling us something we already know, except for the name of this so-called, merciless, violating, heartless wizard. Who are you, anyway? What's your name? Do you have one, or are you just another illusion? Why all this secrecy anyway? Haven't we done enough for you lot? Don't we at least, deserve to know what's going on? No! As far as I can see, it's considered to be none of our business. Ah, just go away; leave us alone before I set the dog on you."

After saying all that, she just smiled and pointed her finger at the wall. The vision of the mountainside then changed to the image of the battling wizards on top of the old Roman fort back home. After no more than a minute, it faded away only to be followed by every single vision Lucia and I had seen during our time together. When they had all finished, the vision of the mountainside returned. The lady then turned to us, held out her hand and asked.

"If I were to ask which one of the visions you believed to be real. Could you answer me?"

I was still in no kind of mood to be bothered answering. So Lucia replied.

"It would be very difficult. So I would say no, we wouldn't be able to."

"You have now seen both wizards Lucia," said the lady. "Gwydion has told you Bleddwyn's version of events. So, once again, if I ask you which one of the two wizards speaks the truth, could you answer me?"

Lucia's reply, much to my breaking point of patience, was, "No, lady. Once again, we would be unable."

The lady smiled again and said, "Well, if you are undecided as to which wizard and what vision to believe in, then why should you believe me? For me to tell you who, why and what would be pointless and only confuse you even more. I have accomplished what I came here for. Now all I can say is; take heed of your ultimatum."

She then turned, stepped back into the vision and walked off up the hill with the vision fading away behind her.

"Ah, what a load of nonsense," I said, turning down the lamp. "If she thinks I'm going to believe one iota of what she told us, she's another think coming. As for my staff, she so kindly tells us, to save our lives, just throw it overboard into the ocean. All I can say on that subject is; so far, my staff is the only thing that has kept us alive and brought us to where we are now. So once again, if she thinks I'm just going to throw it away into the depths of the ocean, she's crazy and probably in with this merciless wizard of hers."

Lucia agreed but did mention that she had never seen me in such a bad mood. I told her that I was fed up and would be glad when it was all over. Then as I lay back down, she gently stroked my hair. She did this sometimes to comfort me until I drifted off to sleep. I loved her doing that; in fact, I loved every little thing about her. I loved the elegant way she walked, her lovely accent, the way she laughed, the songs she sang, her delicate little hands and toes, her long black hair, her pretty face, her loving eyes, her tempting lips and her beautiful smile. I even loved the tiny tears that gently rolled down her cheeks when she was sad. Though I must say, I didn't relish the fact of her being upset. So, all in all, Lucia was the loveliest girl that I was lucky enough to have ever met.

We were up at six in the morning and had a quick breakfast before walking off down the street to catch the seven o'clock train. We climbed aboard, and with Roslyn sitting on Lucia's lap we looked out through the window. It was a cold and wet miserable day we were looking at, but we were reasonably happy. The guard blew his whistle, and we were off, heading to the coast to prepare for what the lady in the vision said, a formidable task, deeper than the very ocean.

It was a long journey, but finally, after ten tiring hours, we arrived in Mollendo at five o'clock. The harbour store was open, so the first thing we did was buy four water containers. We also needed a vast supply of food etcetera, but we had nowhere to keep them. With Roslyn back as our mare, the next thing was to buy a carriage. I did and stocked it with tins of food, some blankets, all-weather clothes and a fishing rod just in case. With that done, we filled our water containers and headed out of the harbour. After taking the north road across the coastline, we stopped a couple of miles away from the port. What was going to happen next, we didn't know, it was all up to Roslyn. All we knew was, according to my world map, the shortest route to Spain was up the coast to Panama and across the fifty-mile strip of land to the Caribbean Sea. From then on it was out into the massive Atlantic Ocean, through the Alboran Sea to somewhere near the port of Aguilas Spain.

Impossible, perhaps? That's what we thought too after looking out into the vast Pacific Ocean. When the lady mentioned us being in a life-threatening situation, she wasn't making it up. Her warnings were true, but we were already in a do-or-die situation. If we attempt the crossing, the chance of us ever making it to Spain alive was possibly slimmer than slim. If we stayed, then we would almost certainly be robbed and no doubt killed. Either way, our ultimatum was much the same. We had to take the chance and sail because after all, surely Vindaguar must have known it was our only way out. We had indeed been lucky up until then, but these natives of South America were poor and were not looking very friendly. Roslyn had never let us down, so we were putting our complete trust in her. Maybe we were not going to like it, but it was in our best interest if we did. So, I told Roslyn that we were ready and to do whatever she had planned and with that, we climbed into the carriage.

"Hold on to me, Gwydion. I'm afraid and so cold," cried Lucia, burying her head in my chest.

Roslyn began trotting along the coastal road, and as she did, I knew by the change of our carriage movement that it had developed legs again. I could now actually feel Lucia's heart beating so fast that it started mine off. Roslyn had picked up speed, left the road, raced across the sands and was now ploughing into the ocean. At that point, I closed my eyes, and we held onto each other until we fell onto something soft. Opening our eyes, we found ourselves lying on a nice soft bed. Lucia's face was white as snow, probably mine too.

"I don't know whether to laugh or cry," she said after a huge sigh. "That was another terrible experience."

"Well, it's all over now," I replied. "Let's go take a look at what's happening."

"Oh, no! Not just yet! Let's take a minute or two to recover first" she begged, pulling me back onto the bed.

It took her an hour before she was ready, but by that time, it was too dark and pointless. Instead, we lit the lamps and walked around the living quarters. There was a log apartment full of fuel, two rooms for the crew and one that must have been for the captain. So along with ours, we thought it a relatively large ship. I can't say that we were not a little concerned, but after a bite to eat, we settled down nicely and didn't wake up until sunrise.

"It's daylight, Gwydion," said Lucia untying our handcuff. "Let's take a look on deck."

We nervously made our way, and after climbing out the hatch, it was as we thought, a ship with sails.

"Look Gwydion? We are speeding across the water, but there is no sign of Roslyn?"

Then just as if Roslyn heard Lucia's cries, a dark brown tiger shark breached the surface.

"There she is," said Lucia, excitedly. "That's our lovely Roslyn. Isn't she beautiful?"

She was, and then as we looked over the bow of the ship, we saw many ropes, twelve at least. Having sails didn't make a lot of sense, for if we were being towed, they would cause a lot of drag, but as I looked up at them, they were blowing in a fashion as if the wind was behind us. I realised then that we had to have sails; otherwise, a boat travelling at about thirty miles an hour without them would be classed as witchcraft, attacked and blown out of the water.

I was excited now and with my confidence high, I just knew we were going to make it. The

Pacific Ocean was calm, and with the air being so warm and fresh, we stood there watching, hoping to see the sharks or whatever it was that was towing us, but we didn't. I said perhaps they were keeping a low profile, away from inquisitive eyes.

"Yes, that makes sense. Good old Roslyn, she thinks of everything," said Lucia and laughed.

All that morning, we were either in the captain's cabin playing quizzes and jackstones or out watching dolphins jumping alongside the ship. In the afternoon, Lucia baked bread in the oven and a jam tart for tea. During all this time, we sailed peacefully across the ocean without a sign of the wizard or his deeds. It was well over fifteen hundred miles to Panama, and it was now six in the evening. I roughly worked out the speed we were sailing and if all went well, we were due to arrive on the shores of Panama the following evening.

"Well, so far so good," said Lucia as we bedded down for the night.

I turned down the lamp, and as we lay down, I replied, "Yes, and if things keep going the way they are, without any hitches, we should be on the shores of Spain in about two or three weeks."

I heard her sigh as if she was thinking, 'Yes, but I can't see that happening.''

"Aww, don't sigh Lucia," I said, putting my free arm around her. "We'll be alright. We'll get there on time. Don't worry."

She gave another sigh, and as she snuggled up to me, she quietly drifted off to sleep.

That night, apart from the usual nudge from her in the early hours asking. "Are you alright Gwydion?" I had the best night's sleep in a long time.

If you can remember, at the beginning of my memoirs, I mentioned that Lucia would wake me almost every night just to ask if I was alright. It was nice she worried and cared about me, but I wouldn't have had so many black rings under my eyes if she hadn't.

Thanks to our fantastic ship, there was a stack of wood already there for the fire. With breakfast over, we climbed on deck to check our whereabouts. There was nothing to see only a vast ocean. So with no sign of land or any other ships or boats, we spent the rest of the morning and afternoon playing games, then later, checking out our route across Panama. Some areas of Panama were lake riddled and swampy, so once again, how we were going to cross it, I had no idea. I was leaving it to Roslyn.

That evening, while up on deck, Lucia pointed out lights in the distance. Whether it was Panama or not, we didn't know, but we were heading towards it.

"What's Roslyn going to do now?" Lucia asked, just as I was wondering the same thing.

We soon found out because soon we were picking up speed and in a matter of minutes we were back in our carriage, running across the ocean towards the coast. Lucia covered her head, and while we clung to each other, we waited in anticipation. After a long dark, claustrophobic ride, we stopped on dry land in front of what looked like a ruin. With our heartbeats back to normal, we stepped out, wondering where we were. The half-moon came out from behind the clouds, revealing other ruins nearby.

"Perhaps this place was one time a settlement," suggested Lucia.

I unhitched Roslyn to let her wander. She was an enchanted animal, yes, but I still thought she needed a rest. The ruin at one time was definitely someone's house and home. The walls were tall and intact, but the roof had caved in. We thought we'd get a candle each and take a quick look. The old black door was intact and wide open, so we went inside and found that the furniture was still there, covered in dust. The staircase was blocked by the caved-in roof, but the downstairs ceilings had held fast. Lucia wasn't too happy.

"That's enough," she whispered. "Come on, let's go. It's creepy in here, and besides, it doesn't look all that safe."

"Ok we'll go in a minute," I said, peeping into the kitchen.

The table was also covered in dust and cobwebs but neatly laid out with four bowls, spoons and a knife beside what looked to be a breadboard.

"Whoever lived here must have left in a hurry," I said, picking up the bowl.

"Yes, they must have, but come on, let's get out of here," insisted Lucia, pulling my arm.

We did, but as we walked back through the living room, either some dust or a cobweb went into my eye. I put the candle down on a chest of draws to gently rub my eye.

"What's the matter, Gwydion? Are you okay?" Asked Lucia, clutching my arm.

I was okay, but as I went to pick up the candle, it flickered and went out as I grabbed it. Strangely, with the light from Lucia's candle, I found now that I wasn't holding my candle. I was holding a small box. Before I could even study it, I felt a stinging sensation in my little finger, causing me to drop the box which opened on impact with the hard floor.

"It's just a little old empty jewellery box of some kind. Will you hurry up Gwydion? Let's get out of here," said Lucia, pulling me out the door.

I wasn't too worried because it didn't feel as if Brynmoroc was involved in any way. If he was, I usually had some kind of intuition. Besides, Roslyn wouldn't have stopped if she thought there was any danger. My little finger was itching like mad now, so I rubbed it for a while until it stopped.

"What's the matter with your finger?" Asked Lucia, taking hold of it.

"I don't know," I replied. "It was as if something stung me, but it's okay now."

We didn't know our exact whereabouts but knew we must be somewhere near Panama. This meant that we had to travel at least another fifty miles across land before reaching the Caribbean Sea. What Roslyn had planned for the journey we didn't know until she came back and stood, waiting to be hitched up. It was two hours to midnight, so whatever she had in mind, she wanted to carry it out in the dark.

"Okay, carry on girl," I said after hitching her. "You know what you're doing."

I told Lucia to jump in and hold on tight, for it looked as if we were in for another surprise. Then with a jolt, we were away again at a fast pace across a mountainside. Another jolt and we were once again sitting on the back of a furry spider, running across a lake. Because of the boggy land, I had a feeling Roslyn was going to do something like that. I think Lucia knew it too because I didn't hear any screams, but she did have her head buried in my back. The night air was warm, a whole lot different to the last time we were sitting on her as a spider. The incredible speed with which she ran across the swampy boggy land and lakes, was something only a spider could possibly do. It seemed no time at all before we found ourselves falling back onto our bed aboard another ship.

Lucia rose and as she lit a lamp, said, "Let's just stay here and go to sleep, shall we? It's a waste of time looking to see where we are for all we'll see is water."

I had no intention of looking anyway. So, she unpacked our sleeping bags, said goodnight and we slept until eleven in the morning. We had a good look around and thankfully found that all our food supplies and utensils, were there in the galley. Next, we were up on deck, checking out our new ship. It was pretty much the same as before, though larger.

"Look Gwydion. Look who our friends are this time," Lucia shouted.

# Chapter 25

nstead of a school of tiger sharks, there were, including Roslyn, seven magnificent orca whales towing us smoothly across the Atlantic. The massive ocean was calm enough to see and hear them spurting water out from their blowholes, and as they swam rhythmically, their large dorsal fins bobbed up and down. Lucia had told me earlier back in the Pacific that whales didn't like sharks and would sometimes attack them. I had been worrying about this. I knew there were a lot of whales' in that particular part of the Atlantic. So you can imagine how relieved we were seeing those seven, twenty or thirty feet long awesome orcas happily bobbing along in front of us. This made me think that Roslyn must have known we were going to encounter whales on the route and had no choice but to use the orcas. The only concern I had was their speed. They were nowhere near as fast as tiger sharks. It was over five thousand miles to Murcia and with the speed our whales were travelling, roughly about eight or ten miles an hour, would take us three weeks. There were only six weeks until the eclipse.

We stayed on deck until four in the afternoon, missing lunch just in case we had trouble with Brynmoroc. We would rather face him out in the open than down below deck.

We travelled on for three more peaceful days until one afternoon, while up on the captain's bridge, Lucia shouted.

"Look Gwydion? There are hundreds of whales out there. We are going to run into them."

Yes, they were whales alright; orca whales and they were heading directly towards us. There was nothing we could do only watch and hold onto each other in anticipation. The closer we approached the orcas the more anxious we became. Then as we held our breath, the advancing whales separated, leaving a clear path for us to sail through. Then, no sooner had we passed the last few whales, we were speeding away again, only this time, a lot faster. Faster, because instead of orcas, we now had our team of tiger sharks back.

"Yahoo Roslyn," we shouted as our brown tiger shark leapt out of the water and back again.

We were travelling twice as fast now, meaning, weather permitting, we would be in Spain no later than two weeks, giving us plenty of time to spare. We were happy now and stayed on the bridge until the day became night. Before sleep, I remembered what Bleddwyn said about Lucia knowing precisely what to do with the staff on the day of the eclipse. So I thought I'd ask if she now knew.

"Yes," was her reply. "I know what you have to do, but I am worried about Brynmoroc and what he'll do to prevent it. So I was waiting to discuss it with my grandmother first. Is that alright with you?"

I said it was okay with me, turned down the lamp and we slept until about three o'clock when I was awakened by a nightmare. I was worried, worried because I suddenly realised that we had no hound on guard now. Roslyn was outside under the waves, tugging away. I couldn't command another hound because my staff was for transport only.

"What's the matter Gwydion?" Lucia asked, flicking out her shield.

"Oh, it's nothing to worry about," I replied. "I can't sleep, that's all. Go back to sleep. I think I'll get my journals and bring them up to date."

I hadn't filled them in for two days. So that's what I did, and it kept me awake until sunrise. For most of that day up until supper, I tried to remember Bleddwyn's words regarding the staff, but after travelling halfway around the world, being through so many battles, mind-boggling secrets and meeting so many people, I just couldn't remember. The day Bleddwyn told me all about my staff was the only day I didn't write down in my journals. I thought I could remember it, but right then, onboard that ship, my mind was a total blank until I mentioned it to Lucia who jogged my memory.

"I thought you told me that after we had found every one of the seven jewels, your staff would become a powerful source of energy."

"That's it, Lucia, you're a genius," I said and could have kissed her for it. "He also told me that up until then, my staff could only be used for ways and means of travel. So, let's try out the staff's capabilities.

"Wait, Gwydion! Don't be too hasty," said my Lucia, sensibly. "Let's wash up first and then we'll sit down and think about it."

With everything cleared away, we sat down to discuss the staff and what we should ask for, but alas, not one of us could come up with anything. We were both afraid that the exact opposite would happen. So after a lengthy discussion, we decided not to risk experimenting until we were safely on dry land, but I couldn't wait. I couldn't wait because there was one thing I was tempted to ask for. Another hound would keep my mind at ease; it would also help me sleep at night. So, as not to worry Lucia, I waited until she was asleep before I quietly and gently unwrapped our wrists. Once free, I held up my staff and commanded it with my thoughts. Then low and behold, sitting by the door was a beautiful bullmastiff hound that barked, waking Lucia.

"What was that?" she said, grabbing her shield. "Oh, no! Not another creature? Quick, Gwydion!"

"It's alright. I tried out my staff," I said and laughed. "She's our new member of the family."

Lucia loved her instantly and named her Adora, meaning lovely. She had exactly the same features and colour as Roslyn you could have even sworn that it was her twin. I was happy now and even more so after waking in the morning from a peaceful night's sleep.

"Yahoo," I said to myself. "What else can this old staff do?"

It was amazing, but then I told myself that I was quite happy with our new member of the family and wasn't going to push my luck again unless I had to. One good thing about having Adora was while we played with her on deck, she made the day go a lot quicker.

The following day, the calm Atlantic Ocean was now the complete opposite, though strangely enough, although the waves were deep and large, our ship just sailed over them with ease.

"Well, at least, we don't have to worry about getting seasick," said Lucia jokingly and we laughed.

It was funny, yes, but our laughter was short-lived, for as we looked out at the raging ocean, it was now becoming a terrifying sight. Noting this, we went below to try and forget about it. I did some calculations; according to the speed we were travelling, we were about halfway across the ocean and in its swell. While we were sat discussing whatever we could think of, one of our conversations was about the Vikings. We were wondering, how on earth they and the like, ever cross the oceans in their small rowing ships. They had sails, but whoa, looking at the height of the waves outside, surely they would have had no chance of survival. All we could say was; they were undeniably courageous beyond belief.

Lucia shook her head and stated that she didn't want to see the massive waves anymore. So we covered up the portholes with any old thing we could find and spent the rest of the day in our cabin with Adora led down on guard by the door.

Two more days had passed before we were brave enough to venture up on deck again. The vast Atlantic Ocean had calmed considerably, but it was still every bit as frightening, for as we looked out across its leaping white crested waves, all we could see was nothing. Nothing, only eternity and a dark grey, miserable sky. So as we lay down to sleep that night, I said to myself.

"I'd rather climb the highest mountain right now than be here, stuck on this ship in the middle of nowhere."

Then just to sicken us even more, the following morning the densest fog I had ever seen crept slowly across the ocean. The miserable stuff swamped us for a further two more days before finally lifting. With the sky now clear and blue again I thought I'd go on deck to look for land.

"After breakfast, Gwydion. We'll take a look after breakfast," insisted Lucia.

Lucia wouldn't do anything until she had her breakfast. So, we had our bread and water with a sprinkle of sugar to make it more appetising, swilled the dishes then went up on deck. We scanned the skyline for ages until I spotted an island in the distance, north of us. We had no idea where we were only that we were sailing east, so the sight of that island encouraged us immensely.

"We shouldn't be too far away now my lovely Spanish Senorita," I said, holding my arms out to her in excitement.

"Yahoo, my lovely Welsh sheep boy," she said as I wrapped my arms around her.

"I'm what?" I said, looking at her grinning. "A sheep boy? Is that what you think of me? Why I…"

"Well, all you think of me is a snivelling big baby," she interrupted, pushing me away and laughing. "That's what you called me back in Peru didn't you, sheep boy?"

Before I could grab her, she ran away, laughing down to our cabin with me running after her. She squealed as I caught her but laughed as I pushed her onto the bed and without thinking, I started to say, "I wish…," then hesitated.

Her lovely laughter stopped, and while looking at me with her beautiful dark Spanish eyes, she asked, "What's the matter? What do you wish for?"

What I was going to say before I hesitated was, I wish I hadn't made any promises, but instead of that, I held her hand and replied.

"Oh, I don't know, but if I was offered one wish right now, I would say keep it, because I have all that I want right here."

She sat up, looked carefully into my eyes and asked, "Do you really mean that?"

"Of course I do," I replied, putting my arms around her, but before I could say anymore, there was a thud against the side of the ship, making us rush up on deck. The fog was back again.

"The thud must have been that old trunk of a tree," said Lucia, looking over the side.

I began thinking, "It's as if someone's watching us and whoever it is, certainly didn't want me telling Lucia anymore."

With the fog being so dense, we were even more vulnerable against Brynmoroc. We had to be on our guard every minute until it lifted. Knowing this, changed the atmosphere for the rest of the day and night.

In the morning, we were awakened by the sound of a foghorn. We quickly dress to check what was happening. Unfortunately, because of the fog still lying thick across the ocean, we couldn't see a thing. I was disappointed, but at the same time, realised that we must be somewhere near the coast for other foghorns were sounding in the distance. All we could do now was trust in Roslyn. Then, while we were looking out and listening, our ship rocked violently sending us sprawling.

"What's happening?" asked Lucia as I picked her up.

The fog now seemed to be swirling around us like a whirlwind until it burst like a balloon, leaving a row of ghostly-looking wizards, one of them, Brynmoroc. They were hovering on one side of the ship with a solitary wizard, who I recognised to be Bleddwyn, hovering on the other. Bleddwyn, while facing Brynmoroc and the other wizards, beckoned them onto him. They responded, and an almighty battle broke out over the top of us. Our immediate reaction was to run for cover, but with our ship being rocked from side to side we couldn't stand, never mind run. All we could do was crouch down, look and listen to loud claps of thunder and lightning booming and flashing above us. It was an ugly, frightening-looking battle, one definitely to the death. Time and time again, as Bleddwyn lashed out with lethal blows, stricken wizards fell lifeless into the waves. The ferocious manic battle went on and on until finally, Brynmoroc too, fell into the ocean from an impact by the victorious Bleddwyn.

"You are a fool Brynmoroc," roared Bleddwyn. "A fool to think you could ever match my awesome power. I'm finished with you cousin, and your lovesick children."

He then looked at us, laughed and said, "And as for you Gwydion, your mission is over son. I don't need you anymore. So thank you, thank you my little fool. And as a token of my appreciation, you can keep the pouch, though I'll take your staff, but only when I'm ready."

Bleddwyn, looking down into the ocean, roared at the struggling Brynmoroc.

"Remember this cousin; I am the power. I always was, and always will be."

With those words, he, along with the fog, disappeared into the clear blue sky, leaving total silence. Our ship had stopped rocking, but we were not moving. We sat there, saying nothing, waiting and listening until we were sure the wizard had gone.

"What's going on now?" Whispered Lucia. "Who was that other wizard? Was it Bleddwyn?"

All I could say was that the strange ghostly image was that of Bleddwyn and why they were all in that ghostly form, I had no idea.

"Unless it's another one of those wizard's tricks again," said Lucia, as she frowned. "Who do you think it is?"

"To be honest, I don't really care," I replied. "One way or another, we are going to finish what we started. What happens after that is their problem, because you and I, my pretty dark-eyed Lucia, are going to…"

I stopped short because I could feel myself getting carried away again.

"Going to what?" she asked. "Why don't you ever finish what you are saying?"

"Err, we are going to forget about them," I replied, somewhat awkwardly.

"That's nonsense!" She said after scowling and giving me a sharp dig in the side. "You were not going to say that at all. Tell me the truth. What were you going to say to me?"

I didn't have time to answer because we heard a cry for help. It was coming from overboard. We stood up and took a look over the side.

"Help me, Gwydion! Help me, please? I'm weak and drowning."

"It's Brynmoroc!" Gasped Lucia. "What are you going to do? Are you going to help him up?"

"Help me Gwydion? Do not be afraid, I'll not harm you. Quickly son," cried Brynmoroc, pitifully.

"Help him Gwydion," said Lucia in earnest.

"Okay, okay," I said, untying a rope ladder. "But get behind your shield. I don't trust him."

I dropped the ladder over the side, down to the spluttering wizard who slowly climbed aboard. Lucia and I backed away, holding our shields in front of someone who looked more like a large drowned rat than a powerful wizard. Adora, who had never left us, stayed by our side.

"Thank you, both of you," said Brynmoroc. "Another five minutes and I would have surely drowned."

"Drown! You are a wizard, Sir. How can that be?" I asked, not believing a word he said.

"There are only two things in life wizards fear," he replied "One of them saltwater, the other snow."

I knew he was talking a load of nonsense and that the ghostly battle was just one of his innovative conjured-up visions. He then stretched out his hand to the ocean and snatched his staff as it flew through the air back to him. In a flash, he was dry as a bone, looking himself again.

"My colleagues and I have just stood our last stand against my powerful cousin. Unfortunately, as you have witnessed, Bleddwyn is far too strong, and soon there will be nothing we can do to stop him. Also, as you are both well aware, you are the true instigators of Vindaguar's prophecy, but you have been deceived by a cunning wizard. Do you think it was your destiny to meet Bleddwyn the way you did son, and that it was he who was to proclaim the prophecy to you? No Gwydion! Your destiny was to be proclaimed by your parents, but unfortunately, they met their fate at the hands of my poisonous cousin. Everything I have told you in the past months is true. Bleddwyn is a wicked evil wizard and at the moment, unstoppable. The only thing left to stop this tyrant is your staff. It is a powerful source now Gwydion, and its energy needs to be stabilised. It holds energy so great; it will kill you the moment you try to activate it. I or anyone of my colleagues will show you how it's done, but we must hurry Gwydion."

I didn't believe a word of it. So, just to get rid of the wizard, I reminded him.

"As we have already agreed, Sir, the staff will be handed over to you, but only when I know that it's safe to do so. When that time comes, I will call out to you. Now, as you can see, Lucia is shivering from fright, so I need to take her below. In the meantime, I'm sure you'll want to check on your colleagues?"

"You are a good young lad Gwydion and you have guarded my lovely daughter with your life. I will make it up to you, more than you can ever imagine and this I promise. I must go now for as you have already pointed out, my colleagues need me. Good day to you now and thank you once again for saving my life," said the wizard followed by a flash and he was gone.

"Rubbish," I said and laughed. "What a load of mumbo jumbo. I'll never give him or any other wizard my staff, not even Bleddwyn. It's ours now, and we are keeping it until after the solar eclipse. Then whoever wants it, can have it."

"Don't worry," said Lucia, giving me a little squeeze. "I don't believe him either. When Brynmoroc stated that there was no way he could stop his cousin, he was really saying; there was no way he can stop us. So come on, let's see why we are not moving.

"There's land," she said, looking over the bow of the ship.

The sharks had left, but Roslyn gave a little splash to let us know she was there. It was now obvious why she had stopped; we couldn't sail into a port without a crew now, could we? We waited until dark before swapping our large ship for a small sailing boat, and within an hour we were gracefully sailing through the Straits of Gibraltar. From then on, we slowly made our way across the choppy Alboran Sea. Whether it was because of the current or from the wind whipping up, the choppy sea was a rough rocky ride, making us think we would never dock until there was a jolt.

"Thank goodness," said Lucia, as we found ourselves back in our carriage, racing across the coast, eventually stopping outside a church. Lucia recognised the place as being Aguilas. She had been there many times with her grandmother."

It was six in the morning, and not surprisingly, the streets were busy with fishermen heading for their boats. It was the perfect opportunity to get an early start on to Lucia's grandmother in Velez Rubio. The quickest route to Velez Rubio was via Lorca Castle, or as the locals called it, 'The Fortress Of The Sun.' This was

Brynmoroc's castle, so that route was not an option. We had no choice but to do it the hard way, cut across country to Puerto Lumbreras. It was only twenty miles, but we had to travel on horseback.

It turned out to be a glorious day, making us feel good as we made our way riding our beautiful Roslyn again. Adora followed and was enjoying herself chasing rabbits as she ran. Now, as I aforesaid, it was only twenty miles, but for any other hound or horse, it would have been a tough task.

There is one more thing I forgot to mention; riding Roslyn, whether she was at full speed ahead or in a slow trot, it was as if we were galloping on fresh air. Perhaps she was? Whichever way, our bottoms were truly grateful, ha-ha.

Eventually, after a fascinating trip through valleys, up and over mountains, we arrived in Puerto Lumbreras in good time. With it being only another ten miles to Lucia's home, we stopped for a long-awaited snack and a coffee in a café there. With Lucia being from around the area, I think she must have known mostly everyone. By the time she hugged, kissed and introduced me to some of her friends, it was time for another coffee. My mouth was dry and my head was wrecked from listening to Lucia's fast-talking, giggling lady friends.

"Dew," I said as we sat down. "You are a very popular girl around here, ain't ya?"

She just laughed and said that she came there often and a few of them were her old-school pals.

After a few more hugs and kisses, we thankfully headed out of town. The road was good, so within an hour of travelling, we were looking at Lucia's home, up on a hill. It was so lovely, but I wondered how her grandmother managed or even afforded to keep the lovely place going.

"I don't know," said Lucia. I've asked her the same question many times, but all she'll say is; it's the same way we royals have always managed."

"You didn't tell me your grandmother's a royal," I said in bewilderment.

"Yes, she's a princess in her own right. So am I. Didn't you know?"

It never dawned on me that they were of royal descent. I was shocked until I remembered something Bleddwyn told me. Neither was of royal blood. It was only because of their adoptive Royal great grandparents; they thought they were.

"Well, your highness," I said and bowed. "No, I didn't. Now, is there anything else you forgot to tell me?"

"No, but I thought you knew," she replied gently holding my arm. "But please don't call me that. I'm no higher than you or anyone else. I'm just me, a princess by right. One who no one knows about."

"Okay, I'm sorry, but that was a shock," I said, patting her hand. "Now let's go and see your grandmother. I'm looking forward to meeting her."

# Chapter 26

The small mansion was a typical Spanish building, constructed very similar to the buildings in Cuzco. Walking hand in hand up the long drive to the door, I counted the windows. There were eight, four up and four down. I sent Roslyn off to graze with Adora along for company.

Lucia opened the dark oak door, walked in and shouted in Spanish.

"Abuela estoy en casa." Meaning, I'm home Grandmother.

"Se que eres," meaning, I know you are," said her grandmother, coming from behind the door. She had seen us coming and was hiding behind it.

"Oh Abuela, I should have known you would have been hiding there," said Lucia as they hugged.

"Gwydion, this is my lovely grandmother. Abuela, this is my hero…."

"Gwydion," said her grandmother, interrupting in English. "So you are Gwydion. It's so nice to meet a hero."

I had never thought of asking Lucia what to call her grandmother, so I called her Abuela.

"It's nice to meet you too, Abuela, but as for being a hero, I think your lovely granddaughter is just excited to see you again. She's been like it all day."

She laughed and said, "My name is Mariana. Now, Lucia, show your hero to his room while I make something to eat."

All the way up the stairway were portraits of people, animals, and religious relics hanging on the walls.

"Here we are, my hero. What do you think?" Lucia asked as we entered a room with a comfy-looking bed and the most beautiful oak bedroom furniture.

I was in awe. It was fabulous and to think that Lucia lived there all her young life was unbelievable and so too was the view. I was looking out at a valley of trees and shrubs that were beginning to flower in the warm spring air. Further on was a gently flowing river meandering its way to a lake in the distance.

"Where are you sleeping?" I then asked, wondering.

"In our room," she replied, flopping onto the bed, laughing.

"We can't sleep together," I said as she laughed. "Not in your grandmother's house we can't. That's not right, and besides, I'd feel terrible. Can't you sleep with your grandmother?"

"Who's going to look after me if I do? Besides, I'll miss you," she replied, pretending to be sad.

"You had better find out what your grandmother thinks," I said, remembering my promise. "Oh, and by the way, why did you tell her that I was your hero?"

"Would you rather I had called you my sheep boy?" she replied, in between a fit of laughter.

"I'll get you for that you little, little, you, ah I'll think of something don't you worry," I said trying not to laugh, but it was impossible.

"What are you pair laughing at? Come on down. Your tea is ready," shouted Grandmother Mariana.

We regained our composure and made our way downstairs. Lucia ushered me into a sunny glass room containing unusual plants. Tea was laid on a beautiful ornate iron table, and as we took our seats on the matching iron chairs, I could see Roslyn grazing in the meadow, with Adora lying close by.

"We don't have rooms like these back home," I was thinking, looking around.

My thoughts were interrupted by Mariana asking if I liked tomato soup. She spoke perfect English which was a blessing. My Spanish was reasonable enough to have a conversation with anyone, but only if they talked slowly.

"Yes, please," I replied. "I love tomato soup, and your bread looks delicious."

It was delicious, and after a second helping followed by steaming hot coffee, we retired to an equally ornate sitting room. At the same time, Lucia caught up with all the news from her grandmother. We decided earlier, not to talk about our adventures until the following day. As for sleeping in the same room, Mariana's reply was as I expected.

"Certainly not. Sleep in your own room Lucia. Adora can look after you."

Much to Lucia's disappointment, I went along with it. Her Granny already knew what I could do with my staff, so it was okay to have Roslyn in with me too

"Don't worry Lucia," I said as we climbed the stairs that night. "The moment there's any trouble, I'll know of it and be in beside you."

"Oh, I don't know Gwydion. I'll be afraid. I know I will," she said sadly, following me into my room. "But I know what we'll do. My room is next door, so if we drag your bed over to the wall, you'll be right next to mine. That way, we can tap the wall to one another and we'll know all is well. It will make me feel a lot safer if we do."

That's just what we did, and we tapped, tapped and tapped until her taps grew fainter and fainter they eventually stopped.

"Great," I said to myself while cwtching my freezing cold hand under the blankets.

I think Roslyn was happy too because after settling down nicely on my bed, she gave a long sigh.

I must say, I felt really lonely that night without Lucia, and because of it, I kept waking up with my arm around Roslyn. She didn't mind, but I found it annoying, especially after poking me in the eye with her cold, wet nose.

"Right, that's it. On the floor Roslyn," I said, putting a couple of soft blankets down for her. "I'm sorry, but it's your own fault."

She didn't mind that either. She just led down and closed her eyes. So did I.

"Wake up Gwydion, breakfast is ready," said Lucia shaking me.

I was disappointed because I was sure I had only just dropped off to sleep. On top of that, it was a miserable wet morning, though later in the afternoon, the warm sun was back out again. I was keen to know the day of the eclipse now and the last piece of the prophecy. So I asked Lucia if she had discussed it with her granny.

"Yes, we have, but let's go and sit out on the porch. I'll tell you there."

There was a lovely view from the porch, and as we sat on a swing bench seat, she began.

"The reason why I had to discuss it with my grandmother was; I wanted to make sure my vision was true and not one of Brynmoroc's. I had foreseen every aspect of the prophecy's conclusion, bar one. The decisive missing aspect is apparently your domain. Maybe in a vision."

"I'm confused now. What missing aspect?" I asked. "What are you talking about?"

445

"It's a black diamond. Another black diamond Gwydion. One only you know of its whereabouts," she replied, shaking her head.

I was annoyed and even more confused now. Finding the jewels from Lucia's visions was difficult enough. The only visions I ever had were probably conjured up by Brynmoroc. Black diamonds were out of my domain, not in it.

"Ah, I just knew you were going to say something complicated," I said quickly standing up. "Now what are we going to do? I don't know where any black diamond is, and if it's a piece of Welsh coal, I'm definitely not going back there. I'm finished with this stupid assignment. I wish I had never taken it on. I must have been crazy."

"Don't worry," said my affectionate Senorita. "Grandmother seems to think it will come to you. You'll just have to sit down and try to remember everything Bleddwyn told you."

I still wasn't happy, and to remember everything Bleddwyn had told me was impossible. I told her that the only black diamond Bleddwyn mentioned to me was the one Brynmoroc absorbed.

"Don't worry Gwydion; it will come to you. I'm sure of it," she said. "Now let's go for a walk down to the river. Perhaps you might remember something then, come on."

So, arm in arm, we went off down the road only to spend the rest of the afternoon until evening thinking and discussing nothing else but Bleddwyn. The only other thing we discussed after exhausting the subject of Bleddwyn, was how did

Mariana cope with looking after the mansion with no servants or a gardener. Lucia's simple answer was, she didn't know; only that she did have a gardener who came once a week.

By the time we arrived back at the mansion, the sun had set and it was time for supper.

"Well, Gwydion, did you remember anything Bleddwyn might have mentioned about the black diamond?" Asked Mariana.

"Not a thing," I replied, wishing I had. I had gone over and over it in my mind, but Bleddwyn definitely didn't say anything about a second black diamond. It was late now and I was tired of thinking, so I said that I was off to bed.

"Don't worry about that old diamond Gwydion," said Lucia following me into my room. "Try and get some sleep for a change. Roslyn will look after you."

I said I'd try, but at the same time, I asked her what I had to do with my staff if we ever did find the diamond.

Her hesitated reply was, "Once we have found the diamond, there will be a rock in the shape of clasped hands somewhere in front of Lorca Castle. It is into these clasped hands you have to place the staff."

My disillusioned answer to that was, "Well, we'll do our best, but we only have five days to find it. If we don't, then we've just wasted our time."

"We'll find it Gwydion. I know we will, but what do you mean when you said that you wished you hadn't taken this mission on? That also means that you are sorry you ever met me. Doesn't it?"

"Well, at least you wouldn't be here with me, worrying about Brynmoroc and the prophecy," I replied.

I wasn't thinking straight and my harmless response turned out to be a mistake because Lucia jumped up and snapped right back at me.

"Is that all you can say? You couldn't say something nice like, of course, I'm not sorry that I met you. I am so happy that I did and now I can't imagine life without you. No, no, you couldn't say that now, could you? All you care about is yourself; I thought you said you loved me?"

Before I could tell her that I didn't mean it that way and that I was sorry, she stormed out of the room crying. I went after her, but she locked her door. It was bad enough worrying about that stupid black diamond never mind worrying about Lucia crying in the next room. So I gently tapped the wall a few times, saying that I was sorry in the hope of a response. Eventually, she did, but it was bang, bang, bang, as if in contempt.

"Well, at least, she answered, so hopefully she'll forgive me," I said to myself.

The loud bangs slowly got quieter and quieter until they stopped.

"Good, I can go to sleep now," I said happily to myself, but then I thought, "What did she mean by saying, I thought you said you loved me? I have never ever said that. She must have dreamt it."

In the morning, it was Roslyn, not Lucia who woke me. This made me think that Lucia was still upset. I wasn't hungry so I didn't bother going down for breakfast, I just led on the bed and while mulling over Bleddwyn's words, I heard a tap on the door and in walked Lucia.

"Did you really mean it when you said you were sorry?" She asked as she sat beside me.

"Of course I did," I replied, tapping her hand. "I was all muddled up from thinking. I didn't know what I was saying. You know very well that I'm happy we met. Didn't I tell you just the other day that if I were granted one wish, I wouldn't take it, remember?"

"Okay, then I forgive you," she said, looking a little happier. "Now I have something else to tell you."

She took me downstairs to the study where Mariana was waiting with a pot of coffee. She poured out a cup each, and we sat down.

"Well, what do you want to tell me?" I asked, in the hope she knew where the black diamond was.

"I now know the last part of the prophecy," Lucia replied. "The rock I was telling you about doesn't exist until after you have found the diamond. Once it's found, the hands will appear on a hill surrounded by seven stones depicting the colours of the wizard's rainbow. It's an enchanted rock and cannot be destroyed. The only problem is; the actual insertion of the staff can only be done at the beginning of the eclipse, fourteen forty-five. Once secured, it cannot be removed."

"So all we have to do now is find this black diamond," I said, much to my tormenting, frustrated, sickening disappointment.

All that afternoon, we sat outside on the veranda, going over everything I had been told and experienced. While pondering over it and our next move, I asked Lucia if and when we find the diamond, what was I supposed to do with it. Did I absorb its energy, or what?

"I don't know," was her negative answer. "I suppose you do the same as you did with the others. Oh, Gwydion, this is a mystery. Come, let's give our minds a rest and go and have our tea, shall we?"

At that moment, there was a flash of lightning and a rumble of thunder. We thought it was Brynmoroc, but it turned out to be a storm, lasting a few hours. The storm reminded us about the wizard and what he was capable of. We thought it strange how he had left us in peace since the last time we saw him. Lucia seemed to believe that he must know about the other black jewel and was waiting to see if we find it, but I was sceptical. Brynmoroc wasn't as stupid as he tried to make himself out to be, but on the other hand, I thought she could be right.

So that night, after Lucia had worn herself out from the tap, tap, tapping, I turned up my lamp and brought my journals up to date. When finished, a strange and lonely feeling came over me. I realised that I had two free hands. Up until then, everywhere we went, apart from during the time at Lord Steiner's house, we were always holding hands. To take my mind off it, I lay there thinking, trying to remember something Bleddwyn might have said or done relating to that black jewel. Unfortunately, without finding a single clue, my eyes grew so heavy and sore from looking back through my journals, I could hardly keep them open until I suddenly felt a cold breeze. I soon came to my senses, and after opening my eyes and jumping off the bed, I was face to face with a black figure of a man standing there in front of me. As usual, I had hidden my staff in a slit in the mattress, but I had my cape on. So, with my adrenaline high, I rushed at him. But as we collided, it was like running into a brick wall. I was hurt, so I backed away a little and threw a punch instead, but at the same time, he threw one back. Both our fists smashed together with such force that it hurt me again. I grabbed him, and we fell into a clinch and began wrestling each other to the ground. We kicked each other away and quickly rose to our feet. I was baffled and moved to the side to see his face, but as I did, he followed me in the same pattern. It was as if I was fighting my own shadow. I then noticed that my oil lamp, which was up on a shelf behind me, was casting my shadow across the room.

"He is my shadow," I said as his every move suggested so. Then, as I looked down to the floor, I saw our joined-up shadow suddenly split. We were now no longer together. Nevertheless, he was still my shadow, and he was alive. Again and again, we clashed in the middle of the room, only to end up stalemate every time. Each time we lashed out at one another, we only hit our own fists and kicked our own feet. It was exhausting, and as I looked towards the door, Roslyn was still lying on the mat, asleep. Then, once again, as we faced up to one another, I realised that he always made sure the lamp was behind me.

So I thought, "Well if he's my shadow, he can only be me with the light."

No sooner had the thought crossed my mind, I heard Lucia scream, making me turn, grab the lamp and quickly blew it out. Next was a rush of cold wind, and my shadowy creature was no more. My thoughts now turned to Lucia and her muffled cries. I blindly made my way towards the door, almost tripping over Roslyn as I went. I opened the door in time to see two burly men carrying Lucia across the brightly lit landing. Her grandmother was there too, desperately holding onto Lucia and shouting for me. I called out, and the men stopped. One of them let go of Lucia and sauntered towards me.

"You're coming too kid, whether you like it or not," he said and grinned.

That's just what I wanted him to do, and as he grabbed me, I lifted him high in the air, making him holler in fright. His astounded friend dropped Lucia, and as he did, I threw his pal at him, sending both of them tumbling down the stairs. They picked themselves up and hobbled away, shouting abuse at me and each other.

Thankfully, Lucia was alright and wasn't hurt, but she was red from struggling.

"Okay Lucia, from now on you had better sleep with me," said her grandmother.

"What's the matter with Adora?" I asked, taking a look inside Lucia's bedroom. "She's sound asleep. Roslyn's the same."

"Look at her tongue? I've seen this many times," said Mariana. "She's been doped. Roslyn must have been too. Don't worry. Leave her; she'll soon come around, and Roslyn"

I went to check on Roslyn and found her flat out, sound asleep with her tongue hanging out to one side.

It was seven o'clock and the sun was about to rise. It was pointless going back to bed, though I could have done with it. Lucia and her grandmother put on their dressing gowns, turned out the landing lamps and decided to have an early breakfast. I let them go and waited alongside Roslyn until she slowly came to her senses.

"Well, did you have a nice sleep, lazybones?" I asked as she stood up and wobbled. "Come on; let's check on the other sleepyhead."

Adora was okay too and was out on the landing wondering where everyone had gone. She gave a woof and another when she saw Lucia running up the stairs to check on her.

"Thank goodness you are both alright," she said hugging the hounds. "Come on. Breakfast is ready."

The hounds, understandably, didn't eat theirs but we enjoyed ours.

All that morning, we searched around the house and everywhere outside, looking for something the hounds may have eaten, but it was to no avail. There wasn't a scrap of evidence to even suggest they had been doped. So we never did find what it was that put them to sleep.

"We had all better sleep in the same room from now on," suggested Mariana. "Gwydion, you can bring your mattress into my room after tea."

In the afternoon, down came the rain again. It was disappointing because I was keen to go for a walk and think. I was never one for hanging around the house, so all I did was pace around, driving myself mad thinking about that elusive diamond. A diamond that I had to find with only three days left.

Searching for jewels halfway around the world turned out to be challenging enough, so looking for a diamond that I was supposed to know where it was hidden, should be relatively easy. The only problem was, I didn't hide it in the first place.

"Ah, I'm sick of thinking," I said to myself. "Bleddwyn didn't mention anything about a second black diamond. There's nothing I can do only wait and see what's going to happen without it."

The night quickly drew in and it was time for bed. For safety reasons, we all slept in Lucia's grandmother's bedroom. Me, on a mattress, while the ladies slept in the bed. Roslyn and Adora were wide awake this time and on guard by the door.

The following day was much the same as the day before. In the evening and as we sat around the table, Mariana wanted to know everything

Bleddwyn told me about the staff. Once again for the umpteenth time, I repeated everything that I could remember, but as I had already told both of them, he never mentioned anything to do with a second black jewel.

"Was the staff his or did it belong to Vindaguar?" Mariana asked, holding her chin in thought.

"No, the staff just grew in my hand," I replied with my hand beginning to pain and itch, thinking about it.

"You mean to say, Bleddwyn knew nothing about the thorn?" She asked after I mentioned it.

"Yes, that's exactly what he said," I replied. "He had the same bewildered look as you have, right now."

Mariana was puzzled and asked no more. So, after a cup of hot milk, we went to bed, worrying. Fretting because tomorrow was the last day before the eclipse. Then while we were led thinking, I felt another cold rush of wind. Thinking it was my shadow again, I stood up waiting as the wall lit up beside me. I backed away to Lucia's bed and stood there ready, but it wasn't my shadow. On the wall in front of me now was the same vision of a lady walking down a hillside. She was strolling, taking her time as if no care in the world until she elegantly stepped out into our room. I turned to Lucia only to find that she and her grandmother were asleep.

"It's no use trying to wake them; they will not wake. What I am about to tell you Gwydion, is for your ears only. The black diamond you seek does not exist. Mariana, as you may or may not have gathered by now, is under the influence of the rapacious violating wizard. Lucia's knowledge of this diamond was fabricated by her grandmother in a dream."

"What violating wizard?" I asked. "Who are you talking about? You turn up once again, telling me something I already know, and if you ask me, we are all probably under the influence of this violating wizard. So tell me? Tell me, why don't you? Who is this menace?"

"My answer Gwydion is the same as the last one. Now take heed of my warning son and do not speak of this night to anyone."

The lady then walked back into the vision and strolled off up the hill until the image slowly faded away.

"What's the matter Gwydion why are you standing there looking at the wall?" asked Lucia.

I turned to find that Lucia and her grandmother were sat up wide awake. Even Roslyn was stretching, looking at me with a look of anticipation.

"Oh, nothing's wrong," I replied. "I thought I saw a spider, that's all. It wasn't one. So, you can go back to sleep now."

"Back to sleep! We haven't been to sleep," said Lucia, as they both led down.

I knew fine I wasn't dreaming and they definitely looked sound asleep, even Roslyn. I said no more and eventually nodded off.

In the morning, I woke still thinking about the lady and that elusive black diamond.

"Gwydion, breakfast is ready, and we only have today to find the diamond," said Lucia as I walked down the stairs.

I hated that word FIND. How can anyone find anything without some kind of clue as to where it might be? The diamond could be anywhere in the world. According to that lady; there wasn't any jewel to look for. Thus, I told Lucia that that was it; no more searching for me. As far as I was concerned, we had accomplished all that Bleddwyn sent me out to do. Tomorrow we were going to this so-called castle, the Fortress of the Sun and I was going to place my staff into a rock, any rock, and whatever happens, happens. I apologised if I was rude, but I didn't want to talk about it anymore.

"Alright," she said, taking hold of my hand. "I won't mention it again. I have told you many times, whatever you decide is alright with me. You look so tired love, why don't you lie down with me on the couch for an hour or two; you'll feel much better after a rest."

I did and while she stroked my hair, it felt so lovely lying next to her again that I fell asleep.

"There now. Wasn't that nice? Let's go. It's time for dinner," said Lucia as I woke.

After dinner and because it was a nice day, we took the hounds for a walk down to the river. We found a nice spot and sat down on the bank watching the rapids race by. They seemed to be competing against one another only to crash into large protruding rocks and logs. In a flash, they were back in the race again, tearing off down the river until out of sight around a bend. It was so peaceful that I wished we could have stayed there forever.

"Let's make our way back now, shall we?" asked Lucia rising to her feet. "After tea we had better get things ready for tomorrow."

That evening, while we were sitting beside the fire sipping some of grandmother's homemade sloe gin, my hand began to itch like crazy and then my shoulder. Lucia asked what was wrong. I said that ever since I took a sip of the gin, my hand and shoulder began itching.

"You must be allergic to sloe-berries," said her grandmother. "Either that or you have touched one of those poisonous flowers down by the river. You had better have a bath, just in case. I'll boil a few pots of water."

I had never been allergic to sloe-berries. I ate them all the time back home. So whatever the itching came from, I was delighted when Lucia told me the bath was ready. I couldn't get in there quickly enough. Her granny had put a bunch of herbs in the water, saying they would help with the itching.

"Well, did the herbs do the trick?" asked Lucia when I returned.

"Yes, thanks and well-done grandmother," I replied. "Now, I think we had all better go to bed. We need to be up early in the morning."

After waking in the early hours, I couldn't go back to sleep. I turned up the lamp and sat there going over my days with Bleddwyn. I picked up and extended my staff to its full length and looked at it. While looking, I once again remembered asking Bleddwyn about the thorn. He said that he knew nothing about its meaning. Even Mariana seemed puzzled. So I began thinking, if it was part of the prophecy, Bleddwyn must have known a staff would grow in my hand, yet he knew nothing about the thorn only that it was part of the prophecy.

You wouldn't believe how deep in thought I was. According to Lucia, there was another diamond to find and I was supposed to know where it was hidden. On top of that, there was another part of the prophecy that Bleddwyn nor I knew absolutely anything about. Finally, after a lot of tossing and turning, I dropped off to sleep only to wake with my hand itching again. I was scratching the scar left by that painful thorn in my finger, and then my shoulder began to itch. It itched so much that I led on my back and wiggled. With my itch soothed, and while I lay there scratching my hand, I had a feeling there was definitely a reason why that thorn stuck in my finger.

"Gwydion, Gwydion," was the next thing I heard. "It's seven o'clock, time to get up," said Lucia, already up and dressed.

I rolled off the mattress, picked up my staff and joined the ladies downstairs. Lucia and I were feeling a little nervous now, so we skipped breakfast and took Roslyn and Adora around to the stables. We were taking Mariana's double horse carriage, which meant having Adora alongside our faithful Roslyn. She didn't mind, and neither did Adora, but I think Roslyn let her know who the boss was.

It was a cloudy dull morning as we prepared to set out on the last stage of our journey. Mariana waved and shouted for me to look after her granddaughter.

"I will," I replied, but said to myself, "I think we need someone to look after both of us."

We took the road east to Puerto Lumbreras then headed north for Lorca and the Fortress of the Sun, twelve miles away. Our plan was to stop a few miles before the fortress and wait a couple of hours. After travelling along nicely and with only five miles to the castle, we pulled over under the cover of some trees. It was ten thirty, and thankfully the clouds had broken, letting through the morning sun. So we led down to enjoy its long-awaited warmth.

"Don't worry Gwydion. We'll be alright," said Lucia, pointing to the sun, "Look, even the sun is saying so. Can't you see him smiling at us?"

I was about to answer but suddenly thought of something and quickly sat up to study my staff. I noticed that in the middle of the staff was a small hole.

"What are you looking at?" Lucia asked.

"Look, Lucia?" I replied, still studying it, "This little hole in the middle of my staff is the hole left by the thorn that stuck in my finger."

"Let me see?" She asked, looking at my finger. "It stuck in your middle finger, and the hole is also in the middle of the staff. It must mean something?"

After saying that, my finger began to itch something crazy again and then my shoulder.

I slung off my jacket and shirt, shouting, "Quickly! Scratch my shoulder Lucia. It's driving me mad. Yes, that's it," I screamed when she reached the itchy spot.

"It's your beauty spot Gwydion. It's all hard and bumpy. I can't scratch that, it will bleed," she retorted.

"I don't care what it is," I hollered. "Scratch the blooming thing, please?"

Then, as she scratched, she shouted, "Oh no Gwydion! You're all bleeding now, but what the...! Gwydion. Oh, Gwydion, it's the diamond. It was in your beauty spot. Look? I've scratched it out."

To my surprise, there, in the palm of Lucia's hand, was a tiny black sparkling diamond.

"YES!" I shouted as she handed me the jewel. "That beauty spot has been itching me for years, but now what do we do with it?"

"It's the same size as the hole in your staff Gwydion," said Lucia.

I was curious now and thought I'd line up the diamond to the hole, then as I did, the jewel shot out of my hand and inserted itself into the hole.

"Yes, yes, yes," Lucia shouted. "I knew there was another diamond, and now we have it. Yahoo Gwydion," she cried again, excitedly.

We were both excited, but as we hugged, lightning flashed across the darkened clouds that had suddenly gathered. It was followed by a huge clap of thunder.

"Quick Lucia, let's get away from these trees," I said, knowing it was a dangerous place to be.

I helped her up into the carriage just as the rain came pouring down.

"Do you think it's Brynmoroc?" I asked after putting up the hood. "Or is it just a thunderstorm?"

She didn't know, but one way or the other we were not taking a chance and prepared ourselves just in case it was the wizard. Fortunately, it turned out to be a freak five-minute storm that soon blew over, revealing a clear blue sky again. The sun in that part of the world, being ten degrees hotter than in Wales, took no time at all in drying up the saturated road we were about to take. So, with the mysterious black diamond found, I put aside every doubt I had about our assignment and pledged to focus on finishing it. All we had to worry about now was meeting Brynmoroc, who was expecting me to hand over my staff. He probably knew I wouldn't, but it was inevitable that he was going to be along soon, asking for it.

We stayed put until noon before starting out again on the last five miles. How we were going to deal with the giant wizard we were going to have to wait and see or in the words of Bleddwyn, the best way we could. Another annoying concern was the final part of the prophecy. I had to wait until the very moment the eclipse began before I could drive my staff into a rock that I would undoubtedly find very difficult to do. That was; if I ever find it.

We nervously travelled on with the midday sun above us, expecting the desperate wizard to pounce at any moment. On our way, we were joined by other traps, carts and carriages, so we had plenty of company. Everything was going well until we were two miles short of the fortress.

"What's he doing?" shouted Lucia, as a large stagecoach headed directly for us.

I shouted at Roslyn and Adora to pull off the road, but they took no notice of me. So we braced ourselves as the six-horse stagecoach ran right through us as if we weren't there. We realised then that we were now, solely in the one-dimensional world, meaning, at that present time, we were no longer visible in our world. It was hair-raising finding ourselves running through anything and anyone as if they were ghosts. For some reason, we were in the wizard's enchanted world, oblivious to any human. It was the weirdest experience anyone could ever witness. Strange animals grazed and ran in the same fields as ours without them even knowing. At one point, a bird flew straight through my face. So now, owing to the fact of this strange phenomenon, we found ourselves in an almost impossible situation, ducking and swerving probably needlessly, but we weren't taking any chances. This went on until we suddenly came to a standstill.

In front of us now, were twelve moving large stone boulders, completely blocking our way, but no one else's. We were trapped, and as the boulders began to roll towards us, my immediate thought was to protect our horses. So with our shields, Lucia and I jumped down and stood our ground in front of them. Then as we watched, the rolling rocks suddenly developed not only legs but also a mouth full of decaying yellow teeth. The stench from their open jaws was almost unbearable. With great urgency, they rushed into us only to be sent tumbling back against each other from the force of our shields. Time and time again, they charged only to be smashed back. It was a pointless exercise for them, making us realise that they were purposely delaying our progress. Then, as the boulders formed a circle around us, they glowed red as fire and began to melt. Within minutes we were surrounded by a river of stinking dirty yellow-coloured liquid that stank like the sewers of Paris. Lucia put her handkerchief to her mouth and mumbled.

"We only have an hour and a half before the eclipse. Why don't you use your staff?"

I had forgotten about my staff and what it was capable of. So we quickly climbed back aboard where I pointed my staff towards the circle.

"Now let's see what you can do," I said and commanded it with my thoughts.

"YES!" shouted Lucia as we raced on and out onto the open road again. The stinking circle of yellow liquid had dried up, leaving nothing but dust. We were away now and happy to be leaving that foul stuff behind. We raced on and didn't stop until the Fortress of the Sun came into view.

"There it is," said Lucia. "That's Brynmoroc's castle, and I hope he's in and staying there."

I was surprised, for it was very similar to the painting of the castle back home in my bedroom, so I mentioned it.

"You have?" Asked Lucia the moment I told her. "You didn't tell me."

"I didn't know until now," I replied. "But forget the painting. I've enough on my mind already. Let's just carry on with what we came here to do."

We unhitched the mares, tied our packs onto Adora, mounted Roslyn and tracked up a hill overlooking the south side of the castle.

"There. That's the hill. Can you see it?" asked Lucia, pointing over to it.

I could see it alright and thought we had better get going for we only had thirty-five minutes left. We headed off back down, purposely taking the longest way to stay under cover of the trees. There was only one patch of open land to cross, which was ideally out of view from the castle.

We arrived at the foot of the hill. With twenty minutes remaining, we began searching until suddenly the whole area changed. We were no longer climbing a tree-covered hill. We were now walking on a cobbled road through weird-looking gates of an ancient abandoned village, surrounded by a cloud. You could say the village was very similar to Machu Picchu. Unlike Machu Picchu, the village was intact, but without any sign of life, not even a bird. We were surrounded by a thick white cloud, yet as we looked up, the sky was blue, and the dazzling afternoon sun was as hot as ever. We trotted on into what must have been the market square. We were thinking and fearing it being another one of Brynmoroc's visions. It was making us nervous, but then the cloud lifted, revealing a tall castle.

"It's in there Gwydion. The rock is inside the castle grounds," said Lucia as we went through the gates.

It was nothing like she had visualised so we had to be careful because that castle looked every bit like a wizard's castle, one you would see in books. It was spectacular, yes, but at the same time, suspiciously unreal. We slipped off Roslyn and cautiously walked towards the castle.

"There! It's over there, in front of the castle. It's a tomb Gwydion. A tomb," said Lucia, making her way towards it.

"Whoa! Hold on, Lucia," I quickly said. "A tomb? I thought you said we were looking for a rock?"

She took no notice and carried on, so I shouted that we should take out our shields.

When we reached the tomb, she was ecstatic. Ecstatic because lying on top of the tomb was the effigy of a wizard with his hands clasped together. The whole tomb was carved out of a rock.

"Yes! That's it. That's where you have to place your staff. You must place it into the wizard's clasped hands. And look! The seven stones are strategically placed around his forefingers and thumbs."

Yes, that's where they were; set around the hole where I had to place my staff. The side of the tomb bore a strange engraved inscription, 'Viendelvin anblenidous buekel sientos.' It was very much the same as the engraving on Bleddwyn's table in his underground cellar. What it meant neither of us knew. I looked at the sun then gave my watch to Lucia to keep an eye on the time. Then, before I could say or do anything else, there was a huge flash making us quickly back away. There now, hovering a distance away, was Brynmoroc.

"Gwydion, quickly, the staff, before it's too late," asked the pleading wizard.

We faced our shields towards him, and with my staff held high in the air, I answered him.

"We have decided to stand by Bleddwyn and carry out the prophecy the way Vindaguar intended."

"Gwydion, you must honour your promise to me; if not, we will all perish. Bleddwyn has deceived you, son. Even as you stand, you are not where you think you are. This place and tomb are an illusion only Bleddwyn can see and create. Quickly now, hand me the staff so that I can place it in the stone on the hill where Lucia predicted."

I wasn't taking any notice of his fabricated statements; neither did I care about his pleas. Besides, I heard him say stone when Lucia clearly said a rock. Maybe I'm wrong, but I always thought rocks were larger than stones. Either way, I didn't care and told Lucia to brace herself.

"No, I am sorry sir," I replied, looking up at him. "We are going to take a chance and finish this the way we were told. If we don't, and things go wrong, we will never forgive ourselves."

After saying this, a mighty clap of thunder roared out, followed by a bright light, making us stagger back even further.

"It's the giant wizard!" Lucia exclaimed as we tried to focus on the shape before us.

Yes, it was a giant, a gleaming, twelve-foot mean-sounding giant, but his face was a blur. He stood on the ground at least twenty or thirty feet away with his bright cloak and tunic shimmering like heat waves across the desert plains. His staff was flickering as if on fire, and as he roared out, his voice was deep and frightening.

"GWYDION! Hand me the staff. Defy me and Lucia will die, but not you. You will live in misery, regretting it for the rest of your life."

"Don't listen to him Gwydion," said Lucia as she pulled me back.

Suddenly, I felt a surge of energy in my staff and through no will of my own, it pointed towards the wizard.

"No Gwydion!" He shouted just before streaks of lightning from my dazzling staff, sent him hurling backwards across the castle grounds. My staff was now lit up like a rainbow and was vibrating with energy. So, with my shield in front of me and Lucia behind, I stood there waiting for his response.

"YOU LITTLE FOOL," He roared, rising to his feet. "So that was your answer. Well, now you are going to pay."

I could see that the gleaming wizard was definitely Brynmoroc. He raised his staff, and as I raised mine, we simultaneously flashed out a bolt of lightning towards each other. The force drove me back into Lucia, but surprisingly, Brynmoroc received the worst end of it and was now struggling to get to his feet. I couldn't understand what was happening because I thought Bleddwyn said that if a wizard uses his wizardry directly to harm any human; it would recoil back against himself. I was no wizard, but Brynmoroc certainly was. So either Bleddwyn was wrong, or I misunderstood him or just couldn't remember, only something about battle engagement. Either way, I was in a fight with an almighty, desperate giant wizard. So, with Lucia behind me and my shield and staff before me, I slowly advanced towards the wizard, but this time, the wizard was Bleddwyn.

"Why you impertinent little imp. Do you think I'll let you take what is rightfully mine? I'll blast you back to your miserable Welsh fool of a gypsy farmer in a bag of ashes," he roared as his staff flashed out a blaze of light.

As the blast hit my shield, it was deflected into a stone pillar, completely shattering it. I hit back with a blast of my own that seemed to sizzle as it sent the wizard reeling up against the castle wall. He rose to his feet, ripped up a stone statue and threw it at me. Once again, my shield saved me by deflecting it away into a tree. The wizard was livid now, and as I advanced towards the tomb, he roared like a lion. Time was getting on, so I intended to reach the tomb and battle from there. The giant knew exactly what I was doing and in a flash, hurled a bolt of lightning from a different angle, hitting Lucia off her guard. The fierce bolt clashed with her shield, sending her sprawling. Then as the wizard rushed in to grab her, I managed to blast him away, sending him thumping into an old yew tree. While he lay there moaning and groaning, I quickly picked up Lucia. She was okay but winded, holding her side. I then turned to face the giant tyrant, who was now standing in front of the tomb laughing, his face constantly changing from Bleddwyn to Brynmoroc.

"Oh, dear, dear, Gwydion," sniggered the wizard. "Kiss her better, son. Take as long as you like because it will be the last kiss you will ever give her. What a shame, but I did warn you, didn't I?"

During all this time he was continually looking at the sun, so I asked Lucia the time. We had less than five minutes. I wasn't sure what to do now except for one thing. He had no defence against my staff, but our shields protected us against his.

"If only I'd been told how to use this staff properly," I said to myself.

Then, as I looked at the position of the sun, I had an inspiration. "Quick Lucia, we have to move to the left…"

Before I could finish, the giant forced us back with an invisible force of energy. I quickly retaliated, with a force of my own that disorientated him long enough for me to execute my idea. With Lucia holding on to my cape, we ran to a stone pillar facing the sun and stopped there. By this time the giant had recovered and was back beside the tomb. With only a couple of minutes left, I needed to get to the tomb and hold my ground. My idea was to dazzle the wizard by using the sun and our shields to hopefully advance and drive him back away from the tomb. At first, my idea turned out to be a bad one, for as we began to dazzle the giant, he laughed and deflected the sun away from him. Then, unexpectedly, it turned out to be even better than I expected because as he raised his staff towards our shields, the crystal tip on his staff flashed, making the wizard cry out in pain. He began staggering around in agony, sizzling like wildfire across the night sky. I was surprised but didn't hesitate, and by using my staff, I sent him reeling back even further.

"Now is our chance, come on Lucia. To the tomb, quickly," I said in haste.

We reached it just as the giant was rising to his feet.

"The sun! Look at the sun. Quickly Gwydion, it's time to insert your staff," shouted Lucia.

"NO! NO!" hollered Brynmoroc as I quickly slipped my staff into the clasped hands of the grey-stoned wizard.

"You little fool Gwydion. You have no idea what you have done. Quickly, before it's too late, take out the staff, or we'll all die."

"It's too late, and even if I could, I wouldn't," I replied as it suddenly began to rain.

At that moment, the wizard rose into the air, roaring like thunder.

"You despicable little snake, I'll make you suffer for what you have done."

With that said, he soared off through the rain towards his fortress, shouting, "It isn't over, not by a long way."

"Yes! He's gone! He's gone!" I shouted. "Come on Lucia, we had better get away from here."

She was still winded. So with our shields back in our pockets, I picked her up and carried her over to an oak tree.

"We'll stay here and see what happens," I said, squinting at the sun.

The eclipse was in its first quarter and the soft and warm rain was gently falling. We had fulfilled our part of the prophecy. All we could do now was wait. Lucia was shivering like jelly, and as she lifted up her pretty little face to look at me, I told her that when this was all over, I was going to give her something.

"What?" she asked.

"It's not over yet," I replied

"Oh Gwydion," she sighed.

Then as a black shadow crept over us, the sky darkened as if it were night.

"Well, here we go Lucia, keep your fingers crossed," I said, looking over towards the tomb and my staff.

She didn't want to look, so as I stood there anxiously looking up through the rain, I put my arm around her. The new moon was visible now, but totally black, with a thin ring of light around it as if on fire. Then, as the sun peeped out from behind the moon, there was a flash of colour revealing a brilliant rainbow arcing its way down to my staff and Lorca Castle. A second later, the Fortress was lit by an explosion of colour with thousands upon thousands of beams shooting in all directions across the semi-darkened sky. As I stood there watching in awe, I saw an old-looking wizard in the middle of it all, holding out his hand to me. Was that Vindaguar, I wondered. I watched him wave until disappearing along with the coloured beams that had been circling the Fortress. In their place now at the top of the castle, had to be the dazzling Sun Giant, waving his massive hand in my direction.

"YES," I shouted, putting my hand up to salute him, but it wasn't my hand that I was saluting with; it was my staff. Then, as I turned to Lucia, my heart must have stopped for a moment. I was no longer holding her. I was on my own; she had gone. Everything had gone. The tomb, the castle, the abandoned village, every single thing had disappeared, leaving me standing on a hill looking over to the Fortress of the Sun.

# Chapter 27

I knew it would be a waste of time calling out for her, but I did, only to find as I expected, no reply. I was more than frightened now, feeling that I was in a world of my own; a weird, frightening world. A world I didn't want to be in and never wanted to in the first place.

"That's it! He's got her!" I cried.

He said he would and that I would live to regret it. But how could he? The prophecy said that the violator would be obliterated. I felt cheated because we had risked our lives for a cause neither of us was going to benefit from. If it were our world we were saving it would have made sense, but to think we had set out to save a world we could have quite happily done without, was ludicrous and I was now regretting it.

"What am I going to do now, Granddad?" I said. "Why didn't I listen t… Hey! Roslyn!" I then shouted after a nudge in the back.

"You little beauty, I thought I lost you too. Where's Lucia and Adora?"

Of course, she didn't reply, but she did give me another nudge as if to say, "At least I'm here."

Yes, she was there, and I can't even tell you how I felt but it was a whole lot better.

"Come on Lass, all we can do is check out the Fortress," I said as I mounted her.

It was a waste of time, for when we arrived, it was just an abandoned castle. There was no one there; in fact, there was no one anywhere to be seen. Roslyn and I were either in the wizard's one-dimensional or another abandoned world entirely on our own.

"What happened? What's gone wrong? Where is everyone? Is this really happening?" I said, looking at Roslyn.

The only thing I could think of was to head back to Lucia's grandmothers and hope by then that things would be back to normal. I was frightened, but at least I had my faithful Roslyn otherwise that lump in my dry throat would have probably killed me. Not knowing what had happened to Lucia was terrible enough, but to be in this forsaken world on my own was something I couldn't bear thinking about. I had a feeling it was a waste of time going to Lucia's home, but I had to.

Strangely, and even more worrying, on our lonely journey down through Spain, every house, street, shop and store were all empty. Not even a bird or any kind of animal did I see until Puerto Lumbreras. Then incredibly, as I looked back, I sighed in relief. I found that in every yard we were taking, the world was coming back to life behind

us. You will never know just how good that made
me feel.

When we arrived at Lucia's home, it was as I
expected, empty, covered in cobwebs with not a
soul in sight.

"Right Roslyn, let's go back to Lorca, Lucia
must still be there," I said after stepping back into
our lovely world again.

I never thought that I would be so happy to
see people out in gardens with smoke rising from
their tall stack chimneys.

When we arrived back at Puerto Lumbreras, it
was busy as usual, so I stopped to get myself
something to eat. Then after dismounting, I got a
sickening surprise, for as I looked behind me,
there was once again no sign of anyone. They had
all disappeared. Even every single occupied house,
shop and building that I had passed a minute ago,
was once again abandoned. To add to my
confused sickening feeling, everything in front of
me was going on as normal. It was as if I was
erasing the whole world that had earlier come
back to life. I was distraught, but quickly
remounted Roslyn and carried on to Lorca,
regardless. My heart was racing now and my
throat was on fire. It was probably the most
frightening experience that I had ever
encountered. Every single person I met, every
thriving household and village I passed through,
simply disappeared behind me.

Eventually, we arrived back at the hill from
where we started. Then as we began to climb, I
found that I was once again back in the abandoned

village, but astonishingly, looking at myself and Lucia. We were over by the tree, underneath the blaze of colour that was illuminating the sky during the end of the eclipse. As I stood there, watching the coloured beams fading away, there was a flash, and I saw myself fall to the ground. At the same time, I saw the gleaming giant wizard snatching Lucia up into his arms. With Lucia now screaming in his clutches, he carried her off to the top of his castle where he stood there waving. That was when I stood up and saluted him, thinking he was the Sun Giant. I now saw myself desperately searching around for Lucia until I saw the most horrifying sight that I have ever witnessed in my life. The giant wizard was holding the screaming Lucia over the edge of his castle. I couldn't believe I was watching this and shouted out.

"No! No! No Brynmoroc! No, Please No. I Beg You. Oh no, Lucia!"

I could hear him laughing and Lucia's terrible screams as he dropped her down onto the rocks below.

At that point, I slumped down in tears, "Oh, no Lucia. No, no, no. Please, no, Lucia…."

"It's alright, Gwydion. I'm here. I'm here. Wake up, he's gone," I heard her say, as I wept.

If I had just experienced the worst moment of my entire life, I was now experiencing the best one I could have ever wished for. I was now looking at my beautiful, lovely Lucia who was trying to help me up.

"It's alright. It's all right," she repeated as I sighed. "After you saluted the Sun Giant you fell, and I couldn't wake you. Please get up Gwydion. He's gone now. We've done it. Look!"

I stood up, but I wasn't going to look at any castle, only my lovely Spanish Princess. I was so overjoyed that I lifted her into my arms and kissed her.

"Oh, I'm so happy to see your pretty little Spanish face again," I said as I held her.

"What do you mean, again? I haven't been anywhere. You have been dreaming, haven't you? I know you have because you are kissing me."

I replied as I put her down, "Well, if I was dreaming and if I ever dream again, just as long as you are there when I wake, I'll kiss you some more."

I picked her up again and ran, carrying her around the village like a fool, and we laughed and laughed.

"Well, that was fun," she said as we led down to recover. "Come on, let's take a look at Lorca Castle, it's in ruins now."

"In ruins!" I asked, surprised.

"Yes. I don't know how, but it's in ruins, and there are loads of people over there now."

"Ah, no, let's just go back home to your grandmothers," I replied. "I don't want to see or know anything that has to do with Brynmoroc ever again. My head's wrecked from thinking and worrying about him."

So after we recovered from our little game of piggyback, I suddenly thought of Adora and asked where she was. Lucia didn't know. After checking out the whole area without finding any trace of her, we assumed, much to Lucia's sadness, she had gone back to the one-dimensional world.

"That's probably what she wanted," I said. "But we still have our lovely Roslyn. So don't be sad, she might think you don't love her anymore."

That did the trick. Lucia put her arms around Roslyn's neck and said as she kissed her.

"Fancy him saying that. Of course I love you Roslyn. You know I do. Don't you?"

Roslyn gave her a little nudge as if to say, "Yes, I know you do," and we laughed.

We were still laughing as we set off out of the village until I realised that I still had my staff.

"Whoa Roslyn, hold on a minute," I called out and dismounted.

Lucia was wondering what was going on. I wanted to know if I could still use my staff. So I lifted it high and commanded it with my thoughts and low and behold, Roslyn was now hitched to a lovely new trap.

"It still works Gwydion. How exciting. I wonder if you can use it forever."

"Yahoo! I hope so my sweet and lovely lady," I replied and laughed. "Now let's go back to Granny's."

We did and after heading out, we were so excited that we waved to everyone we met. I hadn't noticed just how beautiful that part of the country was. So trotting along taking in the lovely scenery was now, more than enjoyable.

Her grandmother was at her door, greeting us when we arrived. Lucia was down from the carriage and was running up into her arms like an excited schoolgirl.

"We did it, Grandmother. It's all over," she said, as they hugged. "But Grandmother, is he gone? Is Brynmoroc really gone? Please tell me he is?"

"Yes, he's gone Lucia and now, thanks to you both, the prophecy has been fulfilled. The wizard's world of enchanted energy will soon be restored to its former glory, and I am sure you pair are going to be well rewarded."

For the rest of the evening, we celebrated with a bottle of Grandmother's elderberry wine. It was a good feeling going to bed that night knowing now that I could have a good night's sleep, but I did have Roslyn with me just in case.

The following evening, while we were all sitting out on the porch, looking at a beautiful sunset, Mariana told us something she had been keeping a secret.

"Lucia, now that you have fulfilled the prophecy, I have something to tell you. Before I do, you must understand that it was essential for both our sakes I kept it secret until now."

She began by telling Lucia all about Bleddwyn and Eluciana and what happened after Brynmoroc captured Eluciana and how her baby Natalia was sold to the childless Empress of Murcia. She paused for a moment before giving her the shocking news. Bleddwyn and Eluciana were her rightful blood ancestors and down through the centuries, there only one child born to each generation, and that child always being a female. In that way, not only did the secret have a better chance of being kept impervious, the wizard's bloodline would stay confined.

I knew what was coming next. Mariana went on to say that Lucia and I were not only born on the same day, the twentieth of October 1880, but also on the last stroke of midnight. Thankfully though, much to our relief, we were in no way related. We were the only children born in the world at that particular time, though, an hour apart. Our birth was another part of the prophecy, passed down in secrecy. It all came as a bit of a shock to Lucia though she did tell her grandmother that she had half expected something strange. With Lucia told, Mariana left her with me while she went to brew up a pot of tea and some sandwiches.

"Did you know Bleddwyn was married to Eluciana and that they were my ancestors?" Asked Lucia. "And why didn't you tell me your birthday was the same day as mine?"

The only answer I could give was that I was sworn to secrecy. Although a little sad and disappointed, Lucia soon cheered up knowing that at least Mariana was her real grandmother. So she felt a lot better by the time Mariana came back with a pot of tea and sandwiches.

While we were sipping our tea, Mariana put her hand on my knee.

"As for you Gwydion. We knew you were born the moment the Orionids meteor shower occurred. It took near six hundred years for this synchronised birth to happen. Eluciana predicted this and that the instigator would come from her home in Wales."

She went on to tell me that after my parents were killed in the mining accident, the coal board house we were living in, had to be vacated for another family. With my Granddad working away in London and unable to care for me, I was put into a foster home. When Lucia's parents heard about this, they set out to Wales intending to adopt me. Sadly, on their journey across the English Channel, their ship went down in a storm, and they were lost. Their journey, unfortunately, turned out to be in vain for two reasons. One, they sadly lost their lives and two, if they had survived the trip, they would have found that my Granddad had since left his job and had collected me.

I just sat there listening, half expecting what she was telling me, except for being in a foster home and the proposed adoption. However, it didn't bother me much because I was so thankful that my Granddad gave up his job for me, and now I was looking forward to seeing him again. When Mariana had finished, Lucia asked if she had ever met Bleddwyn. She said that she had, but quickly went on to ask me how Wales was getting on. She hadn't been there for a long time. I must have spent an hour filling her in on everything.

Consequently, the subject of Bleddwyn never arose again, and neither Lucia nor I said any more about him. However, we did retire to bed that night deep in thought. I was happy but not so Lucia. Although the sun rose the next morning bringing with it a beautiful day, it took her a few more days to get over the revelations.

One morning, a letter came for Lucia. It was from Roisin. It was good news. She was fine and had met up with her brother. He had apologised for whatever it was that he had done and was going to make it up to Roisin by taking her to Finland. Finland was a country where she always wanted to go. Hearing this, a wave of relief came over me, for I had previously promised to take her somewhere special. So now that her brother was treating Roisin to her lifetime dream, I didn't have to worry. Home was where I wanted to be now, but there was one more promise I had to keep, and that was to Cynthia. I had her address, but Vienna was such a long way away, and I had just about enough of travelling. So that night, after supper, I asked Lucia's grandmother if she had any idea what was going to happen now that we had accomplished our mission.

"You can do whatever you want," was her answer. "I thought you knew that. I suppose you want to go back home to Wales now? Your Granddad will be pleased to see you and so too will your friends."

"Yes," I replied. "That would be nice. I think that's what I'll do."

Lucia sighed, stood up and walked out of the room, saying that she was going to bed.

"She's a little upset that you will be leaving, but don't worry, I'll look after her," said Mariana.

I said goodnight and went off to bed, but as I lay there, I heard Lucia crying. I tapped on the wall to let her know I was there. She tapped back, but softly.

"Ah, this is crazy," I said to myself.

We had travelled halfway around the world risking life and limb, and now that it's all over, it was as if it was all for nothing. It had been almost a week and no one had said well done, thank you and here's something for your trouble. I then began thinking the worst. Was it all over? Brynmoroc said it wasn't and that he would make me suffer. So where was he? What's happened to him?

That was it. I was determined that in the morning I was going home to Wales, search out Bleddwyn and put an end to the uncertainty that was clouding my future. As for Lucia, I couldn't ask her to travel thousands of miles again. She was exhausted, and so was I, but for both our sakes, I was heading home no matter what.

In the morning, I told Lucia what I was doing and asked Mariana if trains were running up through Spain and France.

"I am sure there must be," she replied. "There's a station in Murcia where you could find out the best route to take."

I was happy with that, but Lucia didn't seem to be. She stood up and stormed out of the house. I went to go after her, but her grandmother stopped me.

"Leave her be for a while Gwydion. Go pack your things and do whatever you have to do. I'll go and talk to her."

I went up to my room and packed my bag ready to head out the next day. It was passed lunchtime before Lucia's grandmother came in from outside.

"Lucia is still upset and doesn't want to come in," she said and smiled. "I think you had better go out and talk to her. But, wait a while, I'll make you up something to eat and drink to take out with you."

While she was in the kitchen, I nipped upstairs for the little purple feather that Lucia had given me in Machu Picchu and put it into my shirt pocket. Then with a jug of milk and a tray of scones, I went outside where I found Lucia sitting on the lawn in the flower garden, picking petals off a daisy. I put the tray on a little stone table and sat down beside her. She was sad, so I turned her to face mine.

"For you, my lovely Senorita, I will pick the softest rose and gently lay it on your pillow while you sleep."

She threw the daisy down and snapped back at me, "No, you wouldn't. Don't you mean you'll give it to Cynthia? Because that's where you are going, aren't you?"

"No, I'm not. I'm going home," I replied, taking hold of her hand. "Besides, Vienna is miles away."

"Don't lie to me Gwydion; I know you are. I not only heard her tell you that she loved you, but I also saw you kissing her."

I didn't know what to say because it was true. I didn't want to lie, but I thought I had to.

"I um, I couldn't, I mean, she came on to me when I was full of whiskey. My eyes were closed and I thought she was you. By the time I realised she wasn't, it was too late. Besides, that was before I fell in love with you."

"Rubbish!" she shouted. "What a load of rubbish. Had your eyes closed, did you? Thought it was me. I was in the bathroom. And it wasn't before you said you loved me either. Remember that night in the tent?"

"What night?" I asked, but then I remembered. "What! You mean to tell me you were awake that night?"

"Yes I was," she replied, pulling her hand away from mine. "Yes, and another thing, Cynthia also told me that you loved her and that you had been in her bedroom."

"In her bedroom," I said, frustrated now. "Yes, but that was when the pair of you were under the influence of that Lord purple face fella. I must have been too."

She was still defiant, "And what about that ring she gave you? Why did you take it back from her? Don't try to deny it, because I found it in your shirt pocket this morning before I washed it. And what about the one you gave her? Oh, I'm never going to take it off, Gwydion. That's what she said. Didn't she?"

"I told you all about those rings Lucia," I said, trying to think. "And what ring did you find in my pocket?"

"You know very well what ring. The one she gave you," she replied, raising her hand as if wanting to slap me

I was annoyed now and said, "I did give it back to her, and if there was any ring in my pocket, I didn't put it there. Perhaps Cynthia did?"

"Oh, go away, Gwydion, with your excuses. I knew there was something between you two. You don't love me. You just said you did, that's all. It was probably one of Bleddwyn's silly ideas. Just go away. Go on to Cynthia and stay there for all I care. I don't want to ever see you again."

She was about to get up, but I stopped her and held her down. "Don't say that Lucia. I don't want to see Cynthia, and even if I did, it would only be to buy her a house or something. She was good to us. I don't love her; I love you."

"Rubbish Gwydion. Rubbish. Now let me go before I slap you," she demanded

I let her go and watched her run into the house. I knew I gave Cynthia that ring back, but she must have slipped it back into my pocket.

"Why is she like this now and why doesn't she believe me?" I asked myself. "That ring couldn't be mine. I didn't have that shirt then."

I went in to speak to her again, but she didn't want to talk to me. After supper, she said goodnight to her grandmother and went to bed early. Mariana said she tried talking to her, but she didn't want to listen. Her solution was; whatever I had done, we had to sort it out between us. I had nothing to sort out because to my knowledge; I hadn't done anything wrong. Before I went to bed,

I tapped on her door and went to open it, but it was locked. I called out to her, but she told me to go away.

"Oh this is stupid Lucia," I said. "I haven't done anything wrong. Oh, come on, please open the door. I have something for you."

"No, I don't care what you have. Why don't you listen to me? I told you to go away and leave me alone." she replied in anger.

"But I'm off home tomorrow to see my Granddad," I said, hoping she'd open the door.

She didn't, so I went downstairs, told her grandmother that I was going early in the morning, and went to bed.

I was up just before sunrise and thought I'd tap the wall to Lucia, but there was no response. So before I went downstairs, I placed Lucia's little feather on my pillow and left a note.

Lucia, if you can remember, I told you that after we had accomplished our mission, I was going to give you something. Something I had been saving for the right moment. So last night, I intended to give you back your little feather. You know what it means, but you didn't want to listen to me. So I'm leaving it on my pillow for you. I don't love Cynthia; I love you. I'm sorry that I kissed her and I hope you can forgive me.

I then went downstairs, saddled Roslyn, said goodbye to the house and went on my way. It was a misty morning, and after trotting our way across the dirt track road, I turned before going through the trees. I then thought I saw Lucia waving with both hands from her bedroom window, but it was my watery eyes playing tricks on me from all the fog. So we trotted on. When we were out through the forest and onto the main road, I sighed and said out loud.

"Well, Roslyn, we have a long way to go. I only wish we could fly."

With those words, Roslyn began to race like the wind, making it difficult for me to hang on. Then just when I thought I was about to fall off, in a jolt, I was sitting on a giant feathered eagle soaring high up through patchy clouds into the clear blue sky.

"Whey hey, Roslyn! We are flying girl!" I shouted as we flew above the clouds.

It was fabulous, and just like before, there was no wind, and it was really warm up there. I remember that big sigh of relief I gave, knowing that I didn't have to catch any train or boat. It would have taken me weeks. So while we flew at great speed up through Spain, I thought that I could now keep my promise to Cynthia. With that out of the way, my conscience would be clear, but then, as I thought about Lucia, I suddenly remembered that I hadn't given her my address. That was stupid of me and on top of that, I didn't know hers either, not even her surname. No one ever told me, and I never thought to ask. That was a real blow. I couldn't believe it and put my head in my hands, thinking that she didn't want to see me again, anyway.

"Go on, Roslyn. Let's go to Vienna. I promised Cynthia that I would call in."

Roslyn was so cosy that I led down between her feathers and dozed off until she woke me with a squawk. I sat up and saw that we were swooping around the top of a city. I began to panic, but after landing beside a river, I realised that we must be in the one-dimensional world because people were taking no notice of us. In a couple of minutes, I was soon sitting back on my faithful mare. This city had to be Vienna. I felt good and wasn't even tired though you would have thought after flying well over a thousand miles, I should have been.

It was five o'clock, and as we walked along the river bank, people were acknowledging us now making me realise that we were once more back in both worlds. I couldn't speak a word of their language, so I showed a young couple Cynthia's address and they pointed me in the direction of a church. The church was on the corner of her street, and the name of her house was Unwiderstehlich. What it meant I had no idea, but her house was at the other end of the street, detached from other houses.

I walked up to her door, and immediately a strange feeling came over me. I had to take quite a few deep breaths before I could bring myself to knock. It was stupid I know, but that was the kind of effect she had on me and now I was hoping she wouldn't be in, but she was.

"Gwydion! Oh, Gwydion!" She said excitedly after opening the door.

Cynthia looked precisely how I was hoping she wasn't going to. It was as if she was expecting someone and that one just had to be me. I can't describe what she looked like and what she was wearing. All I can say is; my heart was beating faster than usual and I was stuck for words. She hugged me and naturally, I had to hug her back,

"Gwydion, it's lovely to see you again. I knew you would keep your promise and look; there's Roslyn. We'll put her in the stable around the back, and then you can come in and meet Tracy my sister before she goes out."

Tracy, like her sister, was another lovely American girl. A lot younger than Cynthia with slightly different features. She was about to go and meet her fiancé. No sooner than we were introduced, she was away out the door. With her gone, it meant that I was going to be alone with Cynthia, something I didn't really want.

"Relax Gwydion. What's wrong with you?" asked Cynthia. "You look so nervous, and that's not like you."

"Aww, I'm alright," I replied. "Just a little overcome with everything that's been going on.

"Well Gwydion, you couldn't have come at a better time. So now that you're here, I'm going to treat you to a night out in the city. Simon is about your size, so if you go and wash up, I'll find some of his clothes. Tracy won't be back until tomorrow, so you can stay the night.

She was very persistent, and because I didn't want to offend her, I gave in. I hadn't planned to carry on with my journey until the morning. So, a night out in the city sounded interesting. But then I asked who Simon was. He was her brother, who sometimes stays with his sister when in Vienna on business, but was now back home in Poland.

"My oh my Gwydion, don't you look real smart now," she remarked as I came down the stairs in Simon's suit of clothes.

I felt silly, strange and embarrassed; I wasn't used to such a fine suit of clothes. Cynthia had changed and was standing by the fireplace dressed in a shimmery red dress with a white shawl draped over her arms.

"You look lovely," I said and meant it. "Where are we going dressed like this?"

"Oh just somewhere nice," she replied. "Now, can you help me on with my coat please Gwydion? The carriage is waiting outside for us."

Before we went, I had to endure a few lessons on how a gentleman escort treated his lady. So that and the suit I was wearing gave me an incline of where she was taking me. My inclinations were right. The coach pulled up in front of a fabulous building, called the Royal Hofburg Palace.

"We can't go in there, Cynthia," I said as she asked me to help her out.

I had an idea that we were probably going to some kind of wine and dance place, but I wasn't expecting anything as grand as what I was looking at.

"Oh yes we can," replied Cynthia taking hold of my arm. "I have an invite to come here anytime there's a ball. Tracy is marrying the owner's son. We are lucky you came at the right time, because they only have one ball a month."

"How coincidental is this?" I asked myself. "Surely, this is all planned."

It wasn't. It was just my suspicious mind, working overdrive. Tracy was there and had asked her fiancé to put us on the late guest list. It was then that my valid instructress's lesson in gentlemanly manners came into operation. Her fiancé introduced us to probably everyone there. By the time I had finished nodding, bowing and kissing the ladies' hands, I was glad to sit down outside on the veranda.

"Well, what do you think?" Cynthia asked.

"I'll let you know once my head stops nodding and my smile comes back to normal," I replied.

She laughed and said, "After all the guests have arrived, we'll go in, have something to eat, and then we'll join everyone on the dance floor. You said that you could dance, so we'll have a nice time."

It was for one night only, and I certainly wasn't going to spoil the night for her, so I agreed.

"Very well my lady. That sounds absolutely spiffing. It will be an honour to dance the night away with the lovely Belle of the Ball."

She laughed again and said, "Thank you. I'm glad you think so."

I wasn't far wrong because after a small meal, we were on the dance floor and I didn't see anyone as lovely as her, except for her sister. Tracy looked equally stunning in a lovely shot silk green dress that also shimmered and changed colour as she moved around the dance floor. She was dancing with her fiancé and they were looking very happy together.

It was fun and we were enjoying ourselves until Cynthia wanted to go outside.

"Let's go outside to cool down, shall we? I'm hot, and need a rest."

There were other couples outside, but we managed to find a seat.

"Isn't this just wonderful?" said Cynthia looking up at the starry moonlit sky.

She was holding my hand now, and as she looked lovingly into my eyes, she asked, "Will you kiss me Gwydion?"

"Blimey," I said to myself as my heart began to race with anxiety. How could I offend her by not doing so, and if I did, she would automatically think we were a couple? She was so lovely that in those few seconds, I was afraid. Afraid of what I might do. Then when I was about to tell her that I was in love with Lucia, Tracy came out wanting us back inside because after the next dance there was going to be an announcement. So in we went for another slow waltz, a waltz Cynthia made sure we danced a little closer than the last one. When the waltz ended, Tracy's fiancé called for attention, speaking in German. When he had finished, the band began to play and to my surprise, everyone moved aside and began clapping. Cynthia said they wanted us to dance. I thought perhaps we were in some kind of competition or had won one. Either way, I wasn't happy with just me and her dancing around the room on our own, especially with about two hundred people clapping and cheering us. It seemed to go on forever. I had never been so embarrassed in my life, but Cynthia loved it. Eventually the dance finished, and with everything back to normal, I was glad to sit down. While we were getting our breath back, Tracy came over to us.

"Congratulations, both of you."

I didn't know what she was congratulating us for. So I asked what we had won.

"She gave me a strange look, laughed and said, "My sister, of course. Congratulations on your engagement, both of you."

"You what!" I thought as I looked at Cynthia's red face. So to save embarrassment, I went along with it by thanking Tracy, but as soon as the band started up again, I took Cynthia outside.

"What was all that about? Whose idea was that?" I asked.

She broke down crying, so I put my arm around her until she gathered herself.

"I'm sorry, Gwydion. It's all my fault, but I swear I didn't know anything about my sister's announcement. After arriving at my sister's house, Tracy noticed the ring you gave me and asked how long had I been engaged and who to. Oh Gwydion, it was all because I couldn't get the ring off and I still can't. I told my sister that I was engaged to you. It was stupid I know, but you did say you loved me, didn't you?"

She was sobbing now and I was afraid someone would come out and see her in such a state. I looked over the veranda and saw that we were only a few feet from the ground.

"Ah, don't cry Cynthia," I said. "Come on, let's get away from here before someone comes. Do you think you can climb down if I help you?"

"I'll try," she said sadly.

I jumped down and waited for her to climb over. I tried to hold her, but unfortunately she slipped, and as I caught her, I fell with her on top of me. We rose to our feet and ran away between the bushes, out of the grounds and around the corner.

"Are you okay," I asked, but somehow I couldn't help laughing, and neither could she. It was so funny because both of us looked as if we had been dragged through a hedge. Our coats and Cynthia's handbag were still at the Palace, but my sweet dancing partner said she'd fetch them another day. There was a coach by the gates that was waiting for when the guests were ready to leave. I gave Cynthia money to pay the coachman to relay a message to her sister saying that we had left. It wasn't a great distance to her house, so we walked on and dare I say, arm in arm up the street. This was all a mistake, but I didn't want to upset her anymore; besides, I hadn't done anything wrong, and I wasn't going to either.

When we arrived, Cynthia went to the kitchen to make up a cup of hot cocoa each, something I had never tasted. While she was making our drinks, I lit the fire, and we sat sipping the delicious hot chocolate while watching the flickering flames.

"Well, what are we going to do now? What am I going to say to everyone?" Cynthia asked, taking hold of my hand.

I didn't know. All I wanted to do was run or fly away, but at that present time, I couldn't.

"I don't know Cynthia. We'll have to think of something because I'm on my way home tomorrow."

"You're what! Why tomorrow Gwydion? I was going to show you around the city tomorrow. Anyway, I thought you came here to see me?"

"I did," I replied, trying hard to think. "But, I, eh, well, I promised you didn't I, but all of a sudden, I find that everyone thinks we are engaged. You are so lovely Cynthia and if I wasn't in love with Lucia, I would think that I was so lucky."

"What!" She said, quickly sitting up. "You are in love with Lucia? You told me that your interest in her was business only and that you loved me."

As you know, that wasn't me saying that I loved her. I must have been under some kind of spell. So I reminded her of us all being under the influence of that no good Lord Steiner. It didn't help. It only made her break down crying, which quickly put me on the alert of Tracy deciding to come home. So I put my arm around her.

"Don't cry Cynthia. Come on, let's go upstairs and talk about it. We don't want Tracy turning up seeing you this way, now do we?"

She agreed, and we went to her room where we sat on a bench seat in the bay window. Then, after an exhausting couple of hours of explanatory conversations, she finally accepted that it was all a mistake and that I loved her as a friend. She kissed me on the cheek and apologised. But before we went to our beds, I asked her about the ring that I had given her back. She said that she did have it, but it went missing not so long ago. We wished each other goodnight, and I went to my room.

# Chapter 28

We were up at the same time, but neither of us wanted breakfast. Tracy, just as Cynthia told me, hadn't come home from the ball, so we were on our own. I wanted to have an early start, but before I headed out, Cynthia wanted to show me the city. So along with Roslyn and Cynthia's trap, we trotted around the glorious city of Vienna.

During our tour, we went inside many fabulous buildings and churches. I even went into one shop and bought Granddad an unusual-looking pipe and some tobacco.

"He will love this," I said to Cynthia.

"I'm sure he will," she said and smiled. "I have never seen another one like it."

We went further down the street to the house where Johann Straus once lived. I was surprised to know that it was only twelve months ago that he had died. Finally, we landed up walking around the Schönbrunn Zoo, which was on the same street as Johann's house. That brought us up to lunch hour, and after buying a sandwich, we sat outside the zoo to enjoy it. We chatted and laughed about some of the funny things we did when all three of us were together. I felt good, but later that afternoon, when the time came to say our goodbyes, I felt rotten because Cynthia was in such a terrible state. I know I told her that I only loved her as a friend, but I lied a little. She actually meant a great deal more to me than that. With Lucia saying she never wanted to see me again and knowing how I felt about Cynthia and how she felt about me, my head was in a whirl. The way my feelings were at that moment in time, I just wanted to stay there, forget everything and everybody and maybe run away with her, but I had to go home. Firstly, to see my Granddad and secondly to find the outcome of our mission. After that, I was going to listen to my heart. So as you can guess, that tearful goodbye sickened me right down to my stomach. It wasn't until Roslyn and I flew across France that I stopped sighing.

Before I left Cynthia, I gave her my home address and said that I hoped to see her again soon. Whether I would or not, I didn't know.

After reaching the English Channel, we had to fly over a blanket of rain clouds and stayed there until Roslyn dived through them, landing on the heather-ridden mountainside of Blaenafon.

"I'm home Roslyn," I said after changing her into my lovely mare again. "Let's go and see Granddad. He's going to love you."

We trotted off through the heather down over Cefyn-y-Lan and the Cocha to my Granddad's yard where I quickly dismounted.

"Hey Granddad you old codger, I'm home," I shouted, reaching the door.

But when I tried opening the door, it was locked. It was Tuesday, so I thought he was probably down over at the Abergavenny market and was late coming home. It was the only day he ever locked his door. So I went to the stable where we kept a spare key. Mad Luke and the cart were still there, but the spare key wasn't.

"That's strange," I said to myself. "He has definitely gone down over to the market with his old pal, Lyndon Stokes."

They always had a few pints later, especially if they had a good sale. On an odd time, Granddad would stay over at an Inn. I then went and checked all the windows, but they were all shut tight. That was also unusual, making me wonder if he was okay because it was nine-thirty and the sun had gone down. Either that or he had decided to stop overnight at the Inn.

I was tired now, and the only thing to do was get my sleeping bag and kip in the barn. I fed and watered Mad Luke and Roslyn, then settled down in the barn to sleep. With all that worrying about Cynthia, I was so tired I slept until Roslyn nudged me in the morning.

"Good girl Roslyn. Granddad's back is he?" I said and rushed out.

It wasn't Granddad it was one of my pals, Roger Regan. He was in with Mad Luke.

"Wow, Gwydion, you frightened me. So you are back, are you? I'm so sorry about your Granddad."

"Why? What's the matter with him?" I asked.

"Oh no, didn't you know?" he asked sadly.

"Know what?" I asked, fearing the worst. "What's happened to him?"

"He's dead Gwydion. He died a month ago. We couldn't get in touch with you. No one knew where you were. I thought perhaps you'd heard about it and had come home. I'm so sorry pal."

I was devastated and will never forget that terrible day. The very word dead, was the worse sound I have ever heard in my life and the thought of him dying alone, without me by his side, hit my chest like a ton of bricks.

"No, no, no. Please no. Tell me you're joking Roger. He's not dead, is he?"

"Yes, Gwydion," he replied, shaking his head. "He's gone pal, and once again, I am so sorry. He's buried with your grandmother down at Saint Peter's."

I sank to the floor in disbelief, "Oh no. No. Not Granddad."

I couldn't believe it. I just couldn't believe it. I thanked Roger for telling me and for looking after Mad Luke, but after he went away, I sat down on the trough and cried.

Later, after slowly saddling Roslyn, we made our way downtown to Saint Peter's. All my mates were at work, so I didn't meet any on my way, but I did meet a few of the girls from school, Eirlys Whitcombe, Ruthlyn Wilson, Beverly Murray, and Ruth Jones, who passed on their condolences. At Saint Peter's, I walked over to my grandmother's grave on the far side of the cemetery, and then when I looked at Granddad's name on the headstone, my heart sank. It was unbelievable.

"Oh, Granddad, why did you have to die?" I said as I knelt. "I love you so much, and I'm sorry for leaving you. Please forgive me. Aww, Granddad, I don't know what to do now. Life will never be the same without you."

I stayed kneeling there crying for a while, brushing away some leaves and tidying up a few flowers that someone had put there. I then opened my bag, took out the pipe and tobacco I had bought him and buried it in front of the headstone. That's when I got so choked up I could hardly speak.

"I bought you something," I managed to say. "It's a pipe. An unusual one and some bacci too."

Doing and saying that almost killed me. I had never been so sad. Granddad meant more to me than anyone in the world, and now I felt that I had let him down. I must have led beside him for hours until it was too cold to stay any longer.

"I'll have to go now, Granddad," I managed to say. "But I'll see you tomorrow. Hope you like your pipe."

I walked off up the town where I met a couple of my mates, Barrie Protherough and Lawson Allcock who were on their way home from work. They passed on their condolences and said that Lorraine Stokes, Lyndon's daughter, had the key to my house. I said I'd see them down the tavern on Saturday and went off to get my key. Lorraine lived with her parents in Manor House, Cwmavon Road. I knocked on her door and by chance she answered. Lorraine was a quiet, soft-spoken, attractive girl who was very apologetic about granddad passing away. She kindly asked me in for a cup of tea. I thought it was kind of her so I went in and we chatted for an hour. She told me that Granddad had a lovely funeral and that she had been putting flowers on his grave. Her father had Granddad's name put on the headstone. I thanked her for doing that and to thank her father too. Before I went, I said that I would take her out for a meal one day.

That night, it took me more than an hour before I could bring myself to open the door of our cottage. I knew that when I did, it would start me off all over again. I waited and waited until, after a few deep breaths, I opened the door. My feelings as I looked around the quiet lonely house, you wouldn't want to know. All I can tell you is; I wasn't in there two minutes because as soon as I saw Granddad's chair, I did about turn and slept in the barn. I stayed there all week until Saturday when along with Roslyn, now my hound for company, I ventured back in and began cleaning up. After granddad died and because I was away, Lyndon Stokes had sold granddad's sheep and his dog. Knowing I was home, Lyndon came around one night to give me the money he had for them. I told him that he could keep the money, but he insisted on me taking it.

For the next month, I wandered around the hills, sometimes with my mates and other times on my own. During that period, Cynthia had written to me a couple of times with news of what was happening in Vienna. I wrote back with news from Wales and the sad news about Granddad. I also called in to Cindy, telling her all about the mission. She was astounded and wanted to know every little detail and laughed when I gave her a rainbow-coloured broach that I had purchased in France. She said she'd keep it forever. Talking to her cheered me up, and it did me a lot of good.

The next day, I thought it was time to check out the wizard. Up until then, I was going around feeling sorry for myself, blaming him for me ever leaving my lovely Granddad, but it wasn't his fault, it was mine, I should have never left him. Maybe, because of my Granddad dying, Bleddwyn hadn't contacted me. I didn't know, but I was going to find out. That was, if the wizard was still there, something I was beginning to doubt. So, the following morning I picked up my staff and went up to the old Roman ruins. The slab stone was still there, slightly overgrown with grass. Suddenly, a nervous feeling came over me, and I was in two minds about what to do.

"Shall I try to move it or will I just not bother and go back home," I muttered. "I've done my bit, and if Bleddwyns still here, it's up to him to contact me."

Then, as I turned to walk away, I heard the slab move. I half-heartedly turned around to see the hatch slowly opening. I hesitated for a moment because suddenly I didn't want anything more to do with wizards, but something or someone was telling me to go down there. So, after telling Roslyn to stay and wait, I slowly descended into the dark cellar below. The slab slid shut behind me, and as usual, the whole room lit up with candles.

"Welcome, Gwydion, my son. Sit?" beckoned the wizard who was sitting, smiling, pointing to the chair carved in my image.

"Good morning Sir," I said as I walked over and sat down on myself.

"Gwydion," he said, along with a saddened expression. "I am sorry about the sad loss of your grandfather. I know how much you loved him, and now you miss him dearly. He was a lovely man and will be sorely missed by all. Are you ready to talk, or would you rather come another day?"

I told him that I was okay and had accepted my Granddad's passing as a fact of life.

"I'm pleased with you, Gwydion and so too are my colleagues. We will be eternally grateful to you and Lucia for accomplishing such a demanding and dangerous mission. Now before I carry on, I would like to introduce you to someone."

He then pointed to the opposite side of the table. I turned to look and saw, sitting in the chair carved in the shape of a woman, was the very woman herself. That made me jump and go all cold.

"Good morning Gwydion," she said and smiled. "I am Eluciana."

"I thought you were, uh. I thought you were…."

"Dead, Gwydion," interrupted Bleddwyn. "No son. Eluciana did not die as you can well see.

I did not say that she had so. All enchanted people live for thousands of years. My wife has been a captive and confined inside Brynmoroc's castle walls ever since he abducted her. Now, because of you and Lucia, she is free. Free to enjoy the rest of our lives together."

I was astonished, stood up and as I gently shook Eluciana's hand, I said that I was pleased but surprised to see her. She just smiled and said that she was also pleased to see me and was thankful for what Lucia and I had done. Another thing that surprised me about her was her striking resemblance to Lucia.

"Now Gwydion," said Bleddwyn solemnly. "All is not finished. Before we can all enjoy our lives again, there is one more task you have to achieve."

"Oh, no! I thought this was too good to be true. What now?" I said to myself.

"Thanks to you, Gwydion, the Sun Giant was released and is now back in the mountains. After the solar eclipse, it was the Giant who brought Eluciana to me. Also, because of you, Brynmoroc could not receive the centenary supply of enchanted energy he needed to maintain full control of our world. He is however, still very powerful, more powerful than I. The only one that can destroy Brynmoroc is you, but it means engaging in mortal combat…"

"Mortal combat!" I interrupted "That means fighting to the death. I thought Brynmoroc was already dead. Me, fight Brynmoroc. That's just suicidal. I was lucky the last time and if you can't beat him, how on earth can I? Ah, I don't know Sir. I just don't know if this is really happening. It's madness, total madness. Why do I have to do this? Haven't I done enough already for you all? Is it ever going to end? Oh, I don't know, it's just crazy. I've had enough; I'm going home."

I was waiting for his response, thinking that he would be disappointed or maybe angry, but he wasn't.

"Gwydion, I can understand why you are upset. It was as I expected, but before you go, hold out your hands towards the wall beside me."

I held my hands towards the wall, and as I did, flames of lightning flashed from my fingers against the wall and sizzled there. I was in shock and quickly let down my hands. The wizard and his wife gave a little laugh because my face must have looked a picture of amazement.

"Now, point your hands to that cupboard and move it with your thoughts," said Bleddwyn.

So I did, and it moved to exactly where I wanted, the other side of the room.

"This is amazing, but what does it mean?" I asked. "Why is it happening?"

"Now look at the palm of your left hand and tell me what you see?" He replied.

"The mark of a rock that was absorbed into it," I said, looking at it.

"That's right Gwydion. Now look again?"

"It's bleeding!" I exclaimed. "It's bleeding, but my blood is green!"

"Don't be alarmed Gwydion," said Bleddwyn as Eluciana laughed. "You are now a full-blooded wizard. All wizards' and every other enchanted person's blood is green. The stone was ordained by Vindaguar as a gift to the instigator of his prophecy."

"What! Do you mean to say that I'm a wizard now?" I asked, still looking at my green blood

"Yes, son. Both you and Lucia, are now of enchanted blood. If you are not happy or if there ever comes a time you no longer wish to be so, the rock will be removed. It's entirely up to you."

When he told me that I was now a wizard with green blood, it caused a sickening lump in my throat, but I had a choice and thought, "Well, okay, that doesn't sound too bad."

"Now, Gwydion. Eluciana and I will let you mull over your next assignment and await your decision."

I quickly raised my hand to stop him from opening the slab because there was one important question I wanted an answer to.

"Before I go Sir, and before I make any decision at all, I must ask you something. Is it true that Lucia and I are not related in any way, and is she safe now from Brynmoroc?"

He replied, "I can assure you that you are in no way related whatsoever to Lucia and yes, she's safe from Brynmoroc. Now go, and return here when you are ready with your decision."

Then with a swirl of wind, I was back standing on top of the slab again, looking down the mountain. Roslyn was there waiting, and as we walked off down the mountain, I couldn't help fiddling with my hands and flicking my fingers nervously.

"Whoa," I said. "Watch yourself Gwydion; we don't want to set the mountain on fire."

That made me laugh but stopped when I heard someone shouting. It was Roger Regan coming home from fishing. As usual, Roger had caught some nice trout and gave me one. We then walked on down over the heather, chatting and laughing about the time we were chased by the Bailiff while fishing down on the Skenfrith stretch of river.

"See you Friday in the Rolling Mill, Roger," I said, and he went his way, and I went mine.

It was only after a couple of weeks of thinking and discussing it with Cindy that I made up my mind to see Bleddwyn again. I was a little apprehensive about confronting Brynmoroc, but after giving it some thought, I was ninety nine percent sure that I would. So the next morning, I dressed, put on my cape, picked up my staff and with Roslyn my hound by my side, I set off up to the Roman ruins.

Bleddwyn must have known I was coming because the slab-stone hatch was wide open. I told Roslyn to stay, then went down into the cellar.

"Welcome once again Gwydion. Sit and let me know your intentions?" said Bleddwyn as I entered.

Eluciana also welcomed me, and she too beckoned me to sit.

"Well Sir," I began, after a long sigh. "I was a little hasty and upset the last time we met and gave you a rash decision. I really didn't want to listen to you then, but I do now. If I am to do battle with Brynmoroc, so be it."

"I'm pleased to hear it son," he said, also after a long sigh. "Now, I'll start from the beginning. Now that Brynmoroc is no longer one with the Sun Giant, he can now travel the world by day and by night. This makes him more of a menace than he was before. My cousin is still a very powerful wizard. The energy he obtained over all those years is now only in his staff, not his body."

I was confused, "Excuse me, Sir. Something is not making sense. At the beginning of it all, you told me that the violator would be obliterated. I took that to be at the eclipse. Now all of a sudden, Brynmoroc is still alive and probably just as powerful. Were you keeping this a secret so that I wouldn't be discouraged?"

He smiled and said, "You are well to ask me that Gwydion. I was coming to it. I was not keeping anything a secret from you. I, just like you, assumed that the violator would be eliminated at the same time as the eclipse. If you remember, I told you that there were some parts of the prophecy I knew nothing about, one of them being the thorn piercing your hand. I also told you that Lucia knew even more than me. Now I find after Eluciana telling me, that the final part of the prophecy must be performed by the hand of the instigator, you Gwydion. I had no idea it would come to this, and I am sorry, truly sorry. However, we wizards want you to know that you are under no obligation to complete the final part of the prophecy. In time, Brynmoroc's energy will be depleted, but there is no guarantee he will never try anything as terrible again."

I sat there thinking of what my Granddad would have done. He always told me to never take on something that I wasn't one hundred percent sure of finishing. Well, that was a little late now, for I had already done what he had told me not to. So, the only thing to do now was; what he told me to do if I hadn't listened to him.

"If you do go headlong putting your foot in it, you are going to have to put the other one in too and finish it, no matter what."

Well, I had indeed put my foot in it. I was committed now, left with no choice, but to go the full hog.

"Okay. I'll do it Sir," I said, much to his pleasure. "But, is there anything else I should know about?"

"Yes, one more," he replied. "When I informed you that you would be engaged in mortal combat, you must have thought how can this be? Wizards are not allowed to engage in such a battle. This is true, but we can however, engage in such a one if threatened. We are, as you know threatened by a rapacious, power-loving tyrant. I know he is my cousin, but he has no mercy for me, my colleagues or any other enchanted being. This is why Vindaguar wrote in his prophecy, the right to eliminate its violator. You, although you are not aware, are more than equal to Brynmoroc and his power. This was given to you the moment you absorbed the last jewel. According to Eluciana, Brynmoroc knows this and is expecting you."

Bleddwyn didn't say another word which left the room in silence. At that very moment, it once again all seemed like a dream to me.

"Me, a powerful wizard," I said to myself. "This just can't be? It's unbelievable, but if he says I am, then I hope he's right?"

The silence remained as if Bleddwyn was waiting for my response. I had thought of a few other things that I forgot to ask him earlier. One was about all the visions Lucia and I had been experiencing during the mission. So I asked, and he answered.

"Whatever visions you may have had, were probably the work of Brynmoroc, others I wouldn't know. Either way, you obviously handled them well."

Lastly, I asked about Lucia, "You tell me Lucia is safe, but how can she be, with Brynmoroc still around?"

"She is safe Gwydion. Brynmoroc has no use for her now that the jewels have been found. Even if he abducted her today, he wouldn't harm her. He knows that if he did, it would only incite you even more. No, Gwydion, Brynmoroc fears you and is gambling you'll walk away and forget this final confrontation."

I was happy now, and with nothing else I could think of, I asked how and when I was to meet up with Brynmoroc and where was he now.

"He's where you want him to be," was Bleddwyn's delighted reply. "He has to accept your challenge."

I couldn't think, so I asked him where he thought a suitable place would be. He looked at Eluciana, and she nodded.

"My wife would be honoured if you meet him here, where he abducted her."

Thinking it was an ideal place, I then asked how I was to challenge him.

"Whenever you are ready, return here. I will advise you then. Now go Gwydion. Fear no more. Prepare yourself now in mind and body. Bring only your staff for your shield will be of no use to you now."

The next instant, I was back on top of the slab again with Roslyn jumping all over me.

"Hey girl. Come on then, let's go home. I've got a lot to think about."

I did have a lot to think about, and it took me a few weeks until the end of August before I felt ready to face Brynmoroc.

# Chapter 29

On the sunny morning of the twenty-eighth of August, while taking a last look around the cottage, I went over to Granddad's cap, and as I tapped it, I suddenly thought about his lucky penny. I found it in the drawer beside his bed and slipped it into my pocket.

"Okay, that's it. I'm off now Granddad, and yes, I know you think I'm crazy, but I've got your lucky penny."

So, with my staff in my hand and with Roslyn following behind, I walked away up to the old Roman ruins. I stopped just before the slab stone and once more found it wide open. I was off now down into a battle that maybe I wasn't coming back from. So I took the collar off Roslyn and threw it away in the heather.

"You are free now girl, you can go back to your world now," I said. "Thanks, lass for everything you have done for me. I love ya, and I will never forget you."

I then patted her and kissed her lovely nose but as I looked into her eyes, they were sad and watery.

"Hey, what's the matter girl? You look as if you are crying. Don't be sad or you'll start me off," I said giving her another pat, but she pawed me gently as if to say I'm not going.

"Oh, Roslyn!" I said holding her paw. "Well, okay then, if you do want to stay, please don't follow me and I order you not to."

She sighed and as she led down with her head resting on her paws and her sad watery eyes looking up at me. I smiled, gently shook my head and said, "Now that's an order, Roslyn."

With that said, I slowly descended down into the cellar hoping for the last time

"Welcome Gwydion, sit and drink," said Eluciana as I entered.

The room was brightly lit as usual, but the roof now was twinkling with stars, just like the first time I saw it. Everything looked exactly the same. Even the wooden dragon on the table was there with a glass of wine beside it.

"Yes Gwydion, today is exactly the same as the sad day Brynmoroc pierced my heart. Now sip your wine while I acquaint you," said Bleddwyn as I sat.

I didn't want any wine but I did take a sip to dampen my dry throat.

"You are now solely in our one-dimensional world and above you now is our home, the old Roman Fortress where I battled with Brynmoroc. When you leave here, you'll find yourself in the hallway of my castle. In front of you will be a spiralled stone stairway. Ascend this stairway to the top of the castle then rest and gather yourself. Once you are ready and in full control of your mind, point your staff towards the sun and call out for Brynmoroc. He will respond, how he does and in what shape or form, I do not know. So be prepared, for he will come, he has to. He may try and trick you in to thinking that it's all a waste of time. So, keep this in mind. That's all I can tell you."

He then leaned forward, touched my eyes and sat back again, saying, "Now is there anything you are worried about and want to ask me?"

My eyes were tingling a little now, but I blinked a few times and they stopped. I wondered what he had done. He didn't tell me, so I didn't ask, but I did question him one last time.

"If and when I am successful? What happens then?"

"Peace Gwydion. Peace," was his only answer.

Knowing this, I took another sip of wine, told him that I was ready, and the hatch door opened.

"Our hearts go with you Gwydion," said Eluciana as I climbed the steps into the hallway.

"Wish me luck, Granddad?" I said, climbing the stairway while touching his penny.

Reaching the top, frightening memories of the vision came flooding back to me. The statues, seats and the old Roman relics, were all there, and so too was the red and black wizards' flag blowing gently in the breeze. I looked through the turrets down into the large courtyard and immediately felt my legs wobble. I then turned, walked to the centre of the roof, took a few deep breaths to calm myself and thought okay, let's do it.

I took another deep breath, stretched out my staff to the sun and called out the tyrant wizard's name. In the distance now, I could hear a low rumble of thunder as if growling, angrily. Hearing this, and while watching black clouds slowly rolling towards me, my heart skipped and began to race. I was now thinking what the heck am I doing here? The rumbling carried on growing louder and louder until a bolt of lightning flashed from the darkened clouds that had been gathering above me. Another flash and appearing now, who I thought was to be Brynmoroc, was my Granddad. He was about twenty feet away with a staff in his hand, holding out his arms to me. I was stunned, and as I backed away he called out.

"Gwydion, my boy. You are not going to hurt your poor old Granddad, are you?" he said with a pleading expression.

I knew very well that it couldn't be Granddad. It was Brynmoroc in Granddad's form. Besides, Granddad was only five foot ten and now he was about six foot six. At that point, even though our conflict had only just begun, I thought I was doomed. How could I battle against my lovely Granddad? The devious wizard knew precisely what he was doing.

"What's the matter, son? A tough decision, maybe? I too loved my Granddad, and if I were you right now, I think I would be feeling the same way. So, what do you say we sit down and work this out amicably? I am sure we can come to an agreement. Believe me Gwydion, I am sorry for what I foolishly did. I made a mistake I know, but Bleddwyn had a lot to do with it. I have already apologised to everyone and have given them my word that it will never happen again. Bleddwyn knows this but obviously hasn't told you. So, don't be a fool and risk your life for the sake of him. Come to me, let's sit and talk. If you like, I can call on my colleagues to confirm my accepted apologies. What do you say?"

I knew he was talking a load of nonsense, but what could I do? He was a very clever wizard, but impersonating my Granddad made me realise that he was afraid of me. He knew for psychological reasons that I wouldn't battle against my Granddad, even though it wasn't really him. All I could think of was to make him mad because the last time that he was, he showed his true colours. It was going to be difficult because I was face to face, talking to my lovely Granddad. He was a distance away from me, so as I answered him, instead of looking at his face, I looked at his chest.

"Oh dear, dear Brynmoroc. I have never believed a single word you uttered. Obviously, you must have known that your fabricated stories were the silliest ones I've ever heard. The very moment you made your overdramatic exit, Lucia and I would laugh until we ached. We used to sit laughing all night about how we could fool you again the next time. It was so easy and so funny because you believed me every time. Bleddwyn told me that you were not all that bright and easily fooled. Even my Granddad's probably laughing at you now because he never wore wellingtons and even if he did, he'd have them on the right feet."

I then laughed, but at the same time, kept my eye on the scheming wizard, but he just laughed back.

"No wonder your old Granddad drowned himself. If I had a grandson like you, I would have done the same. Oh dear, dear, what's the matter, son? Didn't they tell you he killed himself?"

I didn't like him saying that. Instead of me infuriating him, he did the opposite by maddening me. So I raised my staff and scowled at him, but Granddad's face turned to anguish. I froze, not knowing what to do, then suddenly, my eyes began to tingle and I blinked. To my relief, I found that I was no longer looking at my Granddad. I was looking at Brynmoroc. Bleddwyn obviously knew Brynmoroc's trickery, so he did something to my eyes, enabling me to see the real wizard. I now focused on him and quickly extended my left hand, sending him back against the turrets.

"No, no son, I really am your Granddad. Don't hurt me," he cried as I briefly laughed at him.

"Didn't I tell you Brynmoroc that you were a fool? When are you ever going to listen to me? You are also nothing but a coward hiding behind my Granddad. Is that the strategy of an almighty wizard? No, that's one of a sneak who's afraid of me. A rabbit has more courage than you."

I could tell from his expression now that he was mad, so I braced myself and waited for his reaction. I was right because the wizard roared back.

"I'm no fool sonny boy and certainly no coward. It is you who art the fool, not I. I was trying to settle our differences amicably. So if you don't want to listen to reason, then that's the reason why I am going to blast you to kingdom come."

He then raised his staff, and I too was hurled across the roof into the wall. I wasn't hurt. For some reason, I didn't feel a thing, and as I quickly rose to my feet, our energy clashed sending us both sprawling across the rooftop. The terrifying battle to the death was now on, and as we alternatively blasted one another all over the rooftop, statues and turrets crumbled to smithereens in our wake. Our encounter was nothing like I expected. There were no flashes of lightning or rumbling of thunder. We were thumping ourselves around the rooftop with an energy I couldn't see. So from the lack of visibility, neither of us could evade one another's attack. It came to a stage where we physically engaged, wrestling, leaving our staffs strewn across the floor. Although he was taller and heavier, I was a lot stronger. I managed to hurl him away from me, but as I did, I noticed that he looked relieved. In a flash, he was grappling for his staff, but with the energy in my fingers, I managed to spin him around, giving me a chance to pick up mine.

Every time we clashed, it was just a matter of exchanging blows. We were getting nowhere. Realising this, Brynmoroc backed away and began ranting on, talking a load of garbage. He probably only wanted a rest. I wasn't listening to him for I knew, apart from his physical strength, his energy was only in his staff. With this in mind, I thought the only way I was going to beat the wizard, was to capture his staff. This meant another physical battle. I knew that if I could once again engage him in bodily contact, he was doomed and I was sure that he knew this too. However, after realising this, a strange feeling came over me, and I asked myself.

"What am I supposed to do with him? I'm not a murderer. Apart from those enchanted creatures, I've never killed a single thing in my life, but Brynmoroc wouldn't hesitate one iota to kill me."

So I called out to him, "Brynmoroc, please! There is no need for this. You know as well as I do that you cannot win. I want you to know that I have had enough of wizards and wizardry. I no longer want to fulfil the prophecy in the manner it was set out to be. You tell me that you are sorry and have already apologised to your colleagues. Whether this is true or not, I wouldn't know, but I am prepared to give you the benefit of the doubt. All you have to do is surrender your staff to me, and you have my word of honour that I will leave you in peace. What do you say?"

"Oh Gwydion, Gwydion. That's so touching son, but I never did and never will apologise or surrender my staff to anyone. I will fight to the death before I ever do. Now, how about vice versa? You surrender your staff to me, and I'll let you live, and you can go your way in peace. What do you say to that?"

"That sounds okay," I replied. "I didn't ask to take on this mission, and I should have never accepted it. I've had nothing but heartache ever since. It had nothing to do with me, and you are right sir, it is I who's the fool, not you. I shouldn't have listened to Bleddwyn. I should have let you fight your own battles, but I didn't. For that, I am sorry, but what's done is done, and I can't change it. The Sun Giant is free and the black diamond returned. So if by giving you my staff will bring peace to all, I will gladly do so."

Brynmoroc was surprised, and as he lovingly looked at me, he replied with a soft and gentle tone to his voice.

"Gwydion, that was all you had to do, but it was understandable why you didn't, and I commend you for it. You are a strong and wise boy and by the way, no fool. I only wish you were my son, but we will always be friends. If it is your wish to hand me your staff, then you have my word I will honour our truce."

That was just what I was hoping he would say. So, to assure the wizard that I was genuine, I walked towards him holding my staff upside down by its tip. I had my other hand on my head, and as he eagerly held out his hands to me, I brought my hand down sharply onto Brynmoroc's wrist, subsequently making him drop his staff. I quickly dropped my staff and grabbed hold of him by the arm, but he swung me around, driving me back against the turrets. I still had hold of his arm, and as we wrestled, I was forced back and over the wall and as a result, we both fell down into the courtyard. I was expecting the worst but amazingly as we hit the slabs, it was like hitting a haystack. Neither of us were hurt; in fact, we were up like a flash with Brynmoroc holding up his hand calling for his staff. I saw his staff flying down from the roof, but I caught it, and as I snapped it into pieces in front of him, I asserted.

"Now, pick whatever piece you want, because that's the only peace, you are ever going to get?"

He was fuming now and grabbed hold of me by the shoulders, and we wrestled to the ground with him screaming in my ear.

"You ugly son of a stinking tramp. I'll break every bone in your body."

To my surprise, he lifted me up and threw me thumping against the barrack wall. I was expecting him to be weak and helpless now, but he was still as strong as a horse. While I was getting to my feet, he lifted a statue and flung it at me, which I avoided. Then as I went to blast him against the wall to hold him there, I found that I couldn't. The energy in my hands, for some reason, had gone. I could still feel it within me, but not in my hands. So I picked up the statue and hurled it back, catching him squarely in the chest. In his crazed anger, he rushed in and pinned me against another large statue. I wrapped my arms around his waist and began to squeeze, making him cry out. I thought then that I had him at my mercy, but he savaged my shoulder like a desperate beast. I had no other choice, other than to let him go, but not without grabbing him again.

"Now, it's my turn," I yelled as I lifted him and threw him across the yard in front of the castle wall. Without his staff, there was nowhere he could go now or even fly. All he could do was as he had predicted earlier; fight to the death, but I wasn't going to let that happen. While I watched him pacing around scowling and shouting abuse at me, I repeatedly asked myself, "How can I end this? What else can I do?"

I was so deep in thought; I didn't notice until it was too late. Brynmoroc had somehow summoned my staff from the rooftop, and it was now flying down towards his up-stretched hand. I rushed across, but it was too late. Brynmoroc had caught the staff and had me pinned down helplessly in front of the castle. He had the evilest look in his eyes now and said as he sneered.

"Oh, you are good Gwydion. You're good, but you made one mistake. You should have never broken my staff, for the only way to kill a wizard is by his own staff, driven into his chest. Now, if I am not mistaken, I seem to be holding yours. So what do you think that's telling you, son? You're finished, perhaps? I think it is, so with all my love and best wishes, goodbye and good riddance."

I could do nothing only watch, but as he raised his staff, he was suddenly bowled over. It was Roslyn. Where she came from I didn't know, but she had hold of his arm. The wizard was hollering, trying desperately to get her off. I jumped up looking for my staff, but Brynmoroc was still holding it, and as I watched them rolling over and over, I just couldn't think what to do. Then somehow, Brynmoroc managed to get to his feet and flew off to the top of the castle with Roslyn hanging on to him. I ran into the castle and up the stairway to the top, but by this time Roslyn was limp, held in both hands above Brynmoroc's head. Once again, there was nothing I could do only shout, "No! No! Brynmoroc. Please, no!"

He took no notice of me and threw her off the roof, down into the yard below. The wizard then staggered back, scanning the area for my staff, which I had already regained and was now pointing directly at him. Brynmoroc looked weak now and in pain. His cloak had been torn to pieces, and his arm was covered in blood, green blood. So with the force of my staff, I pinned him against the wall. I then looked down into the courtyard and sighed. Roslyn was lying crumpled up, motionless below.

"I TOLD YOU TO STAY!!" I hollered down to her lifeless body.

In contempt, I faced up to Brynmoroc with terrible thoughts running through my mind, but I refrained myself and scowled at him.

"I was willing to walk away and leave you in peace to do whatever you wanted. I told you that I had just about enough of you lot, but, that wasn't good enough for you, was it? Now, if ever I have hated anyone in my entire life, I hate you the most for what you have just done…."

He interrupted me, "Ah, what are you worrying about an old dog for? It's just a dog."

Hearing him saying that about Roslyn, I could feel my blood boil.

"A dog! Just a dog was she? Well, you're JUST a wizard, and now you are going to get JUST what you deserve. But, JUST as I promised, I'll keep my word and leave you in peace. Only it will be somewhere on the other side of the world. Somewhere, you are JUST not going to like."

I caught hold of his arm with one hand and with all the energy within me, I tore off into the air with him hollering, "Don't do this Gwydion. We'll both die."

The moment he implored me, I felt a sharp pain in my staff hand. It went right through my body to the hand I held the wizard with. Within seconds, a loud cry rang out, and Brynmoroc's arm suddenly felt cold, and with it, the wizard grew unbearably heavy. I slowed up, looked at him and found that he had turned to stone. I lost my grip in fright. There was nothing I could do only to watch him falling down, down and down into a bog on top of Llanellen Mountain. I flew down to where he had landed, but all I could see was his hand. What happened up there I had no idea, but it was not what I wanted. I felt sorry for him, but then I remembered Roslyn and quickly flew back to her. I was grief-stricken, and with my eyes blurred from the wind and tears, I covered her blood-soaked head and stayed there gently stroking her chest. All I could do was bury her somewhere in the grounds. I found a place near a statue of a lady looking down, an ideal spot, and dug a grave with the force from my staff and gently buried her.

# Chapter 30

How long I stayed with Roslyn, I can't remember. I just couldn't believe that another love of my life was gone. So, after thanking her and saying goodbye, I placed my staff on her grave and left it there. I didn't want it anymore or anything else to do with wizards and their wizardry. I just wanted to go home and cry. I looked around and saw that the portcullis gate was open, but before I could even take a step, I found myself sitting back on my chair, down in the cellar. The candles were still brightly burning, but there was no one there, I was on my own. "Now what's happening," I shouted angrily.

Then as my voice echoed, I heard the slab-stone opening. I was now expecting Bleddwyn and his wife to appear, but they didn't. I was happy for I'd had enough of this mysterious nonsense. Besides, I wasn't in any kind of mood to be talking to anyone, especially the wizard.

"Right, that's it. Let's get out of here," I whispered, moving smartly to the steps and out into the open.

"Hey!" I shouted, as I was jumped upon and my face frantically being washed. "Roslyn, you're alive. You're alive. Oh, my lovely girl. How…."

I was then interrupted by a loud cheer and found myself once again, back inside the castle grounds, looking up at cheering wizards and what looked like chambermaids. They were on top of the castle waving and saluting me with their staff. In the doorway of the castle, beaming broadly, were Bleddwyn and Eluciana.

"Come Gwydion," said Bleddwyn as Eluciana held her arms out to me.

I was curious, and as I walked, I glanced across to where I had buried Roslyn. The grave, strangely enough, was still there.

"Welcome to our home Gwydion," said Bleddwyn and Eluciana as they shook hands and embraced me.

"Come, Gwydion," said Eluciana, and I followed them into their living room.

Every piece of furniture in that room, from a candlestick to a Welsh dresser, was beautifully carved from oak. Each piece was unique; even the arms and legs of the table and chairs were different. Bleddwyn and Eluciana had never set foot in their castle since their wedding anniversary six hundred years ago. As we slowly walked around the room, I heard Eluciana say to the very proud-looking wizard, "It's been a long time dear. It's so nice to be home again."

They were in as much awe as I was. You could have sworn it was their first time there and had never seen anything like it.

"Please come and walk with us Gwydion as we reminisce. It has been such a long time since we were here last" said Eluciana.

I did, and as I followed them around their fantastic castle, they ventured in and out of every room. All I can say is; looking at the castle from the outside was fabulous, but inside was breathtaking.

"Now then Gwydion," said Bleddwyn when we returned to the living room. "We will sit and sip wine together. No doubt, there are questions that you surely want answers to."

This was all too sudden for me. One minute I was in an almighty battle for my life and the next I was being shown around a castle, talking to a wizard as if nothing had ever happened. I really didn't want to stop, talk or even listen. I just wanted to go home. I'd had about enough of everything and everyone, but I felt that I had to stay.

So, we sat over by the bay window, and while sipping our wine, Bleddwyn began by once again thanking me for taking on the mission and fulfilling the prophecy. As for Lucia, Bleddwyn said that up to now, although she has been told of her ancestors, she has not entirely accepted the fact that they are. This was understandable, and they were going to leave her to decide for herself. When he thinks she's ready, they were going to visit both Lucia and Mariana together.

We sat for some time asking one another questions. One of the questions I asked the wizard was; why did Brynmoroc have to die and of all things, turn to stone.

His detailed reply was, "At the time of the eclipse, because of the confused un-spiralled rainbow, Brynmoroc could not receive the energy for him to retain the Sun Giant. Consequently, my cousin had no choice other than to release him. However, this was not so for the black diamond collector. Once absorbed, it could not be released."

The wizard stopped then and looked earnestly into my eyes before carrying on.

"Believe me Gwydion. Just as I told you about the thorn in your finger, I knew nothing of Brynmoroc's fate until it happened. Today, while Brynmoroc was in your grasp above Llanellen Mountain, your other hand was also grasping the black diamond in your staff. This reacted with the collector inside Brynmoroc's body, causing his fatality. Why he turned to stone, I do not know. Maybe how he lived was how he died; only Vindaguar knows. The original black diamond no longer exists. It has been replaced with yours, and is now safely in the hands of the Sun Giant."

I was upset that Brynmoroc had to die, especially that way, but I did give him an alternative, and if he had listened he would have still been alive. My final question was; how did Roslyn come back to life?

"It wasn't Roslyn that you buried, Gwydion," said Bleddwyn. "It was Adora. After the eclipse, her loyal assistance to you in your three-dimensional world was no longer needed. Instead she chose to defend you, if necessary, in our one-dimensional. With this in mind, and in that hour of need she gallantly came to defend you and in doing so, bravely lost her life."

Hearing this, shocked and sadden me once again, but at the same time, I was happy that I had ordered Roslyn to stay put. I was exhausted now and felt really drained. I told Bleddwyn that I was all worn out and had better go home to bed. Before I went, he gave me back my staff and told me to return the next day; there was more he wanted to tell me. I looked at my staff, and sure enough, the little black diamond was gone. I was so tired now that after wishing everyone goodnight I can't even remember going home.

In the morning, after looking out my bedroom window towards the old ruins, I found that the fortress had gone. It made sense, and I thought no more of it. For the rest of the morning and most of the afternoon, I spent time riding Roslyn down over to Llanover Village. On the way home I took a detour and came out up on top of Badger's Hill where I sat thinking of Lucia, longing to see her pretty face again. It was going to be autumn soon, and I had promised Barrie Protherough that I would help him with his house after work and at weekends. Barry thought it would take about six months to finish. So I thought spring was an excellent time to go back to Spain in the hope I could change Lucia's mind.

I arrived home in enough time to see the wizard. So at four o'clock, I headed off up the mountain, wondering if the fortress and castle would be there. They were, but as for being visible to anyone else, I doubted very much, and it was something I was going to ask.

Before I went in through the open gates, I let Roslyn off to graze. I was then greeted by a butler who led me into the study where Bleddwyn and Eluciana were waiting. We sat down while the cheerful butler poured out coffee before he left.

"Now Gwydion, I know you are helping your friend construct his house, so I am not going to keep you too long. What are your intentions with Lucia? Do you intend on seeing her again and if so, have you decided when?"

I had been hoping he would ask me about Lucia, and I answer him.

"Well Sir, sadly, Lucia told me that she doesn't want to see me again, but I was thinking around about spring. By that time, Barry's house should be finished."

"That's perfect," he said and beamed. "That's a perfect time for Eluciana and me to introduce ourselves to her. Until then, there will be no celebration in honour of you both. Now, there is just one more thing I would like to ask. Do you love Lucia, Gwydion?"

My heart skipped when he asked me that and I had to take a deep breath before replying.

"If the warm feeling I had when we were together and the longing to be with her again, is being in love, then yes, Sir, I do love her."

Eluciana smiled, leaned forward, touched my hand and said, "That's all we wanted to know."

With that said, and after a few more hearty conversations, it was time to go. Before I left, Bleddwyn mentioned that he had a lot of work to do and it would not be until the spring before we met again. I said goodbye and collected Roslyn, but it was too late to go to Pontypwl to help Barry with his house.

I was only home five minutes when I thought that I should have asked the wizard Lucia's address. I quickly mounted Roslyn and made my way back to the castle only to find that it wasn't there. The castle, the fortress even the slab-stone above the cellar had all gone.

So, that was that. I couldn't get Lucia's address, and she didn't have mine either. In the meantime, I just had to hope she wouldn't find someone else. She did mention that she had a boyfriend back in Spain, but he wasn't bothered much about her leaving. So because of that, she didn't like him anymore. I wasn't going to worry too much about it anyway, because if she did find someone, what could I do about it?

With me not needing a job anymore, though I did pretend that I was looking for one, I would sometimes stack a load of bricks and stones ready for Barrie and Lawson after work. Other times I carried on tidying my place, repairing the side of the barn that I had knocked down trying out my incredible power. I cut a few turfs of grass for my Grandparent's grave and planted snowdrops ready for the spring.

Although I had plenty to do, Lucia was always on my mind, and when my birthday, Christmas and New Year's Eve came around, I couldn't sleep for thinking of her. If it were not for joining in with my mate's fun and games, I probably would have taken off to Spain to see her.

Barrie's house was coming along fine, but the wintery weather held us up. Lawson was always moaning about the cold and probably had on more clothes and gloves than in Fowlers Shop. He was forever moaning but laughed about it after. Barrie and I used to love his little moans; they were so funny. Sometimes we used to think he was moaning on purpose, just to make us laugh. We had great fun together building that house and as Barrie predicted, but only by luck, it was finished at the beginning of April.

By now, with spring well in bloom, my thoughts were on travelling to Spain and Lucia. There was still no sign of the wizard and his fortress, but it didn't really bother me. Whether I saw Bleddwyn again or not, I didn't care. I was going to Spain.

I set a date for around the middle of May, but I had a problem. Just in case something happened to me, I had Mad Luke and my place to consider. Then one night I remembered Emma, the young Irish girl I met in Cork. She had no home of her own, and she wanted a job. Now, I know you may think it a crazy idea, but at three o'clock the next morning, I flew off with Roslyn to Cork in the hope of finding her. I looked all morning, and without success, I went back to the Cork Railway station for a bite to eat.

While there, I met a young guitarist playing and singing in the station hallway. He was a brilliant musician and had quite an audience around him. I hadn't heard a guitar before, and the sound was fantastic. When he stopped for a break, I went over to him, gave him some money, and we had a coffee together. His name was Jim Spillane. Coincidentally, he knew Emma. She sometimes came on the weekends to listen to him and his music.

"She lives not too far from here," Jim said. "It's a wonder she isn't here today."

I listened to him play for a while and then went off in search again. Eventually, just before dark, I saw Emma walking over a bridge just outside the city.

"Hi Emma," I said as we trotted up alongside her, "Do you remember me and my staff? The one you thought belonged to a wizard."

"Oh yes, I remember you Wizard and your staff," she said excitedly.

"Well it works," I said, showing it to her. "So if it's okay with your auntie and you still want a job and a place to live on your own, you can come and work for me. Be my housekeeper. What do you say?"

Before I could even blink, she had hold of my saddle and was pulling herself up behind me.

"Do I want a job working for a wizard? Is this answer enough for you?" She said putting her arms around me.

"Whoa! Hold on!" I said in astonishment. "You don't know me from Adam. We had better go and ask your auntie first."

"Don't worry about my Auntie, I don't live with her anymore, but I'll write. Come on, I know you are a wizard and I trust you. Where are we going?"

She was happy, and I certainly wasn't going to harm her, and if she didn't like it, I would bring her back.

"Well, okay then," I replied. "We are going to Wales, but we are flying. So, are you still coming?"

"Wales! Flying! Do you see me getting off?" She replied, squeezing me. "Fly on Wizard. I can't wait."

She was funny and I liked her right away. So with Emma's arms around me, I asked Roslyn to walk on. She knew what to do, and after finding a nice secluded spot, we were in the air on a giant soft and warm eagle owl, flying across the Irish Sea. Emma squealed with excitement until we landed in my yard. I wasn't going to explain anything to her until the morning. I just showed her to my bedroom and I slept in Granddad's.

In the morning, I showed her around. All she had to do was look after Mad Luke and the house. She was delighted especially when I told her that her wages were two pounds a week for herself, a pound a week for Mad Luke another pound a week for food and a barn full of fuel. In town following that, I bought her all the clothes she wanted.

Emma, who was in her early twenties, settled down well and became very friendly with the neighbours and many townsfolk. She was great about the house, the yard and the stables. Granddad would have loved her because the house had never been so clean and tidy.

A week before heading off to Spain, Lord Rabry was coming to town. He was coming to open Mrs Bowyer's sweet store, next door to Lyndon Stokes butchers shop in Old James Street. To commemorate the event, he organised a playing cards competition in the town hall. The Lord was well known in Blaenafon, not only because of his status but from Welusa's book. He was born and had lived in the large manor house on the Salisbury estate, situated below the coal tips of Varteg. The lord, after marrying Lady Emryl, now lives in Ragged Castle. Lord Rabry loved playing cards, but he was hopeless at it. In fact, he had never won a single game, even though we all knew he cheated.

I went along to the game, and it was a good night. The Lord had generously set up many different card competitions, though the prizes were very skimpy. He probably arranged all those games just to give him a better chance of winning. It didn't do him any good; he was first out in all of them. Lawson and Barrie won a game each though I don't know how Barrie managed to. He was also hopeless at card games. He used to say, "I just can't concentrate." I remember his mother telling me once, "All our Barry ever thinks about is girls, girls, and girls."

I was ready now to head off to Lucia, but before I went, I gave Emma eight weeks' money of thirty-two pounds. I also put another sixteen in her bank account. I told her that if she wanted to go back home, give Roger Regan the key. He would look after everything.

On the morning before setting off, I went down to Saint Peter's to say goodbye to my Granddad. I told him that Emma had the house and yard all tidy and that I wouldn't sell it to anyone. If I ever moved away, I would give the place to Emma because I knew she'd look after it. I would also come back to visit him every month. So I tapped the headstone three times, saying, "See you Granddad," then waved as I went.

I walked back to the house, picked up my pack and staff and said goodbye to Emma. While I was collecting Roslyn from the stable, the postman called with a letter. Going by the postmark, it was from Cynthia, so I thought I'd open it later.

I didn't saddle Roslyn; I just rode her up the mountain and stopped not far from the Keepers Pond. Then, as I was looking around, making sure the coast was clear, I heard a whistle and someone shouting.

"Hey, Gwydion. Come here old buddy? I want to tell you that I am sorry for shouting at you. I had a bad day, but I'm okay now. So come on over?"

It was the dragon. I was not far away from his pond, and I could see him in the middle. I had completely forgotten about him and remembered just how funny he was. So I dismounted and walked over to his pond and asked how he was.

"I'm great," he replied. "But where have you been? I've heard so much about you lately, and I'm disappointed you haven't called by. What's the matter pal? Surely you didn't believe all that stuff I told you the last time. I was only kidding. Sit down and let's have a chat."

I would have loved to stay there and chat, but I couldn't. So I told him that I couldn't stop because I was going somewhere.

"Yes, I know. You are off to Spain to see Lucia, aren't you? But Gwydion, I'm sorry to tell you, you're wasting your time old friend."

I was wondering how he knew about Lucia, especially as he wasn't allowed out of the pond, so I asked him.

"I've friends, haven't I?" he replied. "I have loads of friends. They come here all the time. I know everything that goes on, even all around the world."

I said to myself, "He probably does, but his friends are only the birds."

"Okay, I'll have a chat with you then," I said, to his delight. "What do you want to talk about?"

"First of all, Gwydion, old pal. I am ever so sorry about your Granddad. He was a lovely old fella. We got to know each other well after you went. We used to have a great old laugh together. I remember we laughed so much that he dropped his pipe in my pond. I dived down, found it easy enough and dried it with my breath. Yes, we had great fun, and I sadly miss him, his lovely sheep and his sweet and friendly little dog. I'm so lonely now Gwydion."

I knew he was talking a load of old blarney, so just for fun, I thought I'd see what else he would come up with.

"Well, as soon as I get back, I'll come up here and chat with you just like Granddad. Would you like that?"

"Yes," he quickly replied, "I would like that, and it would be lovely if we could go for a walk together, but I'm too stiff to get out. Will you help me, old buddy?"

Once again, I knew what he was up to, so I replied, "That's no problem I'll fetch my rope and pull you out."

"Oh no, no Gwydion. I'm too heavy for you, and besides, my bones are brittle now and will break. It will be a lot easier and safer if you use your staff."

I pretended to agree and said, "Yes, that's a good idea, but I haven't mastered it properly yet."

So I held out my staff, and by using my thoughts, I asked for a pole and threw it in beside him

"No that's no good, Gwydion. What can I do with this old thing?"

Next, I asked for two poles, then shouted. "What about two then?"

"No! No Gwydion. Poles! I can't use these. I just told you that, didn't I."

I now thought I'd asked for a boat and there it was, a nice rowing boat to which he hollered.

"Ah no, no, that's no good to me either. How can I get out with a boat? I can swim over there, can't I? Pull yourself together boy. Just ask for me to be out on the bank alongside you. It's simple."

"Okay, but I'm trying my best," I said, trying not to laugh.

So, this time, I asked to put the dragon in the boat and plonk, in he went, flattening it down to the bottom. He came up sharply spitting and spluttering.

"What the heck are you doing ya fool? You could have killed me, and my fish. For goodness sake Gwydion, settle down and concentrate boy. I'm getting all stressed now."

I was dying to laugh, but I apologised, "Oh I'm sorry Sir, but I've almost got the hang of it. I'll try again."

The dragon was annoyed now, "Well, alright, but get it right this time because you are messing up my pond."

"Okay, but it's not easy," I said as I raised my staff and with my thoughts, I asked for a ladder up against the bank.

"You idiot Gwydion!" He roared. "What's wrong with you? A ladder! What do you think I am, a monkey or something? Didn't that mindless wizard ever show you how to use that old staff? All you have to do is wish me outa here. For the sake of all the sheep and children, concentrate boy, will you."

I was bursting inside with laughter now and had to get away before I exploded. So I once again apologised.

"I'm sorry, but I don't know what's happening. It's never been like this before. I think it's worn out or something."

"Worn out, my eye. That's nonsense," he shouted. "Your staff will last forever. Concentrate, just concentrate Gwydion? It's as easy as putting your hat on."

"Okay, okay. One more time and I'll have to go," I said as I swirled my staff around impressively. Then, Walla, he went absolutely berserk and hollered out.

"Ah, you stupid clown. You stupid, stupid clown from the coal tips of Abercarn. Take this fool bonnet offa me, you idiot."

That was it. I couldn't hold it back any longer and said in between my laughter.

"It's your fault. You shouldn't have mentioned hats, and now my staff won't work at all. I have to go now, so you'll have to wait until I come back."

I mounted Roslyn, and as we trekked away, he began shouting.

"Why you no good son of a sheep pooping farmer. You, you brainless nincompoop. No wonder Lucia kicked you out and is back with her rich boyfriend. Oh, what a shame. Come back here with that stick you big ugly pansy you. I'll show you how to use it alright, thrashed across ya lousy stinking Welsh bottom. You are nothing but a no good loser. Yeah, that's right, you, you dirty rotten, flea-riddled skunk you. You even smell like one. Do you ever wash? Come back here. I'll wash you alright, ya toad from the ash tip, you."

I laughed so much and loud that it drowned out his crazy rants. But I did hear him tell me that he wouldn't be so kind to me the next time we met. So with aching sides, we galloped on to the top of Llanellen Mountain, passing by the spot where Brynmoroc had fallen. All that was visible now were his fingers. It was sad and I felt sorry for him, but I didn't know he was going to die.

When we were far enough away and with Roslyn now my lovely eagle owl, we soared high above the clouds over Raglan, heading for Spain and Lucia.

Flying across the channel and because I hadn't seen or heard from Lucia for such a long time, a nervous feeling came over me. Lucia did say that she never wanted to see me again, but I always thought perhaps she didn't really mean it.

"But what if she did?" I kept asking myself.

Because of my uncertainty, I told Roslyn only to go as far as Murcia. I wanted to have a night there to think and settle my nerves; if that was ever possible.

We arrived in Murcia at nine o'clock just as the sun was going down. So along with Roslyn, my wee terrier, I paid for a room in a hotel not too far away from the city centre. After leaving Roslyn curled up on the bed, I went down to the bar for a shot of whiskey. I stayed for an hour listening to someone singing. He was okay, and I gave him a tip before I went to bed. It was a nice comfy bed, and I snuggled down nicely into it with Roslyn on my feet. It was strange, although I had nothing to worry about, I still kept thinking

Brynmoroc or his creatures were going to turn up at any time. Funny enough, he did turn up, but it was only in my dream.

I was up early in the morning to another lovely day, but I didn't feel lovely inside. It was eight o'clock, and my butterflies were back. It was silly I know because I was longing to see her. I waited until nine o'clock before taking Roslyn around the back of the hotel.

With her now my lovely mare, we headed on a few miles to where it was quiet before quickly soaring high into the puffy clouded sky, on once again my feathered friend. We flew at the same height and waited until over the mountains before dropping down a little. The small hill farms, tiny chapels and buildings on the way were simply wonderful. Granddad would have loved to have had one of those farms, but only if it was in Wales. There was even a great-looking viaduct across an open piece of land. I would have taken a closer look, but there was a train coming. After that, we zoomed back up and stayed there until flying down outside a forest about a mile from Lucia's grandmother's house.

Roslyn was back as my mare and seemed very pleased with herself as we trotted along towards the mansion. When we arrived, I nervously knocked on the door, but there was no answer. I had a key, but the door wasn't locked. I went in and shouted, but still no response. I thought perhaps they were upstairs and went to check. Both their bedroom doors were open, so I peeped inside Lucia's. She hadn't made her bed and there were clothes strewn all across it. That was unlike her; she was always neat and tidy. I shouted once again, but not a soul answered. Downstairs on the living room table was a hand full of petals in a bowl and a smell of perfume everywhere. I couldn't think, but it was evident that they had gone somewhere special because their going-out coats were still on the hall stand. With it being Saturday, I thought maybe they were at some kind of festival in the local church or had gone away for the day. Suddenly a sickening feeling came over me. I remembered what the dragon said about me wasting my time.

"Ah, he's just a crazy old dragon trying to get out of his pond," I shouted. "I'm not going to listen to him."

I thought then that I'd go out for the day and think. I was hungry, but I wasn't going into Valez Rubio, just in case they were there. Puerto Lumbreras was only twelve miles away. There was a lovely café there; an excellent place to pass the time. Away I went, only this time in a nice new buggy.

Arriving in Puerto Lumbreras, I left Roslyn munching in her food bag while I went into the café. I bought a coffee and ordered a sandwich. Sitting there, I happened to see and hear two of Lucia's friends chatting away across the room. I remembered them from the day we first arrived in Spain. I couldn't forget them because they talked and talked. I quickly turned away in fear that they might recognise me. I didn't want to speak to them. Then I heard one say something that made me spill my coffee.

"It's a shock to me too. I never thought Lucia would ever get married. We had better hurry. Come on."

They were both smartly dressed and in a hurry going through the door. Looking out the window, I saw that they were heading towards the church up on the hill. I had noticed earlier that there were well dressed people going in there. Also, there were more traps and carriages than usual in town. My thoughts immediately went back to the dragon, Lucia's house, the uncharacteristic state of the bedrooms and the confetti-like petals on the table. My curiosity was high now. So I left my coffee, didn't bother waiting for my sandwich and followed them to the church where I was dealt an almighty blow. Inside the church porch were the wedding bands of Agustin Melendez and Lucia Castell. They were being married that day. I did a quick about-turn, and as I did, I recognised a few more of her friends on their way in. I kept my head down and was out of that church and alongside Roslyn in a flash. I couldn't believe it. I was sickened now, just like I was after knowing my Granddad had died. The only difference was, I wanted to hate her now, but I couldn't. I thought I was lonely after the death of Granddad, but now I felt really desolate. It also made me feel inferior, worthless as if I was no one, just the cheap old sheep boy Lucia used to call me. I stood there with Roslyn, and as the church bells began ringing out, I thought at least Roslyn stayed faithful to me. I wanted to get away, but where could I go. There was nothing in Wales for me. Most of my friends were either married or getting married. Then my thoughts turned to Cynthia. I had forgotten about her letter. I took it out of my pocket, opened the envelope and was about to take out the letter when I saw the wedding carriage arriving at the church. The moment I saw her step out of the carriage with a well-dressed gentleman, who was probably giving her away, my heart must have stopped. The bridesmaids came behind and held up her dress and train as she walked into the church. It was only then that I believed it was indeed happening.

"Well, I'm not going to run away," I said to Roslyn. "She doesn't care about us, so I'll just as well go and see her for the last time, and then we'll go."

Roslyn didn't say anything of course, but who else did I have to talk to. So I slowly went inside the lovely church, and as I entered, the usher sent me down the aisle to a bench in the middle. The women sitting there, moved over for me to sit on the end.

Now, I know you probably don't want to know about the ceremony, but I'll tell you anyway.

When I sat down, they had just finished singing a hymn and now the priest was inviting the congregation to pray. This was followed by the Lector reading a passage from the Old Testament. When finished, the choir began singing some kind of responsive psalm. There were about three readings from the gospel, followed by a hymn that made my chest heave with sadness. The priest then spoke about the sacrament, the dignity of married love, the faithfulness to each other and the acceptance of the upbringing of their children etcetera. Then came the wedding vows. At that point, I couldn't stop myself from shaking. I was trying to stay calm, but the beating heart in my heaving chest was uncontrollable. Then, when the priest turned to the groom and asked those devastating words, "Will you, Agustin Melendez, take Lucia Castell as your lawful wedded wife," I couldn't stand it any longer and stepped out into the aisle and shouted, "No! I am!"

The whole church erupted with gasps, and as Lucia turned around, with her veil now up, I was dealt another blow, it wasn't her. I just couldn't believe it, and if I could have died right there on the spot, I would have.

"Let's get the heck out of here," I thought as every single person stared at me. Then as I ran, I heard Lucia call out to me.

"Gwydion! Gwydion! What are you doing?"

She was down a few rows on the opposite side of the aisle from me. There was no way I was going to stay there now, so I quickly turned and ran on. The usher tried to stop me, but I brushed him aside, saying that I was sorry. Roslyn was outside the gates waiting as if she knew what was going to happen. As I ran, I felt a sharp pain in my little finger, making me grab hold of it. Then as I jumped up onto the driving seat, I found that halfway up my little finger was a sparkling coloured ring. I put it into my pocket and was just about to ask Roslyn to get going when I heard Lucia.

"Gwydion wait! Where are you going? Oh please don't go away again. Wait Gwydion. Please wait?" She cried, running up to the gates.

When I heard her asking me to wait, I must have sighed the most prolonged sigh of relief I had ever done.

"Lucia, quick let's get away from here. I thought that girl was you," I said as she climbed up beside me.

I was embarrassed but at the same time, felt great as we trotted away to a nearby park garden and sat on a bench.

"Oh, Gwydion I'm so sorry for behaving the way I did. I was stupid and jealous. The morning you went away I was waving and shouting to say I was sorry. Then when I saw that feather, knowing you wanted to marry me, I could have died. Oh, Gwydion, I love you. Don't ever leave me again."

I then noticed the little feather pinned to her shawl, and it made me smile.

"I see you have your little feather then," I said, putting my hand in my pocket. "Well, now I have something else for you."

I stood up, and as I knelt on one knee, I offered her the little sparkling ring.

"With your little feather, you once asked me to marry you. So now, with this little ring, I'm asking you. I love you, Lucia, will you marry me?"

"Yes. I will. I will. I will. Oh, Gwydion I love you so much," she replied, holding out her trembling hand.

I slipped the ring on her finger but didn't give her time to study it because I lifted her into my arms, kissed her and said with happy tears in my eyes.

"I have been longing to do that from the moment you first smiled at me at the train station."

"But you have kissed me twice before," she said lovingly.

"I know," I said, putting her down. "But not like that. Not like that."

"Well, why did you stop?" she asked as she invited me to kiss her again.

"You were getting heavy," I replied, jokingly.

"Why you little, little…"

Before she could clout me or say anymore, I picked her up, and as the wedding bells rang out, I ran with her in my arms around the park while she laughed and laughed.

"I love, love, love you, and we are getting married," she squealed excitedly as I sat her down on the bench.

"Oh, look at my ring Gwydion. It's beautiful. The seven jewels of the wizard's rainbow are set in it. Oh, Gwydion, where did you get it from? It's the most beautiful ring I could ever wish for. My grandmother would have loved it."

"Would have! What do you mean, would have loved it?" I asked.

"Oh, Gwydion. Sadly, three months after you left, my grandmother died."

I couldn't believe Lucia was mourning the loss of her grandmother at the same time I was mourning poor Granddad. I had no intention of telling her about his passing until later, but now I thought I'd get it over with and told her. With that said, we consoled one another, both believing that they would have been happy for us. The wedding bells were still ringing, reminding Lucia that it was her friend's wedding. So we rushed up to the church for Lucia to see the happy couple before they left. I dropped her off and went away down the road to watch from a distance. I felt like a right fool and didn't want anyone to see me.

After the newlyweds headed off to the reception, I could see Lucia, who was holding red and white roses in her hand showing her friends her ring. The ring I was sure had something to do with that old house back on the outskirts of Columbia. How and why, I wasn't even going to think about. Those days were over.

"Look, Gwydion, I caught her bouquet," said Lucia, running up to me. "Isn't it a wonderful coincidence? Oh, I'm so happy. I can't wait to tell everyone in the world that we are getting married. Come on, let's go somewhere. I've told my friends that I am not going to the reception."

"Well, let's go then," I said, and we headed off up into the hills.

It was a fabulous sunny day, and while we were stopped looking at the lovely view the first thing we talked about was why we couldn't write to one another. It was so silly and frustrating at the time, but we just laughed for we didn't care anymore.

"By the way, what is your surname Lucia?" I then asked

"Tanbonita. Lucia Tanbonita," she replied.

"Tanbonita!" I stuttered in surprise. "That's Spanish for so pretty, isn't it? Well if ever a name suited anyone, it's you."

She laughed, "Thank you, my hero."

Lucia already knew my surname but couldn't spell it, and as for Blaenafon, she couldn't spell that either.

I told her all about my ordeal with Brynmoroc and how Bleddwyn intended to meet her. She felt the same way as I did about Brynmoroc. Neither of us wished him dead, only to strip him of his power, that's all.

"Well, it's seven o'clock," we said, hearing a clock chime in the distance. We were so happy far away talking that we didn't realise it was so late. So we made our way to what was now, Lucia's home and estate.

The very moment we began to walk up the winding road to the mansion, I felt at home and glad to be alive. I couldn't wait to be inside that lovely house and when I was, I found myself back in the kitchen, eating and chatting as if I'd never been away. I can't remember a thing about going to bed only waking in the morning happy and contented. I had the best night's sleep for nineteen months, and now with my beautiful Senorita serving me breakfast, life was wonderful.

That afternoon, Lucia decided to have a picnic down by the river to discuss our wedding plans. She was excited and wanted to get married as quickly as possible.

"Where would you like us to be married?" I asked when I finally got a word in. "That was a lovely church you were in yesterday."

Without hesitation, she replied, "Las Rocas Del Sol. Yes, I would love to be married in the Andes where I gave you my love-token feather. As long as we can make our vows the same as we do here in Spain, then to be married by chief Wabulamba in a tribal ceremony would be the loveliest wedding anyone could ever wish for."

"Brilliant! Brilliant idea. Fabulous, I love it," I said and we hugged.

With that, she playfully tipped me over, sending us rolling over and over in fits of laughter all the way down the bank into the river. Hitting that icy water was some shock, but we didn't care. It was even funnier and waded out laughing, clambering up the bank.

"Well that was fun, but that's our picnic over for the day," said Lucia, still giggling. "Let's pack, shall we?"

We were just gathering things up when there was a sudden gust of the wind, sending us tumbling back into the river again, only this time, not very happy climbing out.

"What on earth was that?" Lucia asked. "Oh, my word! Look at the house. It's all lit up! Oh, no, what's happening, Gwydion?"

I wasn't sure but said that it must have something to do with Bleddwyn. So, nervously, hand in hand, we made our way to the house where a butler greeted us at the door. We were soaking wet, but suddenly we were dry. Inside Lucia's house now was completely different. We followed the butler along a corridor into a great hall where about a hundred wizards were standing on each side of the room, clapping. Bleddwyn and Eluciana were walking towards us with Eluciana holding out her arms lovingly to Lucia. They embraced one another, and as they hugged, the excited wizards cheered loudly.

"Come, let us go into the sitting room a while," said Bleddwyn after the cheering stopped.

The rooms looked very similar to those in Bleddwyn's castle, but with Lucia's furniture inside. We all sat in the bay window and talked for hours. As you can imagine, the main topic of conversation for the ladies was our up-and-coming wedding. How ladies can talk so excitedly and for so long about arrangements for a wedding, was beyond me. Bleddwyn and I had little input to the conversation, only for Bleddwyn to say how honoured and proud he would be giving Lucia away when the day arrived.

When the wedding talk was exhausted, the conversation turned to the present. Bleddwyn had now reached the point where he was explaining how Lucia and I have our own source of enchanted energy and our lifespan. I had forgotten to tell her that we had enchanted green blood. She was overcome with it all, especially having green blood and asked Bleddwyn to explain, for our skin still looked pink and normal.

While he was explaining, the gong went for the feast in our honour to begin. Hence, we joined our new fellow wizards in the banquet hall. I had earlier told Bleddwyn that we didn't want too much fuss or any more rewards. Being able to spend the rest of my life with the lady I loved was reward enough. We enjoyed a lovely meal and a very entertaining evening with Lucia getting acquainted with her great, great grandparents or if you like, ancestors and their friends.

When the time came for Bleddwyn and Eluciana to leave, there was a lovely horse drawn carriage waiting on the lawn outside. Then after a farewell hug from Lucia, they soared off into the starry night sky, and all were gone.

Lucia was relieved and happy to see her house back to normal, and as we made our way up the stairs she stopped and looked at me.

"Gwydion. "Why didn't you tell me that Bleddwyn looks like you?"

"What do you mean?" I asked. "He looks nothing like me. In fact, if anything, it's Eluciana who's the spitting image of you."

"Oh, she looks nothing like me at all, Gwydion," she replied, shaking her head. "Oh, let's go to bed, I'm absolutely worn out."

After the usual tapping of the wall, I lay in bed thinking how strange it was that neither of us could see the resemblance between ourselves in Bleddwyn and Eluciana.

The next morning, we mentioned no more about our likeness to Bleddwyn and Eluciana, but it was on my mind. We spent the afternoon outside on the swing seat, fast asleep. If anyone needed a rest, it was us. We didn't wake until teatime and even after that, we hadn't fully recovered until the following morning.

Lucia was keen to start planning for the wedding. Now, because of where she wanted the wedding, we couldn't invite any of our friends. Nevertheless, she did tell them that we were getting married, but in South America. Thankfully, none of them could afford to come, but they were all excited for her and went around the shops helping her choose her dress.

According to Bleddwyn, I was quite capable of conjuring up anything we wanted, but that wasn't our choice. We decided to give an outward appearance of normality by buying everything instead of wishing for it. What my staff and Roslyn were capable of would be our secret to tell, if we so desired.

We had bought everything we needed and were ready to set a date for travelling. We couldn't just turn up and get married on a particular day; we first had to notify Chief Wabulamba to get his permission. Lucia decided that the eighth of June seemed a good idea, and hopefully the twenty-first being the wedding day. She picked that day because the twenty-first of June was the Peruvian winter solstice.

With the date sorted, my very pretty lady was like a chatterbox during the day and a woodpecker all night. All she did was tap, tap, and tap on the wall until sunrise. Having our own bedrooms meant that I could now turn over, kick the blankets off at any time or even jump up and down if I felt like it. Though after saying that, I was looking forward to having her beside me again, without the ribbon.

On the sixth of June two days, before we were due to head off, Lucia had a party with all her friends while I went for a ride up into the hills. I had forgotten about reading Cynthia's letter, so I brought it with me. After reading the letter, I was thanking my lucky stars that I had hidden it. If Lucia had read the letter, I would have had an immeasurable amount of explaining to do. A lot of her questions would have been unanswerable.

In her letter, Cynthia had decided to buy a small ranch somewhere near a beach. She went on to talk about the lovely time we had together, especially that night at the ball. Along with that, she would never forget me and her ring still didn't come off her finger, but even if it did, she would put it straight back on again. Furthermore, although I had explained to Cynthia about the time I kissed her and what happened at old Lord purple stones place, she insisted that we were both in our right minds and that I knew it. There were quite a few more incriminating pages of the same kind of talk. Finally, she signed off saying that she still had feelings for me and would carry on writing and hoped to see me again one day.

"Dew! I said to Roslyn. "I've unintentionally landed myself in a whole load of trouble."

Bleddwyn did warn me, but how could a man ever turn down a kiss from a beautiful lady? That's my excuse. What about you?

I couldn't keep the letter, but I didn't have the heart to burn it, so I buried it nice and deep. I stayed there for a while before deciding to go into Puerto Lumbreras for a jug of ale. I called into the first tavern I came to and just because I was happy and to pass the time away, I had two jars or maybe three. I arrived back at the mansion an hour before midnight just as the last of Lucia's friends were leaving. They waved as I passed them on the drive.

# Chapter 31

On the very morning of the eighth of June, I suggested that we should name the mansion, Tanbonita. The reason being, that after we were married the name Tanbonita would be gone forever. According to Mariana, she and Lucia were the only ones in the world with a surname like it. With that decided, we designed two signs, erecting one above the door, and the other at the bottom of the drive.

With that done and after packing everything we needed for our journey, we were ready to fly. All we were taking were our wedding clothes, nothing else. As for our everyday clothes, we could purchase them easily enough in Cuzco.

"Well, here we go Lucia," I said, and she laughed. "Go on Roslyn my beauty. Let's fly."

In a sensational moment, we were away, flying high into the sky out of sight of everyone. Lucia was so excited, squealing away and shouting behind me.

"Ooo wee, this is amazing Gwydion. Roslyn's so big and warm, isn't she?"

Yes, she was warm and dry and even as we flew through a storm over the Atlantic, not a drop of rain did we feel. It took six hours before we found ourselves flying over South America and Peru. It was now three o'clock in the afternoon, the same time as we started out in Spain.

While circling Las Rocas Del Sol, all our dear friends were waving frantically. It was as if they knew we were coming. Roslyn swooped down, landing gently in the village square. Milaniah was there to greet us along with the loudest of cheers. Everyone was so delighted and with Roslyn changed back in front of their very eyes; there was another roaring cheer.

We walked behind Milaniah to her lovely little house followed probably by everyone in the village singing and chanting. We were happy to be back among our friends again but couldn't understand why they were all excited until Milaniah told us. Apparently, our wedding appeared in their quipu a few days ago, so Chief Wabulamba knew we were coming.

"Well, at least they know now," said Lucia. "All we have to do now is ask Chief Wabulamba his permission. Oh, I just love this place Gwydion, don't you?"

Milaniah was pleased to tell us that the chief would see us the following evening. That suited us fine because we were so overwhelmed with our very emotional welcome, we needed the rest and time to think. So that night, because the two girls couldn't stop talking about the wedding, the dress and making loads of suggestions, I went to bed and left them to it. Milaniah had insisted that until we were married, we were to have separate rooms. That, we were already doing.

The next day, we spent some time playing games with the children and walking through the forest. In the evening, we met Chief Wabulamba, Lisuella and their family at the palace. It was so lovely to see one another and catch up with events since leaving all those months ago. Although the Chief knew all about our wedding taking place in his village, he was happy that we asked his permission and to honour us by performing the ceremony.

In the run-up to our wedding, because the ceremony was to be held outside, the villagers were busy preparing the area where it was to take place. As a result, we were not allowed on the west side of the village.

I had already told the chief that Bleddwyn and Eluciana were coming. So on the afternoon of our wedding, they arrived on a cloud to a rapturous welcome. With the introductions over, Eluciana went along with Lucia and Milaniah to prepare for the wedding.

The ceremony wasn't until ten o'clock that night, so it gave me plenty of time to get to know Bleddwyn. He was so different now from the severe and commanding wizard I had met back home in Wales. He seemed so ordinary, down to earth. Or did I find him that way because I now had wizard's blood flowing through my veins?

Eventually, Bleddwyn went to honour his duty by giving the bride away. This left me on my own nervously getting ready for the moment I thought would never come. I had no best man, so I was going to pretend that my Granddad was with me and put the wedding ring in my pocket alongside his lucky penny. That made me feel better because according to him, the penny was how he met my grandmother.

At nine-fifteen and while I stood nervously shaking; Chief Wabulamba's personal sedan, draped in flowers, arrived outside the door. The route to our wedding venue on the west side of the village was all lit up with torches and lined with people waving and cheering as I passed. Arriving at the venue, I found that it was also lit with flickering torches. Our wedding was to be held under the flowing branches of a giant willow tree, creating a beautiful archway covered with flowers. Under the willow tree itself, where we were to take our vows, was lit up with candles. The lovely fragrance from the strategically placed flowers, made it seem really special. The aisle which was made up of tightly knitted straw sprinkled with petals led up to two beautifully carved wooden thrones adorned with peacock feathers. Wabulamba and Lisuella were sitting there, waiting for Lucia's arrival. One could say that the wedding venue was set out similarly to a chapel, but without an altar. There were two rows of people all colourfully dressed; even a flower garden would look dull in comparison. Of course, they were all anxiously waiting to see the bride.

They weren't bothered about me, thank goodness. I took my position down the front, holding Granddad's lucky penny in my hand.

While I sat there, watching the gentle movement of branches and listening to the whispering congregation, I heard cheering in the distance. I can't explain why I felt so nervous because I was looking forward to this day. Perhaps it was that I couldn't really believe I was about to marry by far the prettiest and most lovable girl I'd ever met. Then, when the musicians began to play their wooden instruments, and after Chief Wabulamba and Lisuella rose from their seats, I knew she was coming down the aisle. The whispers that were echoing through the congregation earlier now turned to gasps of wonder. I was afraid to look, but when I saw the delight on our host's faces; I turned to see the most unforgettable sight. There, holding the arm of the great wizard Bleddwyn, was my beautiful Lucia. She was all in white, wearing a dress made from an elegant material that I had never seen before. The full skirt was delicately strewn with what I later learned were ostrich feathers. Peeping out from the hem of her dress were sparkling silver shoes, adorned with a single white feather

"Were they a gift from Eluciana," I wondered. They looked very much as if they were from the world of enchantment. In between her small delicate fingers, she carried a bouquet of red roses and rainbow-coloured feathers. Her veil, held in place by a band of silver feathers was down, but I could still see her lovely smile as she turned her head to look at me. The moment we walked up to Chief Wabulamba, Lucia lifted her veil, and her beauty was complete. She handed her bouquet to Milaniah, her bridesmaid, who was resplendent in a red-coloured gown. Following this was Chief Wabulamba beginning the ceremony.

"We are here today to witness the marriage of Gwydion Llewellyn and Lucia Tanbonita. I now ask who gives this bride away?

"I Bleddwyn, with all my heart, do I give this child," was Bleddwyn's proud reply.

In between songs and one of their ritual chants, the chief read out the values of marriage and its sacred bond. Then came the emotional wedding vows, and as we pledged ourselves to one another, I had to blink and swallow many times. I wasn't sad, but I couldn't stop the tears from rolling down my cheeks. Then as I slipped the ring on her delicate finger, Chief Wabulamba announced us husband and wife. We looked at one another, and with tears rolling down our cheeks, we sealed it with a kiss. Loud cheering followed, and as we turned to walk back down the aisle, I could now see the long train that fell from the back of Lucia's dress. That too was edged with those glorious ostrich feathers that I was hoping I wouldn't tread on. It was a wonderful feeling knowing that Lucia was now my wife, and as we walked through the lovely arch, she beamed with delight. Stepping out into the open, we were smothered entirely in petals, happily accepting applause and congratulations from hundreds of cheering people. We stayed there acknowledging them with waves of gratitude until joined by the delighted Bleddwyn, Eluciana, Wabulamba and Lisuella, ready for the reception.

My mind was in a whirl, so the ride back to Wabulamba's palace with my lovely bride was just a blur. It was such a lot to take in, but after saying that, the sight of the feast that awaited, was astonishing. Every Peruvian delicacy you could imagine was on display. It was a feast fit for a king, or should I say a king and a few wizards. I don't think even Bleddwyn in all his long years hadn't seen such a display of delicious delights. Lucia just sat smiling, enjoying every moment. She looked so radiant and beautiful that I couldn't take my eyes off her. Speeches came thick and fast from Chief Wabulamba, Milaniah and the very proud Bleddwyn. I even managed to get to my feet and say a few words of thanks in Spanish.

With the feast now over, came the traditional bridal dance that we enjoyed immensely and so did everyone else. Instead of the usual slow waltz, we danced one of the slow tribal dances that we had learned over our time there. Then as was tradition and much to Lucia's delight, everyone joined in. Peruvian dancing and entertainment followed while Lucia and I had the honour to watch seated in Lisuella and Wabulamba's thrones. It was a fabulous spectacle. Then after exhausting ourselves dancing, I was happy just to sit, holding the hand of my lovely bride and watch the colourful entertainment.

The spectacular evening came to an end with Bleddwyn rising to a gentle roll of thunder that quickly brought everyone's attention.

"Will the Bride and Groom, Chief Wabulamba, Lisuella and honoured guests, please come witness in honour of this day?

Bleddwyn took Eluciana by the hand and led us out into the open where to the roar of the huge congregation, the night sky suddenly lit up in a blaze of colour. The display was amazing, and as we watched and listened to the crackling of gentle thunder, dozens of wizards appeared in the sky with their staffs held high.

"Oh, look Gwydion? Look? They are saluting us. Gwydion isn't it wonderful."

I would have saluted them back, but I had left my staff with Roslyn. Then as the wizards disappeared into the dark beyond, the mountain behind us came to light. There at the summit, was the Sun Giant, waving his vast fiery hand until he too faded from view. Thinking it all over, another roll of thunder crackled and as we looked in the direction it came from, we couldn't believe our eyes. There, waving from the heavens, was my Granddad and Mariana. I was sure Granddad had the pipe I bought and left at his grave. It was nice seeing him again, and as they waved, all we could do was wave back until their images too faded into the starry night. Seeing Granddad again, made me feel like shouting at him.

"Come back here, you old codger you." I didn't, though I wish now that I had.

"Thank you, Grandfather and Grandmother. That was lovely," said Lucia as she kissed them both.

Bleddwyn's surprise brought a spectacular end to the most unforgettable day of our lives. After all the cheering had died, Lucia made a little speech thanking everyone for making our wedding day so special. When the time came to say goodbye to Bleddwyn and Eluciana, Bleddwyn surprised us once again.

"Where ever you are, where ever you go, we will always be with you."

Then as we embraced, they disappeared, bringing gasps of amazement from the assembled crowd. It was as if they had stepped right into us. Everyone stayed stunned for a while until Chief Wabulamba announced the celebrations over. With this being final, the happy crowd of people saluted us with their hands in the air and slowly walked away chanting as they went.

We thanked our hosts once again for the most wonderful day we could have ever wished for. We were then shown to our bridal suite by one of the maids. On opening the door, we were met by the fragrant aroma of thousands of petals surrounding our bed, and on each of our pillows was an image of the sun, made entirely from the most gorgeous yellow petals. It was almost too beautiful to disturb, but after our unforgettable wedding day, sleep was calling. However, as we lay in bed, Lucia began to wonder.

"Gwydion. That was strange how Eluciana just walked into me and disappeared. I felt so light-headed after. How did you feel?"

Then as she took my hand, we felt a tingling sensation. I quickly turned up the lamp and found that both the images of a baby in a womb were no longer there in our hands, they had vanished.

"What does this mean Gwydion? Is it because we are married now?"

"I don't know," was all I could say.

I didn't know, but if it meant what I thought it meant, I wasn't going to worry about it. I was going to lie back down with my lovely wife, put my arm around her and go to sleep. Tomorrow was another day.

In the morning, after a light breakfast, we said our goodbyes, promising to return every year in June. For their kindness, there was nothing we could give them in return, for the whole village was already rich in gold, but we did provide the lovely Milaniah with something. A golden brooch studded with yellow diamonds in the shape of the sun.

With our farewells said and done, all we could do now was give the villagers what they were all waiting to see. So, with Lucia and I sitting happily upon our lovely Roselyn, before their very eyes, we were soaring up and away circling their village on a magnificent golden eagle, waving back to our cheering friends.

# Chapter 32

It was midday when we left Las Rocas Del Sol. Although our journey only took six hours, it was midnight when we arrived safely, trotting up to our home in Valez Rubio. We were exhausted now, so I let Roslyn off in the field to graze. After making ourselves a light supper, we headed off to bed to spend our first night as husband and wife in our lovely Spanish home.

We rose early to the beautiful rhythmic song of birds in the distance that continued until well after breakfast. One thing about Spain, when it was a lovely day it was a beautiful day and that particular day, the twenty-third of June nineteen hundred and one, was just that.

"Let's sit outside and stay there all day, shall we," suggested Lucia looking out the window.

We went outside and sat on one of our favourite swing seats, reminiscing about our time together. Although our adventure was tedious and sometimes life-threatening, we mostly only talked about the fun times we had. It's strange how you find things funny when at the time they were the complete opposite. Even the birds seemed to be joining in as they began to sing again.

"Isn't this just wonderful? Me and you sitting here together. I wish it could last forever and ever," said Lucia, putting her hand on my knee.

At that moment, Roslyn came up to us and as she tapped her hoof on the lawn, quietly neighed.

"What's the matter girl? Are you sad?" I asked.

Instantly, a sudden feeling of sorrow came over me. I thought perhaps she wanted to go back home.

"I believe she wants us to go for a ride," surmised Lucia after standing up and patting her.

"Well, in that case, come on then Roslyn, let's see where you want to take us," I said, also patting her.

As if in appreciation, she gave another little neigh. So I mounted, pulled Lucia up behind me and we trotted off through the woods and up into the hills.

"She's taken us to my favourite place," said Lucia after stopping beside a huge rock. "What does she want I wonder?"

Roslyn had taken us up onto a hill from where a spectacular view overlooked our mansion and the valley beyond. We dismounted Roslyn and stood on each side of her looking out at the beautiful scenery.

"I've been coming here ever since I was ten years old," said Lucia. "If you stand in front of this rock and shout, an echo goes on for ages and ages. I named this hill 'Para Siempre.' It means forever."

I tried it out, and she was right. My echo went on and on. Even after shouting again, I could still hear the other one in the distance. It was amazing.

"I have often wondered what kind of echo there would be if two people shouted at the same time," said Lucia slipping her arm in mine.

"Well, let's try and see what happens, shall we?" I asked in anticipation.

"Yes, that will be fun," replied my pretty excited wife. "After three if you call my name I'll call yours. Are you ready? One, two, three."

We both shouted together, but much to our surprise, our Roslyn whinnied too. The echo was an incredible sound of a jumbled-up version of our names and Roslyn's whinny. Then, as we listened to the nonsensical repetitive sound, it grew louder and louder until it roared over the top of us, and 'CRACK' went a loud noise behind us.

"Gwydion, look? Look at the rock. Our names; Gwydion Lucia and Roslyn are engraved into it."

We walked over to the rock, and as she ran her hands across our names, she quietly read them out.

"Gwydion, Lucia, Roslyn. Oh, isn't that lovely? The three of us together, forever. I love you Gwydion," she said emotionally, then softly kissed me.

"I love you too Lucia and thanks for marrying me," I replied.

At that moment, I thought I was the luckiest man alive. As we walked off down the hill that day, I thought it was an ideal time to gather up my journals and begin writing this story. A story of how I met the love of my life and our extraordinary adventures together.

Now, after looking back and writing our adventurous story, I find myself sitting here bringing that chapter in my life to an end, with the beginning of another. My life with Lucia, the loveliest lady in the world; and Roslyn, of course.

Gwydion Llewellyn
16th February 1906